OMEN OF SHADOWS

Memoirs Of A Living Dead Girl

By NIKI GREGORY

DEDICATION

This book is dedicated to all those who have been ridiculed and mocked for embracing their magical gifts, trusting their intuition, and believing in their own inherent power. Take comfort in knowing that those who downplay your gifts of magic do so because of their own mediocrity. Cast aside their shallow insults and fly high knowing you possess something greater than what they can ever understand.

ACKNOWLEDGEMENTS

I'm truly thankful for my daughters' involvement with the production of my novel's cover. Madison, your expertise in photography enabled you to capture the photo of the model perfectly! Avery, I thank you for being the face of the covers on my, *Memoirs of a Living Dead Girl* series. You breathed life into my vision of the living dead girl.

My editor and friend, Melanie— thank you for your efforts to keep my adoration of the em dash in check—but I know all too well— that you can only do— so much. See what I did there? I appreciate you editing my novel, even if it made you a bit afraid at times. Just know as you feel eyes crawling over you, the shadows are not just a figment of your imagination; they are real, and they are always watching you. You can never really escape their watchful gaze; they remind you that even in the dark of night, you are never truly alone.

Alyssa, my Alpha reader—You juggle the most demanding roles— being an educator, a mother, and a wife. I am so thankful for your precious time spent reading and providing me with feedback on my work.

My Beta and Sensitivity readers: Gion-Karlo, Janell, Charles, Rosario, and Marisol: I can't express enough appreciation for your feedback. I had the best time reading each of your comments and remarks; working alongside each of you was an absolute delight!

TABLE OF CONTENTS

FROM THE AUTHOR

The Memoirs of a Living Dead Girl series will involve confronting some dark and potentially disturbing topics and content. Occult practices, death, child abuse, strong violence, profanity, and phantasmagoria will be integral components of this paranormal story.

I want potential readers to be able to make an informed decision about whether this type of story is suitable for them. Those who wish to access additional information regarding content can visit my website: NIKIGREGORY.com

Thank you for reading my story as I navigate my life as a living dead girl.

My name is Lucinda Holmes, but my friends and family call me Lucy. Not that long ago, a witch lurked in the shadows of my life. She relentlessly sought to steal my soul and its powerful gift of magic. The older I became, my gifts grew stronger, fueling the witch's thirst for my death. Her ambition was clear: she wanted to seize the magic of my breath of life… my spirit. She intended to sacrifice me so she could harness the power of my soul and win favor with the *beast* himself.

The witch burned with ambition, desperate to ascend the ranks and lead the hordes of Satan's Army of Darkness during the *great* Armageddon. Her dark ambition was all that mattered to her, and nothing would stand in her way of achieving it.

The witch lured my body to its death, but somehow my soul escaped her clutches. My spirit laid dormant, safe… somewhere between life and death. Years after escaping the witch, I was blissfully unaware. My soul laid in silence, entranced by a never-ending slumber—until one day, my spirit jolted awake. Suddenly, once again, my breath of life became vulnerable to the witch's power and whatever horrific fate awaited me.

An ominous force far more terrifying than anything I ever could have imagined relentlessly pursued my soul. Through every peril I faced, I slowly began to understand that light and shadow possess an eternal tug of war for dominion over the enlightened souls that roam the Earth. My spirit was hunted like prey. I found myself an agonizing target, just like it was when I was alive inside my body. The witch promised my soul to Satan in exchange for *unholy* power. The darkness felt close and crushing as the witch and her sinister allies closed in—their evil presence sucking away my hope of survival as they once again sought out my very essence.

As the witch closed in on my soul, hope came in the form of my brave sister and her dearest friends. These heroic women ventured deep into the unknown to save me from Hell. Despite the cruel entities that threatened to overwhelm them, they surged bravely onward, determined to protect my soul. They fought with strength and courage, never once giving up hope.

With a final twist of fate, after divine intervention from wisdom passed down from a priestess long gone, the ladies managed to protect my soul and resurrect me. A desperate battle raged within me as my soul sought safety in my body, expelling the witch. As all the darkness and anguish drained away, my body and soul reunited. I felt myself come alive once again. Now, I walk in this world once more—as a living dead girl. I am still haunted by the dark and sinister forces that almost destroyed me. Those harrowing moments have left an indelible mark upon my soul. The shadows are never too far from me; they stalk my every move like a predator, keeping me in a state of perpetual unease and vigilance.

If you feel unseen eyes watching you as you read my story, beware. Your intuition is warning you that something sinister is lurking close by. Invisible eyes are peering into your soul, studying you, learning your secrets, just like they do me. Don't worry, you will know if they are near; you can feel them... their malevolent presence consumes you.

I will tell you what I have learned about this evil force that has made its way into our world. Evil holds a deep-seated grudge against me, and nothing will stop it from achieving its ultimate goal of destruction. I know this. I accept this. My understanding of it is limited, but the uncertainty of what lies ahead scares me to my very core.

As I delve into the mysterious tales of my beloved granny, Izzy, you will discover the extraordinary powers hidden within a coven of witches she was close to. This book is a reverent homage and celebration of their powerful magic and timeless strength.

My granny had an almost reverent kinship with the witches of her coven, but none so strong as with the grand high priestess, Topaz. Alongside her was Victor, a master of arcane arts, Molly, a warrior witch who always stood her ground, Amira, a natural born intuitive sorceress and Devansh, a young man with an abundance of magical prowess and enthusiasm. As I read their tales of supernatural might, I can only hope to grow to be half as powerful in my own pursuits.

The gory details of the occult practices are haunting—from the dark world of drugs and money laundering to sickening blood sacrifices, barbaric human trafficking, and other sickening atrocities.

The depravity of it all is beyond anything you can imagine. With each detail unveiled comes an even deeper disgust and fear that will disturb you, so I will do my best to spare you the details of the horror that I know.

*　✻　*

Whether you know it or not, evil has or will infiltrate your life as well. Be cautious, for it seeks not only to deceive but to devour us whole.

*　✻　*

-Lucy

PROLOGUE

I feel the shadows watching me. They descend on me like a plague, an ominous warning of the horror yet to come. They lurk around the edges of my bedroom almost every night, waiting for me to drift off into sleep so they can approach and bear witness to my vulnerable form. I know when they arrive; the darkness seems to grow as if they swallow all the light in the room, and a chill runs down my spine as I sense their presence near me.

Some nights, as I lay in bed, I'm comforted by a gentle purr coming from outside of my window. The neighbor's cat is perched there, her fur blowing in the breeze, while she loudly declares her presence with a deep rumble. She stands guard over me as I drift off into sleep, warning me with an angry hiss when the shadows approach too close. Despite my unease as I await the shadows, she always manages to put my mind at ease, providing an undeniable calmness and quelling my anxiety.

I jolt awake to the sound of her primal hiss, like the death rattle of a dying animal. My heart pounds against my chest like a caged beast trying to break free. I am trapped between sleep and wakefulness, paralyzed and helpless as they enter. The shadows around me take on a life of their own, with eyes that leer and watch me with disdain. They whisper in a language foreign to my ears, but their presence is ever so familiar to me.

For weeks, I held my breath as I waited for my sister and her friends, whom we jokingly call the crows, to expel the demonic witch from my body. Even then, her presence lingered in the shadows of my mind, stifling and sinister. Then, one day, my soul forced itself back into my body with a seismic wave of energy, banishing the witch away from me.

But what happened to her? Was she still out there somewhere, preying on some innocent child? Or—had she been cast down to Hell, like she so desperately wanted to do to me? My chest tightens as my breath comes in shallow gasps, unable to keep up with the frantic pace of the wicked thoughts that occupy my mind.

My pulse pounds like a raging river in my ears, and the walls of panic close in around me as I think of the horrors I know about and lived through. My breathing only begins to slow down when I *force* myself to accept the reality of the situation. Regardless of what happened before, I am once again reunited with my mother and sister. We hoped the lingering evilness looming over us was finally gone, but is it? After years of harassment by the witch, followed by nothingness, I live again, so for that, I am thankful.

I was thrust from the darkness of purgatory back into the world of living, a reminder of the cruel fate that befell me when I died as an innocent girl. My mother had been tortured with grief ever since my beloved father's sickness took his life. Then, one day, Granny arrived at our door and did all she could to ease my mother's pain; yet she seemed frightfully aware of the witch living across the street, her eyes heavy with fear for me. Granny sensed there was something sinister about this woman and knew all too well that I would need protection from her unnatural fascination with me.

I had naively assumed that Granny could overpower the witch with her protective spells. But when she stepped into the darkness of the witch's domain, I knew my granny would not be able to save me. The wickedness emanating from the witch was so strong, it sent tingles through every inch of my body, and I realized I was up against a far greater evil than I had ever imagined. Granny had tried to warn me, but I was too late in heeding her advice. In one fatal moment, my defiance cost me the ultimate price—*my life.*

My mother, Kezziah, was horrified by the world of magic ever since a nightmare-invading man threatened her. She experienced more than enough turbulent events to turn her away from sorcery once and for all. After so many years, without feeling any sort of magical presence in her life, she had no idea that a wicked witch was tormenting me or that a demonic being lurked in our yard, watching us. She had no idea how close danger really was.

Before my dad fell ill, a dark presence lurked in the shadows of our home, but no one—not even my sister, Mia—could sense the invisible evil stalking me. My mother's grief after his passing created a distraction that allowed the witch to cast her wicked plans against me. Despite her distress, Mia could not see through the mist of her own sorrows and growing pains as a young woman to realize I was being lured towards death by the witch. The truth became terrifyingly clear: neither my mom, Mia, nor anyone else could have saved me from becoming prey to the witch, even if they had known for certain what she wanted with my soul.

My granny's presence was a fleeting respite before her time came. She passed on to me a legacy of white magic for protection and gifted me with the writings of Topaz, Grand High Priestess of the coven—the best teacher in this realm. The books and journals left behind were humming with secret whispers of the powerful witches that once lived and fought against evil. The pages overflowed with spells and hexes—omens of shadows and horrors yet to come.

As I flipped through the pages of these books, I could sense a deeper, hidden meaning that seemed to be designed just for me. Regret swells within me that even with such a precious gift bestowed, I squandered it away in comfort, neglecting to practice what could have saved my life—my very soul. Absent guidance from these very books and journals, my soul would have surely been to be taken into the dark underworld.

When I was on the brink of giving up, my mother, sister, Mia, and her loyal friends swooped in like a flock of crows, ready to protect their own. With an arsenal built from ancient works of magic passed down by my grandmother, and a win-at-all-costs mentality that crows can possess, these incredible women fought for me—to save my soul from the damned. Together, they boldly stood against injustice and used cleverness and courage to ensure we all survived.

The friends of my sister were like angels sent to save me from the clutches of death. Their bravery and quick thinking granted me a second chance—a chance that I will never take for granted again. If any one of those fierce ladies were to be in harm's way, I would march through hellfire and beyond to defend them.

I am now more vigilant than ever before, pouring over the secrets of magic left by my granny and Topaz, and gathering knowledge on how to defend against the many evils that lurk in this world. Death and darkness surround us daily, camouflaged by the façade of normalcy. I keep my eyes peeled at all times, ever aware of their malevolent intentions.

May we all live long enough to face our demons head-on and come out victorious. I have been consumed by my studies, pouring over spells and learning the dark origins of the witch who stole my very body. But in the midst of this bleakness, a bright spot shines through: Charlie, my fellow crow and soul sister. Together, we delve deep into the craft, working magic until the witching hour draws nigh.

When I regained control of my body, I took back what was rightfully mine. Every bit of wealth the evil witch had amassed—every inch of land she had owned—all became forfeited to those in need. And as I watched her empire crumble before my very eyes, I knew in my heart that she had sold her very soul for riches beyond measure that I happily gave away.

But it wasn't enough to simply reclaim what was mine. No, I gave her empire to the children caught in the crosshairs of earthly monsters like herself, who received aid from the properties she had once controlled, while her ill-gotten gains were divided among the courageous women who had helped me reclaim my body. I only kept one thing—the house she purchased across the street from my sister and her family.

Though I knew then that I would forever be changed by this ordeal, I felt a sense of pride—pride in knowing that I could turn even the darkest moment into something beautiful by helping children.

My insides quiver in anticipation of what I know is coming. Even though I haven't seen the witch since regaining my body, something in the depths of my soul warns me this isn't over. I practice white magic rituals feverishly in an effort to protect myself from whatever she has in store for me. She has done unspeakable acts for her malevolent god, and I doubt he will let me go free without a fight.

The ache within my bones intensifies, heralding her return. What other tools do I have to withstand her evil? I must learn more about her dark powers and use them against her if need be. As much as I want to forget, I can't escape this twisted fate—this horror story that began when she stole my life away from my family and condemned them to a living nightmare.

I tore open the pages of Topaz's books and journals, only to be confronted with horrific tales of those who had suffered before me. The evil witch still lingers in my mind; her presence cloys on my soul like a thick smog and haunts my every waking moment. I know that one day soon, her malevolent spirit will come for me. I can feel it lurking in the shadows of my thoughts, biding its time until the moment comes when I have no choice but to confront it. I steel myself against her wickedness, and my only prayer is that I am strong enough to conquer her and whatever nefarious plans she has in store.

I have shed my naive childlike innocence. I am well aware of the looming darkness that surrounds me, and this time, when it emerges from the shadows to consume me, there will be no surrender. I shall not retreat into the abyss; I will stand my ground and face its terror with unyielding courage. No matter what comes, I will stay steadfast in the face of evil.

LET THERE BE DARKNESS

y heart raced as I frantically considered why the evil witch had chosen to haunt me—why she wanted to sacrifice my soul. What heinous crime was I being made to pay for? Why me? No matter how much I pondered, no answers came. When I was younger, I assumed that my innocence made me beyond reproach, but as it turns out, I was wrong. As my best friend, Charlie, looked at me with deep-seated curiosity, a shiver of terror ran through my body when she asked, "Lucy, what could have possibly provoked the witch to target you, drawing you into her sinister web? When did you become so ensnared in her sinister games?"

* ✱ · **How far back should I go?** · ✱ ·

The evil game I was drawn into began when the most beloved angel was kicked out of Heaven. God threw the traitor, Beelzebub, into the bottomless pits of Hell all those many, *many* years ago. As the dark angel passed through the Earth, he fell hard and unfathomably quickly. The Earth shook with such great force that the land rumbled, tearing away from itself. The booming force of his fall even rattled the golden gates in the realm of Heaven.

The angel plummeted into the depths of the infernal abyss, screaming as he was swallowed by a sea of burning embers and darkness. Lucifer plummeted through the searing void, his cries of anguish echoing off the fiery walls as he was cast out of Heaven. He raged against his fate, every muscle tightening with frustration and pain. The putrid smell of death and decay hung in the air. Gigantic lizards decorated the walls, their beady eyes watching as anacondas slithered in the shadows, their hissing echoing in the air like the sneers of the damned. Hellfire blazed around them, searingly hot and untamable. This was it. This will be Beelzebub's kingdom—the eternal prison for those that fall from grace, choosing sin over all else.

The once-heavenly guardian angel was now experiencing an all-encompassing pain that filled every inch of his body. His rapid, reckless plunge into Hell's dark depths created a magnitude of torment he had never before conceived. He screamed out in agony as the searing pain intensified with each passing second.

Hatred, darker than the depths of Hell itself, coursed through him like a raging river, consuming him with malice. His envy in Heaven was nothing compared to this feeling—an uncontrollable fury that demanded retribution at any price.

Satan's venomous machinations resulted in an unforgivable exile of the other fallen angels. Satan and his evil darlings were banished from Heaven. Stripped of their connection to Yahweh and the divine beings they once viewed as family, they capitalized on the freedom to wreak untold destruction with impunity. Thus, it was written: the once-illustrious angel now reviled God Almighty—Yahweh.

Satan and his evil horde of fallen angels, scheming in the shadows, were expelled from the Kingdom of Peace. With voracious rage they disappeared into the abyss of Hell. Now that the Devil had severed his ties to Heaven and the divine creatures he once regarded as family, he would rain chaos without remorse. And so, it was done: the former great angel was now publicly shamed in the sight of God.

Satan fell from grace hard as he plummeted from the Kingdom of Heaven with no sense of good within him anymore. He was no longer an angel but now a *fallen* angel—the Devil. As he fell into the pit of Hell, Satan inhaled the smoldering air surrounding him, and his bitterness amplified. He could now feel and experience physical pain and even disappointment—the same disappointments God must have shared with his once beloved angel's betrayal.

Satan's scarlet veins bulged with white-hot rage as pain and anguish washed over him like a relentless wave. Toxic hatred for God, all of Heaven, and every last trace of the Lord's creation boiled in his belly until it overflowed from the depths of Hell and spread like an unholy plague across the world—the pinnacle of the divine's creation. His vile emotions blanketed the land, poisonous and dark.

Satan felt the tightness around his throat grow as he descended into Hell. His lungs were consumed with heavy, smothering soot, and his three large hearts thundered loudly in his ears. He clenched his fists tightly, feeling the sharp pain of his long, filthy nails digging deep into his palms to keep himself from SCREAMING! Rage coursed through his veins, turning his gray skin into a deep reddish hue that glowed with seething anger. He became powerless against the currents of rage as they surged uncontrollably through him, threatening to consume and incinerate him.

Satan's descent through the starry abyss was swift and relentless. As he plummeted, his body warped and changed into a monstrous figure. His legs morphed to become those of an abominable beast, pounding like drums as they struck the stars, aching in agony from his fall from the heavens above. The Devil stood upon these charred appendages, with rage burning behind his glowing eyes.

Satan's wings were once majestic and dazzling, a crowning achievement of God's gifts. But as he plummeted through the air, his prized feathers gathered filthy soot and grime until they were reduced to nothing more than blackened clumps. His spectacular wings, which had been filled with glorious white feathers, molted away. Every feather fell away—a cruel reminder of what he had lost in his fall from Heaven.

The feathers began to fall from Satan's wings like dried rose petals in the wind. As they reached the ground below, they erupted into flames, their ashes dispersing across the sizzling landscape before him. With each passing feather, his rage and resentment of God grew more intense. He thought that if he had just been given more time, perhaps he could've kept his beloved wings—the ones that carried him through Heaven with such glory and grandeur only the day before.

But then the pain came—a sharp ache that ripped through his spine as thick black thorns pushed out of his skin. His wings were being ripped away from him and replaced by these new horrors, an abomination that felt like a cursed punishment. When the old feathers and wings finally crumbled away completely, all his hope was gone.

Satan's wings were brutally disfigured, as he was cursed by the Mighty One. Growing thick, leathery veins, the wings twitched and quivered, the burnt fur and thinning mange hairs revealing a grotesque form of beauty. No longer beautiful in any traditional sense, these jagged wings betrayed what Satan had become: tainted with evil beyond repair, his transformation into the *beast*.

Satan's skull contorted in agony as his demonic form emerged. His once-handsome face broke apart like glass as the bones underneath shifted and morphed into sharp, monstrous features. His eyes glowed with hellfire, and maggots oozed out of every pore, forming a writhing mass across his flesh. He felt a heavy tail rip through his skin, bristling with dark fur that dragged behind him like a noose. As the transformation surged through his veins, he felt an intense fear gripping within him. He watched in horror as his body turned into a vile and repugnant creature, dripping with malice and hatred from every pore. His mind became corrupted by loathing and despair, until all that remained was a monstrous abomination. The angelic halo that once surrounded his head tore off from the thick bones of his skull and melted into a pool of molten embers at his beastly feet.

Satan felt a searing sensation rip through his skull as two horns, sharp and pointed like spears, plunged through his leathery skin and thick bones. He screamed with agonizing pain as his head throbbed, wracked with spasms that turned his vision opaque. The horns became larger with each passing second, unstoppable in their growth, until they curled up and around the sides of his head like crowning thorns. A cold sweat broke out across the Devil's body, and he dropped to his knees, grasping at the horns as if to pluck them from existence. But they stayed rooted in his skull, an ever-present reminder of God's punishment and Satan's eternal damnation. With every breath, he could feel his hatred for God intensify, his bitter resentment filling him up like poison.

The power of Satan's wrath filled the air, and darkness descended like a shroud upon the army of fallen angels. Desperate screams pierced the walls of Hell as they looked on at Lucifer being morphed into a towering monster, his face twisting in a mask of pure evil. He laughed at the screams of fear that came from his broken army, reveling in their own agony from the fall from above. The fallen angels trembled in terror, cowering before him in submission. They were far too weak to resist; all had been drained of their celestial beauty by the transformation inflicted upon them. As they dragged their limp bodies to the feet of Beelzebub, they could feel his piercing eyes mocking them, daring them to try and defy him. The once-beautiful beings were now enslaved to the beast for eternity—their punishment for trying to overthrow God and rule Heaven.

Satan's army of demons contorted in agony as their celestial forms warped into grotesque creatures of all shapes and sizes. Abominable appendages, claws like daggers, and horns erupting from their heads pulsed with unholy energy. They adopted the forms of other worldly beasts, like amphibious terrors or galactic insects, growing to be large and domineering.

Their shining wings shriveled and molted away, some left transparently thin as if mocking the former beauty that resided there before. Others were left with knotted gaps where glorious feathers should have been—a reminder of the heavens they denounced.

The heat seared their skin, and dried parched mouths cried out to God for relief, their pleas unheard as He turned His back on those who chose the path of exile alongside Satan, His once-beloved Lucifer, son of the morning.

An evil like none other descended upon them, a consuming hatred set fire to those created by the giver of light. The darkness around the rebel angels released unbridled malice. The heat left the new beings—the demons—thirsting for even only a drop of water. Yahweh turned away from these evil beasts and their cries. An unrelenting craving for revenge against the one true creator raged within them as he turned away from the evilness that swelled within each one of his once-beloved angels.

A devastating aura of darkness and terror filled the room, and an atmosphere of pure evil grew. Demons slinked about in the shadows like a pack of feral beasts, feeding on Satan's malicious energy. The once-proud angels had chosen to follow an inferior and selfish leader rather than God and were now permanently cursed to obey their sinister lord.

Satan threw back his head in a wildly sinister laugh, his deep roar echoing through every realm. His curses on God blasted through the air as he screamed with unfettered rage. The other fallen angels—the demons—rose from their knees and joined in with cries of wild abandon. In a wild frenzy, they raised Satan high above their heads and worshiped him. He was now *their* god. The demoniacs began screaming and howling as they praised their horned god. They celebrated their own damnation and the prospect of causing pain and suffering to the world with unbridled glee, behaving like rabid animals wallowing in their own filth.

Satan plotted and schemed, determined to make the innocents in the worlds above into his enslaved entities. He offered them confusion, temptation, greed, and lust as bait. He knew that they would sooner or later turn away from their divine Creator towards him, a wretched spirit of sin and darkness—Beelzebub, The Lion, The Father of Shadows, The Accuser, The Tempter—and his would be the kingdom these creations would serve if they chose to follow him astray.

He seized their thoughts and desires until they followed his will alone. Satisfaction surged through him as he watched more and more of God's creations drift away from His holy light and deeper into the cavernous depths of Hell. After all, he was the Day Star, the one who brought a perverse glimmer of false promises to those hapless souls. He was certain that many would succumb to his beguiling lies without so much as an afterthought.

Beelzebub's mind raced as he plotted his revenge on the almighty Creator. His plan was diabolical—a slow and meticulous process to wean humans away from God. With each human life created, Satan's joy grew, knowing that some of them would be God's undoing. Their souls were eternal gifts from God that Satan wanted to possess and force into servitude.

Satan relished in his plan of using those with divine gifts against their very Creator; the thought of an insidious *human* uprising enthralled him. He became obsessed as he envisioned a *beautiful* betrayal, much like the fall that he and his brothers experienced centuries ago. Satan delighted at the thought of God having to sentence *His* newest creations to eternal fire... much like he did Satan and the other fallen angels. He delighted further, dreaming of the uprising—the battle he so badly wanted to lead against God. Every magical soul could be a weapon, and he wanted to use the very human souls he loathed in his goal to overthrow God.

Satan schemed up a wicked plan to enslave the purest of spirits of the wise beings that held divine, powerful souls. Hungrily searching for those with these bewitchingly blessed souls, he prowled the Earth in search of them, intent on using their magical powers for his own gain. He was determined to harness their magical blessings and add them to his own dark army. Torn from their bodies, these souls were condemned to an eternity of suffering in his malevolent grasp.

Satan had plans to merge these powerful souls with his own creations and birth soldiers that even the archangels would struggle to battle against. Over many years he succeeded, having his witches pluck one soul after another from innocent beings.

The Devil was crafty and calculating, determined to wrench the world upside down with hatred, chaos, and intolerance of one another as an effective smokescreen. He thirsted for hate-filled sins and cursed souls. Satan commanded his sinister, cryptid beings to whisper into the ears of talented purveyors of magic; they sought to sow confusion and doubt, transforming them into vulnerable targets ready to descend into the depths of dark magic.

In some cases, Satan's devils were successful in converting practitioners into wicked witches infused with dark power. The dark forces of Hell roamed the Earth, seeking out magical and gifted humans to enslave for their master's sinister ambitions. Monstrous witches, cursed with unholy strength and power, worked diligently to bring the most valuable souls to their malevolent lord.

As they pillaged innocent lives in preparation for war against God and His mighty angels, it became abundantly clear that Satan had no intention of losing this battle. His determination drove him ever forward in his quest to rewrite the Book of Revelations, replacing God's supremacy with his own. Forcing God to His knees before the celestial angels, he wanted Him to beg for mercy, to plead for a tiny drop of water as his dry mouth thirsts as he and the demons did as they were cast into Hell. With every soul he steals, Satan strives closer to making Yahweh pay for turning his back on them.

The dying light of the sun casts a pallor of doom over the world as Satan rigs his army of the damned and readies them to make war with their Creator. With piercing eyes, Satan thirsts for revenge and hungers to inflict unrestrained pain on Yahweh's creations in hopes of finally breaking Him.

Satan hungers for the oncoming war, eagerly anticipating the sound of the trumpets that will set flames to the world. His eyes gleam in anticipation as he plots his revenge, longing for the day when he can plunge humanity into despair and bring about ruin and destruction. In the depths of Hell, his fiery spirit rages with an unquenchable thirst for bloodshed.

◆ ✳ ◆

OK—Perhaps my destiny with the witch didn't begin that far back...

◆ ✳ ◆

But Charlie did have my mind curious... When was that moment when evil first crept into my life? Was it a moment of choice, or was it something innate within me? Was it an unfortunate coincidence—kismet—or did I do something deserving of all this torment? I have yet to answer this question that plagues me. Each time I begin to wonder, I can't help but feel a strange sense of dread. Was it fate or just bad luck that brought evil into my life?

IN THE BEGINNING

s I laid in my bed, I was overwhelmed by the fearful memories of when evil had first found me. I could swear that something ominous was watching me from the shadows, as if some sinister presence was lurking in my room. My body felt frozen and motionless with fear, but I still held my eyes tightly closed. A chill slowly began to fill the air, followed by strange and moving shadows dancing around my room.

The shadows haunt me still, filling me with dread. Sometimes I feel like a child again, experiencing the same terror that had once plagued my youth. Sometimes, just as suddenly as the shadows would appear, they would begin to leave, disappearing into the darkness. They would scurry away once a more commanding, dominant presence arrived.

The presence carried an allure more powerful than even death itself. The bewitching spirit made me feel protected and safe. After it chased the shadows into the darkness, the spirit would stay nearby, lingering throughout the night, keeping watch over me. Despite its strong and mysterious nature, I found myself drawn towards it in a way that seemed both calming and comforting.

I never felt scared or intimidated by this presence. Instead, I would find myself drawn to its alluring call. It is not like the witch that terrorized me when I was young. This spirit felt like an unstoppable force. It was unyielding and unapologetic. This mysterious figure stays close to me, even after the shadows have dissipated.

I felt a conflicting mix of emotions when I would see its silhouette looming on my wall. On the one hand, it was comforting to be reminded that I was not alone and that something was there to protect me. Yet, on the other hand, I was filled with dread, knowing that I was not safe in my own bedroom, and needed protecting.

The shadows seemed to mock me with their cold stares and whispers. I was trapped in a web of fear and anger. Sometimes, I was so afraid I was unable to move or call out for help. The darkness seemed to take pleasure in the fear that it caused me. My teeth chattered and goosebumps formed despite the unbearable heat around me when the shadows would visit. All I could do was lay still, hoping that my guardian would come soon and dispel the shadows from my room.

After a while, I grew more exhausted than afraid of the unsolicited visits. As much as I tried to stay calm, fury raged inside of me at this unwelcome intrusion into my life, just like when I had been powerless as a young girl.

Many nights, as the witching hour arrived, I prepared for the shadows. It became part of my routine. The neighbor's cat would hiss outside my window, warning of their impending visit. Before I could even take a full breath into my lungs, the shadow people would be upon me. Their hate radiated off them like waves of blistering heat, infecting every inch of the room with a foul stench. Then, one day, I decided I wasn't going to be theirs to taunt: not anymore. I was tired of it all. With courage built up within me, I stood up in bed and faced them head-on.

The shadows moved fast as they scurried to the corner of the room, huddled tightly together. They appeared darker than any other shadows cast by the moonlight that shone through the window. Yet still, I felt relieved to see mere shadows rather than something more sinister. Summoning all my strength, I put the entities on notice, my voice becoming commanding and stern.

"I see you," I declared boldly while glaring at them with determination in my eyes. "I know you're here, and you won't defeat me!" My voice echoed through the room as panic and fear coursed through my veins.

They remained silent, but their malevolent energy continued to swirl around me, threatening to overwhelm me with its power.

Despite shaking with fear, I cussed at them and yelled until they finally began to disappear back into the darkness from which they came. As much as I tried to convince myself that this wouldn't be how I spent my time back on Earth, deep down inside, I knew there was no escape from their insidious grasp.

My heart was pounding in my chest as I stood in the dark, willing my courage to grow. No longer was I the living dead girl who was taken away from her family. I was a powerful woman, and nothing would take me away from them again. My fear of death no longer haunted me, and I refused to be intimidated by any force that tried to threaten my peace. At least, this is what I told myself every night as I faced and conquered my own fears.

The lifelessness of death had been my home for far too long, and I was determined to not be dragged into Hell without a fight. It was then I decided... I needed to do my best to be my own guardian. It was me who had to continue forward, and I didn't need to rely on an unknown entity for protection.

It was then that fear no longer had control over me; I would stand my ground and face whatever came next. I shouted at the shadows, and sometimes they would retreat, other times they would not. After a while, they did not flinch or flee like they did when the mysterious figure would come to my aid or when I would initially confront them. I knew they were testing me.

My agitation grew as I flipped on light switches, illuminating them; yet still, they remained unfazed. The shadow people would come to look in on me, and it would be me that began chasing them away. I got fairly good at standing my ground against them. The guardian began showing up less and less as I took more control over my fear.

After a while, the presence only began showing up in times of utter desperation and helplessness. It was almost as if the bewitching spirit was summoned by my overwhelming fear and worry. The more I could manage my own fear, the less I would feel the presence of the guardian spirit.

Sometimes the shadows were too overpowering for me. The guardian appeared like a specter, unleashing an unearthly power that banished the shadows away from me as my screams echoed through the house. Evey so often, when the shadows were chased away by the guardian spirit, their presence were revealed by flickering lights, illuminating their ominous, monstrous shadows. My mother would bolt into the room, her eyes wide with panic as she took in the scene—barely missing the shadows as they exited my room. I clung to her like a lifeline, grateful for her warmth and steady breathing that anchored me to reality.

"What's wrong?" Her voice would shake, barely louder than a mutter. I always lied through my teeth, assuring her everything was fine and that it was just bad dreams causing night terrors. But the truth was far worse. The shadows had been watching me—even in my sleep. They were dark, hateful beings that sucked the light out of every corner they touched.

I couldn't tell my mother about them, though; she was already worried enough as it was. If she knew what lurked in the darkness beside me, she would never let me leave her sight again. I knew the danger wasn't going away anytime soon. It was only a matter of time before something terrible happened. And when it did, I knew I would need to be ready. The evil would not go away on its own; I never had that kind of luck.

* ✳ *

Every morning, I woke up with the same dread and exhaustion that I had gone to sleep with. My eyes drooped heavily from a night full of harassment, troubled dreams, and endless insomnia. I haven't been able to sleep properly since I returned to my body—a body that feels so foreign and unfamiliar, despite being my own.

Regardless of all my efforts, I still feel like a stranger in my own skin. After having died at such a young age, it was difficult to come back and inhabit the same body as an adult. It felt like I was living a life that wasn't mine—like I was living in someone else's house, sleeping on their couch, when they didn't even want me to be there.

I stood in front of the mirror, looking at my reflection with a critical eye. I'd gone to Charlie for help in updating my look. After reaching for the scissors, she had chopped off my long locks that the witch, Lacy, grew out when she possessed my body, leaving my hair falling just above my elbows. The brown lowlights that she added to give definition to my face were my favorite part of the new style. Shopping with her was a bit of a battle, though, as I tried unsuccessfully to hang on to my comfort zone of nineties grunge clothing, which had found its way back in style again.

The music that blared from car radios, the movies that lined theater shelves, and the television shows that filled prime time slots were a far cry from what I remembered before dying as a twelve-year-old. Time had moved on without me while I was in limbo, leaving me to catch up with the world and unable to make sense of the massive changes that had occurred.

My social queues felt out of tune; emotions and conversations were like foreign languages to me now. I knew I needed help getting back into step with society, but it was overwhelming. I still lacked patience and understanding. So, as best as I could, I tried to ease myself into the ever-changing world. I tried my best to be a mature adult.

• ✸ •

The legacy of Granny Izzy and my mother, Kezziah, burns inside me like fire, setting my soul alight with their gifts of magic that have been passed to me. With each breath I take, I inhale the power of the witches who came before me, each syllable calling forth the potency and strength of their ancestry. For my family, friends, and the witches that have come before us, I live on.

Studying the books and journals of sorcery is how I realized I learned and became educated through observation of Mia when I was in purgatory. I matured and learned this way unknowingly. My mom had never been religious or spiritual, but her mother practiced magic handed down from the grand high priestess, Topaz. Because of her, Granny Izzy knew how to make a doll in my likeness—the one that safeguarded me when my soul was hunted.

I hadn't realized it then, but the doll was a tether to my family home. With Mom and Mia bustling around me, packing and cleaning in preparation for Mom's move, my senses sharpened, and I stirred awake. I was somewhat... stuck between two worlds—one of semi-conscious dreaming and another of full awareness. My soul was in the realm of—the in between—asleep in limbo.

Granny had followed Topaz's instructions to make the doll, just for me. After being stirred awake, I clung to the doll out of desperation. My soul latched on to it, so I wouldn't be left behind. While my soul was being sheltered inside the doll, I was protected and well-aware of everything going on around me.

Being in the doll was different than when I was in limbo. While in limbo, I was blissfully unaware of my own death and imprisonment. My soul slept in a void; unaware I was dead. Nevertheless, I was still able to observe the outside world, I just didn't know it. It was almost like, being tucked away in a womb; I was safe and protected. I could hear things but had no understanding or awareness as to what was going on around me.

As I study magic, I believe that, at least one journal is missing... maybe more. I also suspect that I do not have the complete collection of books given to my granny that were passed down to me.

Granny always wanted to shield me from the consequences of dark magic; I wonder if, perhaps, she purposefully hid away some of the books or journals. All the books and journals have been invaluable sources, providing a wealth of knowledge and insight that have helped me gain clarity and understanding of the underworld. *The Golden Book of Sorcery*, written by Topaz, was filled with useful information, almost as if it was written for me. This journal was my favorite.

I have already learned so much through the immense amount of information within each book. While poring over every page, my mind raced with newfound understanding, absorbing every word. As I recount what I have learned of Granny Izzy and my mom, Kezziah's life with you, I will make my best effort to refer to them by their given names. That way, I can share their perspectives more vividly.

My great-grandmother, Lucrecia, was born gifted with light and magic. Even at a young age, she knew there was a fine line between dark and light magic. Izzy always said that her mother was kind and loving, but she had suddenly changed into a distant, cruel person who was not the woman she once knew. Izzy shared her mother's story by explaining that it was not really her mother when she turned cold and hateful—it was the influence of dark magic.

Izzy had such complex feelings when it came to her mother. Though she knew in her heart that her mother was not a naturally evil person, Izzy faced the reality of her mother's behavior and how it had been influenced by dark forces. Izzy admitted, when she was younger, she desperately wanted to make excuses for her mother and believed that she would never do anything as malicious as turning to the occult. Yet, she just couldn't ignore a nagging feeling that something sinister was at play.

When Izzy was a young lady, she loved her mother dearly and felt a deep sadness for her. She knew that her mother wasn't inherently evil; she was misguided and influenced by dark forces. On one hand, Izzy wanted to accept her mother as the woman she used to know and love; on the other, she feared that the darkness had taken over completely and there was no going back. Izzy desperately wanted to make excuses for her behavior, but at the same time, she knew that if she had really gone down the path of the occult, nothing would ever be the same again.

Izzy had always known there were secrets lurking in the shadows of her family, but she had no idea what those secrets were until years after her mother's death. Izzy hadn't realized years of psychological torment and abuse consumed Lucrecia, leaving her with little hope when she was a young girl. She desperately fought to keep her tragic past hidden from her husband and children, burying it deep within the depths of her soul. She did her best to try to keep the darkness she once experienced from eating away at her happiest moments.

Izzy kept these secrets hidden for many years, never having the courage to share them with anyone other than her siblings. But just before Izzy passed away—she told her daughter the truth of our family's history, allowing these dark secrets to step forward into the light.

Kezziah was determined to pass on the vital knowledge she had acquired, protecting me from the evils that lurked in the shadows. She knew it was futile to attempt to hide magic from me any longer, for she accepted that it would forever be part of our lives. She deeply regretted not taking Izzy's stories seriously, but given what she had learned, Kezziah wasn't sure if those tales were fantasy rather than reality at the time. Now, she has resolved that I should know all that Izzy imparted.

After all that we had been through with the witch that hunted me, she now knew that the stories of our family's history were true. She knew I had to know everything, even the darkest parts. Of course, we would rather not have to face the past, and sometimes we fear the future, but there is nowhere to hide from any of it.

She stared at me with an eerie calmness, knowing I hungered for the truth. Her voice was a low whisper as she spoke in measured tones, each word landing like a heavy blow. "You want to know everything? Fine. But let me warn you, what lies ahead is darkness beyond the worst of nightmares."

With that warning her eyes glazed over, and she began recounting horrors that were not in the journals. Stories passed down to her, so awful Topaz did not want to put them in writing. The stories of Satan worshipers, so grotesque my mind recoiled from them. Yet, I listened with rapt attention as she continued speaking, unflinching in intimate detail about every twisted turn of events that led to our present situation.

The journals warned of evilness that was determined to follow the family. We were hexed, no doubt. Izzy had taught her daughter about the magic that came with being part of our family—a magic that gave us strength and protection from those that wish to break us. I knew it was important to learn the magic within the books and journals entrusted to me.

Kezziah chose against using magic when she got older, hoping her gifts would disappear. She was sure by doing this, the world of enchantment would leave her and her family alone. This would be a decision she'd regret.

Of course, after everything, she wishes she didn't cast her magic aside. Her father didn't want her around magic, so she never was a practitioner. Now, she tries desperately to recall the forgotten spells and incantations she would hear Izzy recite. In her mind, she faults herself... if she had kept practicing, surely then she would have known about the witch living across the street. Now, after so many years of abandoning magic, Kezziah felt as if all of her magical prowess had been sapped away, leaving nothing but an empty void where her knowledge should have been. Casting her gifts away has become one of her biggest regrets.

Izzy always told her daughter to use magic cautiously and carefully, making sure not to be consumed by its power. As she passed the journals filled with secrets of magic to me, she stared deep into my eyes while she solemnly warned me to keep that advice at the forefront of my mind.

My mom was not the only one filled with regret. I had neglected my gifts and intuition, completely disregarding that uneasy feeling in the depths of my stomach about the witch. I should not have settled into a misguided comfort and neglect my protection spells. Little did I know, succumbing to my day-to-day life and comfort, was just part of her malicious plan. The witch had expertly positioned herself in my blind spot, out of sight and out of mind—all part of her calculated plot. Her intentions hidden behind a façade of innocence, waiting to be revealed in the most devastating way possible.

If, younger me, had been smarter—if I had listened to the warnings of Izzy, I would have surely noticed the wickedness that lurked in the shadows—I probably wouldn't have been led to my demise. I was always left to ponder "what ifs," yet at the same time, life had already forced me to accept the harsh reality that it was too late. It already happened and now, I can only move forward and stop looking back.

I know Izzy and my mother, Kezziah, were both haunted by the dark side of sorcery and enchantment in their own lives long before me. It took my death to teach us a lesson—not all magic is terrible. Just like prayer, some magic can be used for defense and tranquility. Sometimes, magic is necessary.

Before I passed, I was blessed with "gifts" of magic. As a young girl, I believed it was all in my head, but soon I learned otherwise: hearing stories, reading about events, dreaming of things to come—all these were visions that had happened or would occur in the future.

So, as I hear, read, and share the tales, I witness them as they truly are, were, and will be—finally understanding the power of my gifts. Clairvoyance, clairaudience, claircognizance... sounds like they're wonderful blessings, and I guess they can be. These gifts of magic can also feel like a huge... pain in the ass too!

Thanks to old journals and retelling of spells and magic, Charlie and the crows were able to save me from a witch who wanted my soul. But there were many other tales yet to be revealed between the pages of the journals Izzy left behind. When scouring the journals, these stories were unread by Charlie, Mia, and the others. They were looking for spells and instructions on saving me. They didn't have an interest in the diary and tales of the life of Topaz. They needed quick answers.

I have, however, taken an interest in these stories left behind, written before the high priestess passed away. For many years, several books and journals were packed away with so many other sentimental items that Izzy saved. Before she died, Izzy had lovingly packed them away. She placed them among her most valued possessions, items like old photographs and trinkets she'd collected over the years. As the dust settled around them, these precious mementos lay tucked away in her storage for a long time.

Kezziah confided in me how she tried to avoid Izzy's storage unit, especially after my passing. She dreaded the emotions of coming across items of her parents, her deceased husband, and, of course, her deceased child, me. Each time she had to go there to look for something, or to put more things away, her heart would sink as she would lift the door. The smell of the stale room made it even more somber. Sometimes when she would have to go there, she would end up stumbling out of the unit disheveled and tear-streaked, vowing to never go back echoing in her head.

After my death, she didn't have the strength to relive the years. In the wake of my passing, she desperately tried to shield herself from the memories that could stir her sadness. Everyone grieves differently—she went into survival mode, trying not to allow herself to think about the lives or deaths of her loved ones. So, my bedroom, the storage room... remained mostly untouched. She didn't rummage through things too often, in fear of what she may come across that could trigger her heartache.

Although she didn't like going to the storage unit, she felt a faint tug, a stirring inside that told her it was time to go back. Now that I had been resurrected, the journey ahead didn't seem so daunting for her; yet her heart still pounded against her chest with every thought of what we may come across. My sister's husband, Tyler, watched their son Jacob and my sister drove us to the unit so we could go through Izzy's possessions. Even though I had a number of books and journals already, we knew I needed the rest of the books.

Mia and I worked in silence, gently handling boxes and items that hadn't been opened for years. We held up photographs of long-forgotten relatives, old toys our mom had played with when she was a child, and a battered guitar belonging to Izzy's father. Mia and I loaded some boxes of books into the car as my mom continued to look around.

I noticed her standing still as she looked down. Watery-eyed, she knelt and lifted the top off of a small box. She pulled out a thin book and what looked to be a personal diary. She ran her fingers lovingly over the bindings before setting them down on the floor. The fear of unearthing memories that had been kept hidden away churned in her stomach as she slowly opened it.

As she flipped through the diary, I picked up the book. I knew I needed to read it; there was so much more I needed to know, and it called to me. Perhaps that, too, is what filled my mother with dread. Most of the books and journals I had at home were all written, hand-bound, and ribboned by Topaz or Izzy. But... these were not. This book and diary belonged to Izzy's mother. These were written by Lucrecia.

ONE WHO BRINGS LIGHT

Once we made it back home, I took the book and diary to my room. I ran my fingers over the leather cover of the diary and gently opened it. My great-grandmother's name, Lucrecia, was inscribed in faded gold leaf on the first page. I paused, taking a moment to reflect on what her name meant—*one who brings light*—before turning to the entry that began her story. I could almost feel her presence as I read: a young girl crossing an ocean with her father, so full of sorrow for the mother she never knew. A new life and hope waiting for them in America.

Lucrecia was almost two when her father remarried after courting a lady named Helen Jackson. Helen had deep-set hazel eyes and amber freckles dappling both cheeks, like brush strokes of burnt sienna on eggshell-colored fabric. Her hair, the color of rusted metal, was swept up in a tidy, soft bun, but it was inevitable that stray escaped curls would drift across her forehead and into her eyes. She kept constant vigil over her ruby-red lips, which were usually chapped from constantly chewing on them while she schemed.

Lucrecia had been living with her stepmother for years but was never able to form any kind of bond with her. No matter how hard she tried, Helen always seemed to keep her at a distance, and Lucrecia could feel the covetous gaze of her stepmother watching her. The three lived in a small town where rumors about witchcraft surrounded their family. Lucrecia would often hear the heated arguments between her father and Helen, making her feel even more isolated and lonely. She would shelter away with fright over the rumbling disputes.

Lucrecia had been fighting tears for weeks, feeling helpless in her own life. She eventually came to the conclusion that she needed to tell her father, hoping he would be the one to save her from her misery. But instead of comfort, Lucrecia was met with hostility from her father's wife, Helen. Even though she expected an argumentative response, it still crushed Lucrecia's already fragile heart.

Helen's words felt like a punch in the gut to Lucrecia. Her beloved father had abandoned them both, leaving her with a gaping hole in her heart where his love used to be. She could not comprehend why he wouldn't take her away with him, or why he would leave her alone with Helen. Her tiny frame trembled, and tears ran down her face as her heart was ripped out of its chest cavity with a white-hot knife of anguish.

Lucrecia worshiped her father as if he were a god among men. Even after he left, his shadow loomed over her like a dark cloud. But when her stepmother arrived, the clouds grew thicker until they suffocated Lucrecia's spirit. Helen's cruel words became daggers that pierced her heart, while the beatings left bruises that never healed. The pain of being forgotten was almost unbearable; it felt like she was slowly fading away into nothingness. But even as hope dwindled and despair mounted, Lucrecia gnashed her teeth and vowed to survive no matter what.

Lucrecia stared into the mirror, trying to find a hint of her mother's features in her own face. Despite being much too young to remember such things, she yearned for some kind of connection with her missing parents. As if an answer to her silent prayers, Lucrecia found an old chest of her father's when Helen was away. While rummaging through it, she discovered a worn photo of her mother. Her beauty was breathtaking. Lucrecia's breath caught in her throat as she took in the beauty of the faded picture held tightly against her heart.

Linda, Lucrecia's mother, had long, flowing brunette hair with the same familiar curves on her face. Her smile was easy and lit up her eyes. Lucrecia's nose and soft, plump lips were just like her mother's. They seemingly had identical tall, slender builds. Although the photo was black and white, Lucrecia could tell they shared the same faultless, smooth skin.

Lucrecia would sneak the old photograph of her mother out any time Helen left the house. Lucrecia had never known her mother, who had died when she was very young. She could not remember the time before her mother's death, but that did not matter now.

Lucrecia looked at her mother's face as she touched her own. Her mother's eyes looked full of kindness, soft and almost glowing, despite being half-closed in a gentle smile. There was a light on in Linda's soulful eyes, as if the photographer had captured a burst of joyful energy there and put it into a picture for Lucrecia to see. Her mother's gaze made her feel inexplicably protected and loved, like an invisible embrace that seemed to wrap around her until all her worries melted away.

It made her feel happy to think that maybe this was what her mother might have been like. She studied the photo carefully, looking at Linda's features, knowing she inherited many of them. The only spot of color in Linda's image was the startling flashes of citrine in her dark maple irises. It seemed to pulse with life. Lucrecia knew her eyes matched her mother's, since they were not like her father's.

Lucrecia did not know it at the time, but Linda was not only beautiful... she was also a wonderful person. However, as it turns out, her extended family was not. There was a long line of witches in her bloodline. Some were good and innocent, but there were many who became practitioners of dark magic. The darkest magic, in fact.

The witches of the family bloodline were consumed by rage and deceitfulness as the witch-hunts in Europe raged on. Not only did they strive for mere survival, but they were pulled into the darkest corners of the occult, where Satan dwelled. The maliciousness that coursed through their veins shifted them from ordinary witches to wickedly powerful sorcerers.

The more they were hunted, the more determined their fight for survival became. Each step of evasion and hiding felt like a rat running away from a hungry cat. But soon enough, these persecuted witches no longer ran but rose up in rebellion to protect all who faced accusation. With vigilantes' hearts, they manipulated witch hunters to track down rapists, murderers, and thieves instead, while also directing them to kill innocent accusers if it meant ending the hunt for the witches so that they could finally stand tall and proud.

Linda's family used their magic to manipulate those around them and embraced the darkness within them. Hexes, curses, and manipulation were all part of their repertoire to protect themselves from being hunted by the witch hunters. To further their escape, they used these magical tools to draw attention away from themselves and onto less skilled witches whom they doomed with hexes and cursed spells to be discovered at the hands of the witch hunters. Destruction was imminent for these unfortunate souls while Linda's family watched in satisfaction, as they would remain spared from a fiery demise.

Linda's family had been plagued by generations of evil witches, but Linda and her mother were the exceptions. They kept to themselves, silently practicing healing magic and avoiding the prying eyes of witch hunters. When Linda was little, she discovered her special gift—a powerful ability to dream of things before they happened. Her father deemed it wicked and forbade her from using it. So, over time, she pushed those dreams down until they became faint and distant whispers.

Lucrecia's father, Leonardo, had a peaceful aura that radiated from him like a glowing halo. His curly sandy-brown hair and brown skin complemented each other, as if they were two pieces of a puzzle that fit perfectly together. The color of his eyes mirrored the steel-gray sky on a cloudy day. Leo had a kind heart and worked tirelessly to provide for his family. He yearned for nothing more than to find a loving mother for Lucrecia, but he never could have guessed that Helen would be so cold and malicious. Even though he tried his best to make things work with Helen, he couldn't help but compare her to Linda, the one true love of his life. Helen loathed being in Linda's shadow and resented Leo's profound love for her.

From an early age, Lucrecia was aware of her stepmother's obsession with dark magic, a practice that made Helen increasingly wild and out of control. The house began to fill with a parade of strange and savage men, brought in by the wicked stepmother who spent most of her time in a drunken haze. Fed up with being exposed to the dangerous and chaotic environment, Lucrecia confronted her stepmother and refused to put up with it any longer. But Helen only laughed at her and berated her. As Lucrecia woke each morning, the smell of vomit filled the air as her stepmother's guests passed out on the floor, leaving her feeling helpless and trapped.

While getting ready to go to school, Lucrecia would often find her stepmother passed out on the bed with blood spattered all over her body. No doubt from dabbling in occult hexing. Lucrecia frequently had to step over drunken men asleep on the floor too. One morning, as she stepped over a drooling man, he reached out and grabbed for her leg. The gesture made her feel uncomfortable and scared. But as she stopped in her tracks, staring down at him, she felt something else: a sense of power.

Without hesitation, she lifted her heel and crushed his hand into the floor while he shouted in pain. She laughed as she fled before anyone could hear her, but she couldn't help but feel troubled by this satisfaction that came with someone else's suffering.

Meanwhile, Helen was growing increasingly careless in her practices of magic, and this negligence left behind evidence of dark deeds around the house—an undoubted reminder of what Helen was capable of when intoxicated and practicing magic.

Helen's family had been targeted as witches and persecuted for centuries, with many of the witching women in her bloodline burned at the stake. Even as times changed, and these same neighbors kept their distance from them, a deep-seated fear of witchcraft remained. Lucrecia, despite not practicing any magic, was still shamed and bullied by the townsfolk as if she were a modern-day witch—a reminder of days gone past that no one could escape from.

The relationship between her stepmother, Helen, and her half-sister, Iris, was one of deep-seated hatred. All those around them felt the chill of their malice, radiating like a dark haze over the whole area. Transgressions against Helen and Iris were harshly dealt with, but even those within their Satan-worshiping clan weren't safe from their ire. Lucrecia later discovered that it had been Helen and Iris' doing that had dragged her and her father into the unending cycle of darkness in which they found themselves, unable to escape Helen's grasp.

The two witches unleashed a powerful spell that plunged Leo and his daughter into the hands of the merciless Helen. I felt sad for her. She had succumbed to the deadly curse immediately, unable to fend against its might due to her lack of magical experience—a gift Lucrecia's mother had been born with but dismissed at the stern request of her father. This fateful event locked away any chance of protection Linda could've imparted onto her baby girl before she passed away.

With the death of Lucrecia's mother, her father was utterly broken. The pain that saturated him day in and day out gradually numbed him until he was ready for a new start, free from any reminder of his beloved wife. Helen and Iris used their dark powers to draw Leo and his special child across the briny Atlantic Ocean. Bewitched by their malicious intentions, Leo and Lucrecia set out on their voyage, enticed by the call of wickedness. Lucrecia's father thought he had found love and a new mother for his *lovely* light, Lucrecia. Helen and her sister, Iris, had a different plan for them. There would be no happy life; they would make sure of that.

Lucrecia clenched her fists as she walked down the desolate street. After an agonizing day of being tormented by her peers and feeling completely invisible in the eyes of her neighbors, she dragged herself home to cry uncontrollably. She silently mourned for her father's absence each night, while her empty stomach emitted its desperate howls—a reminder of their newfound poverty.

The terrifying loneliness stalked Lucrecia's entire life, casting a dark shadow that seemed to linger with no end in sight. The echoes of unrecognizable voices haunt her mind constantly, beckoning her to respond to the visions that only she could see—feelings and experiences that were too powerful to keep from Helen. Helen knew Lucrecia's gifts were developing, and this pleased her.

In blind fury one evening, Helen told my great-grandmother she had conjured her and her father, Leo. She demanded an enchanted daughter to keep with her forever so they could share their supernatural powers and grow old together. Or she would just sacrifice her soul and harbor it safely away in her body. Helen would laugh and shrug her shoulders as if she were deciding between the two options.

Izzy told my mother that Lucrecia truly believed what Helen said were ramblings of drunkenness at that time. Lucrecia loathed her stepmother more and more each day, wishing she could run away from her as soon as possible, with no intention of growing old by her side. Reading these things was so hard for me. I could feel and hear the sorrow of these upsetting events that Lucrecia experienced as if I were there.

Helen would guzzle alcohol day and night. The repulsive strangers would lurk around. Lucrecia would retreat to her room and plug her ears as her stepmother stayed up all night with these filthy criminals while servicing them. Helen would moan, scream, and indulge in seedy sexual acts with the brutish men all through the night. Lucrecia would lay in the back bedroom hearing slapping sounds of their bodies giving each other pleasure and the debauchery of their vulgar conversation. Incessantly, different names were repeated lustfully in the dead of night—Charles, Robert, William, and Frederick—as Helen kept company with the various town drunks.

It was always one of them—sometimes all of them—throughout the day. Lucrecia would call them out by the wrong names if she unintentionally crossed paths with them. "Oh, hello there, Harold," she would say, rolling her eyes wildly, knowing none of their names were Harold. Lucrecia enjoyed making them uncomfortable and poking at Helen to upset her. She knew Helen would never beat her in front of the drunken men.

Helen held each man in disdain, taking what she wanted and discarding them without a care. She had no use for love and romance, instead focusing her energies on the dark spell work that would soon create her own sinister design. Lucrecia would be nothing but a memory, buried beneath the ground, with only worms and maggots to keep her company. Helen's wicked plan was getting closer to taking shape.

Lucrecia could feel the ominous presence of one man in particular as soon as he entered her home. He was not a town drunk; he was something far worse. His dark aura filled the air, and his voice sent shivers down her spine like icy fingers. He came at night and left before dawn, lurking in Helen's room with her all night long. Lucrecia suspected something sinister was going on in that room. The house thundered with loud shrieks and demonic voices, and when the sounds faded off into the night, she knew that they had been practicing some kind of dark magic together. She was terrified to be in the same house with this man and felt a real fear for her safety every time he appeared. It seemed like evil had taken hold of her home, and she wanted nothing more than to escape it.

Helen abused Lucrecia after her dad left them, but Lucrecia's stepmother grew ever more abusive and torturous as the young girl got older. The woman would exact her wrath by forcing Lucrecia to sit outside in the biting winter chill with nothing but the fog of her own breath for company. Shivering, she would be left to bear the cold gaze of the cruel night sky while enduring her punishment.

My great-grandmother Lucrecia was engulfed in a frigid shower of cold vengeance as her stepmother hurled cup after cup of frigid water at her. The coldness seeped through her skin like daggers, making her tremble and cry out in agony as each droplet hit her flesh and formed prickles of ice on her face and hair. With every wave of pain she felt, she became increasingly numb from the torturous chill.

Lucrecia's body convulsed uncontrollably from the cold as she stood outside in the biting wind. When she finally made it inside, Helen viciously grabbed her and hurled her into a scalding hot bath, burning every inch of her flesh until it felt like a thousand knives were piercing her skin. But that was just the beginning of Lucrecia's nightmare. The sadistic abuse became a regular occurrence, with no one coming to her aid—not even the neighbors, who turned a deaf ear to her cries for help. It was as if some kind of evil spell had been cast, sending her pleas out into an endless void, unheard by anyone. Lucrecia remained trapped in her living hell with no hope of escape.

Lucrecia was beaten one too many times by Helen. She had endured enough of her stepmother's cruel wrath and wanted to spare the wildlife that seemed to vanish around Helen from any more pain. But when Lucrecia approached her, hoping to halt the hollering and howling, Helen struck the back of her head hard with a broom. As she stumbled to the ground and felt the warm blood trickle down, Lucrecia's rage steadily built up inside of her. Helen lunged at her again with a feral ferocity, swinging wildly and aiming each punch with an unbridled savagery against Lucrecia. When Lucrecia didn't cry, Helen spit on her, and in that instant, Lucrecia knew it would be her last night in that house.

As Helen lifted the broom above her head, it was as if time had stopped. She watched with a sense of hatred as she brought it down heavily on Lucrecia's face, splattering her nose with a fountain of blood that ran rampant down her cheeks. With an angry cry, Lucrecia ripped the broom from Helen's grasp and wielded it like a weapon against her.

Trying her best to dodge blows, Helen stumbled backwards and into the filthy pigsty until she landed in a deep pool of manure. Lucrecia pulled at a tattered end of Helen's dress with both hands, creating a jagged rip. She paused and wiped away the blood that had smeared across her face. Lucrecia watched Helen as she stared into the distance; she was in shock at Lucrecia's rebellion against her. Helen's chest began heaving as she drew in sharp breaths. She was too afraid to stand up and confront Lucrecia and unsure of what to do.

Helen sat in a state of shock as she looked on in horror and amazement as Lucrecia whispered an incantation, conjuring up a powerful enchantment to lift the broom off the ground. Lucrecia raised her hand and the broomstick trembled beneath her palm. She mounted it gracefully and lifted off the ground, soaring through the night sky. The cool wind rushed by her cheeks as the stars twinkled above, and she let out a sigh of relief mixed with sheer delight. The full moon glowed in anticipation as Lucrecia flew away.

Helen stood up from the slop, bruised and defeated. She felt a pull within her chest as she witnessed the sheer force of Lucrecia's magic. She recognized the unparalleled finesse and precision of her mystic abilities, something Helen had always longed for but lacked herself—a talent with no need for stolen innocence or selfish desires. Helen's envy of Lucrecia's gift was almost too much to bear.

Ever since she was a little girl, Helen wanted nothing more than to have that kind of magic. She practiced, pleaded, and sacrificed for those abilities but didn't have the magic that ran through my great-grandmother's veins. Lucrecia came from a family of magic, but they dismissed their gifts and tucked them deep into the embers so no one would know. They feared the burning and feared being separated from one another. They wished for their gifts to go away. Over time, their magic, like all of our magic, faded.

Lucrecia was kept in the dark about her own secret power—a magical gift she inherited through her mother's side of the family. She had no knowledge of this power until, one night, an unsettling vision snuck into her dreams and unlocked an inner awakening that unleashed a force she never knew she possessed. That fateful night, Lucrecia finally found the strength to break free from the grasp of Helen and embark on a journey to build a life of her own, despite the obstacles in her way. She fought through every trial with courage and resilience, determined to finally take back control of her destiny.

Niki Gregory

SLY TEMPTATIONS

Lucrecia was surrounded by loneliness for years until, suddenly, something changed within her. She found herself smiling widely and often, taking joy in the smallest of things. Lucrecia, now free from Helen, started to take more care of her appearance—wearing nice clothes and fixing her hair. For the first time in many years, she began interacting with other people. Soon, she felt a sense of home when a kind family adopted her, offering her support and security. With renewed purpose, Lucrecia attended school, worked hard, and embraced life again.

Lucrecia was taken by surprise when she met a hard-working man and fell in love. They married only months later, starting their family of three children—the eldest being Izzy. After her chaotic childhood, Lucrecia craved the normalcy of everyday life that allowed her to settle down. She fiercely avoided any magic in her new life, believing it evil, keeping magic away from her life as she started her own family. Lucrecia had gentle, sun-kissed hands that were often found cradling her children's faces in soft caresses. She spoke to them with respect and kindness, never raising her voice or using aggression when disciplining. Her home was cozy and full of love—everything they could need for a comfortable life.

Lucrecia soon noticed flashes of supernatural occurrences surrounding Izzy when she was only a child. This would frighten Lucrecia. Conversations would unravel, which revealed Izzy's magical gifts. Those conversations left in their wake fear and pain in Lucrecia's mind. Izzy told my mother about the talks she shared with her mother and how it had slowly led to Lucrecia instructing her to cease sharing any further experiences with those otherworldly forces—out of love, not spite.

Izzy was too young to understand at the time, but after her mother learned of her daughter's magic, she hung a broom over Izzy's bedroom door, assuring her that it would bring good luck and protection. Lucrecia hoped the broom would be a reminder to dark forces that she, too, had magic.

The broom had a long handle crafted of twigs bound tightly together with dark thread, ending in thick straws and feathers that seemed to whisper sweet nothings as Izzy would fall asleep at night. Lucrecia and Izzy added the beautiful feathers when Izzy was around seven. Izzy always loved the mysterious crow feathers that she meticulously added into the project, feeling a sense of magic in their beauty.

Izzy shared that when she was a young girl, she always felt the broom watching over her... like an extra guardian, offering security throughout her childhood. It wasn't until years later that Izzy realized it had been the very same broom that had saved her mother's life, allowing her to escape to safety and begin again. And, for this reason, Izzy treasured it more than anything else. She wondered if, perhaps, the broom of protection could be the reason she was never harmed.

Izzy's given name was Aliza, a family name. Her parents called her Izzy, and the grandkids simply called her Granny. Izzy's lush, dark brown hair danced in a captivating mix with sparkling platinum strands, creating a subtle halo of color that framed her delicate features. Her eyes that looked out from beneath her smooth locks were identical to her mother's—the same eye shape, color, and show-stopping starburst of bold embers that illuminated when she became happy or excited.

Lucrecia felt a special connection to her daughter, Izzy; she felt as if they shared a specific kind of bond. Lucrecia knew they shared the gift of magic. This thought, the thought of magic, brought up memories of Lucrecia's stepmother, Helen, whom Lucrecia escaped and sheltered away from many years ago. Whenever Lucrecia would do mundane tasks, such as cleaning, cooking, or otherwise going about her day, the image of Helen would come to mind from time to time. The surprise on Helen's wicked face when Lucrecia whisked herself away in a flurry with the very broomstick Helen beat her with never failed to bring a smile to Lucrecia's sweet face.

Lucrecia knew Izzy began to have vivid premonitions and dreams of warnings; she would always tell Izzy not to have *those* dreams anymore. She could see Izzy having visions and would scold her to stop, as if she had control over her gifts. Lucrecia was afraid of Izzy possessing abilities and turning evil. Lucrecia knew even good magic could open doors to dark magic and godless practitioners.

Izzy's mother did all she could to keep her children away from the dangerous realm of sorcery. She feared its sly temptations of easy power would take hold of them and plunge them into a dark abyss of despair. However, Izzy found herself irresistibly drawn to it, with its promise of freedom and potential. Torn between the love for her family and the call of the mysterious world, she was stuck in an inner battle as she tried to find a way out.

All seemed good in their worlds, until one day it wasn't. As much as Lucrecia tried to hide and tuck her family away from the world and its evil people, evil people found them anyway. Lucrecia turned from magic and never saw it coming for her. She never saw that the witch would forever want to ruin her family.

The night Izzy saw something shift with her mother was a night of pure dread and terror. Lucrecia felt a chill run through the air just before an unexpected visitor arrived at her door: Helen, her stepmother. As soon as she stepped into the humidity and stickiness of the evening, the winds began to howl like a vicious predator. The trees shook violently as the leaves began to vibrate in fear, ripping off branches and spiraling around in a frenzy. They clung to the house like a plague, announcing the terror that awaited Lucrecia that evening.

Lucrecia's heart raced as the heavy knocking on the door echoed through her home. She cautiously approached, fearful of whom she would find on the other side. Her husband was away at work that night, and a sense of dread came over her. When Lucrecia opened the door, to her horror, there stood Helen—a face from her past she had desperately worked to forget. An anger built up in Lucrecia's chest as she remembered all the torment Helen caused her in her youth. She wanted nothing more than for Helen and her cruel memories to vanish forever.

Izzy shared that she became very upset when she heard her mother quarrel with Helen. I could see into that memory that moment Izzy endured—just as Topaz could see events as they happened. Izzy snuck into the darkened hallway and peeked into the living room. She only wanted to ensure her mother was OK. Until that day, she had never heard her mother raise her voice in anger or swear. Helen had fallen ill and had a dark confession she wanted Lucrecia to know before her impending death.

With her hot, foul breath, Helen whispered a dark secret into Lucrecia's ear. Lucrecia seethed with anger, her lips trembling and her eyes ablaze. As Helen drunkenly taunted her with her repulsive secrets, Lucrecia's hand darted out like a striking cobra. Her palm collided with Helen's face so hard that she spun around and crashed to the floor, cackling madly as she fell.

With a smug smirk on her face, Lucrecia asked for more and this time delivered a crushing blow that sent Helen hurtling backwards with a jolting force. The impact of Helen's body colliding with the table caused an echoing crack to reverberate throughout the room. An ice-cold chill settled over the entire house. Deathly pale, Lucrecia looked on in horror as she realized the magnitude of the situation. Helen was gone.

With tears streaming down her face, Lucrecia dragged Helen out into the yard. Uttering prayers of repentance under her breath, she tipped over the metal barrel and stuffed Helen inside before lighting it on fire. The smell of searing flesh filled the night air, and Lucrecia's sobs could be heard from miles away as the flames engulfed her normal life in one agonizing moment. Izzy watched in terror as the flames licked away at what remained of Helen, the only sound being the symphony of crackling embers.

Izzy told Kezziah of the small rainstorm early in the morning. She did not sleep that night. She couldn't. Izzy watched as the rainstorm blew in, cooling off the reaming ashes that slept silently in the barrel.

Just before her father came home, Izzy watched quietly as her mother, covered in filth, discarded what remained of the evil witch's body under the oak tree—the body of the evil witch that bedeviled her for many years. Izzy was traumatized from watching the hellish events unfold, never telling her mother what she had witnessed.

The other kids slept with ease but not Izzy. She quietly stayed in her bed, knowing the big, awful secret that was lying under the tree in her backyard with fragments of ash and burned bone, sleeping in the barrel that rested in secret for years. Sometimes, as Izzy would lay in bed sleeping, she could hear whispers around her. Izzy felt as if Helen were telling her that it knew she saw her mother's dirty little secret. She felt taunted by the large oak tree and the barrel resting beside it anytime she caught a glimpse of it from the corner of her eye.

The day that the unwelcome visitor arrived, Lucrecia was changed forever. As the beastly presence lingered in her family's once-happy home, a dark energy began to seep through the cracks. Izzy wrestled with her conscience, eventually succumbing to the realization that Lucrecia gave into the temptation of learning dark magic.

Animals went missing, blood spattering around the kitchen while her father worked late nights. An enormous dread clawed at her throat and a heaviness sank into her bones as she realized her mother now practiced this forbidden craft under the cover of night, desperately trying to keep it hidden from her innocent siblings and pious father, who would surely bring the church crashing down on them if he knew what lurked in his house.

Izzy's father, with his bushy eyebrows and white whiskers around his mouth, fell ill one day and passed away soon after that hellish night of Helen's passing in the family home. The house dipped into empty silence. Lucrecia didn't speak to the kids much anymore. She completely withdrew and struggled not to think about anything. Everything in the home became messier—the dirty dishes piled up in the sink, and the children's coats left tossed on the floor behind the door.

An outsider would think it was the sudden loss of her husband, but Izzy knew that was not the reason why Lucrecia changed. Izzy knew it was a result of Helen's visit. After that night, Lucrecia—the mom she once was—seemingly died. The once-loving home was now disheveled—no longer a haven for Izzy, her brother, Isaiah, and Izzy's sister, Kezzie.

All the children sensed the abrupt change in Lucrecia. Once gentle and caring, she transformed, becoming unreasonable and mean to each of them. Izzy suspected the shift resulted from being overcome by the guilt of killing her stepmother; even if it were an accident, her actions took a life. As a young woman, she did not fathom that the changes were a result of occult magic.

Lucrecia practiced dark arts with obsessive fervor after her husband's death. Izzy watched in fear as her mother scoured the neighborhood with a suspicious eye, radiating hatred from every pore. The once kind and loving woman now loathed anyone who displayed even a hint of joy, her resentment becoming a hellish rage that threatened to consume her. For this was not the mother Izzy had always known.

As Izzy grew older, the strange things happening in her home became unbearable. Lucrecia's envy had become palpable and sinister as she began using dark sorcery to sabotage anyone who dared cross her path. The transformation of Izzy's once-loving mother into a bitter woman was hard to take in. To make matters worse, Lucrecia's behavior took an abrupt turn when she started heavily drinking—a substance that she had always spoken out against, forbidding it from ever entering their family home. Her sudden change in attitude and preference puzzled Izzy to no end.

But what truly broke Izzy's heart was witnessing her kind and nurturing mother slip away before her very eyes. Some days, Lucrecia was herself again, only to slowly change as the hours of the day inched along. There were spouts of the mother she once knew, infused with this short-fused and unhinged temperament of the new Lucrecia that was enthralled by the occult. After the passing of her father, Izzy struggled with depression and solitude. Her family began to unravel at an alarming pace, and everything spiraled out of control after Helen's visit.

Izzy became the caretaker for her siblings and the household. The sight of what was happening to her family was unbearable, and it left her feeling conflicted and alone. Izzy trembled as she listened to her mother's raging voice echoing through the walls like a dark storm as she often argued with herself.

One particular night, the rage was out of control, as it sounded like things were being forcefully thrown around her mother's room. Frightening demonic voices swirled around her, drowning out Lucrecia's words while she argued with invisible forces. Creeping closer and closer to the door, Izzy was about to open it, when Lucrecia shouted for the Lord Almighty to watch over her children. Then a chilling silence descended upon Izzy as she heard her mother plead for mercy on her soul to God. "To be absent from this body is to be present with the Lord," she pleaded as she wept.

Lucrecia's life came to an abrupt end in a flash of gunfire. Izzy watched in horror as her mother's blood slowly oozed to the ground, painting the room with its crimson reminder of death. Topaz explained that it was the only way for her soul to be released from the witch and demons that took possession of her body, holding her in a living hell until the day would come when Helen would need to find another vessel to inhabit. In one final act of courage and defiance, Lucrecia chose death over life on her own terms.

Helen was left suffocating in a lifeless body now. The wrathful demons that once befriended her would now take her soul to Hell. Helen's screams tore through the air as they dragged her down to the unfathomable depths of Hell. These were no friendly guides but henchmen of Satan himself whose hunger for her soul had reached its peak. She was doomed to a wretched end for failing Satan again, discarded into an abyss full of other wretches doomed to be tortured for all eternity. Once again, Lucrecia had the upper hand as she ascended into Heaven.

◆ ✳ ◆

It wasn't until Izzy met Topaz that she realized the depths of the changes that consumed her mother, who, overnight, morphed into a cold, distant, and withdrawn person. The flutter of their budding friendship was like a breath of fresh air for Izzy. It wasn't long before Izzy fell into her warm embrace, drawn in by her bright smile. My grandmother's new friend took her in and tucked her safe into her coven of protectors and healers.

Topaz could feel Izzy's untapped power surging like a raging river, begging to be put to use. Together, they trekked to Topaz's house and began exploring the forbidden corners of magic, working with Izzy as their guardian. With every passing day, Izzy's powers grew, learning how to curse and hex with an adeptness that left Topaz in awe. As the darkness swirled around them, Topaz taught her the most valuable lesson: you must learn the shadows if you ever hope to overcome them. Wearing all black—the only color capable of absorbing negative energy and warding off malicious spirits—they practiced until their souls seemed to echo with a new dark power.

Topaz's coven called her Witch Master, for she was gifted with a mastery over most styles of magic, even occult spells which she never sought to invoke. But her power did not come from gatekeeping knowledge; she saw it as her purpose to teach and to strengthen all who showed genuine interest in the craft with pure hearts and honest intentions. Topaz had an impeccable eye for differentiating crows from grackles, only trusting the crows enough to make them part of her inner circle.

The witches within the coven were taught the sinister magic of shadow casting by Topaz, and another gifted witch, Victor. But the witches within the coven were warned to guard their souls against demoniacs trying to steal them away. When you cast your soul into a shadow, the body you leave behind is very vulnerable.

Running in the shadows was a way to stay safe, and this way of evading predators was a secret known only to a few witches. It was Victor who passed this lesson to Topaz, as his mother passed it to him when he was only a young boy. Tucking your thoughts into a living nightmare could protect your soul from demoniacs. For no one willingly wants to be inside the depths of their own personal hell, the demons may not think to hunt in such a place.

I knew this secret too well, something I thought I accidentally did when I was being pursued by the witch and demons. Now, I suspect there was a spell upon me that lured me there to protect my soul. Izzy never believed in coincidences, and neither do I, so I know I did not stumble into the shadows of my mind by accident.

I've since learned that the shadows of your nightmares can be somewhat of a refuge, a sanctuary. The shadows of my nightmares safeguarded me. It works much like latching onto a doll, a talisman made to ward off evil, hide you away, and protect you from harm.

It's true, it's a form of witchcraft. Some may think of it as dark magic, weaving an intricate spell that wraps around you like a shield, but it isn't dark magic at all. It is a form of protection; it is white magic. You do what must be done to keep yourself safe, even if it means courting the world of forgotten spells. Doing this is another way to hide and protect your soul.

Topaz felt a burning passion for white magic—third eye open magic. Her youthful soul was an untarnished beacon of light, yet there was more she wished to accomplish. She strove to do what was right and to make sure all people could lead lives of dignity and purpose—not only those who looked like her or shared her values but all human beings that shared this world. She wanted everyone to feel joy and safety in their lives, knowing it was their fundamental human right on this planet.

Topaz was a force to be reckoned with. Her beauty and larger-than-life personality couldn't compare to the dazzling aura she shone with. Brilliant shades of yellow, orange, deep pinks, bright blues, and soft grays shimmered around her like glittery dust, leaving an unmistakable impression on all who encountered her. Even those who could not see her aura were entranced by her kind smile and welcoming demeanor, which seemed to shine brighter than any star in the night sky.

Izzy was enchanted by Topaz's beauty, and in looking back at the pictures of the coven, I could see why. Her thick hair, like a mane of spun gold, cascaded down her back in luxurious locks. The light rose-brown tendrils were kissed with glistening streaks of ginger and flaxen that shimmered beneath the moonlight. A fragrance of sweet honey drifted from the tantalizing curls. Her entrancing eyes were like those of celestials—one a sparkling crystal blue, which she told Izzy she got from her mother, and the other a stunning emerald green, which she was told was like her father's mesmerizing eyes. One thing was for certain: all who looked upon Topaz felt entranced, captivated by her alluring gaze.

Topaz stood strikingly tall—like her parents—and she boasted an athletic build. Running and working out was a part of her daily routine. For her, physical strength was paramount to her sense of power and vitality. She pushed herself beyond her limits with each workout, striving to become stronger than she had ever been before. Topaz was determined for her body to be a temple of unstoppable force.

Topaz could clear her mind and relax as she ran, worked out, and ate healthily. She encouraged others who practiced magic to care for their body—their temple—the same way. She preached that tending to your body and soul was the key to unlocking a sharpened mind and strong intuition. Self-care was not an option, but a mandatory ritual for cultivating intellectual resilience and spiritual growth.

Every morning, she gauged the day by her exercise routine: how much did she run; how many sets could she do of push-ups and crunches? The gauge had an effect on how she handled people; she became more patient with students and peers in magic, if she had been able to work out that day.

Izzy attended many practice sessions at Topaz's home or the woods nearby, where the other practitioners would meet up. They all worshiped differently, but many of the spells were the same in their craft.

After the coven had left their nocturnal celebration of magical blessings and offerings of gratitude, Topaz called for Izzy to meet her. As Topaz sat her down to speak in private, Izzy knew it was going to be serious. The grand high priestess laid out all she knew about Lucrecia's situation. Veracity can never be manipulated, but maybe it could finally be corrected.

Topaz proclaimed unequivocally that Lucrecia had indeed murdered her stepmother, Helen. This revelation stunned Izzy since she had never revealed what she saw to another living creature, not even her own mother. Topaz also confirmed, yes, it was an accident—but one provoked by something far more demonic than any mortal being: Satan himself. With malicious intention and a twisted agenda lurking within our darkest nightmares and anxieties, he, too, played his part.

Topaz's words cut through the air like a knife as she explained Helen's wicked plan. Young Lucrecia hadn't even taken her first steps yet when Helen was determined to crush her spirit and challenge her for her soul. Her rage would open a portal from innocence, allowing Helen to rip away her life and trap her enlightened soul in Hell so the evilness in Hell could feed upon it and use it for a more sinister plan. Helen would keep the body left behind for herself. The thought of it filled Izzy with dread as Topaz spoke of the inevitable fate that awaited Lucrecia.

This plan would allow Helen to honor a promise she made to Satan many years before Lucrecia came to America. It would also allow Helen to gain power within the occult and perhaps distract her mind from her own dark thoughts. Once she forced her soul into Lucrecia's young, strong body, she would snatch her life away, living it as her own. Helen planned to sacrifice Lucrecia the very night she did retaliate—the night she escaped upon the broom Lucrecia commanded—foiling Helen's malicious plan. Izzy listened intently, believing the truth Topaz spoke of.

Topaz grabbed Izzy's hand and whispered sternly, "Close your eyes, Izzy." The night fell into dead silence. As the ritual began, the frogs croaked no longer, and the chirping of crickets could be heard gradually fading away; even the howling wind seemed to slink back into the shadows like a timid mouse. Fireflies swarmed around Topaz's small campfire as she started her prayer, then, slowly but surely, the fireflies began dissipating one by one until all that remained was darkness. The dull embers in Topaz's fire suddenly raged with flame as they were reignited, and the trees shook their branches frantically against a sky full of stars as the conversation about Helen turned grim.

Izzy's heart ached as she realized that her loving mother, Lucrecia, had been subject to the burden of servitude imposed by her wicked stepmother. With a crackle of fire, Topaz ignited the ritualistic flames, and a blaze of light soared high into the moonless night. "Tonight, we will look back in time so you can witness your mother's plight," Topaz declared. Izzy felt her skin crawl with anticipation as she came to understand the hand her mother had been forced to play. As Topaz wove her powerful magic, Izzy was granted an eyeful of the pain and suffering that formed her young life.

Topaz explained to Izzy that Lucrecia's mother was also abundantly blessed with magical gifts. Linda's death left Lucrecia's magic exposed, like a seedling in the sun, its stem and leaves browning and dying. Linda never thought anything of her third eye closing many years before she gave birth. She certainly couldn't have fathomed her daughter being abused and used for wickedness.

Chapter Five

THE PLAN

Helen and Iris planned to sacrifice Lucrecia. They were drawn to her power like moths to a flame. They followed the demon's directions deep into the shadows of a distant land, where they offered up the blood of animals in a Satanic ritual. With every drop of life that was spilled, the demon sucked away, feeding upon the offerings from Helen and Iris. They fed the beast in exchange for his assistance in hunting enlightened souls.

Topaz explained with sadness and remorse that Lucrecia's father did not run away; he was sacrificed and murdered by the Devil's whores so they could have his vulnerable daughter. Helen needed to sacrifice Lucrecia's magical soul once she was mature enough. The demon by Helen's side, her nightly visitor, fed on Lucrecia's father.

As Topaz spoke, Izzy felt engulfed in the story. Her vision blurred as she watched Helen and Iris work with the demon. As Lucrecia's mother, Linda, succumbed to her sudden illness, Lucrecia's fate was sealed. Tears spilled from her eyes like rivers of regret that cascaded down her face, but she refused to give voice to her grief as Topaz continued to share the tale. Izzy forced herself to remain composed among an overwhelming range of emotions.   Izzy was utterly horrified as Topaz revealed the truth about her great-grandmother. She had resorted to dark magic in order to make herself stronger and break free from an unbearable environment, but it had come at a tragic cost. When her great-grandmother eventually gave birth to her daughter, Linda, the Devil's forces exacted their cruel revenge.

At the time, Lucrecia's grandmother

53

had no idea of the consequences of her decision to engage in the Devil's magic. Little did she know that, decades later, her daughter Linda would pay the ultimate price. The consequence of opening the door to Satan's magic caused her daughter, Linda, to fall ill soon after giving birth to Lucrecia. After seeing the sparks of magic within Lucrecia, the Devil put events into motion—events that would send Linda's magical daughter away to America, sending Lucrecia into the eye of the storm of 'Hurricane Helen.'

Topaz spoke in a menacing tone. "Beware, for when it comes to dark magic, there is no escape from the consequences. No matter how hard you try, the one you love will always bear the burden of your mistakes. Dark magic can open portals that can never be closed again. Do not use it unless in dire need."

Izzy's face twisted with fear as Topaz warned against the danger of practicing dark magic, knowing all too well that even the slightest mistake could come with unforgiving repercussions. I think that is why Izzy would practice protective magic but feared magic in general, especially after Topaz died. Izzy thought of Topaz as her safety net, but after her passing, she never wanted to accidentally invoke self-serving magic and open doors to the underworld.

Izzy watched in horror as Lucrecia's life slowly unraveled. She saw Leo shower his daughter with love, unaware of the danger lurking in Helen's heart. The little girl blossomed and matured, unknowingly walking further and further towards her tragic fate. With each passing day, her stepmother's desire to consume her power grew stronger, until it became an undeniable force of destruction.

Helen craved the power inside Lucrecia, obsessing over her every move until she was consumed with paranoia that another witch would steal it away. Helen imposed tight boundaries, forbidding almost anyone from getting too close to her daughter—even Helen's own sister. Izzy could see Helen's intense protection of Lucrecia, hovering around her like a hawk ready to dive and snatch away its prey if needed.

Helen had planned to sacrifice Lucrecia at a younger age, but her selfishness won out; she relished having free labor around the house and refused to part with the girl. Helen believed that the older Lucrecia was upon being sacrificed, the more powerful the ritual would be. But time began to take its toll on Helen's ambition:

Lucrecia grew stronger instead of weaker. She became too strong for Helen to contain; she broke away from her cage and flew away into the night sky in a blaze of glory. That was a vision Izzy could never forget.

Terrifying visions haunted Izzy's mind, revealing to her the vile power of Helen and Iris. As mirror images of each other, the two could easily pass as twins, yet they shared an odiousness that made them grotesquely distinct. Helen grew stronger under the guidance of their dark family; her father embraced the occult, while Iris felt inferior due to her father's refusal to frequent the occult. With malevolent intent in their eyes, they secretly conspired against each other, determined to beat the other with any means necessary.

The sisters made a blood pact with Satan to give up the powerful souls of others in exchange for eternal life on Earth and insurmountable power. Helen burned with ambition to become queen of all the occults, believing that sacrificing Lucrecia's soul was her surest path to success. Iris did not have sacrifice yet, but hunted for one whom she could claim as her own.

Iris finally saw an opportunity: to win over the gatekeepers of Hell and lay claim to an innocent young boy. The young boy Iris had been observing displayed a sharp intellect, but his lack of magical ability left him undesired by the beast and he sent his demon to see Iris.

A demonic messenger descended from the dark depths of Hell, sent to deliver a message from the dark lord himself. With a voice rumbling like thunder, the entity spoke of an infant child. The demon's red eyes glowed with malicious intent as he revealed that Satan's thirst for the child's soul was unquenchable and warned her not to fail.

The demon's message sent shivers down the spine of Iris and Helen. The revelation washed over them. They knew that no other soul that roamed this world could compare to the intensity and power of the child the demon spoke of. The women were overcome by tales of the might and strength of the powerful human, feeling humbled in comparison.

The air around them seemed to quiver with an invisible tension between the sisters. Excitement at the news of the child delighted Iris. She would no doubt have the ultimate sacrifice now. This realization filled Helen with envy, as she had been so sure it would be Lucrecia's soul that would garner favor with the demons and even Satan himself. Now, it would be Iris who wielded a stronger soul to offer up in an unholy deal. An enlightened soul that she didn't even seek out on her own, one practically gifted to her. This infuriating gift ignited a fire of bitter resentment deep within Helen, causing an ache that she could not shake.

Iris befriended the young mother named Faye. Little did Faye know that her innocent friendship was a pawn in Iris' sinister plan, orchestrated by a devious demon lurking in the shadows. Faye was born in Ireland, though her family was comprised of descendants all over Europe. She lost her young husband to illness and had no other family nearby.

Faye had a brother named John. They were twins and very close growing up. John had moved to England two years before and started a family. With so many miles between them, they would exchange letters to keep in contact with one another. After losing her husband, Faye and her infant daughter began to financially struggle. Though she had written to her brother, she never revealed her plight. With no other nearby relatives to turn to, Faye found herself alone and penniless, struggling to provide for her young daughter.

The call of magic stirred within Faye, but her strict, religious upbringing had instilled in her a strong sense of shame. She was always told that magic was for fairytales, and those were stories only meant for children. Faye realized, as so many of us have, that her gifts would not stay with her if she refused to nurture them. With each passing day the power within her grew weaker, and she could feel it slipping away like sand through her fingers.

It happened in my very own family, so I know it to be true. With each generation our ability to perform magic faded and the truth of what we were hushed into silence. Every day we surrender a piece of our mysticism, an essential part of ourselves, if we refuse to acknowledge it. We sign away the very essence of our being with every moment of neglect and denial of our special gifts.

Darkness shrouds us all, blurring our sight and numbing our senses. There is no escape from the *blind spots* that haunt our minds; not even heavenly angels or demonic entities can see through them. We are all vulnerable to ignorance, but when we ignore our natural gifts, these blind spots grow larger like an insatiable void. The more we hide from our intuition, the less we're able to sense visions of what's coming, leaving us ever more exposed and helpless.

As a young girl, Faye picked up on the subtle hints of the nun's auras in school and would comment on them. Her older brother John quickly hushed her with stern words: "Faye! Don't talk about auras or dreams; people don't like it. Just keep those thoughts to yourself, like I do. Whenever I get these weird feelings, I tell them to go away, or else we'll both be in trouble."

Faye took his advice and learned early on that magic was not accepted by the church. She was taught to distrust and fear her own God-given gifts, and as she shushed the voices more and more, they began to fade into silence within her mind.

Faye felt a flutter of excitement and anticipation as she held her baby daughter and stepped onto the boat bound for America. When the ship docked, Faye was overwhelmed with uncertainty about her future. She had no money, no job—she was very afraid. But, thankfully, an old neighbor from Ireland—a kindly woman who had come to America years before—sent word that she had a room awaiting them in her home. With hope in her heart, Faye and her child headed for their new home in a new country.

Once there, Faye worked hard to repay the woman's generosity by cooking meals, cleaning, and caring for the household in exchange for food, shelter, and stability. It was more than Faye had ever dreamed of. The remarkable kindness of this generous soul gave Faye the chance to establish a better life for herself and her daughter in a country full of exciting opportunities.

Faye's older brother sent for her and the baby girl once he received word of her husband's passing but missed them as they left for America less than three hours before she and her infant departed. He had fallen ill and had a hard time getting around. Faye's former neighbor passed away shortly after Faye and her baby arrived. They would soon be homeless in an unfamiliar country. Izzy watched; she saw how Faye cried. Faye felt devastated by the loss but also had nowhere to go; she and her baby were soon to be without a place to stay. Faye was a young mother without help in a strange country she didn't know.

As luck would have it, she crossed paths with a lady named Iris— Helen's sister, Iris, as luck would have it. Not all luck is good, unfortunately. Iris and Helen greedily welcomed Faye and her newborn daughter with the promise of help, their true intentions hidden behind false smiles. They wasted no time using powerful magic to lull Faye into a false sense of safety. The two women slinked through the shadows, cackling their evil intent to capture the innocent child's soul and sacrifice it to their devilish lord. Their mission was fueled by a sick need for power, a longing to please Satan with the sacred offering of pure innocence.

Helen and Iris seethed with jealousy as they looked upon Faye. She possessed a baby with gifts bestowed beyond any ordinary life—her own sparks of magic and unmatched beauty. Her legs stretched endlessly, her hair was as soft as molten silk, and her bright cerulean eyes sparkled like jewels in the night sky.

A demon sent by Satan himself had enlightened them of the gifts—a blessing Helen and Iris were all too thankful for. The malicious duo silently plotted to ensnare the innocent child in their clutches before her mother fully realized the power within her.

Helen's heart ached for the pure joy radiating from the infant in Iris' arms. A part of her longed to keep the child for herself, yet she knew it was impossible, as she had already made her promise to the dark lord. Lucrecia was much closer to sacrificial age than this new innocent soul, and Helen begrudgingly accepted that she would have plenty of time to hunt and collect more souls while using hard magic before this baby reached her physical peak.

Helen seethed with impatience, waiting for Lucrecia to turn a year older so she could finally sacrifice her to Satan. Each day, Helen felt an addictive rush of pleasure as she terrorized Lucrecia, shoving her around and belittling her mercilessly. The thrill of tormenting someone weaker gave Helen an unnatural high that filled her veins with sick delight and jubilation.

As Topaz detailed the abuse her mother suffered, Izzy felt a pang of revulsion pulsing through her veins. Topaz needed Izzy to know, to really see the cruelty Helen was capable of. Izzy listened and watched with the gift of visualization Topaz provided. Izzy observed. She watched Iris coo over the baby that was destined to be ripped away from her arms one day and sacrificed to Satan. Every gesture toward the baby was tainted by the knowledge that, in the future, this child would be discarded without remorse. Helen and Iris' cruelty had no limits, and it chilled Izzy to the bone.

Iris and Helen were always competitive, so knowing Helen felt jealous of the baby being Iris' sacrifice delighted Iris. Both ladies knew the baby girl was so strong, and her soul would no doubt appease Satan. Her soul would be far more valuable than that of Lucrecia's. Though Lucrecia had the gift of magic, it was subpar compared to the gifts the young baby held. Iris was confident her offering would secure her future with the occult they belonged to.

Iris's heart swelled with sickening pride. Knowing that the innocent baby would soon be sacrificed provided her with a disturbing sense of excitement. She flaunted the little girl in front of Helen, who secretly prayed for her death before she could be claimed by the twisted game they played with people's lives.

While Faye prepared dinner, Iris brought the child to Helen and Lucrecia, dolled up and boasting of her beauty and supposed gifts. Lucrecia immediately took to the baby, holding her tight and playing with her as if they were long-lost friends. The child giggled and laughed in a moment of pure innocence, while Iris watched on with joyless glee.

Lucrecia desperately awaited the arrival of the beloved baby each morning when Iris would bring her by to flaunt in front of Helen. At almost six months old, the precious child had already developed a strong personality and was never content unless Lucrecia was holding her and cuddling her close. As the baby kissed her cheek with slobbery lips, Lucrecia's heart would fill with joy despite the drool dripping down her face. This little life brought indescribable happiness to Lucrecia's heart; the baby was the highlight of her day.

Iris descended to Helen's home the night of ill-fated news: her newborn baby girl had mysteriously taken her last breath, and the mother took her to be buried back home next to her father. Iris appeared to be consumed with grief, and she left without a word, leaving Helen in stunned shock. Helen felt relieved that Iris would not have a sacrifice more powerful than her own, but she also felt frustration. She felt confused by their lack of sight. How did they not see this coming? How did the demon not know? Why was it they couldn't see beyond what had already been done? The baby died, and it was too late to undo her untimely passing.

A wave of spite and rage swelled inside Helen as she watched Iris slowly walk away into the dusk. Helen realized an invaluable gift—a pure soul meant for selfish gains—had been stolen from their grasps by death. Helen hated being so helpless against their greatest adversaries: death and free will. Helen did have some sadness for Iris. Now she was left without a sacrifice and would likely not be in a position to find a replacement that was worthy.

Lucrecia's heart was heavy with grief. The baby girl had been the joy of her day, and now she was gone. The pain of the loss felt unbearable, but at the same time, a part of her wondered if Helen or Iris—or both—might have had something to do with it. Lucrecia was desperate for answers yet terrified of what she might discover.

Iris felt the cold breath of Satan on her neck as his wrathful gaze bore down upon her. She knew he was owed an empowered soul, and if she failed to deliver, she feared she would be cast into the depths of Hell. Hours bled into days as Helen and Iris scrambled to locate another enlightened child, but each failed attempt only served to heighten Iris' desperation.

Her borrowed time was running out, and Satan's tolerance was wearing thin; any hope for mercy had long since faded away. With every mundane young life that crossed her path, a sense of dread crept over her until regret for past decisions was almost palpable in the air. As each morning brought a new day of unending anguish, Iris knew that soon enough, her debt to the dark lord must be paid.

Iris had made a promise to Satan—a deal she was determined to keep. Iris felt the creeping terror of failing Beelzebub. Every nerve within Izzy could feel the desperation that coursed through Iris as she struggled fruitlessly against the promise she couldn't keep. Her fear was palpable, like an ominous shadow that surrounded her in the darkness.

Iris felt a growing sense of dread as she stopped practicing dark magic, hoping to be forgotten by Satan. Every attempt to take the soul of a young innocent had failed, and it haunted her each day. She was raised in the world of magic, and yet something inside had begun to shift.

The guilt weighed heavily on her. Lucrecia had been in danger ever since Helen appeared, yet Iris had done nothing; she simply stayed silent, hiding from her own responsibility. For years, she'd used manipulation and evil tactics, but now something was different.

She could have repented for her actions and tried to make amends, but at the core of who she was—cruel and evil—Iris wouldn't have considered surrendering to a God she resented.

The dark lord was coming for her, and there was nothing that Iris could do to stop it. With every breath, she felt heavy dread settle in her bones, knowing that the punishment for her decision would be unbearable. No spell or incantation could keep the looming darkness away as the newborn slipped from her grasp. She shivered as fear clamped on her heart, understanding too well the discomfort of something wicked on the horizon.

Iris clenched her fists in defeat, resigned to fate, knowing that there would be no place to hide from her ultimate truth. She had embraced the occult and sold her soul for power; she knew what she was getting into. The thought of forgiveness skirted across her mind, but with a bitter laugh, she rejected it. God could never understand the craving for power that burned within her veins. Honesty, integrity, and goodness?

No, such virtues were foreign to Iris. On the contrary, all she wanted was to follow in the footsteps of Helen, the dark priestess who always seemed to outperform her in magic since they were young. There was no chance for salvation or redemption. Iris had chosen her fate long ago.

Iris's fear began to consume her, making her unable to bear the thought of being alone. Her eyes darted around for any sign of movement, but there was only stillness as she peered out of her window. Each sound seemed magnified, and her nerves jangled as if a storm brewed inside her. The witching hour arrived like an omen as Iris awoke from a nightmare. Voices in her head roared, the fear pounding in her chest like drums as she ran to Helen's house for refuge. The dark streets were alive with shadows that followed her every move, bubbling with fear with each step she took.

Terror ran rampant through her body as Iris sloshed through the murky mud. Every step brought a searing pain from the sharp pebbles cutting into her flesh, bringing a crimson flow of blood in its wake. The chill of dread radiated from her bones, an instinctual knowledge that something sinister was determined to consume her. But a faint glimmer of hope lit her way, urging her onward with hopes that Helen's mysterious powers could ward off the evil spirits that doggedly pursued her. But even as she reached the sanctuary of her sister's front yard, she feared it was not enough. Helen's dark magic may not be strong enough to repel the demonic darkness intent on devouring her wicked soul.

The premonition of a looming disaster flooded her senses. Once an evil witch, now she was the one terrorized by something much more powerful than herself. Helen opened the door when Iris arrived, shocked and worried at the sight of her sister's cruel face. A sense of foreboding hung heavy between them, as there was something that Iris had kept hidden deep within her, telling no one.

Iris was terror-stricken with fear as she thought about the truth that lay dormant inside her—a secret of lies and betrayal that she had desperately tried to keep hidden from even Satan himself. She knew he would never forgive her if he found out what she had done—a decision made in haste. Her mouth opened, ready to speak the shameful secrets, but it was too late. Iris had already been interrupted by an incoming visitor, and her dark confession remained unheard.

A deafening roar, followed by a thunderous shadow, filled the sky as an imposing figure stalked closer to the home. It came to a halt at the bottom edge of the porch, shifting from a monster into a towering man. His cold gaze scanned Helen and Iris with contempt.

The man pulled out a cigar and shot an ominous smile towards the sisters. He inhaled deeply before lighting it. He took a puff of the cigar, releasing a noxious cloud of smoke around him. His eerily still eyes settled on Iris's trembling form, and even Helen felt terror for her sister as the man—Satan—looked at Iris, who was now cowering and trying to avoid eye contact with the man. As Topaz narrated the story, Izzy sat in harrowing silence as she waited to hear about his next move.

Topaz shuddered as she recounted the story of Iris, powerless to her Lord's will. Without warning, Iris jumped from her place and bent in submission beneath his shadow, knowing he had come for her soul. The Lord of Hell had no intention of giving her time to prepare or hide; he had come to take her immediately. Her fate was sealed, and she knew why.

Helen's limbs grew heavy, her bare feet rooting themselves to the floor as she watched in horror. A chill ran through her veins like lightning, and a wave of terror crashed over her entire being. She knew if she ran, the darkness would follow her; she was unable to escape Satan's clutches. All their lives, they'd wanted to be with Satan, but never did they imagine it could come at such a price. As the shadows began to consume them, Helen realized that this was a fate from which there was no escape.

Beelzebub took a deep drag of his cigar, savoring the pleasure as the smoke trailed from his mouth and curled into the air. The women in front of him trembled uncontrollably, eyes wide with horror, as their throats constricted like a tightening rope. Silence filled the room as their pounding hearts raced faster and faster, feeling a terror that was akin to the innocent animals they would often sacrifice to the beast during their rituals. Fear and panic consumed them just like it would consume an animal or an innocent person. Now it was them who got to experience the fear.

The sisters felt a deep fear and trepidation sink in as their hearts pounded faster and faster. The searing panic was engulfing them, making them feel faint from the sheer dread they couldn't escape. As if mocking their terror, Satan's laughter echoed around them. But still, there was something else—something deeper than fear—that lingered in each of their minds, as though some part of them refused to give in completely.

Iris' desperate pleas for mercy were immediately silenced by the cruel and snarling beast. Satan was unmoved, like a stone statue with no emotion, as he coldly questioned Helen about why he was there. His booming and harsh voice echoed in her ears, making it clear that Iris had failed him, and now she would suffer the consequences—to be made an example of. But it wasn't just about punishing Iris. He wanted to make sure Helen knew *exactly* why he was there: PUNISHMENT!

Helen was mute with terror as her monstrous lord demanded her to answer him. He hoisted Iris up, her feet dangling helplessly, and she pleaded for mercy. Her delicate frame was like a doll in the palms of his hands, and fear coursed through her veins as her body started to convulse uncontrollably.

"Iris promised me a soul." The night stood still as he uttered the words, and Iris stared at him in a paralyzing trance. She willed her shaking body to stand strong but could not summon the strength to move away from his imposing figure. His eyes, filled with menacing authority, burned into hers.

Satan's laugh was like a deadly cackle, and raining chills flew over Helen. He glared at her with an unbridled rage that seemed to come from the darkest depths of his soul. His voice boomed and shook the ground as he spat out, "Your dear sister fell in love with the baby she swore to me, and she let her go! She sent her away with her mother to protect her from… ME!" The trees along the property line swayed back and forth as if in fear of his immense power, their branches shaking uncontrollably from the breaths of Satan's lungs. Helen felt her body become paralyzed with dread as the ground trembled beneath her feet. A cold sweat poured down her forehead, and bile rose in her throat. She was stuck in a horror story she couldn't escape from.

Izzy watched in horror—able to see all—as the beast spoke of the fate that awaited Iris, who had failed him. Iris had sworn her soul to Satan, and in return, the demon promised her power within the dark ways of the occult.

To gain such power, Iris had to sacrifice the baby girl—a pure, magical soul—with an untainted soul. Unlike Lucrecia, they wouldn't wait for her to age up before sacrificing her. Iris was supposed to manipulate and trick Faye into consenting to the sacrifice on the baby's first birthday.

~Izzy stayed rooted in fear as she had a *dark vision*. She saw Iris slowly walking towards the cradle, ready to damn this sweet, innocent being to Hell before… something stopped her. ~

Satan burned with a raging desire for the newborn child; her brilliant gifts were overwhelming and irresistible. Her soul was of an intensity that far exceeded any of his loyal followers, perhaps even matching that of the fallen angels who had followed him into damnation those centuries before. Satan yearned to secure the powerful soul of the baby as his own, ensuring ultimate loyalty and obedience when the trumpets sounded.

Satan's arrival filled Helen with worry, her fear ratcheting up even more as he calmly smoked his cigar. As she realized the dark lord hadn't come for her, but for Iris, she selfishly felt some relief. Helen had promised Lucrecia to Satan and knew it was only a matter of time before he would require her soul. Helen trembled at the thought of what his retribution might be if she failed to deliver on her promise.

In stark contrast, Iris did not hesitate to elevate her love for the baby over her duty to the Lord of Darkness and embraced the child protectively, as if knowing this was her one chance at experiencing motherly love. Her heart overflowed with compassion and empathy as she cradled the infant in her arms, uttering words of kindness that she had never spoken to anyone else before.

Unknowingly, Iris had fallen head-over-heels in love with the baby. This vulnerability revealed her true intentions to her mother, Faye. Something in the pit of her stomach began to warn against Iris. Faye dismissed it at first, but the nagging warning persisted. The warning tipped Faye off, and she followed her protective instinct. Faye, rusty with her magic, put a spell of protection up to safeguard her daughter, sending Iris away from her crib the night she planned to harm her.

To Helen's shock, Satan revealed that the little girl was alive and thriving. This angered Helen. She knew Iris broke her pact and wasted away a golden opportunity to rule the world for years to come. Faye's spell had saved the baby from the clutches of evil, but the girl was not out of danger yet. She would be hunted until the end of her days. Satan wanted her soul above all else.

Satan shared with Helen how Faye confronted Iris, and a flicker of fear in her eyes gave all of her secrets away. This was something Helen never thought was possible for the fierce warrior she thought her sister was. Faye snatched her precious child with panicked urgency, spurred by the thought of the treacherous entities that were surely coming for her. She ran as fast as she could, away from Iris and Helen, desperate for protection under the Divine, Almighty Lord.

Finally, Faye found refuge in a quiet convent far outside her native country; their secret hiding place guarded against any evil influence that sought to steal her daughter's soul. Satan's anger boiled like molten lava when he discovered he had been betrayed by his own servant, Iris—someone who had sworn fealty to him countless times in the past.

As the Devil drew closer to collecting his dues from Iris's debt, Helen understood that her days were numbered too. Her mind was plagued by thoughts of Lucrecia's disappearance—had she died? Escaped into a convent? Became too old to be valuable to Satan? She grew increasingly desperate as the seconds ticked away, fear gripping tightly at her heart but not speaking her thoughts out loud.

Satan stepped closer to Iris as she was levitating in the air, looming in the darkness. Helen watched in horror from the shadows. "What kind of mistress of the dark shadows would pity a child?" he asked rhetorically as his cloak flared out around him.

Iris remained unmoving just beneath him. She stared at Satan, as she was unable to speak or move. He gazed upon her with cold eyes. Iris was unable to answer, and she looked at Satan as he shook his head.

"A child that could be used to fight with us upon the trumpets of Revelations to aid in the defeat of God and His proud and arrogant followers?" He paused, waiting for an answer.

"What kind of mistress of the dark shadows would pity a child? A child with a soul so strong and powerful that it could be used to fight with us upon the trumpets of Revelations to aid in the defeat of God and his *proud* and *arrogant* followers?" Satan rhetorically asked an immobile Iris as Helen watched in fear.

Satan shifted his form in a dizzying blur, taking on the semblance of an ordinary man. The transformation was complete as he stood tall and powerful, looming over all with an aura of menace that seemed to fill the area like a living shadow. He put the cigar into his mouth and drew in smoke with delight. The bitter taste of the tobacco on his tongue was satisfying and relaxing for him. He blew out the smoke, leisurely watching it disappear into the dark. As he finished off his cigar, he put the fire out with his tongue and discarded the cigar on the ground.

Helen stumbled down the steps, propelled by raw determination, as she forced her way to kneel before him on the frosty grass. Her unsteady hands scraped his feet as she begged for mercy and emptied her heart of everything she had left until she felt hollow inside. She couldn't look away from his piercing gaze as her desperate eyes searched his face for a merciful reprieve. The cold ground slowly bled through her dress, while Iris hung in the air like an omen of doom.

Satan roared in agony as his body twisted and contorted, transforming back into a monstrous visage of terror... an unholy beast. His eyes burned with an unearthly fire. He reared up on his haunches with an earth-shattering scream, ready to unleash his fury on Iris. Satan extended his arm, beckoning Iris closer with a sinister hiss. An evil sneer curled his lips with sinister glee. His expression seemed to carry centuries of hatred, the depth of which could not be measured.

The air was thick with anticipation as Satan watched his prey, knowing that this was the moment that would seal her fate and bring about her ultimate demise. With a cruel smirk, he made an example of Iris. Satan opened his mouth and released an unearthly growl as it widened, stretching beyond its limits like a gaping abyss. The putrid stench of sulfur filled the air as razor-sharp teeth emerged from the darkness, snarling and gnashing, ready to end her life.

With ferocity, he began consuming Iris' soul. His tongue licked her essence as it seeped from her body while she convulsed in agony. After consuming her soul, he left her emptied and lifeless on the cold hard ground.

Helen stood frozen in horror, fear gripping the very core of her being, as she heard the last wail escape her sister's lips. Iris' limp form now rested dejectedly in the mud beneath her feet. Helen knew that at any second, Satan could consume her, and she trembled with dread at what may happen to her now.

A maniacal laugh escaped from his devilish lips as devouring Iris made him recall how he had once tricked a cherub into helping him— long ago. His shapeshifting abilities had transformed him into the most pathetic creature imaginable, yet it was all a ruse. Once the trusting angel came to his aid, he revealed himself in his true monstrous form and clamped down hard on the cherub, no matter how hard he desperately struggled to break free. Hot tears streamed down the cherub's face as Satan sank his fangs deep into its belly and immediately began feasting on the anguished celestial as his chaotic screams filled the air. The beast feasted, leaving behind only a few bones for the grackles to pick at until nothing was left of the cherub.

Helen was paralyzed with fear as she watched the Prince of Darkness stand in his sinister glory, savoring the thought of past atrocities. With a vicious snarl, he violently snapped out of his trance, and an unearthly growl ripped from his throat as foam and spittle began dripping from his mouth.

Satan bellowed furiously, "Iris is your sacrifice; you must go now and hunt Lucrecia. If she won't surrender to you willingly, threaten to take her children. She will have no other choice. Make a pact with her that their lives will be spared in exchange for her own."

Helen knew as soon as Satan's booming voice echoed through the room that this would be the only way she would survive. With a trembling voice, she responded, "My Lord, I shall bring Lucrecia and her children."

"I DEMAND that you have her return to you, or you will pay the ultimate price." He spoke with wicked menace, his words dripping with sinister power. Satan's voice thundered and shook the ground with a wrathful promise. Helen felt a chill slither down her body as he spoke, reminding her of the unyielding punishment she would endure in Hell should she fail him: "You will suffer eternal anguish within the pits of darkness, stripped of your dignity and authority, as you become an outlet for every wretched creature that inhabits the flames. Your screams of pain will echo through the abyss of Hell, and your body will be violated without mercy until you beg for death. If Lucrecia does not cooperate, I shall send my demons on that fateful hour to drag you away; let it be known that her children's fate is intertwined with hers—set them alight, and she will yield to you," Satan declared.

Chapter Six

THE VISITOR

elen thought about how Lucrecia had soared high up into the midnight sky, her broom silhouetted against the full moon and stars as she flew away in defiance. The wind howled through Lucrecia's hair as she escaped on the broomstick to seek safety and freedom. Helen thought back to that night with fright. Lucrecia was untamed and wild, her fingers gripping the handle of the broomstick for dear life as she rode into the night, faster and faster until the landscape below her was just a blur.

Helen shuddered at the visions of that night. Her imagination ran wild with what powerful dark magic Lucrecia must possess and how far she would go to exact her revenge.

She pushed her memories aside, suppressing her fear of Lucrecia as best she could.

Helen was both thankful and fearful of Lucrecia's children. She knew the children would provide her with leverage for manipulation, giving her an opportunity to seek revenge on Lucrecia. On one hand, she was glad that Lucrecia was blessed with magic so she could use her soul for sacrifice but feared it all the same; Helen knew Lucrecia wouldn't use magic against her—she resented witchery. Without practice or guidance, Helen was well aware that Lucrecia had blind spots that left her vulnerable to Helen's plotting. With a reluctant nervousness, Helen prepared herself for the battle ahead.

Helen's skeletal hands trembled as she dragged her withered body up the stairs to Lucrecia's home. She paused at the door, her breaths shallow and labored from a lifetime of neglect. Her yellowed skin hung loosely over her frail frame; evidence of the many years Helen had wasted on not taking care of herself. With iron determination, she steadied herself and stepped onto Lucrecia's lawn, her eyes burning with a hunger for her stepdaughter's vitality.

Helen trudged forward, her feet dragging on the ashen ground, guided by the vile demons of Hell to find Lucrecia. Fear grasped at her throat—fear that Lucrecia wouldn't recognize her in the decrepit state she was in now. Over the years, Helen's lifestyle had slowly carved its way into every facet of her face and body, leaving behind a frail and withered figure. With death closing in on her, and no time left to waste, she looked forward to sharing something with Lucrecia—a dirty little secret she had been hiding for so long.

Helen's heart was colder than the darkest night, as her soul filled with a raging hatred. She was ready to carry out Satan's evil tasks—snatching innocent Lucrecia's body away and damning her soul to Hell. Helen knew that all the innocents captured by witches around the world would be hidden away in eternal darkness. These poor damned souls would suffer without end, forced to battle alongside the demons of Hell in preparation for an epic war between Lucifer and God—a war that has been raging since time immemorial.

Helen's bloodthirsty ambition was her driving force, and selecting only the most powerful of souls to inhabit was her sacred mission. She had years ahead of her now that she had a body to call her own, and she would not let any opportunity to secure the perfect vessel pass her by. With her burning gaze, Helen knew that, soon enough, another unsuspecting soul would fall under her predatory spell.

Topaz detailed the story with urgency, her hands gesturing wildly in the air as if to capture the moment for Izzy. "When Lucrecia escaped and Helen could never find her, Lucrecia won. She proved herself stronger than Helen before she could be taken, and your mother stayed tucked away without a trace. Helen frantically searched high and low for any sign of Lucrecia, but her attempts were in vain.

"The dread of failure stirred in Helen's gut as she continually came up empty. Refusing to give up, her frustration built until she began to look for other children worthy of Lucrecia's favor. But on the night Satan arrived, Helen was filled with terror. It seemed Satan had been watching their every misstep and was beyond angry at the sheer number of failures from them both. Helen knew their punishment would be severe. Satan had come to collect."

Topaz's voice rang out as she explained. "Night after night, Helen called for your mother, yet each time, her cries went unanswered. Lucrecia turned away from all that was familiar, leaving behind the haunting memories and experiences. Unwilling to look back, she trudged on through the darkness, with only the thought of a brighter tomorrow spurring her onward. As Lucrecia's feet touched the soil of Texas, the cacophony of Helen's cries faded in the distance. Lucrecia knew she could never go back. She had won her freedom, but nothing could erase the agony of being trapped and alone at such a tender age. It was here in this land of unforgiving heat and savage beauty that she would make her stand. And so, she did.

"Once the demons ushered Helen back into your mother's life, Lucrecia was left without a choice. Her body shook with fear as she felt their malicious presence lurking around every corner, waiting to pounce. If she didn't agree to allow Helen's soul to find refuge within her body, she knew that her kids would be in immediate jeopardy.

"Lucrecia could already imagine the horror of watching her children being tormented and dragged down to Hell by the demonic forces. She knew she couldn't fight off Helen and the demons alone; without any experience practicing magic, she was completely ill-equipped to defend herself or her children." Topaz's voice shook as she spoke, her eyes wide with terror at what had transpired.

"Lucrecia could do nothing but submit to Helen. Helen attached herself to Lucrecia's limp form and filled it with a wicked spirit, inhabiting the vessel while your mother's breath of life lay dormant, unable to escape." Topaz explained it all in one nightmarish breath.

Izzy shivered as a deep chill ran down her spine. She slowly asked Topaz, "Is my mother's soul in... Hell?" Izzy could feel the anger well up inside her as tears filled her big, sad eyes. For all these years, she thought that her mother had snapped and become evil, never understanding what Lucrecia had sacrificed for the safety of her children. Topaz's words brought forth a whole new reality to Izzy, yet at the same time, she couldn't accept that her own mother would ever be stuck in such a place.

Izzy's grief was palpable, but Topaz spoke quietly yet undoubtedly, her words giving a voice to the truth that Izzy already knew—Lucrecia had been a remarkable mother and person. Izzy could not contain her tears of joy and relief that came pouring down her face as Topaz's wisdom broke through like a bolt of lightning.

The priestess, Topaz, had studied every religion and every faith from around the world before finally settling in America. She embraced and adopted all of the various teachings that she learned during her journey, and it was this powerful combination of knowledge that made her so skilled and enlightened, so she had the gift of seeing things as they happened to a person, even without knowing them or being there to witness the situation. Topaz assured Izzy that Lucrecia was, in fact, in Heaven among the celestials.

The inferno of Topaz's blazing fire surged with scorching heat. Izzy felt the air wavering around her as she watched Topaz spill out her soulful revelations about her mother, offering a bittersweet kind of closure to Izzy. In one move, Topaz had ripped Izzy away from every false veil that had been cast over her mother's memory and revealed the darkness that lay beneath.

Topaz was desperate to talk to Izzy about her future, but there was no more time. She could sense the supernatural and see beyond this world—a force that few mortals can comprehend. Topaz wanted to provide Izzy with closure on her mother's death and show her something far worse than anyone could imagine: the horror of witch-hunting.

The witches of the coven cast their meditation spells with an intense focus, moving their minds swiftly from Gamma to Beta and then finally Alpha. Victor, one of the male witches, dove even deeper, delving into Theta state in mere moments, ready for his shadow work. His heightened sense of clarity and power was highly respected within the coven.

Victor had first encountered Topaz during one of his many treks to Peru, a place he had grown up learning the traditions and rituals of magic. Topaz was only visiting briefly; crossing paths with Victor was serendipity. They would cross paths many times over the years before forming a coven in America.

Victor's gifts were incredibly unique. He was like no other witch in the coven, and Topaz favored him above all others. Topaz and Victor had grown close over the years, and their relationship followed a steady course toward friendship. Victor was much shorter than Topaz, barely grazing her shoulder, but she looked up to him like an older brother and would jokingly refer to him as 'her little big brother' to which he would tease back, referring to her as his 'giant little sister'—always with a big smile on his face.

Victor had a sun-drenched complexion, his tanned skin radiating a subtle tangerine hue. He kept his face closely shaved and smooth, though the wrinkles of years of experience around his eyes betrayed his age. His eyes were an entrancing umber color with dark, mahogany specks that seemed to draw one in with untold secrets ready to spill. Victor's head was crowned with thick, wavy hair, black as night with streaks of silver like stars in the sky—no doubt from all the unpredictable adventures he endured alongside his sister in magic, Topaz, and the love of his life, his beloved wife Ana.

Over time, his wife Ana crafted beautiful tattoos on Victor's arms that chronicled their journey in life together—a glory to God in every case. In between these details were swirling ensigns, intricate designs and symbols that further spoke to Victor's character. Each symbol embodied a moment in their lives together: a rose for her acceptance of the truth, a bird of paradise evocative of their first date, and the number seventeen, indicating his age when he realized his earthly duty was to be a protector of children.

As a young boy, Victor watched in agony as his father's frail body was swallowed by the raging sea. His heart died, as he knew he would never return, and he was now alone with a mother, both tormented by grief. Although Victor had strong abilities from an early age, they drew attention from those who sought to use them for dark purposes. His mother could sense his impending danger and did her best to safeguard Victor.

Victor was relentlessly pursued by an evil witch, intent on claiming his soul as her own. His mother bravely challenged the wicked woman in a desperate attempt to save her son. The two clashed in a breathtaking battle, blades and fists clashing against each other with fierce determination. In a final act of courage and sacrifice, Victor's mother flung them both from the highest point they could find in a daring leap, killing them both immediately. Both women— both witches, one good and one wicked—leaving their sons behind in a cold world. Victor found solace in knowing his mother had found salvation in Heaven.

The evil witch who wanted to cause harm to children descended to her own eternal damnation in Hell, burning forevermore for her sins.

Victor and Topaz had a connection that was nothing short of extraordinary. With every practice session, they deepened their bond, unlocking hidden secrets and knowledge from one another. Victor's mother had passed down her magical gifts to him, a legacy she held with great pride like those before her. Meanwhile, Topaz was bestowed with the greatest of earthly blessings. Topaz's power was unrivaled, and she never abused it; instead, she humbly accepted her blessing with grace and appreciation.

Victor and Topaz were both elite magicians, but it was Topaz that had a gift like no other. She could bend magic to her will and read the minds of those who dedicated their lives to religion, magic, or even science. For years, they practiced magic together in different villages around the globe, learning new ways of worship and techniques of spell craft from others.

After Victor and Ana moved to America, Topaz stayed behind with her ailing mother. After her mother passed away, Topaz had an undeniable feeling across the ocean—a calling that only she seemed to feel—urging her to move with Victor and Ana to America. Leaving behind her old home with no family close by, Topaz embraced her destiny as she set out on a journey that would change her life forever.

Victor and Ana took Topaz in and treated her like family, and Topaz looked up to them and loved them very much. Topaz opened a market, selling produce and herbs from her garden, which did very well and flourished, and Ana helped there every day. The two ladies were close friends, often communicating telepathically with one another. They shared a strong bond; these ladies were sisters in magic.

Victor's wife, Ana, was a wonderful wife. Victor had known Ana since they were children, growing up together. Their bond was one of deep friendship that turned to romance then marriage after some time.

Ana was born into a silent world, unable to hear the conversations and laughter of others. Yet she found solace in Victor and Topaz, who could communicate with her beyond spoken words. Their connection was so intense that they shared an unspoken language as thoughts flew back and forth between them. Vibrant expressions lit up their faces as they exchanged ideas, emotions, and memories that bound them together like two halves of one soul.

Ana had tight mahogany curls that seemed to be arranged by nature into ringlets that surrounded her face. Her skin was light brown. When she smiled, her warmth seemed to fill the entire room, chasing away any darkness in an instant. Her frame was petite yet very strong. She was beautiful in every way.

Topaz formed a coven of fierce witches, who met under the cloak of darkness to practice powerful magic, their rituals filled with ancient incantations and potent elixirs. Every member was gifted in their craft, wielding pure magic with unwavering devotion to protecting the land and blessing their loved ones and neighbors. They were fiercely loyal to one another, bound by love—not by blood and sacrifice. With unbridled intuition, they could discern between a grackle and a crow, keeping their circle small as they plotted to stop evil practitioners from doing unspeakable deeds. The air around them crackled with energy as they tapped into the primal forces of nature as they worked their magic.

Victor and Topaz pushed their abilities to the limit, each feeding off the other's strength. Ana never practiced meditation, and the other witches grazed into other consciousness; they were unable to descend into a deeper realm of sentiency like Victor and Topaz. Topaz explained to Izzy how Victor could reach the furthest depths of the Theta state while meditating. His focus was so strong, he could even dip into Delta, but never far enough to access what lies beyond Delta, when one's soul leaves its body and crosses realms.

Topaz revealed her secret to Izzy with a sly wink, explaining how she could drift effortlessly into Delta and beyond. With no need for practice or mastery of spells, simply by following the guidance of her innermost intuition, Topaz could traverse realms unknown to even the most experienced mages, straying far from Earth while her body remained in an ethereal state of suspended vivification.

Topaz took a deep breath in and clenched her jaw tight. Nervousness ran through Izzy's body as she watched Topaz sit in the firelight, her eyes shut tight. Izzy knew she was about to witness something extraordinary.

Suddenly, her attention was diverted to a commanding presence lurking in the shadows of the woods. With every step, it crept closer until it was nearly upon them. Izzy felt nervous as she watched Topaz, who remained seated and calm. Topaz was unafraid, which provided some comfort to Izzy.

Before she could ask Topaz what was happening, Izzy felt her heart leap into her throat as a figure emerged from the shadows. Paralyzed by fear, she watched as Victor stepped into the pale moonlight. He strode towards them and embraced Topaz tightly as she stood to her feet. Izzy stood back in awe, realizing Topaz was calling out to Victor in her mind—calling for him to join them. Topaz and Victor turned to Izzy and held out their hands to form a small circle. In that moment, it dawned on Izzy that Topaz felt her to be trustworthy enough to include her in their secret ritual.

Izzy closed her eyes, squeezing them shut in anticipation. She let out a deep breath, shuddering as she slowly released her shoulders before opening them again to stare at Topaz and Victor. "What now?" Izzy asked tremulously, fear lacing her voice. The night air had turned chillingly cold, seeping through Izzy's light clothing. The wind howled through the trees of the nearby forest, echoing off the lake like a banshee's scream, and the moon shone down disconcertingly on the three below.

Topaz held Izzy tightly, feeling her quivering subsiding. "Victor will be here with me to keep me safe as I dissolve into a trance, piercing barriers of reality," she whispered in the darkness, curving her lips mischievously. Victor stepped in and explained to Izzy how this out-of-body experience would blur the boundaries of existence.

Izzy felt her head swim, struggling to understand what was happening. Her heart raced faster and faster as Victor sat by the fire, a compassionate smile gracing his steady face. As Izzy watched him, she saw that he was taking long, slow breaths, inhaling deeply until his chest filled with air before releasing it in a languid exhale. He seemed to be willing himself into a calmer state of mind as he looked at Topaz, who seemed distant—almost like she was now in a dream and totally removed from our reality. He explained to Izzy that Topaz's soul was a solitary dark figure in the infinite abyss of shadows in Hell. Her soul—invisible and obscure to the hostile shadows that lurk within. In a sea of sadness and darkness, her soul was just another entity stalking the abyss.

Topaz remained in deep meditation for hours. Once she began to wake from her trance, her body began to jerk, her chest heaving as she gasped for air, causing Izzy to jump back in alarm. Topaz felt like her insides were being pulled out of her body; her muscles had gone limp, and her vision blurred. She was desperately trying to keep herself from getting sick while Izzy watched, her face full of concern. Victor stopped Izzy from moving closer, his voice gentle but firm. "Give her a minute. She needs space right now. Let her get some fresh air."

Topaz gained her bearings, and after a few moments, she stood to her feet. Topaz stepped closer to the fire, her face glowing with rage and perspiration. "I won't let the witch become more powerful. She's gained the trust of the demoniacs, even Satan himself. Her rituals of stealing innocence from hapless souls grow stronger each night. I have to stop her before she causes irreparable damage on Earth. I will make her pay for every innocent soul she's taken! She will not take anymore!" Topaz hissed, her disgust seething through her words.

Topaz's heart thumped erratically in her chest as she told Izzy and Victor that the witch completed another ritual.

Violet, the witch, had wickedly taken over her last host. Her evil sorcery snuffed out their lives, as if a candle were being put out with a sharp breath of wind, and she would bring their spirits into Hell. The malicious witch had already leapt from body-to-body multiple times, stealing power with each enlightened, doomed soul she devoured.

The story of Violet was an eerily familiar memory for me. An evil witch had once terrorized me with the same intent: to host in my body as my soul would be damned in Hell. Violet was eerily like the witch who stalked me—the witch whose origins are still uncertain.

Ramona, Ruby, Lacy—all one and the same: a powerful witch who had invaded my own body as a young child, claiming to be Lacy. My family thought I was dead, gone forever. They were unaware of the witch living inside of my body as she roamed the world unchecked among a sinister cabal. They kept her shrouded in secrecy. The nightmarish truth hidden from view, evading any chance of rescue or retribution of my body being stolen away by the witch.

Violet's clout within the occult was immense, her wealth unparalleled, and her reach extended far beyond any mortal realm with businesses spanning continents. The riches she accrued could not be contained, and her followers lauded her as a divine being, just like the witch that once tried to sacrifice me.

She was half a world away, so Topaz had to meditate to spy on her. Topaz warned Victor that they had to keep the witch from crossing into the shadow realm and taking innocent souls with her all the way to Hell. Victor's hand clamped down on her shoulder, his fingers digging into her flesh like sharp talons. "We have to stop her," he growled, his eyes locked on Topaz.

Topaz nodded, her eyes darkening with fear and worry. "We both know what happened the last time a witch became this powerful," she whispered hoarsely. The memory of that cataclysmic event still haunted them both. They couldn't let it happen again. With grim determination, they stepped forward together to face their foe.

Topaz held Victor's hand tightly as if it were her only lifeline. "I must go alone, and you must stay here with Izzy," she demanded sternly, her voice dripping with determination, though Izzy noticed a hint of fear lurking beneath. "I will be OK, I promise," she proclaimed, although they all knew the risks involved in her plan—but none more so than Topaz herself. With a final squeeze of assurance, she let go of Victor's hands and steeled herself for the daunting task ahead.

She exhaled heavily as she settled onto the ground near the warmth of the campfire. Closing her eyes, her chest rose and fell with deep, concentrated breaths. A light breeze ruffled the hem of her dress, and she seemed to venture far beyond the realm of ordinary consciousness, once again leaving Victor and Izzy behind as the night began to draw to a close.

Victor frantically pounded his chest, feeling the staccato thud of his heart racing as he started pacing around. His breathing became increasingly erratic with every step he took. Izzy's voice shook as she nervously asked, "What is going on? Where is Topaz now?"

Victor's eyes locked onto Izzy's, searching her gaze with frenzied desperation as he shook his head in sorrow and shrugged his shoulders in resignation. His expression quivered with fear and anguish, conveying a deep-seated worry that no words could express.

He cleared his throat, shifting his weight from one foot to the other. Izzy's eyes narrowed, and she asked him again, her voice tinged with frustration: "Where did Topaz go now?"

Victor sighed heavily, looking anywhere but at her. His fists

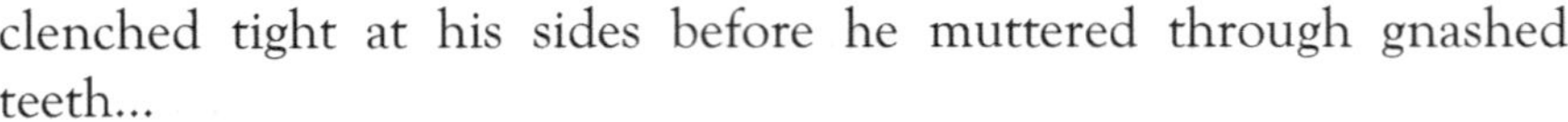

clenched tight at his sides before he muttered through gnashed teeth…

"To Hell…"

DUNGEONS OF DRY BONES

As Topaz stepped into the dungeons of dry bones, a wave of unbearable heat engulfed her body and soul, burning her with an intensity so strong that she thought she would combust. She felt her energy quickly being drained as the searing blaze made her feel weak and helpless.

Despite her fear, Topaz stood fast in the realm of Hell and pushed forward, determined not to fail in her mission—even if it cost her own life. But she was poorly equipped for this journey and soon realized she had underestimated the power of the unforgiving heat. She could feel herself melting away little by little as the flames licked at her skin, threatening to consume her whole.

Topaz's breathing was heavy as she tried to stifle the fear that threatened to overwhelm her. She knew she had to be brave and strong, but as much as she wanted power and control, fear still lingered. She was determined not to let it consume her, but it felt like an almost impossible task. She needed to find her courage and stand firm against whatever danger might come. If she failed, the consequences would be too harsh for her to bear, yet still, she lingered in the shadows of Hell, hoping no one would detect her presence.

A rumble shook the entrance of the suffocating abyss as some demons swarmed in. Their wings were loud, like large plagues of locusts. The creatures came from a dark tunnel that was cracked open, and even though they looked like monsters to Topaz, they could shift into humanoid form as they exited and re-entered Hell.

Over the centuries, the beasts learned to move between Earth and

Hell easily. They'd spend time in both worlds for various lengths of time, both feeling like home to the monsters. Being on Earth and interacting with humans makes them more efficient at demonic possessions and luring mankind into a false sense of trust.

Topaz was well aware that some demons masqueraded as humans, making it difficult to distinguish between a true human and a shapeshifter. Even she could not tell the difference between them at times. Topaz also knew some of the demons lived perpetually in human forms, capturing the likeness of their victims that died while they were possessed. The demons wore their victim's likeness, as a grotesque trophy while they walked through Hell. Their menacing faces echoed the eternal torture of the body they infested as they paraded through Hell, sneering at their victims.

As Topaz crept through the blazingly hot cave, trying her best not to tremble, she heard a loud thud. A group of grotesquely tall creatures stormed through the entrance with the witch, Violet, in tow. The witch's body glowed, and shadows writhed around her, as did the tortured souls that had been fused together with hers. The demons sniffed the air, their eyes scanning for a source of fear to feast upon, only to find an intruder standing in their midst.

As Topaz peered into the depths of Hell, her eyes widened in disbelief. It was an infinite abyss of darkness boiling with molten lava and belching out plumes of smoke and immense heat. The fires were bright enough to challenge the light of the sun, burning fiercely in a never-ending inferno.

Topaz could not believe that she had navigated right to where Violet entered at that very moment. How could she be so fortunate? She shuddered, wondering if she had received divine assistance or if it was just blind luck to find herself exactly where she needed to be.

She gasped in shock as millions of piercing screams from the gates filled every crevice of the canyons—the demons scuttling around like frenzied insects. Topaz felt an eerie presence prickling inside her mind, whispering words that seemed to come from an unearthly language. But somehow, they made sense to her: telepathic messages conspiring with sinister intentions. It was the demons communicating with one another telepathically, and yet she knew what they were saying.

Winged snakes, the color of blood with eyes that glowed like rubies, slithered around the witch, and the demons, hissing, hoping to consume the beaming souls that were tucked away within the witch. The snakes sensed the powers—the essences of the souls the witch escorted into Hell for Satan.

In Hell, souls and even demoniacs take their post-Heaven or post-earthly form as they were in their prime. Most humans cannot see these demonic entities on Earth, only shadows, unless they are revealed to them before their death or to intimidate them into submission. But in Hell, they revealed their true selves to the humans they manipulated into Hell, much like Satan did to Iris the night he consumed her. He did not shapeshift into a beautiful human to manipulate her. Satan did not shapeshift into a familiar, earthly beast to appear common to her. If she had to face him that night without knowing what would happen, she'd be most afraid of his face. So... Satan showed her one of his many grotesque forms.

Topaz felt a tug of conflicting emotions as she stood in the smoldering cavern. Below her, the screams of the damned filled her ears. It was these same people who had ruthlessly taken so many lives without mercy or remorse. Now, they begged for water and mercy, praying for respite from their brutal plight. In an ironic twist, Topaz found herself sympathetic to their call while at the same time knowing they did not deserve the consideration they were asking for.

The prisoners, the damned souls, who had devoted their lives to serving the dark lord on Earth, were now condemned to a tortured eternity. Their cries of despair pierced through Topaz's heart, stirring chaotic emotions within her. But she could not afford to be paralyzed by fear; she mustered every ounce of courage inside her and approached the demons that had been sent to punish the souls and to release the enlightened souls captured by the witch to their new resting place—Hell. She steeled herself against the darkness and made her way forward.

The demons quivered with fear and anticipation as an oppressive darkness rose from the blazing abyss. Topaz watched the creatures bow before the figure, trembling in reverence for its presence. Unearthly glory enveloped the scene as they rejoiced in its arrival. The beasts appeared grateful that the witch had successfully fulfilled her mission of delivering more cursed souls to Satan's domain. Helen and Iris had failed to meet Satan's expectations and were consequently punished according to Satan's law.

Once Topaz emerged from the darkness, a hush descended over Hell, and all its inhabitants' paid attention to her with shock on their wicked faces. There was no mistaking it—she let her guard down by mistake and now she had been seen. The entities watched her as she tried to blend in with the shadows.

The demons howled as Topaz strode boldly through the gates that guarded the entrance to hell. Knowing of the dark lord's relentless pursuit of her since infancy, the demons all assumed that she had come to surrender and join forces with them. Their howls and screams echoed off the walls of the pit as Topaz marched ever closer, her strength and determination radiating off her like fire.

The ominous entity that commanded the demoniacs laughed as if he were delighted. As he approached closer, the hairs on the back of Topaz's neck stood up. Her fight-or-flight mode kicked in.

The ground beneath Topaz trembled as the shadowy demons coalesced around her. "You!?" The powerful demon roared, his voice reverberating in an all-encompassing echo. His face was a macabre mask of hatred as he pointed at Topaz with an accusing finger. "We've been after you since before your first breath, and now we have you." He spat with malicious glee. "Iris thought she could protect you from us, but here we are," he taunted as his demonic cohorts shouted threats and promises of pain. Pointing to the ground with a trembling hand, the demon demanded that Topaz bow down and surrender.

Topaz advanced menacingly towards him, her expression darkening as she spoke. "You think Iris sent me away out of the goodness of her heart? Oh, no. My mother, Faye, saved me from Iris. She confronted Iris. Not even one of Satan's trusted witches could withstand Mama's wrath! There was no way Iris would get away without supplying us with a means to get home. My mother was prepared. If Iris didn't comply, she'd skin her alive!" Topaz cackled fiercely at the thought of her mother's strength and bravery against an adversary so formidable.

"My mother held her gaze upon the witch Iris as she confronted her. Tension flooded the air as they exchanged words, each trying to outwit the other. Then a smile slowly grew on Iris' face, and she nodded in agreement. Little did she know that my mother had manipulated her into letting us go. I saw the surprise on Iris' face when she realized what had happened. But it was too late; we were already free."

Topaz boasted this with a fierce glint in her eyes, emphasizing each and every word to make sure the demons understood. "My mother saved me. She manipulated Iris. But rest assured—if Iris refused to help us leave, my mother wouldn't let her stand in her way. My mother, a gentle and kind soul, would have taken that sorry witch apart piece by piece if she tried to hurt me." The air was thick with tension as Topaz stared the beasts down.

The demons roared in defiance, infuriated by the truth that Topaz dared to speak into their ears. Their eyes flashed with burning malice as they shook their heads, refusing to believe her words. But the truth was far greater than what their limited minds could comprehend: Satan himself was blind to the reality that Iris had been played by Topaz's mother. The two were under the protection and guidance of God, shielded from Satan's grasp and those he sent to hunt for their souls. The demons seethed with frustration, unable to overcome the Divine will that protected their prey.

Topaz faced the hellions with bold confidence, her voice dripping with sarcasm. "My mother, Faye—just an innocent believer in good—was stronger than one of Satan's own chosen witches of the occult." She watched as rage burned in the eyes of the demons before her. "Be sure to let your daddy know that too," she scoffed with a smirk, each word inflicting more pain and humiliation. Her tone was unyielding and ruthless, pushing the boundaries of respect.

Topaz continued; her voice laced with menace. "Your brothers came to hunt for me, and I trapped them with a box and buried them deep in the woods. Let your papa know that also!" She cackled, as if drawing strength from the demon's rage, as she taunted them. The commanding demon was blind with fury as he stood in front of the earthly witch, as if he were guarding her. His rage seemed to feed Topaz's energy, much in the way demons are fueled by our terror when tormenting humans on Earth.

Anger boiled through her veins as she screamed, "I'm here for her!" She jabbed a finger towards the evil sorceress who pilfered and enslaved the souls of innocent mortal with sick satisfaction. Teeth bared, Topaz snarled, "I'm going to obliterate this sick bitch!"

The demoniacs erupted into a frenzied cackle as the witch

shuddered in fear and sought shelter within the inky shadows of Hell's tormentors. A booming voice from among the horde boomed out: "You will MEET your DEMISE here today, and you shall never leave this place except to join us as one of our own, to serve your father, who awaits you eagerly, craving the souls of the innocent." The dusk pressed thickly around her until the figure before Topaz stepped away, and suddenly, an immense, darkened silhouette loomed ahead, drawing nearer with each step and sending a chill through her very being.

Topaz glared defiantly at the demon, her fury and contempt etched into her face. "You are no match for me, demon!" she spat in a commanding manner. Her words were met with a deathly silence by the other demons around them. She continued her scolding of the false Satan, her voice dripping with scorn. "You're not fooling me," she sneered. "I know you want me to believe you're Satan, but you're just a soulless vulture like all these others!"

The beast roared with fury and let out a warning snarl as if he was about to attack her. Topaz refused to back down, standing tall against him while laughing mockingly. "Go get your dad," she jeered, intentionally belittling him to reduce his status in front of the watching demons.

The imperious demon crawled from the abyss, illuminated by the infernal flames that rose like great towers of orange and red. All around his feet were massive serpents encircling him in a tight, protective embrace. Even Topaz felt her courage waning at the sight of the beast—horns like spears protruding from its skull and claws sharp as razors. Its feet were soot-blackened with thick nails like daggers, prepared to pierce any who dared challenge its might.

The sight of this beast was so unbearable that one could mistake him for the Devil himself. This creature was certainly trusted by Satan but was far from holding the most powerful position in the dark army that will march against God on judgment day. When time crumbles, and the world catches fire, we will all bear witness to these demons who have chosen to stand with Satan against our Creator.

The true horrors of Hell lay beyond the wildest nightmares. Far more sinister than anything imaginable. The demons take form on the very pits of evil, wielding limitless power over anyone unfortunate enough to dwell in their domain.

Topaz's gaze was steeled and unwavering as the imposing demon attempted to stare her down, but she refused to be intimidated. All of a sudden, a monstrous anaconda slithered toward Topaz with determination in its eyes. It curled around her body tightly like a noose, hissing words that were not of this world meant to hex her. But despite the overwhelming fear coursing through her veins, Topaz stood tall and unflinching, refusing to give in to the serpent's intimidating tactics.

The demons and serpents recoiled in fear as she reached out for the massive serpent that lay like a coil of greasy rope around her frame. He was larger than life, stretching his enormous length— over sixty feet—and possessing nine hundred pounds of pure muscle. His tongue flickered from his mouth as he watched her approach with an intensity that betrayed her fear. She opened her mouth impossibly wide—like a snake, like Satan himself when he'd consumed Iris—and inhaled his soulless essence deep into her lungs. With one swift movement, she cast his lifeless body onto the burning embers below, creating an eruption of sparks that shot high into the abyss of Hell.

Topaz's presence caused the demons to retreat until they were practically shoulder-to-shoulder, fear radiating off of them in palpable waves. None of them had felt this type of terror in epochs, and it was an unwelcome sensation.

Topaz's voice rose with a ferocity that resonated through the shadows of the abyss. "I'm done fucking around! Hand over Beelzebub's whore!" Her eyes burned with anger that froze the very air with dread as she called for the evil witch, Violet, to be surrendered. The demons shivered and cowered; they knew they couldn't deny her request, for if they did, Topaz would let loose a fury of fire and brimstone on their heads.

Topaz roared in defiance and desperation, daring Satan to come to her himself and take the innocent souls away from her. She dared him and his fallen angels to come into her presence, fully aware that she was tempting fate and death itself. But even brimming with courage, Topaz knew deep inside that she could not face off against the dark lord and his fallen angels alone. Yet still she tried, determined to save as many souls from an eternity of damnation as she could, even if it cost her own life. She refused to back down.

Shocks pulsed down Topaz's spine as waves of Hell's intense heat poured over her. Satan was oblivious, secluded in his own domain deep below the pits, away from the prying eyes of the demons he saw as nothing but peasants. She quickly concluded that he had no intention of associating with the worker bees who were forced to toil under his rule. Satan was oblivious to her being in Hell.

That night, as Topaz stepped through the threshold of Satan's home, he was surrounded by a bevy of demonesses, each vying for Satan's attention. Satan, in all his wickedness, frolicked with his harem of demonesses, unaware of the intruder as they pleasured him and courted his attention. In his lustful state, he remained ignorant of Topaz's presence, blind spots forming around his already darkened heart, not seeing her unwelcome invasion.

As Satan plummeted from the sky, he was cursed with a million weaknesses that all stemmed from one horrible vice—lust. Uncontrollable urges wrecked his body and mind, dragging him deeper and deeper into depravity. He knew he must hide his weakness from his damned in the Underworld, yet every moment brought new thoughts of coupling with demonesses in ways unimaginable. His unquenchable desire dragged him closer and closer to defeat.

Satan filled his palace with voluptuous demonesses to provide unspeakable pleasures for himself. He created other twisted, submissive creatures of the night to breed and entertain his loyal subjects. The Devil also created an army of succubi and incubi, to prowl the dark corners of the world. They were always ready to tempt and corrupt mankind with their sinister plans of unworldly pleasures. Satan's creations wielded power of lust to breed with humans, producing and tainting bloodlines of humankind, making them more susceptible to falling into sin.

Topaz crept into the depths of Hell—a place no mortal should dare enter. Satan lay entwined with his demonesses, captivated by their seductive touch and oblivious to any other presence in his foul domain. The walls of doom shook with each moan of pleasure from his harem of unholy consorts; he was never to be disturbed and had trained them all to know this. Little did Satan understand that his momentary distraction from his wicked desires could spell destruction for his disciples.

Topaz's desperate attempts to assert her power were met with disapproval from the demons in their own home. The sizeable and menacing demon seethed with impatience as he slammed his blade-like horn against the shattered stone along the wall. "Satan is far too busy to be disturbed by trivialities such as you, mortal. Your time here has come to a close." The fury of the underworld roared around them as another demon emerged from the darkest depths of the dungeon, ready to unleash their fury upon Topaz.

The demon that materialized from the depths of darkness was no negotiator; he was a ruthless warrior. His sinister figure lacked the horns of a commander; his disfigured face covered in raw burns and oozing wounds, suggested he was a force to be reckoned with. With an intimidating gaze and menacing stance, he stood there, radiating hostility and instilling fear in Topaz, who quivered in terror at the sight but stood tall as she faced him.

The demon's grotesque eyes shone with wicked brilliance, threatening to devour Topaz in its depths. They danced eerily in the darkness, vanishing like a ghostly apparition until he stepped back into the light, and they glowed with malevolent fury. His spine was clad in scaly armor from his neck all the way down to his broad shoulders, and his large feet were adorned with singed fur like a mane of fire. Long, bony legs encased in green, thick flesh, reminiscent of the reptiles that scaled Hell's walls, completed the demonic figure, an image of pure terror.

Topaz stood eerily still, her eyes scanning the demoniacs surrounding her. She took a deep breath and steeled herself against their ugly forms. She forced a smirk onto her lips as she locked eyes with the largest one of them all. His scaly gray skin was mottled and covered in patches of fur on his feet and hands. He flashed his fangs at her in an apparent attempt to intimidate her and puffed out his chest.

Topaz laughed out loud. "Don't you look like something from another world?" she condescendingly asked, with disdain dripping from her voice. "You look like a patchwork of leftovers—Goulash!" She cackled with a mocking laughter, her voice ringing through the dungeon as she belittled the demon. Topaz was determined to strip him of his power, refusing to let him intimidate her. Her body grew rigid as she faced the demons head-on, brimming with a fierce confidence that made her stand tall and unyielding.

The larger demon let out a guttural, menacing laugh. "Clever, but

I am about to devour you! Goulash is going to shred your skin and suck away your marrow," he growled, as Goulash bared his fangs in anticipation. Topaz glared into the demon's eyes with hatred and spat a defiant laugh.

She stepped forward, her head held high despite the overwhelming fear pounding in her heart. Her voice came out strong as she spoke to him. "Let's make a deal." The menacing creature laughed at her, but his laughter was cut short as her eyes locked with his and she stood her ground. He could see that she was not afraid of him; instead, she saw through his façade and showed no sign of backing down. He felt himself drawn in by her unwavering stance, and he involuntarily straightened up in response, feeling power radiating from her.

Topaz realized she needed to deceive the horned beast in order to gain her desires. She boldly pushed the issue, daring the monstrosity of Satan's trusted lieutenant to believe he was weak and even foolish, thus luring him into a false sense of security. He may have been one of the largest demons among his peers, with horns that curled like a ram and muscles that strained beneath his tattered skin, but even this grotesque monster wanted what all creatures do: to be king, just as Lucifer himself had desired before his descent from heaven.

The entity shrank in fear, knowing he should never dare disobey the Beastly Father's orders, but his pride fueled a rebellious instinct that prevented him from admitting it. He quickly weighed his options. Calling for Satan would bring the full force of wrath onto himself. He had witnessed what happened when others dared to disturb Lord Satan and his whores—their bodies were mutilated beyond recognition while their souls were condemned to an eternity of pain in Hell's cavernous depths. The demons knew their place, and none dared to contest Beelzebub's authority, knowing he would humiliate and punish them.

"I'll bet you..." She paused. "Unless you are unsure if you are entrusted to make decisions?" He sneered at her while approaching her even closer. Topaz glared defiantly at the two monsters standing before her. She could already feel their hot breath on her face as she clenched her fists and boldly announced, "I will take on either one of you, and I'm sure I'll be the one standing victorious when it's all said and done."

Goulash, the lizard-like demon with deep-set glowing eyes, stepped menacingly forward, eager to rip her apart. His brother, a hulking horned beast, sneered down at her with contempt in his voice as he asked, "Why bet us if we can just pitilessly tear you limb from limb right now?" His eyes slowly trailed downward to his long, wicked claws, which seemed to gleam in the eerie light from the moon above. Topaz did not hesitate for a second as she faced off against them both.

Topaz's mind raced as she scanned the group before her. She was outnumbered, and she knew it. If they wanted to fight, they had more bodies and more power than her—by far. Although far from the most powerful demons, they were still much stronger than Topaz.

There had to be another way. Topaz decided to use manipulation rather than brute force. Suddenly, a flame erupted from the tip of her finger, and with a few muttered words of magic, she disappeared into its depths. The demons roared in surprise that she'd vanished, but before they could act, she reappeared out of the smoke, triumphant. "Either we agree to a wager and battle," she declared authoritatively, "or I leave, and you can tell your daddy I came here to fight, and you felt too apprehensive about battling me, and I slipped away— AGAIN!"

He snarled. "What's the prize?" His voice deepened into a growl as he glared at the other demons. Their voices grew louder as they discussed Topaz's challenge, and anger boiled in the commanding demon's blood. He seethed with frustration, subordinate to a mere mortal on his own turf. Every second reverberated his ire. How dare she face him down in front of his peers and servants?

Topaz smirked cruelly, her eyes blazing with malicious delight. "If I win the bet, you shall surrender the souls to me, and the witch will be banished to the darkest depths of Hell for all eternity." The wicked witch trembled with fear at this demand, but she refused to back down, instead standing defiantly behind the demons. Seeing this act of defiance, the demons hissed in rage, their red eyes shining like embers from a raging inferno.

The demons snarled in unison as they circled menacingly closer to Topaz, their eyes piercing her with a look of dark intent. A host of sinister rumblings swirled around her as the demoniacs began an unintelligible chant that filled the air with dread. Suddenly, the sound stopped, and the atmosphere became still as a telepathic conversation took hold between them, blocking out Topaz's attempts to read their thoughts. Not even her special ability could penetrate their thoughts now.

She desperately tried to pry into the minds of the demons, but now their communication was closed off from her. She began to fear that Hell shackled her power or that they could be immune to its effects. Her anxiety mounted as each second passed, knowing that every moment she spent there was potentially a step closer to a confrontation with Satan or some other menacing agent of evil. She had to act fast and find an end to this living nightmare before it was too late.

Topaz felt the air thicken around her as she contemplated her own fate. "If I am defeated tonight, I will surrender willingly to Satan. He shall take my soul and the magical gifts that have been bestowed upon me since childhood. But if you win, demon, then I shall become your most prized possession." Her eyes burned fiercely into the horned creature's face, daring him to accept her offer.

Topaz unbowed, and a dark defiance rose in her chest as she faced the demon horde. A hush descended as her words echoed through the cavern: "We accept your challenge." The other demons cowered in fear, for they knew if Topaz were to be victorious, their father of embers would learn of their defeat and the consequences they would face for failing him. Worse still was the thought of incurring the wrath of the BEAST.

The horned demon was hell-bent on conquering Topaz and gifting her soul to his father as a tribute to his loyalty and servitude. Beelzebub, fueled by power-hungry rage, eagerly pursued her with the hunger of a predator, ready to devour Topaz's soul since she was only a baby.

The demon's insatiable desire to consume the soul of someone who had denied Satan for so long only intensified his already savage nature. He snarled at the mere thought of failing, allowing such a prize to escape from his grasp as if she were nothing more than a fleeting dream. It seemed that the demon felt confident and believed he could be the one to capture Topaz.

The demon knew that Satan and his powerful beasts had hunted

Topaz for years, tirelessly trying to find her as she was shielded by the nuns and her fiercely protective mother, Faye. The knowledge of his failure to capture her filled Satan with a rage so intense that it seemed to take physical form, coiling around him like thick black smoke. His humiliation became an obsession, as if Topaz and those who sheltered her were purposely mocking him, deliberately taunting him with their success in outsmarting him.

Satan was enraged that Faye eluded capture, and his vendetta against her endured. The horned demon was delighted at the possibility of taking Topaz to Satan. He wanted to be the hero who enslaved her soul and knew that Satan felt entitled to her.

The menacing demons encircled Topaz as they taunted her with sinister hisses. Sephinone, the horned demoniac leader of the demons who lingered in the shadows at Hell's gates, arrogantly swaggered in circles around her while Vladizimone—or Goulash, as Topaz tauntingly named him—was ready to pounce on her at a single command. Sephinone then spoke in a voice that was beyond mortal comprehension, filled with absolute hatred and malice towards Topaz.

Topaz demanded, "Reveal yourselves to me." The demons angrily revealed themselves at her demand. "I am Sephinone," he boomed, "and this is my servant, Vladizimone. Now—which one of us do you think has the power to kill you?" The menacing question echoed through the atmosphere like thunder. The other demons and the witch, a thief of souls, mocked Topaz.

Topaz's aura burned a furious scarlet as her confidence transformed into a raging inferno. She threw down the gauntlet and spoke in a deep, booming voice laced with brimstone. "I fear no one here," she snarled, her eyes blazing with wrath. "You pick; I'm ready to tear the flesh from either one of your bones!" Her words seemed to enrage Sephinone even further, his presence looming heavy in the room like a menacing storm.

Sephinone stepped back as Vladizimone, the menacing reptilian demon, emerged from the shadows. He crouched low and hissed with rage, looming over Topaz, who stood before him. With a devilish sneer, he kicked up a cloud of thick ash and soot directly into her face then bared his sharp teeth at her in the challenge of hand-to-hand combat. The other demons laughed jeeringly from the shadows, where Sephinone stood nervously but ready to intervene.

Vladizimone was incensed, his rage boiling with ominous hatred for the woman who dared slay his beloved pet snake, which she discarded on the floor of Hell. He swore to take her life in revenge and ensure that no one could ever enter the dreaded dungeons of Brimstone again. The commanding demon took a bet on behalf of the underworld that Vladizimone would prevail in his endeavor to slaughter Topaz. The witch, Violet, remained lurking in the shadows, still holding the innocent breaths—the innocent souls—captive.

The encircling demons' eyes began to roll back in their heads, and they began to convulse erratically, their tongues flickering in the air as if they were serpents. They shook their heads enthusiastically and began to snarl wildly, taunting Topaz. All were sure she would be defeated with ease. They could barely contain themselves with anticipation of her surrender.

The horned demon snarled as it laughed with disdain. "Very well, then. If you are victorious, we will honor our agreement and allow you a chance to rescue the souls. But... be aware that your victory is impossible! WE will win, you will be dragged down to the depths of Hell, and your soul will belong solely to Satan. You shall regret ever being born!" Sephinone's eyes lit up with anticipation for the impending battle between Vladizimone and Topaz. Deep within him, he felt there was no way that Topaz would survive against his soldier, his servant. She knew there was no guarantee that they, nor Satan, would honor any bets, so the wager was trivial.

Time was of the utmost importance for Topaz, and she needed to move quickly with the wager—entering the battle—in order to escape before Satan or other more powerful demons than the ones confronting her arrived. The demons nervously gathered around, stepping into the light of the fire. Though scared of angering Satan, they hoped to win this battle in order to be rewarded with more power and rank among the demoniacs. The demons became increasingly frenzied, howling and cheering on their brother with confidence that he would defeat Topaz.

As the battle ensued, the demons were chanting and hollering for their brother's victory over Topaz. Vladizimone lunged towards her, weighing hundreds of pounds more than she did. But instead of retreating, she caught him mid-air, throwing him to the ground with a thunderous roar that shook Hell's walls. The demons were filled with fear as they stumbled backward with cowardice. Vladizimone stood up and grabbed hold of her arm, slicing it open and drawing blood. He positioned himself to deliver a killing blow.

Topaz bravely stared into his eyes and smiled. "Damn Goulash!" She yelled mockingly as searing pain ripped through her body. She grabbed him by the throat and lifted his massive frame effortlessly, throwing him back onto the floor with unsurmountable force, before realizing that in Hell she was only limited by her own mind.

Topaz roared and seized him with a grip of iron, her fingers tearing into his fragile wings like claws into parchment. She yanked them off with one firm tug as the demon screeched in pain, writhing to escape her vice-like grip. As he scurried away from Topaz, Sephinone refused to join his brethren in hiding.

Instead, fire raged in his eyes as humiliation transformed into anger. His breath came in ragged gasps against the cold night air as he faced Topaz, ready for battle. Taking a step forward, he challenged her with a chilling glare that would make even the bravest of warriors quiver.

"I defeated the demon; he is unable to continue the fight. I am giving him undeserved mercy. I have decided not to kill him. I thought it best to humiliate him and deface him so he could explain the defeat to Satan," Topaz explained.

Disgust flew all over Sephinone. He wanted to renegotiate the deal as the defeated demons groaned with disappointment. Topaz nor the demon died, so he felt strongly that the wager was incomplete. Vladizimone groaned in anguish and despair. Sephinone, the beast, adamantly demanded, "Face me now, or your dear coven will endure agony."

Topaz froze in fear as her mind raced to consider the proposition before her. She knew if she stayed, she would risk not making it out alive. With a heavy heart and lightning speed, she declared, "Perhaps you and I will meet again" before thrusting her soul into an inferno of Hellfire flames, consumed by the blaze until nothing remained but a wisp of smoke that vanished before their eyes.

The demons were incensed as they watched her vanish, their hands scrabbling helplessly in the air. All that was left of her presence was a mangled demon and a slain anaconda. Roaring with rage, some of them spilled out of the brimstone gates in search of Topaz. The demons planned to forcefully bring her back to Hell so that they could finish the fight she had started. Fear twisted their faces at the thought of explaining their defeat at the hands of a mere mortal to Satan's unforgiving wrath.

The demons guarding Hell's gates were met with a devastating shock as Topaz, a mere human, emerged victoriously. The victorious warrior stalked through Satan's kingdom, leaving a gruesome wake of destruction behind her.

The demons trembled in fear as news of their defeat spread through the underworld. They knew that when Satan found out, heads would be lopped off their shoulders in a frenzy of rage and retribution.

CONJURING OF MAGIC

The demons were fooled by her ruse and carried on their treacherous acts, all unaware that the battle before them was only a distraction. Topaz stood toe to toe with the demons to allow time for Victor to work his magic.

Victor pushed his palms towards the fire and chanted a powerful spell, sending its reverberations through the flames. The orange hues of the blaze seemed to gain intensity with each echoing note, swirling around Topaz's body as she lay in meditation. Izzy's gaze fixated on the magical inferno; she had never seen anything like it before.

His demands for Violet to be dragged out of Hell along with the enslaved souls echoed around the dismal abyss. With an earth-shaking roar, the evil witch materialized from the flames, and Victor took immediate action. As Violet and the souls that she harbored emerged upon the call of his spell, he sent Violet's soul immediately back to the underworld, liberating the souls she escorted into Hell at last.

The souls were swept away from the darkness, finally given the peace they deserved, soaring straight into the arms of Heaven, thanks to the heroic witches who braved the night and extracted them from their prison of sorrow. Despite being considered wicked by some, these witches saved the lost souls and led them back to the path they were destined for, reuniting them with their Creator.

Topaz felt the veil of the living world fall away from her as she drifted towards death. She was plagued with visions and dreams of Hell, as if it were engulfing her in its fiery embrace. With a jolt, she had visions—all-knowing visions—about what happened the night she left after her battle with the demons. As these visions intensified, she began to share them with Izzy, writing frantically in her journal as each horrific scene came into focus. With every moment closer to death, Topaz added more and more details of the carnage she left behind in Hell.

Topaz told Izzy that as Satan reached the peak of his pleasure with his whores, a sudden disturbance caught his attention, sending him into an all-consuming rage. He flew through the dungeons of Brimstone with relentless fury, and when he reached the entrance to Hell, not even the serpents dared cross his path.

Satan's rage thundered through the underworld as he stormed away from his dalliance with his demoness whores. His claws dug deep into the stone floors of the dungeons in fury, and he knew that the demons had disturbed him while he was enjoying his sexual pleasures. He was determined to make them pay for their insolence and so flew down into the hellish depths of the pits and caverns towards the entrance of Hell. All around him, he felt their fear as he passed by a dead anaconda draped across the floor, which had been slain by some unknown force.

Satan's eyes glowed with a fierce fire as he surveyed the cowering demons. He noticed Vladizimone, writhing in pain and fear on the ground beside his beloved brother, Sephinone. Then, a glimpse of what transpired flashed before his eyes. In one swift motion, Satan snatched up Vladizimone and yanked him away from his brother, drawing an agonized cry of terror from the demon. The air around them quaked in response to Satan's booming voice. "You were beaten—by HER!" His rage ripped through Hell and up into the realms above Heaven, shaking even the foundations of God's kingdom.

Sephinone trembled as he looked up at the menacing figure of Satan, who had come to mete out punishment for his loss. The demonic forces cowered in terror at the sight of their king.

Satan reached down, and with a wave of his hand, brought the demon face-to-face with him as he sucked the essence from the defeated demon as he screamed while being evaporated. The unfortunate demon that faced off against Topaz was wiped from existence by Satan. He looked upon the other demons in the crowd with hatred. His disdain sent ripples of humiliation through the gathered crowd.

Rage exploded from his lungs as he roared with frustration. A raging inferno blazed around the Devil like a vengeful aura, causing the very foundations of Hell to quake with fear. His voice bellowed through the cracks of the underworld. "You are all worthless! You all stood around as a woman entered your home and dominated you!" With this, he let out an earsplitting scream that echoed throughout Hell. The entities cowered in fear from the intensity of his voice, which rippled through the air like thundering chaos.

"Vladizimone no longer exists," Satan declared in finality, his voice reverberating through the depths of Hell. "To speak his name will be punishment by annihilation." Fear descended upon the demoniacs as they stood in silent shock.

An eerie figure, smaller than a demon but with a ferocity greater than any other being, emerged from the shadows—a cryptid standing nearly eight feet tall, smaller than the demons surrounding him. The creature looked strange, although immensely ominous. Although he had a slender build, he was nearly three hundred pounds of solid muscle. The creature had an abnormally small head with large wings that towered behind it like two giant sentinels. Its *alienesque* eyes glowed an ominous red as it stepped towards Violet, its gaze unwavering. It brought forth her offering of souls to Satan in an attempt to placate him in this tense moment.

Satan's eyes burned with unbridled anger as he confronted the cryptid looming before him. His rage was palpable as his voice rose to a fevered pitch, spitting out scathing words. "That bitch, Topaz, defeated a legion of demons; you are all a bunch of cowards. I've sacrificed enough dark angels to her machinations, and now she has slaughtered beasts and humiliated you all here in Hell." He clenched his fists tightly, saliva frothing at the corners of his mouth, speaking with deep suppressed rage. "Who allowed this? Who made a bargain with that deceitful bitch?" Satan cast an accusing glare over the assembled demons, knowing one of them had been foolish enough to wager against Topaz's victory before the battle began. "You have all failed me," he growled with contemptuous disappointment. Too angry to witness their shame, he furiously turned away from them. They had failed him—again. Topaz had once again evaded the wrath of an enraged devil.

Sephinone shivered as he stepped closer to his father, desperately trying to change the subject before the beast erupted again. "The ritual has been done, Father; within the witch are the souls you have been waiting for." Satan's eyes glowed with anticipation as he snatched Violet from his servant and cradled her in his gnarled hands, a malicious smirk creeping across his face.

Beelzebub's grip on the witch tightened as a cold laugh escaped his lips. His laughter built into a thunderous howl, echoing through the darkness with an intensity so powerful that even the demoniacs couldn't help but tremble in their wake. His skin was seared by dark maroon flames that engulfed him and unleashed a beastly dragon from within. Spewing lava and fire from his lungs, he roared in rage—a harbinger of death, destruction, and retribution to all who dared cross its path. The monster had arisen; no one would be left unscathed.

The walls of Hell trembled with a deafening roar as Satan's wrath boiled within the dark depths of the cavern.

"You FOOLS! You were duped, the souls are saved, and all that remains is this washed-up witch!" He bellowed, throwing Violet into the undulating wall of flames that snaked around the demons like an infernal moat.

Satan's monstrous hands curled into fists so tight, his veins bulged from his skin as he trembled with uncontrollable rage. His eyes became wild and feral as a soundless howl of hatred erupted from his throat.

Satan's face began twisting into a menacing sneer as he reached out with an iron grip that clamped around Sephinone's throat. The other demons present shivered in fear and bowed their heads as they felt the power radiating off him. It was enough to keep them in line; no one wanted to be subjected to the wrath of their ultimate commander. Meanwhile, Topaz crept closer.

Eerie silence of the underworld hung heavy with dread as Satan began to laugh and mock Sephinone for being tricked by Topaz. The other demons followed suit, joining in the berating and jeering; even though they pitied Sephinone, they chose to side with Satan rather than stand up against him. His humiliation seemed never-ending as Satan paraded him about, dragging him through the grounds of Hell while all the other entities watched on, snarling and snapping.

Satan seized the demon's prized horns with a singular, powerful grip. Sephinone shrieked in terror as Satan's grip tightened around his horns, feeling the skin rip away from his skull. The pain was unbearable as he let out a tortured scream, the pressure intensifying with every tug of Satan's hands. Blood dripped down the demon's face, and his body quivered until, finally, both horns were torn off and cast into an inferno of flames.

Sephinone scrambled away in agony, stumbling far into the shadows to hide from his shame. His brothers denied him any comfort, turning their backs on him in disgust. Even the serpents slithered away, not wanting to be near Sephinone's cursed form. He was consumed by his hatred for Topaz and her coven—the ones who so cunningly defeated Vladizimone, freeing the souls from Violet, and making fools of the demons that were present that dreadful night.

As Topaz recounted her bone-chilling experiences, Izzy embraced and consoled her. Izzy shared with Topaz how loved she was and how fearful they felt the night she transcended to Hell. She recounted watching in the distance, faint streams of sunlight peeking through the daunting darkness. Izzy watched, transfixed, as Victor swept his hands into graceful arcs as he chanted. His motions stirred deep purple flames that thrashed at the edges of the fire. He repeated his spells of protection... again and again.

The flames surrounding them eventually began to dwindle away as the misty air threatened to snuff it out. Victor was beyond himself with worry and started to pace around the smoldering remnants of the fire. Izzy watched with panic as Victor's pace quickened. He began storming around the smoldering fire with rage and worry battling within his heart. His mind spun with visions of Topaz's soul tortured and wailing in Hell, and guilt clawed at his chest like a rabid animal.

He ran his hands through his hair in frustration as he cursed himself for not forcing her to allow him to go too. He paced frantically with a wild look in his eyes, muttering to himself as if trying to make sense of the situation. He knew he needed to stay behind to free the souls and to bring Topaz out of a trance if she needed help.

Izzy remembered what happened next, like it was yesterday. Topaz's breathing was labored as she rolled to her knees on the ground and vomited a thick purple sludge that seeped out of her mouth. Victor quickly grabbed the essence of the anaconda she had inhaled while in Hell, throwing it into the fire to get rid of it for good. Topaz's arm shook uncontrollably as bruises spread across its surface, effects from her battle far below in the realm of Hell. Victor, relieved to see her alive, pulled his sister close in an embrace and whispered, "My sister!" in her ear.

Izzy was in disbelief as she watched the scene unfold before her; it was like a surreal dream that she wasn't able to wake up from. She stumbled into Topaz's embrace, and Izzy grinned at her with excitement. Topaz turned to Victor with a small chuckle on her face. "I killed a giant snake and beat up a demon, though I didn't kill him. I wanted his father to see what I did and let him explain how he lost to an ordinary human being." She then shrugged her shoulders as Victor smiled. It was as if he wanted to say something but held back and let the moment pass.

Topaz collapsed onto the ground, her legs shaking uncontrollably as she tried to soothe the blistering heat coursing through her veins. Although it was only her soul that descended into the underworld, the hellfire scorched her flesh like a branding iron, leaving its mark long after she returned to the physical plane. Clutching her arm tightly, Topaz could feel the fire still raging inside of her, burning brighter each second.

Victor could hardly contain his excitement when Topaz announced her victory. "Which ONE, Samuel? Mikal? Bezaliel?" he gasped with awe. With an air of mischief and glee, Topaz replied, "Which one looks like a lizard?" Joyous laughter accompanied their high-fives. She continued her story with a sense of pride. "Not even Mann or Iikin dared to show up! If they had been there, I can only imagine how disappointed they would be to get their asses kicked by me," she joked.

Suddenly, she felt a pang of intense agony in her hands. Even though she was capable of healing herself, the memory of the fiery pain stayed with her until the day she died. Steeling herself against it, she pushed on. Topaz was good at choking back agony from her many battles.

Izzy remembered how scared she was when Satan emerged out of nowhere that night. Topaz breathed life into the fire, causing it to blaze until it was almost blinding. She muttered under her breath, "We must become one with the flame; he is on his way."

He stormed into the room, an inferno of rage radiating from his body. Fire sparks erupted from his mouth as he yelled, "Where are you bitches?" He surveyed the area with a feral glare, knowing full well that they had cowered away from his burning fury. The smokestack sputtered and died in the wake of his approach. He demanded they show themselves, but no one emerged from their hiding places. Taking a deep breath and crouching low, he scooped up the ashes from the ground and placed them into his gigantic palm. His face twisted into a sinister sneer as he spat out, "Victor! Where are you? You think you can rescue souls now?"

The wind whipped through the air, howling like a banshee as it picked up the ashes from their fire and scattered them into the sky. Satan seethed with rage, his face twisted in anger, knowing he had been tricked once again by Topaz. His teeth gnashed together as he imagined her death one day—a slow and agonizing demise that would render her enslaved to do God's bidding.

The trio jolted awake on a bed of damp leaves, the acrid smell of charred wood filling their nostrils. "Teleportation," Topaz managed to gasp, her voice rasping like burnt paper. "I couldn't go as far with you two. I need to practice more," she suggested weakly, her body wracked with violent shivers. "I've only been able to teleport physically one other time; it's not something that comes easy for me." The memory of searing pain and suffocating darkness was still fresh in her mind as she struggled to catch her breath.

Topaz forced a smile as her old friend recounted the last night they had all worked together. It made her think of Victor's passing. Topaz thought of Victor grabbing her hands tightly, his fingers cold and clammy, the night he passed away.

Victor shared how honored he was that, of all the witches, she selected him to help save the souls from Violet. Only moments later, Victor lay in bed, still holding onto Topaz's hand, before drawing his last breath. His grief was so great that it broke him from the inside out until, finally, Victor passed away of a shattered heart that even magic couldn't heal.

His beloved wife, Ana, had already gone to the great beyond after a short-lived battle with cancer, leaving him with a grief so deep that his heart couldn't bear it any longer. He stayed alive just long enough to see their plan through—to save innocent souls from Violet's wickedness. In the end, Victor at last succumbed to his broken heart.

SHOOTING STARS

After Victor passed away, Topaz was broken. She went on about her life with a hollow imitation of what it used to be like, attending the weekly meetings of her coven. Things felt different for her without Victor and Ana.

Topaz threw herself into teaching magic to Izzy. The other witches would stay with them, and they would practice late into the night, but even so, Topaz couldn't distract herself from the thought of Victor or the secrets he shared with her—secrets that allowed her to enter the gates of Hell.

After one particularly trying meeting, Izzy noticed Topaz looking up at the moon and stars, seemingly enraptured. "Telling the moon your secrets?" Izzy asked softly. Topaz slowly nodded her head in agreement and hugged her arms around her body as if to keep whatever she was feeling inside. "She's an enigma," Topaz murmured, almost reverently. "She knows all my dirt and has not once ever told another soul my secrets." Izzy smiled a sad smile and looked around them before saying, "She knows some shit about me too." They laughed as they softly bumped shoulders and leaned onto one another.

Topaz's thoughts raced as she did her best to stop thinking of Violet. She closed her eyes and imagined Violet, and other witches like her, stalking through the city streets like a dark mist, searching for innocent victims to take against their wills. With each life stolen, the witches grew more powerful as they consume every ounce of their victim's magical essence.

Reading her thoughts was eerily familiar for me; an evil witch had once terrorized me with the same intent: to host in my body as my soul would be damned in Hell. I shiver with dread, reminiscing of the witch who stalked me—a witch whose origins were still uncertain. Ramona, Ruby and Lacy, all one and the same—a powerful witch who had invaded my own body as a young child, claiming to be, Lacy. My family thought I was dead, while she roamed the world freely amid occult members who shielded her from plain sight until she was older.

The stars gleamed brightly against the endless abyss of black that draped across the night sky. Topaz gasped as a shooting star rocketed through the sky, trailing glittering stardust behind it as she pointed it out to Izzy. "I can't help but think about Victor every time I see a shooting star," she murmured with an air of dread. "My thoughts always drift towards my mom and even my dad, whom I never met—not that I remember, anyway," Topaz continued in a quiet voice.

Izzy nodded in agreement before asking curiously, "So... you don't know exactly what happens when we die?" The silence that followed was heavy as their eyes connected, both desperately searching for an answer that neither had.

"We will understand what happens to us after death when we are at its doorstep. Until then, it's one of life's big mysteries." She smiled. "I'm excited for the chance to live in Paradise and reunite with my loved ones. I especially miss my mother around the holidays; her absence is felt more acutely at this time. I also can't help but think of Victor too. Doing magic and working spells without him just isn't the same."

"Why didn't you just kill Helen before she came for my mother?" Izzy snarled; her jaw clenched in anger as she bluntly inquired. "You were the child that Iris desperately desired, but your mother helped you, and you managed to break free. But what about my mother? How could you not have done more when you became older and more knowledgeable in order to protect her? You might have special powers, but why couldn't you find a way to save her?"

Topaz looked away, hanging her head low with shame. She was a witch, but she knew that even with the power she wielded there were certain laws of magic that could not be broken. Free will must be honored, and lives left to their own devices. She had done all she could do to protect Lucrecia from Helen, creating a powerful spell for her to fly away on a broom when she was a young adult. But Topaz still felt guilty and responsible for Helen's choice to pursue Lucrecia.

"Lucrecia was doomed to her fate the moment Satan stepped in, his dark powers far more potent than the magic within me," Topaz explained with sadness in her trembling voice. She explained to Izzy that she was powerless against his immense strength and had no idea the demons and Helen were hunting Lucrecia. Topaz explained that her visions, as powerful as they may be, were swallowed up by the black void of Beelzebub's evil intentions, shielding her from the ability to look in on Lucrecia.

"The world is an unpredictable and even cruel place at times. But then, it can also be magical and awe-inspiring. In a single moment, one's choices can ripple and have unforeseen consequences—for better or worse. I have been on the edge before and done things that had dire results. I want to fix the pain and suffering of all but know it is impossible without assistance from above. All of us struggle with this same conflict. How do we save the world when we can't even understand why we're here?" Topaz sighed sadly, knowing she was powerless to make any real change—but like many of us, she would fight on in search of answers.

Topaz added, "I like working on magic and protecting those I can when I can. Sometimes, I will make a jerk spill coffee on themselves or trip; nothing too terrible." They laughed. "Same," Izzy confessed. "What's the worst thing you've done to someone?" Topaz paused before answering Izzy. "I've done some sketchy shit, but I really try to stay away from things that interfere with free will. Interfering can have a ripple effect that would impact an innocent person in a harsh and often unjust way."

Topaz let out a sinister laugh as she stood still, the smirk on her face lingering. In a low voice, she told Izzy of the stories she had kept to herself—vigilante tales of hexes cast to reveal the true colors of those who crossed her path, exposing people who were like grackles—liars, thieves, and users—to people they wanted to take advantage of, in the name of *justice*. As she spoke, she felt the warmth of karma coursing through her veins, overpowering every thought that threatened to steer her away from her righteous duty. Karma was hers alone, and it was a sweet comfort.

Izzy's eyes burned with hatred as she glared at Helen—the one who had caused such despair to descend upon her mother, Lucrecia. Her previously kind heart was filled with a venomous wrath that she never thought herself capable of containing.

Every action Helen had taken against her mother fueled Izzy's seething rage, and though she had never wished anyone harm before, she wished Helen would suffer for all eternity. Topaz could feel the malignant fury radiating off Izzy in waves, her words cutting through the air like a blade. "Our time in this world is nothing compared to what awaits in the afterlife." Topaz tightly clutched Izzy's hand. "If you want to keep score, think of it this way." Izzy felt a chill run through her as Topaz continued. "Helen being sentenced to an eternity in Hell, never to be able to live out the life she so desperately wanted—all while Lucrecia won and was granted the eternal bliss she was entitled to. Lucrecia is at peace in Paradise." This thought did bring a smile to Izzy's face and happiness to her heart.

Topaz changed the topic to one of celebration. "Your wedding day is so close! Aren't you so excited?" They talked excitedly about the ceremony and the days leading up to it, each detail more exciting than the last. Before long, it was time to part ways for the night, yet the excitement and adrenaline shared between them lingered well into the wee hours.

Topaz entered her bathroom, the cool tiles tickling her toes. She turned on the shower and adjusted the temperature to just below scalding. Steaming water poured down on her as she stepped in and let out a sigh. The warmth of the water soothed her sore muscles, and she closed her eyes, tilting her head back into the spray. The room filled with steam until she could no longer see outside of the glass door from inside her shower. Topaz gathered her long hair into a loose bun and continued to stand there, unmoving except for the steady flow of tears streaming down her cheeks.

She stepped out of the shower, her skin still damp from the hot water that had been a momentary reprieve from her emotional turmoil. With trembling hands, she wiped the tears from her face and quickly dried herself off before slipping into her comfortable bathrobe. Taking a deep breath, she heard something loud in the front yard. Pausing for a moment, she then heard three loud knocks. Fear surged through her body as she felt for her slippers in the dark room and proceeded quietly in the dark to her front door.

Topaz feverishly scooped up the baseball bat that lay next to the entrance, her heart pounding in anticipation. Gripping it tightly, she pulsed with magical energy—ready to unleash a torrent of power if an evil being was present. But if it was a human, she needed her baseball bat to beat the shit out of them if necessary. She had to be prepared to do whatever necessary to protect herself from malice of man or demon, if need be. Always wary, Topaz knew better than anyone that humans could be the most dangerous creatures on this planet.

Topaz often warned Izzy about the dangers of human beings, saying that even a single encounter could prove disastrous. Free will gave humans an edge, which made them so incredibly unpredictable. Every version of each person's character could be hidden with intent of deceit, and while trust can be a good thing, it can also be your very demise.

The deadly silence on the porch filled her with dread as she stepped out. Even the crickets were too afraid to break it. She gripped her bat so tightly that her knuckles turned white, ready to swing at any moment. Steeling herself, she called out into the darkness, "Who's there? Show yourself, or I'll knock you senseless!" The bat was clutched in her hands like a lifeline, ready to crack skulls if need be.

A tall, mysterious shadow emerged from the darkness. Topaz trembled and held her breath as it advanced closer to her. In a sudden burst of joy, she recognized the figure that had come to save her. "Seth!" she shouted as he raced towards her and gathered her into his powerful embrace. She felt safe in his arms as he sprang up onto the roof with her securely in tow, never missing a step. He carefully laid her down on the shingles beneath the full moonlight, their eyes locked in an unspoken understanding. The midnight sky was illuminated, but not a sound could be heard between them except for the beating of their hearts.

Seth was an absolute vision of masculine beauty. His towering frame cast a gigantic shadow over Topaz, and she trembled in anticipation. His broad shoulders were chiseled with muscle and strength, and his chest boasted only the slightest amount of chest hair that begged to be touched. His arms bulged with unbridled strength, veins popping beneath the surface and radiating a sense of power. His strong arms radiated power and authority but were still full of tenderness, exuding warmth and security. Everything about him seemed perfect, and immediately, Topaz wanted him with burning intensity.

She was captivated by his velvety, soft, fair skin. She yearned to run her fingertips through his sepia-colored locks that framed his incredible ice-blue eyes. Her heart raced when she pushed his hair back and looked into the depths of those gorgeous eyes, like two azure oceans where she could bask in blissful admiration. His wild mane had delicate waves with a brilliant golden honey hue, and she was mesmerized by his beauty.

Topaz drank in Seth's handsome features with her eyes, his chiseled jawline and closely shaven beard captivating her. His full lips moved as he talked to her, revealing his perfect teeth in a way that made her heart flutter. Seth's wings were a thing of wonder; a slate blue-gray mix of colors, they were large and powerful. When he would walk, his glorious wings would sweep along the ground like a majestic cape as he walked.

Seth's voice dropped as he spoke, weighed down by the sorrow in his heart. "I had to come and see you, make sure you were OK," he whispered softly, knowing Topaz was crushed by her recent loss. "Your parents, Ana, and Victor—they're all doing fine. They've taken off on their adventures and are soaring to greater heights. I am sure Izzy is aware, but her treasured parents are living in the magnificence of Heaven," he shared as he smiled at Topaz.

Topaz breathed a sigh of relief. She was so pleased to hear how her loved ones had managed since arriving in Heaven. "Lucrecia has been in France, protecting a family there," Seth explained with admiration. "She's become incredibly strong; all the difficult life lessons have prepared her for her journey in Heaven. She's even started taking care of high-level tasks, though she doesn't have wings yet. God gave her a beautiful set of bronze armor and a crown of jewels for her accomplishments." This news made Topaz beam with joy.

"We already know she needs no wings to get around—Lucrecia just snatches up a broom and flies away!" He laughed as Topaz smiled widely with happiness as Seth teased her, knowing Topaz had something to do with that.

Topaz's heart swelled as she listened to Seth describe the glorious lives of Victor and Ana in Heaven. Ana had always wanted children but found the world too wicked, so she and Victor chose not to have their own. Watching Victor and his wife care for innocent souls dramatically highlighted Topaz's excitement about their life in the Kingdom. Seth assured her, "Your loved ones are all beloved and highly favored by the archangels in Heaven."

Suddenly, an idea sparked in her mind, and a mischievous glint appeared in her eyes. "When I die and go to Heaven, I will be their favorite too," she laughed. Seth leaned closer to her, his voice thick with admiration. "You are already a pretty big deal. You help more as a mortal than some aids in Heaven that have been in practice a while."

His words felt like soft velvet on her skin, and she could not resist the urge to lean into him as he continued. "You're already favored," he added softly before locking his gaze with hers. An electric charge passed between their bodies, and they shared a tender kiss that left them both trembling with anticipation. Although tempted, they knew it would be complicated—even, possibly, forbidden—so reluctantly, they allowed the moment to pass.

Topaz dedicated her life to helping save souls, never allowing herself to experience the heartache of romantic relationships. Her beauty was undeniable, and men longed for her affections, yet she remained strong in resisting any advances. That is, until one fateful day, when she laid eyes on Seth. His presence sparked an intensity in her soul that overwhelmed her body and mind. In the stillness of the night, Topaz's thoughts were consumed by Seth, her desire for him transcending mere physical attraction. This was something much more meaningful. She yearned for the intimacy shared between them, like a beacon guiding her home.

Seth wasn't a divine angel, as his wings would suggest. He had never been a sacred, celestial creation. He had never been a blessed creature of the heavens but an ordinary human. Seth was a human spirit with wings. His altruism and bravery caused him to come to the aid of an elderly woman whose car had broken down on a busy road.

In one terrible instant, a drunk driver plowed into Seth as he was helping her move the car, sending him flying across the street. He lay in agony, blood pooling around him, before finally succumbing to his injuries. The intoxicated motorist drove straight into a telephone pole, ending his life right alongside Seth's, their souls entering Heaven side by side, despite the tragedy. The remorseful driver met Seth briefly in Heaven before they each began their separate paths through eternity. Seth was almost two years older than Topaz at the time of his death.

Seth stood tall and majestic. His handsome visage is filled with a stern purpose as he vehemently guards those under his protection. Seth watches over people like a vigilant guardian, divinely appointed to protect and guide those that need help going into the light.

His rise through the ranks of the afterlife was unprecedented, a feat that made even the archangels stand in awe. He worked tirelessly to aid those making their way into the Kingdom. God was so pleased with Seth and his sacrifices that He bestowed upon him a rare honor among heavenly humans: angelic wings. His wings spread wide and glorious with pride. Seth was one of the few human spirits from Earth gifted with such an extraordinary offering from Yahweh.

The archangels' voices swelled with a chorus of admiration, their glowing wings shining like starlight. They knew firsthand the immense blessing that came with the bestowal of wings. Gabriel, the Archangel, stepped forward and placed his hand on the Seth's shoulder, saying, "Your valor has earned you this sacred gift." A chorus of resounding praise filled the air as other angels joined in, each admiring the new appendages with awe.

The archangels understood the grand design that Seth's life had been meant to follow. They were privy to the visions flitting through his mind when he was on the brink of death. The archangels knew how much he'd lost in his untimely demise. They also knew Seth mourned all that he would never experience. In this moment of joy, they knew Seth's mind immediately thought of the woman he was supposed to spend his life with.

It was when Seth's life began slipping away that he experienced a multitude of memories and visions. In a flash, his mind was overwhelmed by the memories of his childhood dreams, the most joyous moments he'd ever experienced, and the potential paths that he could have taken if given the chance. As he drifted through the haze of his most cherished memories, he stumbled upon a haunting vision of the woman who was meant to be his wife—Topaz.

As Seth lay dying, his heart quivered with sadness at the injustice of it all. In that instant he could almost smell her perfume, taste her lips, and feel her warmth in his arms. But then reality crashed down on him, crushing him beneath the weight of what could have been as Seth took in his last breath.

Seth and Topaz were meant to be together in an earthly life. As Seth made his transition to the Kingdom of Light, more visions of his unfinished life on Earth flooded his mind: visions of future milestones—moments he and Topaz should have shared, had someone else's free will not changed the course of his life.

These visions raced before him like lightning yet burned into his mind like fire, and he would often find himself dreaming of her and their *almost* life together. Seth's hard work and dedication in Heaven did not go unnoticed, and the archangels eventually granted him a unique privilege: When he returned to Earth for his tasks, they allowed him additional time to spend with Topaz.

Topaz felt an incomparable bond with Seth, as if their souls had been inextricably linked. It was like an invisible thread that held them together. Her body ached, and she yearned for him with a passion she had never experienced before. It would have been clear to anyone that saw them together that they were meant to be husband and wife, but fate intervened when another person's choices ended Seth's life too soon.

When Seth passed away, Topaz felt an unfamiliar yet undeniable emptiness within her chest that seemed to expand with each breath. Although she hadn't met Seth before he passed away, Topaz's entire world shifted when he died, and yet she was oblivious to the change in course her life would take. In a single breath, her entire world was altered irrevocably; the fate of her future forever changed.

No longer fated to be with Seth, she followed a new path, her alternate life path. Unlike many young adults her age who focused on dating and the ordinary problems of life, she focused on saving innocent souls from cunning witches. Her fiery passion was unleashed to protect the innocent from the unforgiving clutches of Hell.

Topaz had taken on a new quest, an unending mission to safeguard those in need, regardless of the risk to her own safety and well-being. She willingly sacrificed a life of normalcy and embraced an existence dedicated solely to guarding the vulnerable from the depths of evil. This, too, is why the archangels allowed the two to spend time together.

Seth first met Topaz when he was already in Heaven. The archangels sent him to protect her before she traveled across the ocean to America. He watched as she and her friend, Victor, chased away a dark magic practitioner who had been menacingly stalking two innocent children. He quickly realized Topaz was not just an ordinary person. Even though Topaz thought of Seth as her guardian angel, he knew his true mission was to protect the woman he was supposed to share a life with before destiny stepped in between them.

Topaz worked tirelessly to keep the witch away from the precious boys. The menace of the old crone's plans weighed down on her shoulders. Every time she stepped into town, Topaz kept a vigilant eye on the witch as she slunk through the streets, looking for someone to sacrifice to Satan.

Finally, one fateful day, the evil sorceress came across the twins while they were in the company of their mother. The dark practitioner sensed the power within them and envisioned two souls for her dark lord—an unprecedented prize! With burgeoning strength from her magic—her dark arts—keeping the witch at bay would be trying, even for Topaz. She steeled herself against the onslaught of spells and hexes, summoning all of her strength to repel the witch.

Topaz awoke that morning with a feeling of dread and knew this would be the day she would take on the witch. She was determined to protect the boys from any further harm; she had to put an end to her taunting, bedeviling them with nightmares once and for all. As Topaz prepared to leave her home, there stood Victor, watching her with concern. She could tell he wanted to stop her, but she was resolute in her mission; this wicked witch needed to be stopped before she caused anymore suffering. A wave of determination washed over Topaz as she set out to confront the witch.

Victor was determined that Topaz would remain safe, no matter the cost. He was aware of the cunning and treachery of the Devil, so he feared Topaz could easily be tricked into a deadly trap if Beelzebub discovered her plans. With great care and caution, Topaz crafted her ideas, bending the laws of magic as she formed her scheme to prevent the witch from carrying out her nefarious deeds, remaining undetected by even Satan himself, for Satan, too, has blind spots.

Topaz and Victor had crossed a line they should never have dared cross. Without warning, they'd meddled with fate, disregarding the free will that even wicked witches and wicked people possess. Face-to-face with the witch, Topaz was determined to stand her ground without Victor's help. Despite his final oath of loyalty to Topaz, he could not bring himself to turn away from the inevitable battle between these two formidable ladies, knowing that only one would come out alive. Fearless and fierce, Topaz readied herself. She was prepared for a fight to the death.

The witch's eyes sparkled. She had a malevolent glee about her. The witch drew up her most powerful spell against Topaz. The thick vortex of dark energy seemed to crackle as it hummed with deadly intentions. But Topaz was ready for it, snarling with defiance as she raised her fists in challenge. The spell surged forward like a tsunami, slamming into Topaz with all its fury, but Topaz declared, "No spells can stop me. I'm going to kick your ass, Bitch!" In a blur of motion, Topaz darted over to the witch, who cowered in fear at Topaz's unexpected aggression. As Topaz loomed over her prey, waves of raw power emanated from her body, causing the witch's heart to race with terror. She began to sweat profusely as Topaz closed in on her.

Topaz's power radiated from her, shaking the earth beneath her as she glared menacingly at the witch who had caused so much pain to innocent young souls. As her rage filled the air, the witch lost all courage and struggled to draw a breath. Topaz saw the fear in her eyes as she desperately tried to make an escape, only for every movement of hers to be thwarted by a ferocious Topaz. The witch dropped to her knees as she began clutching her heart. Topaz towered over her, and she was unmoved. She met the witch's eyes with a piercing glare and a mischievous smirk. The witch dropped to her stomach and curled into a fetal position. Topaz then unleashed an invisible force that ripped through the evil witch's heart. Paralyzed with shock, the wicked witch perished. Topaz interfered with free will, and she was the sole cause of the witch's death.

Topaz and Victor desperately tried to bring her back, but it was in vain. Her spirit had already been claimed by the Father of Lies in exchange for the invaluable souls of the two boys she swore to him but failed to deliver. The deed was not complete, and the witch was cursed to a futile eternity in Hell, robbed of any hope that she may have held onto from her years dedicated to the dark lord. Satan now owned her soul, an insignificant one among billions that paled in comparison to those he was promised by her. Sadly, for every witch that failed him, there were many that succeeded in their promises to Satan.

Satan burned with raw fury when a witch was killed, or a demon banished from a soul he desired. Lucifer's rage reached its boiling point when a witch failed to ensnare the souls of the enlightened for his grand war against God. His obsession with Topaz and her soul started when she was an infant, never wanting a human's soul so strongly before. He could feel their disobedience when they boldly confronted the witch, usually flirting with danger, but this time, they went too far. Satan wanted Topaz and Victor to pay for their defiance.

Satan's anger flared as he finally laid eyes on Topaz after she had the gall to reveal her true identity when stopping the witch's dark magic from reaching the twins she was caring for. Having crossed the line first, Topaz and Victor were now his prey, and he would be sure to visit upon them both a reckoning of wrath like no other before. His rage burned brighter with each passing moment, until it seemed an inferno of hatred was blazing in his wake.

Satan prowled forward with a sly grin, his intimidating presence rippling through the air. His eyes blazed with a feral intensity as he inched closer to Topaz and Victor in an effort to recruit them. His massive stature seemed to shrink before them, as if reducing his figure would lessen the fear they felt from his overwhelming presence. He slowly extended an arm, offering a hand of friendship as his lips curled into a sinister smirk, daring them to accept or reject him, and knowing that, either way, their souls were his for the taking. With nowhere to hide and no time left, they could only watch as Lucifer approached with deadly intent, offering up his gestures of deceit and deceitful intentions.

Topaz laughed, unfazed by the sight of Satan. Her flippant attitude only served to fuel his rage. Seething with anger, a thick cloud of smoke filled the air as Satan's body began to mutate and seethe, growing larger and more gruesome as each second passed. His wrath seemed to envelope the world, and for one horrifying moment, Topaz and Victor both thought that Satan would obliterate them with a single sweep of his arm.

He felt now that he was entitled to their lives—they had played God when they killed an innocent witch without her consent—no matter how noble their intentions may have been. They had attempted to incapacitate Satan's witchy woman from causing more harm, but instead they took away her free will and thus claimed her life instead. Now it was Satan who felt he had the right to take what wasn't his, exacting revenge against the two mortals standing before him.

Satan's frustration built like a raging inferno, fueled by the audacity of Topaz and Victor to not cower before him. His mind raced with thoughts of punishment as Beelzebub's voice grew even more menacing, deep and stern. The demonic language that spewed from his lips was so convoluted, it felt like he was speaking in tongues—English became Latin, which quickly turned into Spanish before switching to Portuguese. As Satan's eyes rolled back into his elongated skull, the sclera transformed into a blinding white while deep red illuminated just behind his pupils—a clear sign of the rage that boiled within him.

Topaz and Victor were rooted to the spot in terror. Satan's grip was like iron, paralyzing them with fear and refusing to let them flee. His eyes, hate-filled and menacing, burned right into their souls. Topaz had already been through a great deal; her mother had braved the convent and hidden her away from evil years before. But... even *that* had not been enough to keep her safe from the clutches of Satan.

The beast wanted her power and her magic. He wanted her to fight him until she was completely under his control—or broken forever. Satan wanted her to be his own warrior in the ultimate battle of good versus evil and felt that now, with her before him, her soul would be his at last.

They fought against Satan's hypnotic trance that had bewitched them. Without warning, a blinding light penetrated the ominous scene, brighter than any color known on Earth. The light seared their eyes, and even Satan himself cowered in fear from its incredible intensity, unable to pierce through its overwhelming brightness that overpowered all darkness.

The fading light illuminated an angelic figure from the heavens. Topaz gazed at the glorious being who radiated with raw beauty and kindness. His slate wings expanded behind him—a proud angel ready to face off with Satan. Lucifer stepped forward, sneering at the smaller creature in front of him.

Satan's obsidian wings spread wide as he bellowed out his challenge. "Know that I am the mightiest angel, more powerful than any godly gift you've been given!" The air crackled around them as evil reigned, and pride spilled from the Devil's lips.

Seth's voice boomed like a clap of thunder. "Lucifer is dead to those of us in Heaven. His once glorious wings wilted into the hideous appendages you now have." Satan's eyes blazed with fury as he turned his gaze toward the sky, fists raised in defiance. "They sent you to protect her? Not even a real angel? Come on, Michael, Gabriel," he bellowed. "Come face me yourselves! Don't be cowards!"

With lightning speed, Seth snapped his fingers aggressively before Satan's face and smirked as he watched the fallen angel seethe with rage and disbelief. The audacity of this false angel, a former mortal man—the defiance was almost too much for Satan to bear. As Seth stepped back, an unearthly growl escaped from Satan's throat, and he stepped towards Seth with all the force of a hurricane.

Seth stood fearlessly in front of Satan, his voice a booming proclamation. "They will come with their armor and swords, but at the end of the day, it will be your head decorating Heaven's walls as punishment for daring to challenge Yahweh." As he spoke, Seth felt no fear, only firm conviction in the righteousness of his mission.

Satan trembled with rage, his skin turning an intense scarlet, and his wings reverberating with energy while he took deep breaths to keep himself from unleashing total destruction. With every breath, he seemed more infuriated, and even the false angel's mocking laughter was almost enough to set him off.

Stoking the fire, Seth taunted Satan further. "You think you can achieve many things, yet all you manage to do is fail embarrassingly. I'm embarrassed for you with every one of your failures!"

Satan's angered voice echoed through the underworld: "I have many of Yahweh's creations in Hell with me. Looks like Mr. Perfect is a failure too!" Satan knew the creations had free will, as did he, and it was their failures, not God's, as he hoped to draw Seth into a debate. Once he saw Seth didn't feel the need to explain or defend God, Satan grew more irritated. "They sent me a mortal to fight me for this bitch," he mumbled to himself, pointing at Topaz.

She smiled. "Big ego you have there. You weren't even smart enough to know that my sweet, angelic mother manipulated your witch Iris to send me away, right under your nose," she mocked. She and Victor wildly laughed, intentionally infuriating Satan. He would still think of how Iris deceived him. If not for the betrayal of his own witch, he wouldn't have lost Topaz. If not for the buffoonery of Iris, Topaz would already be in his grasp.

The malicious plan struck terror into Faye's heart as she held tight to her tiny, defenseless daughter after realizing what almost happened to her. She recognized that the Devil wanted Topaz from the day she was born—waiting with rabid hunger since she took her first breath, so that he might drag her down to the depths of Hell. If Iris were able to snatch away the innocent soul and offer it up in sacrifice, then Satan would have had the most gifted soul with him the day of the end of the world. But those seedy plans fell through, like so many others he sets into play.

Iris, aiding the escape of Topaz when she was a baby, and betraying him for her safety, flew all over him and his controlling ways. Topaz stood beside Seth. "Now you know how it feels when you give trust and get betrayed by someone you thought was loyal to you," she sneered. "At least God is all-knowing and knew what a traitorous fool you and your sorry-ass demons were! But you, BELIAL, were easily fooled by a measly little witch!" Her eyes flashed as she laughed mockingly.

Her words bounced off Satan like bullets as he silently seethed with anger. Topaz knew she was pushing her luck but took confidence in the fact that Seth was there to protect them from Beelzebub. She would never have been so bold if it wasn't for his presence.

Satan felt a swell of rage crash into him at the thought of a mere "mortal angel" being sent by God to stand up to him. His voice descended into an incomprehensible growl as he spoke backwards in different earthly languages.

The king of darkness threw back his head and let out an unearthly howl as he warped his body into new shapes, transforming himself into something even more terrifying. A mouth appeared from the side of his face, snarling and spitting out blasphemies in languages that hadn't been heard in millennia. With a crack of bone and a sickening wet peel, another head tore through the flesh of Beelzebub's neck, its eyes black pools of pure evil.

Sinister faces of powerful tyrants appeared from the murky depths, morphing from Hitler to Stalin and Vlad to Himmler in an endless cycle of terror. Each face contorted with unimaginable evil and spoke backward in low growls and grunts that reverberated through the depthless abyss. At their feet was a chorus of tortured, damned souls crying out in agony as the body of Satan loomed ever larger.

The head of Satan contorted and morphed back into its true form, towering above everyone with an air of menace. Topaz and Victor quaked in absolute terror as they witnessed the unholy transformation. Electric energy crackled through the atmosphere as Satan prepared to face off against Seth, who stood strong and resolute. Satan's spine tingled with a strange sensation—a hint of God's power radiating from Seth. In that moment, he knew that his adversary had been sent by the archangels and must be powerful enough to defeat him. "We will meet again," he threatened ominously as Seth continued to guard Topaz and Victor from the depths of darkness. With a final snarl, Satan disappeared, taking only his witch's damned soul with him.

Seth turned to Topaz and Victor. "He's not afraid to fight me or you. He's just not going to indulge his brothers," he said, gesturing to the sky. "He won't give them the satisfaction of getting his ass kicked or kicking mine, because even if he beat me or ended up killing me, a former mortal... Well, there's no notoriety in that. He knows me being sent to protect you both was a mockery to him," Seth explained.

He flexed his biceps and grinned, revealing a set of beautiful white teeth surrounded by smooth, tan skin. His eyes twinkled with mischief as he added, "But I'm sure I would have won." He struck a playful pose, one arm pointing to the sky while the other held an imaginary sword victoriously above his head. He winked at Topaz, who blushed and looked away, enjoying his wit, even though she found his joke corny.

Seth slowly and deliberately met the eyes of Topaz and Victor as he passed along the warning he had been sent to deliver. He emphasized that their interference with free will was not a game but a consequence with far-reaching ripple effects, capable of changing courses for people and even generations. "Help when you can, but remember that taking lives, even accidentally, comes with a heavy price. I'd hate to see anything happen to you," he warned emphatically, his gaze lingering on Topaz as if conveying an underlying meaning beyond his words. His expression shifted into something more mischievous as he added, "I'd truly hate to see you suffer such a fate; you're too precious for that."

She felt a jolt of electricity pulsing through her body as she laid eyes on Seth. His gaze was fixed on her, full of passionate intensity and admiration. She could feel her cheeks reddening under his affections, her heart thumping wildly in her chest. Every inch of Seth's being ached for her; he wanted to take her in his arms and never let go.

Seth had only glimpsed the depths of beauty his soulmate adorned, but now that his vision was unfettered, he fell head-over-heels in love with her all over again. He cherished the visions he experienced of having a family with her—something he would never experience now after his life had been cut short.

The instant Seth laid eyes on Topaz, and he felt a jolt of electricity shoot through his veins. Even the archangels were moved by the fire that burned between them; this passionate flame was too powerful for Heaven to keep apart. But when it was time for him to return home, he felt an unbearable pain that could only be soothed by thoughts of holding her again. In the depths of his soul, he longed to drown in her eyes once more.

It was soon after that encounter that Topaz began to hone in on her magical abilities, making them stronger. She was a force to be reckoned with, preventing many from straying down the treacherous path of dark magic. Even when she fought for others, she could not shake the constant longing for Seth, an angelic being that infiltrated her every thought. Guilt gnawed at her for entertaining lustful thoughts of him, but it was nothing compared to the loneliness that consumed her when she was alone. Tears would flood her eyes as she thought about her mother gone from this world. Her heart would ache with loneliness thinking about Victor and Ana, half a world away in America.

Seth's words echoed in her mind like a battle cry, fueling her determination as she trained relentlessly with the most powerful of magicians and holy practitioners from around the globe. Her determination grew with each passing day as she prepared herself for the epic showdown with Satan that was sure to come.

* ✳ *

Seth and Topaz lay side by side on the roof under the light of the midnights of Topaz's house as they admired the star-dappled night sky above. Seth turned to her and reminisced about their first meeting years ago, when she had put herself in harm's way to save sweet souls from certain death. His eyes held a mixture of admiration and fear, concerned that she might not be so lucky next time. Playfully, Topaz swatted away his worries. "Have more faith in me!" she teased, knowing his concerns were valid.

Topaz narrowed her eyes, knowing the danger of what they were up against. "Satan's power is limitless," she muttered under her breath. He smiled back at her and whispered, with a voice like ice, "Luck and good timing will not be on our side. As careful as you are, he can outwait you. His patience is infinite; every second that passes is another chance for him to find a way to fool you." A chill ran through Topaz.

She realized there was no turning back now. As the moment grew tense, Seth broke the awkward silence with a laugh. "Do you know why a succubus seduces human men?" he asked. Topaz felt a wave of dread wash over her as she tentatively replied, "Are you about to tell me a demon seduction joke?" She giggled. Seth wasn't a dad but had a plethora of dad jokes.

"No, no!" he sneered, his face twisted in mockery. "I've heard rumors." He winked. "I hear they seduce men to make up for what Satan lacks in the bedroom. It's been suggested that he's cursed with two tiny dicks?"

He smirked as Topaz gasped in shock, with muted laughter as she shook her head. "But for real," he continued, leaning closer. "I heard that Satan has two dicks, but I'm sure they're both puny." He laughed as he ran his hand through his luscious hair. "You're LYING!" she spat, and he merely shrugged, unfazed. "Damn it! If I'd known something like that before, I would have told Satan to SHUT THE HELL UP with his two little dicks!" She squealed.

Seth confessed he had heard Satan had two dicks, but he had never heard they were small. "I just assumed they were two small dicks, or maybe they were floppy and didn't work. Maybe that's the real reason he's so angry," he suggested jokingly. "Seriously, though. Demonesses pleasure Satan, not succubi like most people believe. People also believe a succubus will only seduce men in their dreams to make them think of lustful, or troublesome thoughts. But... that's not entirely true; that's not the real purpose. Succubi and incubi are Satan's creations. These entities serve a far grander purpose than sexual dreams and sex."

He bellowed, "These unholy abominations, the succubi and incubi, were spawned by Satan himself to twist and distort God's creation. Flawless in form but soulless in nature, they roam the earth, preying on humans to create cambions—unholy offspring of sin and lies. Their sole purpose is to spread corruption and damnation, to bring forth destruction and death!"

Topaz listened intently, but she was already aware of succubi and incubi, and for some reason, she didn't want to talk about them; she was tired of thinking about the evilness of the horrors that lurked in the shadowy realms between life and death. Besides, there were very few things about the undead that Topaz didn't know.

"Satan is so fucked up," she said while shaking her head. Seth stretched out his arm and beckoned her back to him, and as they both lay still under the night sky, a brilliant bolt of emerald fire streaked across the midnight blue canvas above them. Topaz gasped. "A shooting star!" Her eyes glowed with wonder as Seth whispered, "No, not a star. That's Zadkiel, Archangel of Mercy." His words echoed in her heart as Topaz placed her hand over her chest in reverence.

Realizing the beauty of that moment, they stared into each other's eyes. "Moments like this are what I yearn for with you," he whispered to her, his voice filled with emotion. "Moments like this are why I chose just you," she responded passionately as her heart raced. Seth knew it was time for him to fulfill his destiny and depart.

"I can't stand this, but... I have to go. I wanted to make sure you were doing well. I know how much pain you're in," he said with regret while standing up. "I must now follow God's will and help those in need, but rest assured, I'll come back to see you soon," he vowed.

His words seemed to lay heavy on her heart as he prepared to leave, something he had not intended to do so quickly. Seth swept her up in his arms. His gaze shifted to hers, and he could see starlight reflecting in her eyes. The soft moonlight illuminated their faces as he held her close. They were lost in one another's eyes for a moment, before Seth steeled himself, then jumped from the edge of the roof. His free arm was securely wrapped around Topaz as he landed with a thud in the soft, dewy grass. Seth let her down slowly and steadied her body against his. They locked hands briefly before she pulled him close and rested her head against his chest. Topaz leaned close and tried to hear a heartbeat or feel a breath against her skin. But there was nothing—his body that once housed his human spirit, now contained an immortal, angelic being.

As they hugged, he surprised Topaz as he dipped her back, holding her tight in his strong arms. He pulled her close and kissed her gently. The sweet kiss turned passionate and deepened as his hands explored the curves of her body. His left hand firmly pulled her body against his. She could feel his fingers slide through her hair as he caressed her. Seth held her face in both his hands and looked deeply into her eyes, full of an insurmountable longing that could only be mirrored by a passionate kiss. His kisses were slow and meaningful while his grip on her tightened, conveying the immense love and longing that he had kept hidden for so long, determined to risk any complication to be with her once more.

The world around them seemed to fade away as their lips melted together in a sweet and fervid embrace. Topaz broke away reluctantly, tears welling in her eyes at the torrent of emotions that threatened to overwhelm her. "I know you have to go," she whispered, never breaking eye contact. "But promise you'll come and see me soon." Her voice trembled with an intensity that shook him to his core, her eyes wide with fear as she begged him to return to her soon. It was as if every word she spoke was a knife twisting in his gut, the weight of her desperation almost suffocating him.

Awestruck, they held each other in the moonlight. With a heavy sigh, Seth replied, "It's moments like these that I dream of. I am whole again when I'm with you." His words lingered in the air until she spoke up again, joining him in his desire. "Yes," she whispered, their gaze intensifying with every second that passed.

Torn between his longing to stay and his duty to go, Seth reluctantly stepped away. "I must answer my call. But before I did that, I wanted to make sure you were alright," he explained, still embracing her and feeling her warmth radiating throughout his body.

Reluctantly, he stepped away and watched her silently turn and step onto her porch.

Seth felt his breath catch as he stepped closer to the porch, mesmerized by her luminous beauty in the moonlight. His eyes widened and his heart raced as he drank in Topaz's flawless skin and her sexy, womanly curves that left him speechless with desire. His thoughts derailed into a world of passion and longing as he admired her long, athletic legs, firm stomach, and voluptuous breasts. She was so captivatingly beautiful that it made him vulnerable; he wanted nothing more than to be with her and unite with her in body and soul like a husband would be able to with his wife.

She pulled the robe tight around her body and looked him in the eyes. "You have people to protect!" she sternly reminded him. He shook his head and snapped back into reality, then laughed. "I have two minutes until I have to go," he whispered, moving closer. "Kiss me for two minutes." Her heart raced as she shook her head 'no' and shooed him away with a wave of her hand. "Come back to see me soon!" she called after him as he began walking away, fading into the shadows of the night. He glanced over his shoulder one last time and smiled. "That robe needs to go," he growled before completely disappearing.

Topaz watched him walk away, not yet knowing how long it would be until his return. With a shaky breath, she whispered "I love you" one last time before stepping inside and locking the door. She took a deep breath, holding it in for a moment before slowly exhaling, releasing a shuddering sigh, her chest heaving with the pain of his departure. Her tears pooled and spilled over her cheeks before she could stop them, creating salty rivulets down her pale skin. Topaz desperately wished he had stayed—not out of sorrow but because she ached for his presence.

She stood in her room, the moonlight spilling over her naked body. Her hand reached up to her hair, brushing it ever so softly, while she let out a deep breath and stared into the mirror before her. Topaz knew the only man she wanted was Seth. She knew she would never marry or have a child with another man. Unbeknownst to her, she was fated to become a mother, but the path of her destiny completely changed with his premature death.

Now she was walking a different road. Her path in life was

different—not better, not worse... just different. Topaz knew it was ultimately less important to create a child than it was to be a warrior for children, protecting those who counted on her from satanism.

Topaz let out an exhausted sigh as she crawled into bed, her body heavy with the thought of Seth. She couldn't help but feel like his opportunities were scarce, and he was fighting against the odds just for a few moments with her. It was maddening not knowing how long it would be until they met again. Hugging her pillow tight to her chest, Topaz closed her eyes and found solace in the ebb and flow of her breaths as she drifted off into sleep.

IF ONLY...

Topaz was in a dream-like trance when she suddenly jolted awake, her heart pounding madly with terror. She found herself in a hospital room, almost as if it were a vision from another realm. She was like a ghost, drifting through the background of the cold, sterile environment unnoticed and unseen.

The family circled the bed of the dying man, their faces drawn and haggard. The stench of impending death hung thick in the air like a shroud as the rattle of death reverberated in his chest. He heaved for a breath, his lungs burning and chest rumbling with every shuddering inhalation. The noise ricocheted off the walls, reverberating around the room until it felt like his own deafening agony was all that existed.

His family stood around him, hands clasped together as if that would keep death at bay. Tears streamed down their cheeks, but none dared to speak for fear of breaking the fragile stillness. The old man's hand reached out as if grasping for something just out of reach. And then, with a final gasp, he drew his last breath and was gone, leaving his loved ones in the room utterly heartbroken.

There was a sudden chill in the air as *death* stepped into the room. Its silvery feet glided across the cold hospital floor. A bright light radiated from him. The family of the dying man was blind to the momentous occasion, not noticing the angel of death. He did not reveal himself to them; that's not who he came for. The angel brought his hands together, and a bright light shone from his fingertips. His wings were wide and cascaded down his back onto the floor. As the angel moved closer to the man, he whispered sweet nothings to him and touched his gentle lips to the man's cold forehead.

Topaz watched in awe as the *angel of death* lulled the man away into an eternal peace, and she was overcome by a feeling of familiarity. Despite death's intimidating presence, she felt nothing more than comfort from its compassionate embrace.

A wave of euphoria washed over the man as his spirit lifted from his body. The years of sickness melted away as his spirit glided into eternity. The man stepped through the blinding light where his parents and a young child that preceded him in death were waiting for him with open arms.

I know death is often seen as something we must fear, but it is truly a liberating reward for having enjoyed life. However complicated, sorrowful, and painful it may have been, life brings its own lessons, joys, and exciting moments—an amazing conclusion to our tale. Life may be tumultuous and painful at times yet filled with magical moments we cherish. When death comes for us, it is our ultimate prize, and at the end of our journey, we should feel proud of the life we led on this earth. I, for one, don't fear death. I've already been dead, after all. I fear not living my life.

Topaz lay in bed, thoughts swirling in her mind and a deep ache in her chest. She had woken up from a strange dream that she couldn't shake, feeling as if it hadn't been a dream at all but a reality. Rolling over to check the time on her clock, hoping for some sort of solace, Topaz was surprised by the sight of Seth, sitting on the edge of her bed. His face illuminated in the soft orange glow from the streetlight outside her window, and he seemed to pull the last breaths of air out of her lungs. "I saw you tonight," he whispered as he reached his hand toward her face, gently pushing back strands of hair that had fallen across her eyes. "I invited you there. I wanted to show you what it is I do. My sole purpose. I am an angel of death—one of many.

"Now, you know. I am not a guardian angel. God granted me these glorious wings as my reward for services of transitioning mortals into the next life. I shepherd and guide humans who are too scared to take the plunge into Heaven that awaits them. People look upon my wings and feel comfort. I lived as a mortal man, and I understand their fear and suffering. I feel joy that my presence alone brings them solace. I crossed over with doubt and trepidation in my soul. I strive to comfort them as they make their transition on the path to the heavenly paradise that awaits them," Seth explained as Topaz intently listened.

"Where is your scythe and black cloak?" she taunted, smiling as she teased him. "You are too pretty to be an angel of death. You are... an angel of life."

Seth hung his head, and his voice turned grim and serious. "I am not an angel of life, but a collector of souls," he whispered in a voice that seemed to scrape against her eardrums. "And I will come for you when it is time. Whether it is beautiful or peaceful remains to be seen."

Topaz shuddered, unsure if she wanted his words to comfort or horrify her. "That night I met you," she asked with trepidation in her voice. "Were you there for me? Was my life on the line?"

"I was there for you, but not to take you or Victor. The archangels knew I could protect you; they knew I wanted to see you, so they allowed me to go so I could be the one to protect you and Victor," Sabastian explained as she took in what he was telling her.

Topaz gazed into his eyes with disbelief. "You never knew me before that night?" She scrambled, crawling closer until she was mere inches away from him. He tenderly swept her hair aside and leaned in close. His pink lips brushed across her earlobe like a whisper of fire. Her eyelashes fluttered shut as he cupped her face in both hands, the kiss intensifying until their tongues intertwined. When he finally pulled back, his gaze drilling into hers, he commanded softly, "Close your eyes." Without hesitation, she complied; their foreheads touched as her breath mingled with his.

Topaz closed her eyes, and Seth showed her visions of his life coming to an end. She witnessed his last, living moments as they grasped one another's hands. She was nearly overwhelmed with sorrow. After this passed, she was met with images of what could have been. The first date that never happened, the first kiss they might have shared. She saw their marriage and the life they might have had together had he lived. The power of the moment left them both longing for more, wanting more visions of a happy life together.

Topaz's visions betrayed her. No matter how hard she tried, all of her efforts to see into the future with Seth were for naught before that night. Like a door shutting out the truth, Seth's death barred her visions from ever seeing his fate or what may have been. But he had to show her; she had to bear witness to the revelation. In one swoop, the life they could have lived together was changed by someone else's actions.

Topaz felt her heart contract as she shared the visions of his life—their life. The most heartbreaking vision for her to witness was the moment he was in the room with her as she was giving birth to their daughter.

At that moment, she opened her eyes and looked at him, her hands trembling as they broke free from his and moved across her stomach, knowing now that their baby would never grow and live within it.

"I'm sorry I died and couldn't give you those things." Seth sighed as tears dripped down his face, and he attempted to look away from Topaz, but she reached out and pulled him into an embrace. He let himself be engulfed in her warm hug, refusing to pull away until Topaz had finally released some of her sadness in quiet sobs against his chest. "It's OK to cry, Topaz. Crying shows that you care and are compassionate and strong; it's a beautiful way to show how you feel. I am sorry." He let out a heartrending sob as despair and regret engulfed him, the anguish in his voice echoing off the walls. Tears spilled from his eyes, running down his cheeks until he was left trembling in quiet sorrow.

The silence in the room was almost unbearable as Topaz fought to control her tears. "It is an unshakeable regret, one that will haunt me for eternity," he said, his voice shaking with emotion. "But... you can still have those things with someone else. Just because our story ended before it began doesn't mean you can't find another ending. Our destiny might not have been written together, but there's still a chance that you can have something better." Seth did his best to console her, stroking her hair gently as she cried.

Radiating an aura of strength and courage, she looked at him with loving eyes and proclaimed, "No story could ever be as beautiful as ours." No one could deny the power that radiated from her. Seth smiled at her. "Well, you kicking witch ass and whooping up on demons is pretty hard to compare to," he jested. "You rattled their cages, and the demons fear you. Their brothers come up missing when looking for you, and now, after seeing you challenge and fight their brothers in Hell, they think—no... they KNOW—you are something special from God, and they fear you," he said as she shared a shy smile with him. "You are special, Topaz. Your story now is one without me, and you are saving and protecting people's souls, which is something special. You are... You are the angel of life!" Seth insisted as he pulled her close to him.

The moment seemed to stand still as the two gazed into each other's eyes, neither wanting to be the first to break the silence. Seth didn't need any more assurance than what was written in her heart and finally found the courage to ask the question he'd been holding back for so long. "Will you marry me?" Her answer was immediate and passionate. "YES, Seth!" She threw herself into his arms and their kiss felt like a promise of eternity. In that one eternal moment, they both knew their union was blessed by God and rejoiced by the angels. Their love was perfect in its own way.

Seth's voice shook as he spoke. "A multitude of scared young men, barely even boys, will need comforting and guiding to the light. They'll be thrown into chaos, confusion clouding their minds from the trauma of war. I must be the beacon that leads them towards redemption, despite how much it may tear me apart. I will not be afraid; my soul is safe. You must bear with me as I cross over for however long this duty takes me. Days in my world could be years in yours, but with every life I usher into Heaven, I will know it is bringing me one step closer to seeing you again."

Topaz was compassionate towards Seth's mission, yet she felt aching grief swell within her chest as she grasped onto his words. How many years would she wait for him to return? She wondered if the day would ever come when they'd reunite while on this earth. Her heart tore open, knowing he may never come back in her lifetime. But... those innocent, scared, young people would need his comfort and guidance, and asking him to stay would be selfish—and she was anything but selfish.

The leaders of our governments within our world sit smugly atop their thrones, carelessly sending the innocent young souls to their graves. With an aching heart, Topaz swallowed her emotions. She offered her condolences and understanding to Seth, the chosen one who must carry these young, innocent souls away. He stood there before her, knowing he was breaking her heart, and it's then that she whispered, "Be with me."

She began to undress herself slowly, never dropping her gaze from his soulful eyes. There was something so potent in the air—a desire calling out from deep within her soul. Despite him being dead, and a being of Heaven now, she wanted him to make love to her before departing, knowing she may never feel his touch again. She began to slowly inch her silk teddy off her shoulders and down her arms, letting it slither down to the floor. His eyes never left hers. Her breath became shallow; she could hear it in the silence.

He leaned over her, taking in the sight of her face as if he were soaking in each second. His soft lips met hers in a tender kiss that seemed to last an eternity; his hands ran down her neck and sides, tracing her curves with reverent admiration. She responded by running her fingers along the intricate feathers of his wings, feeling each individual one as they fluttered against her skin. Topaz shared that she was completely mesmerized by him; she wanted to be with him as if he were her husband and not a man that death claimed long ago in its cold embrace.

An explosive flame of passion raged between Seth and Topaz as they explored each other's bodies with a star-crossed love that felt like it would never end. A lifetime of inexplicable emotions burned within them as they tasted, caressed, and embraced one another; wave upon wave of pleasure consumed their being, until time melted away into nothing but ecstasy. With the rising sun came the harshness of reality and the realization of what must come: goodbye. A goodbye, yet not for eternity, as their longing for one another would ripple through the ages until they were reunited again. Seth clung to Topaz with an ember of hope that some way, somehow, their seemingly impossible destiny could be reunited.

Each thought of how things may have been different if things unfolded differently the night he was killed felt like a hundred blades, cutting deep into Seth's soul as he replayed the night he died over and over again in his mind like a broken record. If only he had left five minutes earlier. If only he had seen the car stalled on the street sooner. If only he could have moved faster. If only he could turn back time and make it all right again.

        •   ✱   •   If only life was kinder.   •   ✱   •

Regrets clawed at Seth's insides like a ravenous beast as he gazed upon the wreckage of twisted steel and shattered glass the night of his death. If only the man hadn't lingered at the bar like a drunkard, pouring bourbon down his throat until he was blind to the dangers of driving. If only the woman's car hadn't stuttered to a halt on this busy street, drawing him into the tragic intersection. If only one or all of these wretched things hadn't happened, he would be alive today. He and Topaz would have been able to sing lullabies to their precious little girl with her long, soft curls and magical gifts inherited from her mother. Her electric-blue eyes would have shone with love and laughter, reflecting back her daddy's captivating smile. If only she had been born before that fateful day, she would have spread warmth and compassion throughout the world instead of leaving it behind in cold silence, never having been born into the world.

The weight of their loss crushed him. It wasn't fair. It wasn't right. It was life, though, and it can be very unfair and hard at times. Seth drew Topaz close to him as he whispered into the night, "If only."

Chapter Eleven

THE ANGEL OF LIFE

As weeks of daydreams and anxiety passed, it was time for a wedding. Topaz laced up her lilac gown with trembling fingers. She brushed her hair into an updo, each stroke precise and intentional as she secured it with a spray of hairspray before adding dainty flowers from her garden to her updo. Softly patting blush on her cheeks, she made sure to blend it in just right, finishing her look with a swipe of lipstick. With one final glance in the mirror, she tried to suppress a sigh. *All dressed up... but for who?* she wondered, knowing that despite all this effort, Seth would never see her. It didn't matter if anyone else noticed.

In that same instant, Seth felt the familiar tug of souls being pulled from the human world as he traveled to the chaos-ridden battlefield. He saw it all around him: the fear in their eyes, the acrid smell of smoke and gunpowder in the air, and the blood staining the barren ground. But then, for a moment, as Topaz stood in her mirror, Seth thought of her. An image of Topaz materialized in his mind as if she were standing right there in front of him. Her lilac gown flowed delicately around her figure like a gentle breeze, her auburn curls dancing gently on her shoulders. He longed to stay with her, bathing in the glorious light that seemed to cloak her. But before he could take a step closer, she dissolved into nothingness, and Seth's heart sank. He shook himself out of his trance and returned to his task of escorting young souls back to Heaven. With love and compassion, he whispered words of reassurance, promising them a peaceful journey beyond this life of pain and suffering.

Topaz's high heels clicked against the stone floor as she entered the church. She saw Izzy, standing in a room tucked behind the altar in an ivory gown with a large bouquet of lilies. Izzy's brother and sister, whom Topaz had never met in person before, stood next to Izzy, looking teary-eyed just before the ceremony began. Topaz hugged Izzy tightly and told her, "You look absolutely stunning! Isaiah is a very lucky man!" Izzy's siblings smiled at her warmly as they exchanged introductions.

Neither of Izzy's siblings possessed any powers of the supernatural, just the same traits that their father passed on. They favored him in physique and a gentle kindness that made them extraordinary. It was Izzy's joy to have them with her on her big day.

Weeks before they arrived, she had explained to them the years of abuse Lucrecia endured at the hands of Helen—a truth that left them shaken but determined to forgive their mother for her suffering. Love for Lucrecia swelled within their hearts—a love that could only be matched by their fury directed towards Helen for the life she had taken from their beloved mother. They felt somber hearing the horrible abuse that happened to Lucrecia in her youth at the hands of Helen's cruelty and how it changed all of them after that fateful evening so many years before, but knowing this provided them closure.

*　＊　*

The church fell silent as Izzy and Isaiah stood before the minister. The coven sat together and watched as my granny looked into her beloved's eyes, her beautiful dress billowing in the gentle breeze that came through the open windows. They recited their vows with emotion-filled voices, each word spoken with love and commitment. Gleaming streams of tears cascaded down the guests' faces as Izzy and Isaiah passionately embraced—their first kiss together as husband and wife.

Topaz's voice of blessing hung heavy in the air as Izzy and Isaiah departed on their long-awaited honeymoon. The day was brilliant with a promise of a new journey, yet beneath all that joy bubbled an underlying current of nervousness as Izzy was now a wife, and she would be busy, building a life with her new husband.

Izzy embraced the coven less often, dedicating herself to her new life. The only magic she practiced now was simple magic. She mixed her teas with meticulously crafted spells, wishing luck and fortune for her husband each day he went out to work. In her hands, she carved out simple spells of vitality and growth for the garden, as well as good health for her loved ones—though it was nothing compared to what she could create when she practiced magic with the coven.

Izzy was a cauldron of anticipation, bubbling and boiling with an energy she hadn't felt in a while. She had missed several visits to her coven, but that was not enough to quell the excitement building within her. She decided to visit her close friend and spiritual sister, Topaz; there was something special she couldn't wait to share but strongly suspected that Topaz already knew. She had that special gift of *'knowing things'* before you told her. Of course, Topaz already knew; visions had come to her in the night, telling her of Izzy's pregnancy. This made Topaz so elated for Izzy.

Izzy set off to visit Topaz in hopes of reconnecting and sharing her exciting news: Izzy was pregnant—with my mother! She drove to Topaz's home filled with anticipation and surprise, expecting her good friend to be just as excited as she was. Izzy told her siblings over the phone, but she didn't have a mother to share the excitement with. Izzy felt a sense of awe towards Topaz, like a mother figure. After all, her very own mother loved Topaz when she was only a baby. Topaz had a very special bond with the family.

Izzy wanted to ask Topaz to do a reading for her; she wanted a peek into the future. Izzy enjoyed it when Topaz did tarot readings for her. She also hoped Topaz would indulge her and try to see if Topaz could see if the baby would be a boy or a girl.

Izzy arrived at the house and felt something strange. She shivered as she knocked on the door, waiting for an answer that never seemed to come. With each passing minute, Izzy grew more uneasy. She knew Topaz had to be home; her car was parked in the driveway. But why wasn't she answering? After what felt like an eternity of waiting, Izzy knocked again, louder this time. Part of her wanted to turn around and run as an uneasy feeling crept over her, but another part needed to know why Topaz hadn't responded.

As she stumbled towards the door, Izzy's heart raced as she reached for the doorknob, her body trembling. As she slowly extended her hand towards the knob, her heart pounding in her chest, the door creaked open. Stiffly, it peeled back slowly and steadily like a curtain, unveiling its secrets.

Izzy stepped inside, a wave of nausea surging over her as the smell of death hit her nostrils. She felt her skin blanching with fear as the crimson blush faded from her cheeks. The feeling of dread intensified as she took hesitant steps into the house. The living room was engulfed in darkness, but Izzy could feel a presence lurking inside. A sharp glint caught her attention in the corner of her eye, and as she took a cautious step forward, a feral roar ripped through the stillness, a deep growl resonating in her bones.

She spun around to face whatever creature lurked in the shadows and spotted its silhouette ahead of her. Izzy grew cold with dread as she realized that retreat was no longer an option. Izzy knew that if Topaz were alive, she had to rescue her from whatever maleficent beast lay before her.

With trembling hands, she steeled herself for what might come next. Izzy felt her heart thud in her chest as the demon emerged from the shadows. His melted skin drooped off his long face, revealing blistering burns underneath and colorless eyes that glowed with a sinister white light. Two tall, dark brown horns protruded from his forehead, nearly grazing the tall ceiling. Long, frizzy hair obscured some of the injuries inflicted on his face. His legs were thick and robust, like those of a horse. The smell of sulfur invaded Izzy's nostrils as she beheld the creature towering before her.

"Topaz!" she cried out. He mimicked her. "Topaz!!" She watched in terror as he threw back his head and cackled at her. "She's not here... I've been waiting for you," he rasped in a deep, menacing voice. Izzy opened her mouth to speak, but before she could utter a word, her stomach dropped as the horror of his words pierced her like a searing dagger. "She's dead," he urged with conviction and a hint of enjoyment in his voice. Izzy shook her head in disbelief, unable to comprehend what she was hearing.

Her hands trembled as if they had been shocked. She took another step backward, desperately wanting to get away from this monster that was standing before her. The sickening smell of raw meat wafted off him, and he opened his mouth wide, exposing rows of long, sharp teeth. "I've waited here for you and your baby all day," he taunted as he pointed to her stomach. "Aww, a baby girl. *Mmm!* I bet she's delicious. Topaz was delicious; you should have heard her screams—it was beautiful. Quite a mess in her bedroom!" he chuckled wickedly as he shifted his eyes towards the direction of Topaz's room.

Izzy's eyes widened as two distinct figures slowly emerged from the shadow of the horned demon. One had a long, pointed nose and chin, a small, wiry frame, and leathery wings that draped past its shoulders. The other had coal-black eyes, heavy horns curving from their forehead, and claws for hands. They both seemed to be emanating dark, smoky energy. Izzy shuddered as she realized this was likely one of the demons Topaz had warned her about—Satan's angels. Her mind scrambled for a name as fear prickled up her spine. "The watchers—the onlookers," Izzy's intuition warned her as she stood in shock.

He stood, looming closer in the darkness. The demon's eyes flashed a bright yellow as he chuckled sinisterly. Izzy shivered as the icy chill of the wind sliced through her bones when the door slammed shut at the bidding of the demon. Fear washed over, paralyzing her in place as she felt as if her heart plummeted to her stomach. And then, much to her surprise, the door flew open again with such force, it barely missed her fragile frame. She stumbled back, trying to regain her footing, but she found it difficult with her hair wildly blowing into her face and the stench of defeat already filling the room.

Izzy turned towards the door, and to her relief, it was Molly. Aside from Topaz or Victor, when he was living, Molly was one of the powerful witches in her coven. Molly held her hands up, and the room glowed with a magical energy. The unclean spirit wailed, banishing to the depths of hell and far away from Izzy.

Molly was a formidable figure, despite being 5'1" with a dainty build. She had long silver hair, lightly tanned skin, and intimidating eyes that were light brown with dark yellow and tangerine flecks. During the cold, dark months of the year, Molly was very fair-skinned, but as soon as the long days and the warmth of summer approached, her winter complexion always transformed her soft skin into a deep sun-kissed complexion without fail. She often wore classic biker leathers and rode a motorcycle like she owned the road when she was not casting magic. "You need to stop missing sessions; you almost got yourself and your baby eaten by a damned beast!" Molly scoffed with a sassy tone.

Izzy pointed to the bedroom, her eyes brimming with tears.

"Topaz is in there! It killed her!" she screamed in panic, her voice shrill and high-pitched as the realization set in. Molly's eyebrows shot up in surprise. She marched down the hallway, hands clenched into fists and muttering, "This poor lady believes a damned, lying ass demon," under her breath as she shook her head in annoyance at Izzy's being so gullible. "Topaz isn't dead!" Molly declared as she rolled her eyes wildly.

Molly had been studying the mystical arts since she was a child, and not many were able to deceive her. Not grackles, not other witches, not even demons. She had a strong gift and many talents she had developed over her time practicing sorcery. One of her most beloved tools was her scrying mirror. It shone in the dim light of the midnights as if it were filled with stars, and Molly would gaze through its depths to view hidden truths. Topaz mentored Molly in much of witchcraft, but even Topaz would watch in awe as Molly moved her hand in circular motions across the glass, chanting incantations that made the surface hazy and ethereal. Crystal balls were useful too, but they couldn't be used for long-term observation due to their multidimensional nature. Spirits could easily see back or cross through, so Molly utilized the mirror to scry into the future most often.

Molly went into Topaz's practice room—a secret sanctuary buried deep within the walls of her home, her own secret fortress, made to keep out malicious magic and unwelcomed presences. It was a place of protection, a refuge from malevolence.

After a few moments, Molly returned from Topaz's practice room, breathing heavily from the effort of carrying a large, dusty box. She carefully set it down at Izzy's feet and continued to explain. "Topaz sent me here to give you this. She sensed you were coming today but had an emergency that pulled her away and had to leave urgently." Izzy knew Molly was sent to save her from the demon when she arrived to see Topaz. She also knew the box was important, as Topaz instructed Molly to remove the floorboards of her practice room to retrieve the box.

"Inside this box are books she wrote, multiple notepads full of information for you, and a small doll. This is for Topaz if she needs it." Molly ran her fingers over the smooth wood of the box as she spoke, a wistful look on her face. "All of these are meant for you to safeguard while she is away. She needs you to go through it all; read the material," Molly demanded, lowering her voice. "*Learn* the material," she warned.

Izzy opened the box and carefully pulled out a doll, gasping in awe at its resemblance to Topaz. Molly snatched it away, her face set with determination as she placed it back in the box. "This doll has a spell cast upon it," she began gravely, her voice shaking despite her attempt at a confident façade.

"The spell upon this doll is so that evil entities will not be able to easily sense its presence. This doll is an escape route for Topaz's soul. She created it so that she could use the vessel to tuck herself away to hide if she were to find herself defeated by death and trapped between worlds.

"She made it just in case her soul needs to hide from those who seek to trap her soul's gifts into darkness. If the dark entities, a black magic witch, or demon capture an enlightened soul before the soul can cross over into Heaven, and they take that soul to Hell for sacrifice." Molly paused, shuddering as a chill ran through her body, her eyes clouded with fear.

"You must go into the shadows of your mind—somewhere no one else knows about. Run into the shadows for your safety," Molly explained. "It's better to linger unknowingly in the shadows than to be forsaken in Hell as the demons pillage your soul for its God-given magic. For me... it's a recurring nightmare I've had since I was a child—a living nightmare of a sad life." Her words hung in the air like smoke, an icy reminder of her own dread.

Molly wore an ornate black robe adorned with silver jewelry and a colorful woven shawl that draped over her shoulders on this night. Her long gray hair was tied back into a tight bun, and her wrinkled hands were clenched tightly together. "Now, you must take this seriously," she warned. "Topaz is out there dealing with something complicated, and it affects us all. Before I go," she continued, taking a stack of books from an old side table. "Read these books of magic, too, so that you understand exactly what we're up against. If your husband has any objections to witchcraft, kick him out. We don't have time for his narrow-mindedness." She said it *half*-jokingly as she rolled her eyes.

She grumbled under her breath about double standards and

judgmental religious people as she was preparing to leave. "The Pope can wear his big ole hat and do his rituals, but when we wear our hats and do our rituals, we are evil. Probably more witches in Heaven than judging religious ass men," she muttered.

Molly was fiercely devoted to her faith but detested how religious beliefs had been warped over many decades by politics and greed. Her righteous resentment of the holier-than-thou churchgoers drove her away from God, until Topaz's kind interference brought her back into the light of the coven's sanctuary, where dark magic is not permitted.

Yet despite this newfound serenity, Molly could never quite shake away the dark magic that continuously lurked in the shadows. Her intuitive powers often warned her of forthcoming dangers in her vivid dreams, and it was only due to Topaz's guiding hand that she ever managed to break free from the Devil's grip. Yes, long ago, Molly herself was a practitioner of the underworld's magic.

Molly crossed the room in haste, "Let's get going; my grandson has a baseball game I must attend. You don't need to lift this while you are with child, just take it easy," she said in her no-nonsense way, picking up the box. They locked up as they headed outside. Izzy watched quietly as Molly placed the heavy box in the trunk of her car before turning back towards her.

"Topaz will be gone for a while, and you must read and study this information," Molly explained, once again reminding Izzy as if she wanted to make sure she understood the importance. "Topaz will call for you upon her return," Molly said. Her voice softened as she added, "If we don't hear from her in the next few days—maybe even weeks—we will know she isn't coming back."

With one hand on the door handle, Molly paused and looked at Izzy intently. "Next week you will feel worried and upset because you'll have light spotting when you go to the bathroom. Go to the doctor if you want, but it's normal, and your baby is fine. Oh! And he was right, by the way: it is a little girl," she said with a twinkle in her eye before getting into her car and driving away.

Naturally, she already knew the basics. Tarot cards: A witch's tarot cards are almost like a treasure map; they lay out in plain sight—all that one needs to know—and helps them find their way through the dense forest of daily life. Sage: Cleanse your space with sage after a ritual or when a negative presence has been in your space. Crystal

Ball: Covering your crystal ball so another witch may not gaze upon you is necessary for defense against any dark magic that might come from the jealousy of another practitioner or from a maliciously intentioned trickster. Salt: The circle of salt for protection should be laid around you while you do spells that involve money or property or any kind of spell work where you don't want negative energy to affect your intentions. Izzy also knew that salt acts as a repellent for such energies, which is why it has always been used to cleanse and likewise sends vibrations into the ground to help clear away discordant vibrations.

Izzy was also certain of one more thing: No amount of sage and salt could rid a powerful spirit, let alone a demon, not for long. No herb or protection spell can keep the darkness away forever. Evil is the smothering smoke of corruption that lingers in the air; it is unrelenting as it looks for any opportunity to weave into our lives.

Izzy's belly swelled as the weeks of pregnancy turned into four months. Despite their desperate attempts to locate Topaz, with Molly at the lead of their coven, they could not break free of Theta state. A dread realization encroached upon each witch like a steadily thickening fog: Topaz would not be returning. From all corners of the world, each witch had brought their own brand of magic to bear on the situation, yet nothing seemed to work. Night after night, they called for her in vain. Where was she? In Hell? Purgatory? Soaring among angels? Was she no longer as her body was becoming one with the earth? No one had any answers and that terrified them all. Izzy held Topaz's doll, hoping to feel some connection but feeling only distant emptiness.

Izzy's due date came and went as she became a mother. There was still no sign of Topaz, and an oppressive sorrow settled into Izzy's chest like a heavy stone, knowing she may never see her beloved friend again. One night, as Izzy lay alone in bed while her husband was working nights, she heard the faint whimper of her sweet baby girl, Kezziah.

Izzy's breath seized in her throat as a wave of terror washed over her. Her feet moved faster and faster until she was sprinting to the living room, only to discover the walls trembling. The walls drew in shallow breaths as if the house itself were alive.

Fear raced through her veins like a river of ice as she pushed past her fear and rushed into her daughter's room. Whatever horrors awaited there; Izzy had to face them. That's when she saw the demon from Topaz's house looming in the corner with glowing red eyes. The cursed encounter with him at Topaz's house flashed back to Izzy as if it were happening again in real-time. All the while, Kezziah had fallen silent, which sent a chill even deeper into her bones.

Izzy approached her daughter, where she stood guard before the crib while staring at the demon before them. The beast laughed in delight at Izzy's futile efforts to protect her child, and he lunged forward, a blade materializing from thin air in his hand. Her eyes widened as she saw it coming toward her throat. She summoned every reserve of power that she could muster and cast a shield between them. She had no idea if it would be able to stand against the power of a demon, but the white magic did not fail her, safeguarding her from the blade of Satan's demon. He snarled, "Turn over Topaz, and I will spare you and your child."

Izzy took control of herself. Her hands shook uncontrollably, and her eyes darted back and forth in the dimly lit room. Her thoughts were running wild with fears she couldn't keep from rising into her mind. They swirled around, strengthening their hold on her imagination. The thing in the corner kept moving. Izzy's teeth chattered as a cold wind blew through the window—her breath visible like thick smoke. "I don't know where Topaz is." The demon seethed in frustration, knowing Izzy was telling the truth.

The room grew more uncomfortable and sinister with each passing second. Izzy closed her eyes and drew a deep breath, taking control of herself. She felt power begin to charge into her body like electricity coursing through it, electrifying her movements and thoughts. Her hands trembled as she fought to regain control of her emotions. She breathed out slowly as she tempered the racing pace of her heart while maintaining eye contact with the beast.

Hearing her baby whimper created urgency. She wanted to scoop her little one into her arms and wrap her in a warm blanket. The demon chuckled, knowing he was causing the freezing room to feel unbearable as the stench of his rotten flesh lingered. His chest rattled with his deep laugh. His eyes glowed like hellfire. Pus oozed from his deep abscesses from the searing burns. "Hand Kezziah to me now, or I'll kill you both," he threatened Izzy.

She looked into his grotesque and misshapen face, at the bulging eyes and wide, flat nose. Izzy stepped away from her daughter's crib as she made her proposition. His eyes followed her as she moved about the room. She cleared her throat before speaking, for fear that if she swallowed too quickly or too deeply, she might puke from the overwhelming smell of the demon.

"I am not going to give my baby over to you," Izzy insisted, contempt and disgust dripping from her voice.

The unholy beast was angered, wanting her to be afraid and unable to protect herself and her child. The monster knew she was an ally of Topaz, and he knew Lucrecia was her mother. He wanted to surrender Kezziah's soul to Satan. The demon came to settle a score for his dark lord since he knew Topaz was not there to protect Izzy. Though Izzy was stronger in her skills of magic, she was no match for this beast.

"You are a stupid bitch," he seethed. Pressing his hands into tight fists, he leaned in close to her, crowding her personal space and letting his powerful body language distract from his words. "Where is Topaz? I want that bitch, and if she's going to hide, I will just take you and that crying ass baby of yours!"

"I don't know where Topaz is, but I do know that if she were here, she would kick your ass like she did the other demon that wanted to spar with her. You know; you were there." Izzy taunted him as she tilted her head up, trying to balance on the bottom of her heels as she leaned away from him so that there was no risk of skin contact. "We aren't playing fucking patty-cake here. You need to leave my home," Izzy demanded with a force that took the demon off guard.

The demon's eyes flared. His face was inches from hers, his lips pulled back in a snarl revealing his fangs as though he were a rabid animal about to bite into its prey. The beast began speaking backwards as he gazed upon her before calming himself.

She nervously stared unresponsively at him. A single droplet formed along the edge of her lashes and fell onto her cheek. Her fear was bubbling over her—fear for her baby, not for herself. She stepped back abruptly, removing her feet from their precarious position.

"You can't have my baby; she is off the table. But you can have me," she said with a devious smirk playing on her lips to hide the contempt that welled up inside of her. It appeared that he was pleased. The pause grew long as Izzy looked at him intently.

Her eyes glinted ominously as she challenged him with a smirk. "But only if you can win the bet." He clenched his fists even tighter. Her voice dropped to a whisper, thick with danger and temptation, as she added, "If you fail... you'll pay dearly." Izzy winked, knowing this would enrage the demon who was there when Topaz wagered a bet that infuriated Satan with his beasts that lost to her. Izzy shot a sly, mocking wink in the direction.

The unholy demon reared up on its hind legs and roared, revealing pointed fangs and his soulless, glowing eyes. Izzy stood frozen in terror until the beast slowly backed away, his heavy steps shaking the ground beneath her feet as Izzy watched him melt into the darkness of the night and slink away from her home.

Chapter Twelve

COVEN OF SHADOWS

After Faye made her escape from Iris with her daughter, she found protection in a covenant near where she went to church growing up. When Faye arrived at the convent with her precious baby, the nuns welcomed and tucked them away for safety. The baby's name was Grace, but it was there that she was given her nickname—a name that shone like a radiant gem in the light of day.

Each morning, the nuns washed her and prayed for divine protection to keep her safe. They ushered her into the hallowed sanctuary where an array of beautiful, colorful hues radiated from her in waves. It was as if she had been transformed into a living jewel—a Topaz that shone ever brighter in the early dawn's glow. She became known as Topaz Morning among the nuns that safeguarded her.

As Topaz began to grow, it became clear that Topaz's gifts went beyond what the nuns understood, though they never spoke of magic or the ability to see auras. But Topaz's powers were undeniable. At a young age, she began predicting events with astounding accuracy, leaving all who watched in terrified awe. Topaz continued to amaze everyone around her with her otherworldly abilities.

The nuns at the convent huddled together in hushed concern, their contemplative faces etched with fear of Topaz and the unearthly power she possessed. Yet beneath the apprehension lingered a glimmer of awe and reverence for her gifts—a spark that no amount of shame or admonishment could extinguish. The nuns loved Topaz and believed her to be a gift from above.

In my family, we are all named after people from previous

generations. My name, Lucinda, combines Lucrecia and Linda, my great-grandmothers on my mom's side of the family. My middle name was Topaz's given name, Grace. Topaz was practically family. Of course, I was always called Lucy, except for Granny Izzy, who always called me Lucinda.

My father, Jack, was named John after his father. He was the fifth John in his family line but the only one they called Jack. My sister Mia named her son John Jacob, but we call him Jacob most of the time. He only gets called by his full name when he's in trouble, just like me when I was a kid. When my full name came out, I knew I was in trouble! My mother's name, Kezziah, was from Izzy's sister Kezzie and her husband and brother, who shared the same name, Isaiah. My father named Mia after his mother, Amelia, who always got called Mia as a nickname. Mia had Izzy's middle name, Aliza.

Topaz held an irreplaceable place in our family. Despite not having grown up with her, Mia and I had heard countless stories of her—tales of how she used her power to save Izzy's mother's soul. Her absence on the day Kezziah was born was felt heavily by Izzy, who said she would often remind Topaz about it... giving her a hard time, of course. Izzy never told us why she was not there when we were younger, yet we all knew that something momentous called upon her so strongly that it demanded her immediate departure.

With a heavy heart, Topaz made her way to the market before leaving. There, she encountered Molly, who worked for Topaz in her market. Molly was the formidable maiden of the coven. She was a naturally gifted witch. After Victor and Ana crossed over, Molly held the highest rank in their order below Topaz. Molly was an expert with herbs and potions.

Concerned for Topaz's safety, she scattered various mysterious herbs around the stall—an arcane ritual performed in preparation for Topaz's fateful mission. In that moment, Topaz felt overwhelmed by the weight of responsibility, unsure if she would ever return. Topaz trusted that her calling was by something greater than any of them and buried her fears deep within herself.

Topaz had a lingering worry about Izzy when she was leaving. Molly pledged Topaz an oath that Izzy would be taken care of and equipped with the resources needed to make it safely in Topaz's absence. Knowing how often Molly had been saved by Topaz in the past, she accepted and promised to get Izzy through whatever came their way.

Thankfully so, Molly showed up to keep the demon at bay the day Izzy went to tell Topaz of her pregnancy. Without Molly, Izzy would have been defenseless against the wicked creature that threatened her life. The thought of what could have happened without her presence still sends shivers up and down my spine.

Topaz was gone for longer than the witches had anticipated, worry gnawing away at them every day, yet none knowing what exactly happened to her or when she'd return. The details of her mission were held in secret, and much of her journey remained untold even after she returned. Eventually, Topaz would reveal her experiences, but I think it must have been a lot for her to unpack and process.

As Topaz went on her journey, Molly and Amira, who was also a witch and part of the coven, took turns watching over Izzy for her. Amira joined the coven after Victor ascended to the afterlife and reunited with Ana, so she never had the luck of practicing magic with Victor as one of her teachers.

Amira was the newest addition to the witch's coven, coming from a long line of powerful witches. Though she was young in comparison to the other members, Amira had already made her mark. She couldn't control magic, bend magic, or manipulate the elements like Topaz, but her intuition far exceeded that of many of the gifted witches within Topaz's coven. She had an uncanny ability to read people and situations, relying on a sixth sense that few possessed.

Though still quite young, Amira carried wisdom beyond her years. Her kindness was only matched by her expertise in sniffing out grackles, fake friends, and selfish witches. Amira was extraordinary. Although she had only been part of the coven for a short while, she grew up around many of the witches in the coven, including Topaz.

Amira's childhood in Texas was filled with tales of Topaz, the mysterious witch who ran a local market. Her mother would swear that Topaz was powerful and brought a sense of security to her family and community. Though Amira never ventured within the coven's bounds, she could feel its power radiating outward, protecting those enthralled by its magic.

Amira had olive skin and dark cherry hair, just like her mother. Her petite frame was delicate compared to that of her mother and aunts, but her small stature didn't lessen the strength inside her.

Amira had the cutest dimples and a bashful smile. She was blessed with a full pout and perfect, heart-shaped lips. Her eyes were amethyst with hints of lilac, and seemed to be sparkle when she smiled. Everyone wanted to talk to her and be her friend. Her confidence was palpable, drawing others in with her magnetic aura. Her spirit was powerful and mesmerizing, drawing others in with an irresistible magnetism. She smiled easily and often, especially when she was making others laugh. Izzy said she looked like an angel.

Amira never felt more alive than when she stepped into Topaz's market. With her mother, Gloria, beside her, the shop filled with magical wares suddenly became a haven of security. Their visits to the market were filled with vibrant spices and potions. Gloria enjoyed spending time with Amira and showing her how to make oils, candles, and potions of protection.

Gloria's passion for mixing potions to protect her family was matched only by the terror that lurked in her mind's eye. Amira was born in Arizona. Her mother was pregnant with her when, in the dead of night, Gloria and her sisters fled Mexico—and with good reason. The wicked witch, far more powerful and sinister than anything they ever witnessed, had begun lurking around their homes. Casting shadows and watching them—drawing plans against them all. Gloria feared the witch, Ramona, who she knew coveted the daughter she was carrying in her womb.

Ramona seethed with anger and hatred towards Gloria and her sisters. They were blessed with powerful, supernatural gifts, yet they clung fiercely to their faith. Ramona's blood boiled every time she saw them, and her heart was filled with a sense of utter loathing for the sisters. They could feel the burden of her hatred heavy on them.

Gloria shrank in Ramona's presence, feeling her dark aura even from several feet away. She could never bring herself to look into Ramona's eyes, instead looking away or twiddling her own hair nervously when near her. It was clear to Gloria, even at a young age, that Ramona harbored a wickedness deep within her soul. Every instinct told Gloria to stay away from her, and she followed the warnings of her sister, who had seen the evil effects of Ramona's magic on others and didn't want Gloria to be next. The mere thought of befriending such an insidious being.

Even though she was young, Ramona evoked terror with her wicked spirit throughout the town they lived in. Everyone feared the power she channeled through her magic. Gloria's sisters became frantic and felt an urgency to keep her away from Ramona. They knew fully well the evilness that lurked beneath the surface of Ramona's soul. They didn't want Gloria to get too close and risk unlocking something they, with their limited magic, may not be able to contain.

Gloria's sister hissed darkly about Ramona's family and their affiliation with the Devil's magic, a force which was now threatening their own kin. Despite her devout faith, Gloria's mother and aunts were no strangers to practicing magic of their own—albeit *lighter* magic—and would not hide their disdain for Ramona's more insidious path.

Molly and Amira were unwavering in their pursuit of the craft, but little did they know that the shadows and demons they would encounter would far surpass their darkest nightmares. When Amira was a child, an eerie entity began to haunt her, fueling a fear that seemed to grip deep into her soul. Although Topaz was able to chase away the evil presence, it left an unforgettable mark on Amira, teaching her the grave consequences of prematurely experimenting with powers one doesn't fully understand.

The malicious demon that invaded Izzy's home was the same one she faced at Topaz's—the same beast that Amira encountered before her rescue. Izzy knew he was searching for Topaz, and when he found out she was nowhere to be seen, his rage turned to Izzy's baby— Kezziah. He wanted to drag her soul down into the fiery depths of Hell as punishment to Izzy and the coven for hiding Topaz. Izzy was haunted by her nightmares of that terrifying night for years afterward.

Amira awoke from a strange nightmare in a drenched, cold sweat, the stench of sulfur and brimstone still heavy in her nose. She knew something was amiss. Her pulse was pounding in her ears as visions of the demon filled her mind. It was the same entity she had seen hovering over her as a child when Topaz stepped in and chased him away. Without hesitation, Amira grabbed her coat and raced to Izzy's house, trusting her instincts that the demon was watching over Izzy's baby.

Molly followed suit; she too was awakened by an ominous feeling she couldn't shake. Both of the ladies screeched up to Izzy's house at the same time, both of them sprinting towards the house. As they reached the doorstep, thick smoke began billowing from every window, accompanied by a noxious stench and piercing shrieks. Fear gripped their hearts as they feared they were too late to save Izzy and her baby.

Just as they reached for the door handle, it swung open with Izzy holding her baby in a vice-like grip. "Damned demon!" Izzy spat out, her eyes blazing with anger and defiance as she welcomed them into the house. They immediately began to chant powerful spells that echoed off the walls of the home, cleansing it of the dark aura that had taken hold. With every exhale, Izzy opened the windows to release the cloying stench of rotting flesh that filled the air.

"What on earth happened here?" Molly asked, cradling Kezziah tightly in her arms. Izzy and Amira looked at each other silently, both too scared to speak. A few moments later, Izzy nervously began to tell her story. "A dark entity came for Topaz, threatening to take my baby to Hell," she shared, as tears streamed down her face while she grasped desperately at her head, trying to make the dizzying room stop spinning.

"Deep breaths," Amira insisted as she tried to calm Izzy. She bent her head towards the floor and pushed the hair back to cool herself. A bead of sweat trickled from her bangs along her temple, and a small pool collected at the top of her hairline. Amira blew gently at her forehead, her soft lips tickling Izzy's flushed skin. Izzy later shared how she took solace in Amira's calming breath that blew gently across her face, as if Amira were breathing a calming spell over her.

Molly came close and wrapped an arm around Izzy's shoulders; the strength of it felt like a lioness protecting her cubs. The three ladies then hurried to the kitchen, each grabbing something from the fridge—Molly a beer, Amira a soft drink, and Izzy a glass of cold water as she settled into a chair and began nursing her baby girl.

As they sat down at the kitchen table, Amira asked with great admiration, "How did you do it?" The air hung heavy with tension while Molly listened intently, waiting for an answer. Izzy smiled proudly and confidently said, "I guess it's good I haven't missed practice sessions," as she passed a sly wink to Molly before gulping down a tall glass of water.

"You are a warrior for standing your ground!" Molly exclaimed, her voice shaking with admiration. Izzy smiled weakly as she felt lightheaded. Her voice was barely more than a whisper as she shared her experience with the demonic entity who was looking for Topaz and willing to drag her and her baby into Hell as punishment.

Molly spoke up harshly. "Take caution of these entities. They will want to destroy you—possess and control you. They could even mess with your mind and manipulate you to cause harm to yourself or even hurt your baby. They will try to do whatever they can to cause you chaos. Even worse, if they possess you and talk into your ear to kill your own child and sacrifice her to Hell, they'll win." A feeling of nausea radiated throughout Izzy at the ominous thought.

Amira nodded in agreement with Molly, her expression solemn. "It's like they are calculating plans to cause harm to any or all of us until they can cause harm to the one they hate the most—Topaz. This sick monster covets control and approval from Satan. He would love for you to harm your child and the devastation that would bring to not only your lives but also your husband's. It's something no one should ever have to face. It wouldn't just be hard to reconcile; it may be impossible," she uttered, letting out a heavy sigh, knowing Kezziah was now in jeopardy too.

The ladies sat there, worrying about what could have been, what was next, and about Topaz. Where was she, and why has she been gone for so long? The witches were alive with anxiety because they didn't know what had happened to their grand high priestess or what was to follow next with the evil that swirled around them, heavier than ever now.

Izzy and the coven met upon the next moon's rise. They discussed their plans to try to locate Topaz again through meditation, since Molly was unable to view her through scrying. Amira entered the clearing at a run, stumbling out of her car. She leapt into Molly's arms, nearly knocking her off balance. "They followed me here!" she gasped. The trees sighed in the distance as they swayed in the wind, which became violent.

The coven huddled close, forming an unbreakable circle of chanting voices. The air was alive with the cacophony of their prayers as the demons flew in like a ragtag army. The coven held their ground despite the seeping fear in their hearts and would not flinch to find shelter in shadows—a secret they could never escape from with the monsters lurking around them. Not a single witch flinched as the monsters descended upon them—not one stepped into the shadows to evade their grasp; they stood strong in solidarity.

The demons swarmed like predators to the coven as they dove down towards them. The demon's leathery wings buzzed closely to the witches as they would take shelter in their circle. The witches huddled together while the demons flew overhead, barely missing them by inches and sometimes snapping the air with their bat-like wings. The heat coming off the monsters was stifling, like being too close to a raging bonfire; it made it hard to breathe. Their flapping wings sounded like a thousand angry locusts flying at once, making a terrifying sound that demanded attention. As the witches chanted in unison, they hoped to banish the devilish monsters away, as they were aggressive and domineering.

The size of the demons was immense, looming over them like an executioner's ax. Their muscles were swollen and bulging beneath their calloused skin. The witches' hands trembled in horror as a cacophony of unearthly shrieks filled the air. It pierced through their flesh, pummeling their eardrums until it felt like they were going to pop. Every muscle in the witches' bodies froze in fear and terror, and all of them dropped to their knees. The terroristic event was unbearable, threatening to crush the witch under its terrifying might.

Molly reached her breaking point as she and Izzy's hands broke only for an instant. A giant demon scooped Molly up with a long, thin hand and cast her across the circle, where Izzy scrambled to grab ahold of Molly. Amira quickly grabbed ahold of Izzy's empty hand now that Molly had been plucked from the circle to close the circle back as the chants began to grow louder with fear. Molly's shrieking screams shook their souls hard. The air thundered with energy from the witches within the magic circle that was pleading for help from the beasts that descended upon them.

The ground rumbled beneath their feet as a sonic boom split the night sky and the cacophonous screams of terror silenced. Izzy fervently shouted for them to keep praying, not daring to break their trance-like chanting for fear of the consequences if they failed. Wild panic coursed through their veins, fear of their own safety mingling with dread that Molly had been dragged to Hell, where Satan would wreak his vengeance upon her and—by extension—the coven.

The witches stood in the vast darkness, straining their senses for any hint of sound or movement. Fear kept them frozen, clutching onto one another with strong grips. Then, finally mustering their last bit of courage, they hesitantly opened their eyes, never fully knowing what might lurk in the shadows around them.

A prominent shadow stood in the distance. As it approached Izzy, she instantly saw the familiar aura beaming as relief washed over her. Amira gleefully ran towards Topaz. The coven was elated to know that she was safe and to have her back home. Their shadows danced around the moonlight as they celebrated Topaz's return. Their cheers echoed as they saw that she was carrying Molly in her arms. As Topaz approached the coven, they looked up at her with excited smiles on their faces—until they realized Molly's body was without breath.

Topaz gently put her down and began performing CPR, breathing life into Molly's lungs as she did chest compressions, while Amira listened for a heartbeat. Topaz's hands trembled with determination as she balled them into tight fists and slammed them down onto Molly's chest. She tightened her jaw and sent an electric surge of energy through her fingertips, pushing life back into Molly's body with every ounce of strength she had.

Molly screamed in agony as she threw up on the ground, her body violently shaking with each heave. Topaz wiped Molly's mouth and kissed her forehead, her voice thick with emotion. "My angel." Topaz sighed as she hugged Molly tight in her arms.

"Those sons of bitches were about to take me to Lucifer himself," Molly murmured in shock as she clung to Topaz's shoulders. Topaz only smiled with determination, knowing that the demons were trying to locate her whereabouts by harassing her coven and allies. As the witches rejoiced their safe return, Topaz knew they had much to discuss, but more importantly, she desperately needed rest.

"If the demons come hunting for me, they will have to find me at my home when I awaken." Topaz spoke with a weary smirk before bidding goodbye to them all. Without hesitation, Topaz began walking home barefoot through the darkness of night, feeling each blade of grass beneath her feet and determined to reach her destination. She left the coven of witches behind as their minds raced with a hundred questions about where she had been. Those answers would have to wait as Topaz made her way home to rest her exhausted eyes.

Molly nodded with understanding. Despite nearly being dragged into Hell, she was still cracking jokes... "She's going to enjoy feeling the grass between her toes until she gets a sticker in her foot." Amira giggled before adding, "Or until she steps in a big pile of dog shit." They laughed as Topaz walked into the night. Their teasing and laughter put a smile on her face—one that could be seen even in the darkness.

Topaz laughed as she extended her arm and waved goodbye to her coven before gesturing to the ladies—flipping them her middle finger in jest. The witches hooted and howled at the moon in delight like a pack of wolves. Topaz walked into the night, the beautiful moon filtered through the treetops, shimmering off the dew-laden green leaves, at its radiant light escorted Topaz home.

Chapter Thirteen

THE ENTITIES

As Izzy opened the car door to leave, Molly grabbed her arm and pulled her aside. Their voices were low and hushed as Amira slowly approached. She slowed her steps when she saw the other witches take their leave, cautious of interrupting a private moment. Just as she was about to turn on her heel, Izzy called out for Amira to join them. Molly gestured her closer with an exhausted wave of her hand, her face drained of color from the night's adventures.

Molly winced as she pulled up her sleeve, revealing three deep gashes that seared through her skin. Her burning wounds still pulsated and steamed with a heat as intense as molten lava. The ladies gasped in horror at the sight of Molly's agony, knowing full well how agonizing these injuries must have been for her.

The welts were radiating heat, and the smell of singed flesh lingered in the air. Struggling to hold back tears, Molly began to tremble as she recounted her story. "The screams of the demon filled my ears," she whispered. "It was like the Devil himself hovering over me, ready to take my soul to Hell. I felt its claws digging into my skin, tearing through it like razor blades. Then all of a sudden, I saw another being fly into the tree next to us, and before I knew it, I was pushed off the branch and freefalling... until Topaz swooped in and caught me."

Amira's eyes widened in disbelief. "She was flying?!" she exclaimed. "No, no," Molly replied, wincing as her memory replayed the scene. "Topaz was on the ground and caught me as I fell. I'm sure I hurt her just as much as the fall did me."

158

That night, Topaz was finally making her way home and back to unite with her friends. She hastened onward, eagerly anticipating the gathering of the coven. She began to feel a strange force looming in the air, and as she looked up, an invisible shockwave pulsed through her veins. Above her, something unseen seemed to be hunting down the demons, who shrieked and scrambled away in fear. Topaz felt a wave of dread rise within her, and she quickened her pace towards the coven.

Molly's voice wavered as she spoke. Her hands trembled at her sides, and her eyes glazed over with the memory of her experience. She went on to explain that her guardian angel was watching over her, and Topaz was there waiting for her rescue like a beacon of hope in the darkness. Izzy and Amira gasped in shock, their eyes widening at the thought of an angel swooping in to help Molly escape from the clutches of the nightmarish creature that had stolen her away.

Molly thought to herself that this was no coincidence but a divine intervention that saved her from being taken by the beast. With a newfound appreciation for angels, she gazed up at the stars in thanks.

Topaz had saved Molly's life countless times; this was far from the first time. The darkness of her past came back to haunt her when entities threatened her on that fateful night. Molly dabbled in *dark magic* at one time, and it haunted her. After turning away from the *Devil's magic*, she started helping Topaz. Molly helped Topaz protect those close to them from falling prey to evil, which only provoked the malicious forces further. Her voice trembled as she spoke of her fear of going home, and dread rolled off her in waves. The night air grew cold around them as they stayed close together, clouds enveloping the lone moon in a heavy blanket of darkness.

Izzy lifted her gaze to the heavens as a fierce gale howled through the trees and their branches thrashed wildly in its wake. Heat rose from deep within her chest, causing her nipples to tingle with anticipation for her baby, who was eagerly awaiting her meal back home with her husband. "If I don't leave now," she giggled, "my shirt will look like I'm taking part in some kind of lewd wet t-shirt contest!" With a firm press of her forearms against her bulging breasts, Izzy set off to go home to feed her baby, while Amira and Molly stayed behind visiting.

Amira's heart pounded as her car approached her home. Fear and dread twisted in her stomach, warning her of the unseen danger that lay within the walls of her house. With trembling hands, she surveyed the property, searching for any signs of life in the darkness. She watched shadows lurk along the walls inside her living room as she sat in her car and gazed into the windows. Overwhelmed by a sense of duty, Amira knew she would need to bravely make her way towards the door and be ready to confront whatever evil lurked inside. She sat only a second longer, taking in the silence of the night, before she steeled herself with one purpose: to rid her home of any dark forces that were present.

Amira held tightly to the rosary her aunt had gifted her, pleading for protection. Taking a deep breath, she stepped from the car and gingerly grasped the handle of the door. It opened with a squeal before slamming shut like thunder. Her heart was racing as she tried again to open the car door, but the handle felt like it was glued down when she tried to open it. She jimmied it again, and just as it started to crack open, a rough hand yanked her into the backseat by her hair. She heard an audible crack as her wrist connected with the unforgiving floor of the car.

Amira's heart was pounding in her chest as she made her way to the rear passenger side door and grabbed blindly at the handle. Through the corner of her eye, she saw the figure next to her take form—a giant goat-like man with deep black eyes and pale skin that smelled of death and decay. He didn't speak, but his malevolent energy filled the seat like an invisible force field, warning her away. But Amira was determined—he wouldn't keep her from protecting those she loved. She had a duty to protect her family.

Amira's eyelids drooped, fatigue weighing heavily on her body. Her speech was thick and slow as she began to recite prayers of protection. She tried with all her might to muster the will to cast out the demons, but no matter how hard she tried, words would not come forth. Izzy yanked open the car door and pulled Amira out onto the street. Her eyes widened as she saw a large, dark figure crouched in the backseat, watching them with an eerie stillness. Izzy started to chant words of protection against the entity, but he showed no reaction besides those unblinking eyes.

Izzy could feel him watching her as she began to recite a banishing spell, but he didn't flinch or show any sign of fear. With nothing else to do, Izzy screamed out a defiant "Fuck you!" before slamming the door shut and dragging Amira away from the horror in the car and up to her porch. Once Izzy and Amira were standing on the porch of Amira's home, they observed long shadows stretching across the walls. The ladies watched them in silence, their faces solemn in the fading light.

The ladies tentatively stepped through the doorway. They could feel the cold air freezing to their bones and knew, without question, that evil lingered within the home. Amira raced to her parents' bedroom. Her father had already left for work, leaving her mother alone. Gloria lay asleep in the frigid cold, when suddenly, her eyes flashed open, and a startled gasp escaped her lips. Amira accidentally woke her up. Her mother huffed, exhaling icy-cold breath from her mouth. "Hace frío bebé, por favor enciende el calentador.," she begged as Amira scrambled to turn on the heater in an attempt to warm the house.

Amira nodded and stepped out, silently shutting the door behind her. She could see Izzy kneeling on the living room floor in prayer as she hurried over to her brother's bedroom. Peeking in, Amira saw him suspended in mid-air above his bed. His eyes were shining solid white, and he was trembling. Letting out a terrified cry, she lunged forward and dragged him onto the mattress. It was as if a shock of electricity ran through his body as he convulsed. Miguel involuntarily arched his back, letting out a series of low growls and grunts. His chest heaved with each exhalation, the deep guttural rattle echoing off the walls of his cold room.

Amira's mother was jolted in fear by the echoing clamor and rushed towards the bedroom of her son. As she passed through the living room, Gloria was stunned to see Izzy banishing the dark specters that surrounded her. With courage like no other, she fearlessly confronted the shadows until they scattered.

As the ghostly figures made their way through the living room, the ladies pressed on, stumbling into Miguel's bedroom. He was clawing at his sheets and convulsing as he spoke in an unfamiliar language. The monstrous growls of a dark entity seemed to get louder as Miguel desperately begged for help between sobs. Miguel began to flail around on his bed in a panic. His eyes were wide and glazed over, and his lips moved rapidly as he muttered incantations in Latin.

Amira grabbed her younger brother, who was shaking and whimpering, to try to calm his convulsions. Gloria shouted "Ramona!" in protest and fear, as she had a looming feeling the witch was present in the home. Booming growls from the overpowering demon shook the walls of their home, consuming Miguel's cries for help.

Izzy began praying for salvation, but she never got the chance to finish. Topaz crashed through the door; her eyes were wild with fury. "All of you are so predictable," she said with contempt to the shadow people watching the demon that entered Miguel's body. She stood in the center of the living room, with Molly walking through the door behind her. "I knew you would fuck around with my coven and their loved ones," she scoffed at the entities lingering within the home.

The demon hunkering down in Miguel was enraged, spitting and clawing at the walls with venomous rage. Topaz demanded everyone leave immediately—their faces pale and their bodies shaking in fear as they scurried out of the room. Everyone was so afraid; no one needed to be told twice to flee, and every person staggered away, trembling in terror, with the exception of Molly who stood beside Topaz.

Molly stepped closer to Topaz, her expression pleading. "Let me stay with you," she begged with desperation in her voice. Topaz met Molly's eyes and firmly shook her head. Topaz's heart raced with fear as she felt the demon's dark power emanating from Miguel's quivering body. She knew that demons were at their weakest when they first possess a human, but once they acclimate, their strength returns and grows as they consume the energy of their host.

Topaz's mind buzzed with urgency. If she didn't banish the demonic entity now, it would take over Miguel completely, and saving him would prove even more difficult. With a reassuring smile, Topaz gestured for Molly to step back. Molly brandished the dybbuk box with both hands, staying just on the other side of the door, ready if Topaz needed her. She sat quietly on the other side of the door as she listened to Topaz getting berated by the demonic entity inside of Miguel.

The demon possessing Miguel became increasingly violent. The monster began pulling gobs of hair from Miguel's head while Miguel's soul was asleep within his own body. The demon viciously pulled his hair and began banking his head into the wall while cackling with malicious glee. "You're no priest, Topaz—you're evil at your core like us. You can't cast us away," the beast snarled, throwing books directly at Topaz, who desperately tried to fend off the onslaught.

Heaving with rage, Topaz stared in disbelief as the demon spat in her face. His words rang in her ears as he sneered again, taunting her. "You're not good; you're no priest." The air around them suddenly felt heavy and charged as his eyes turned solid black... then he rose off the floor, levitating. With a sudden burst of frustration, she forced Miguel back down to the ground with her mind, and then held him firmly by the shoulders. The air around them thickened with her wrath. Her voice crackled like lightning as she growled a warning to the demon.

The demon's eyes flicked back and forth, from solid white to solid black, as fast as the flickering of an eyelid, until they finally settled on utter blackness. A grin slid across his face. The demon clamped down on Topaz's arms and began snarling viciously. She didn't flinch from his grip; instead, she pulled him closer until she could feel the immense heat radiating off Miguel's body. As he stared into her eyes, he realized he had made a grave mistake. His grip loosened and his expression softened, replaced by a burning fear that spread like wildfire through his veins.

Topaz tightened her grip on the demon, her energy surging through Miguel's body, causing it to quiver in fear. The terrified creature tried to move away, but Topaz continued to hold him tightly as his face contorted, revealing his terror. Miguel's form was nothing more than a mere vessel for his spirit, as he wanted to steal Miguel's soul for Ramona. Miguel's body began convulsing, and Topaz had just about enough of the demon's defiance and unwelcome presence

Topaz's eyes morphed to an unnatural shade of black, mirroring the same glare the demon radiated at her through Miguel's evil gaze. Her voice was a thunderous roar as she stated confidently, "I am not a priest. I am a priestess! I am THE grand high priestess of the *Preston Hollow coven*, and I now banish you from this young boy." With an effortless gesture, she yanked the demoniac towards her, her mouth agape as if it were unhinged from her face. She howled in triumph as she began to inhale the demon out of Miguel's body. The demon squealed with wretched cries echoing in her ears.

Miguel sat on his bed, eyes closed and arms crossed, stifling a heaving sob as he tried to contain whatever emotions were bubbling up inside. He lurched up in a frantic motion, as if he had just received an electric shock. His eyes darted around wildly as his mind raced to make sense of the situation, desperately trying to remember what just happened. Thankfully, he could not recall what transpired, which left him utterly confused as he rubbed his throbbing head.

Topaz flung the door open with a dramatic swing, and Molly hastily turned away from looking at Topaz as she handed over the box. Molly knew Topaz was now hosting the wicked entity in her own body. Gripping the ancient, wooden box that was carved with symbols of good fortune and protection, Topaz opened it and breathed out the demon, unleashing the ancient terror from her lips and casting him into the sacred dybbuk box. The lock clicked shut, sealing the horrid demon away, along with the shrieking shadows that clung to the dark entity.

Her hands trembled as she sealed the box. Topaz made her way to the ladies waiting in the living room as Molly followed behind her. Gloria was nervously pacing as Amira sat with her head in her hands. Topaz's voice was low and her eyes wide with fear. "Yes, Ramona, the witch you uprooted your family to hide from," Topaz explained urgently. "She's growing desperate, unable to consume an enlightened soul and has sent an allegiance of shadows and the demon she is so fond of to look in on all of you. They are hunting; I'm afraid they now desire your son." She glanced around nervously, lowering her voice to barely a whisper. "You must keep him safe."

Topaz cleared her throat. "I can feel their dark presence everywhere, hunting for something new to satisfy Ramona's hunger. Miguel is strong, and his soul is in peril if she is able to get her grasp on him."

Molly's heart quaked with terror as Topaz warned her. They could also target her beloved grandson, who also was an enlightened soul. Molly would have to protect him from the forces of evil lurking in the shadows, seeking a young vessel for their unholy acts, just as Gloria would need to guard Miguel. "We must keep an eagle eye upon the boys, keep them safe." Molly growled, her gaze steeled and unwavering. Topaz nodded, reminding them all, "No dark magic, no meddling in matters beyond this realm!" Her voice echoed through the room like thunder, leaving no doubts about her intent.

Gloria snatched Topaz and crushed her in a frantic hug, the force of her embrace leaving an imprint on Topaz's skin, pressing a kiss on her cheek. Gloria then sprinted to Amira and Miguel. Her heart was loudly pounding with fear as she reached out for her oblivious son and embraced him.

Miguel shoved the intruding ladies back with a loud shout and demanded to know why they had barged into his room. Amira felt a wave of relief wash over her, and she smiled as she watched her baby brother stand up for himself. She had always doted on him, indulging in every whim and treating him like the prince he was, and now he stood there frustrated that these ladies were invading his space.

Amira smiled big and rubbed his arm in a noogie-like fashion. "You were having a nightmare and cried for Mommy," she teased. Miguel denied that possibility as the ladies chuckled, closing the door behind them. Amira paused at the door, exhaling in relief.

As the women entered the living room, Topaz shivered with dread. She shared with them how, as soon as she reached her house, she began to sense ominous eyes leering at the coven, and in that instant, she delved deep into her innermost thoughts, searching for answers. She felt the weight of a premonition crushing her chest like a boulder. Without hesitation, she rushed out the door with her dybbuk box in hand. Topaz told the women how she nearly knocked Molly over in her haste as Molly pulled up to Amira's at the same time.

Like Izzy, both Topaz and Molly knew something was seriously wrong. These crows—united by unspoken loyalty—hastened to make right whatever had gone awry at Amira's. Within minutes, other witches of the coven arrived. Their spirits warned of danger surrounding Amira's family.

Izzy said nothing but silently queried why the entity in the car didn't leave when she asked it to. It had worked on the demons who had come to her house before. Was this creature different? Topaz glanced at Izzy. "The incantation used against the demon can only be used once; these fiends won't go away with the same spell again. I will need to conjure up a new one," she muttered as she grasped the dybbuk box tightly, as it held the wicked spirits inside.

"Ramona's desperation has grown, and she's joined forces with other powerful creatures. I can't save everyone from her wrath, but

I'm doing my best to shield our loved ones and cast spells that will hopefully impede her from snaring and preying on the defenseless," Topaz explained.

Molly and Topaz tore down the street, desperate to be rid of the dybbuk box that held raging entities inside. The demon and shadow entities screeched their sinister whispers into the witches' minds, promising power beyond imagination if only they were released from the imprisonment of the box. But the witches stood tall and resolute, their wills like iron against the onslaught of the entities' deceitful words. With a fierce glare, they silenced the entities' pleas and crushed their hope for escape.

Amira escorted Izzy out to her car in haste so she could return home to her family. Both were mentally and physically exhausted. Meanwhile, Izzy's husband was no doubt already asleep, oblivious to what had transpired among the darkness of the witching hour.

Amira felt thankful that Miguel was safe and grateful to her coven for banishing the demon from him. She turned to see Gloria, her mother, lighting a black candle. Amira threw herself at Gloria and knocked the candle out of her hand. "No!" Amira ordered, shaking her head emphatically. "No... No dark magic! This will open the door for the demons to come back in!" Gloria stood looking down at the floor, trying to regain her composure.

"Ramona," Gloria spat, her voice laced with venom. She clenched her hands and began to cast a powerful hex onto Ramona, but Amira managed to stop her just in time. With an ice-cold glare, she remained motionless, the hatred radiating from her strong enough to penetrate the air between them. In that instant, Gloria conceded, knowing that Amira was right and her desire for revenge would be met with a greater act of revenge in retaliation. Ramona was far more powerful than Gloria, and Gloria knew this for certain.

Amira shivered as her voice rose to a fevered pitch. She warned Gloria not to invite evil into their home with malicious magic; every spell must come from a place of goodness, or else risk consequences unknown. Fearful energy crackled in the air as she held her mother firmly in her gaze, her words ringing through the air. Amira warned her mother that any magical act of evil could open a portal to the Devil himself, one that would leave their home vulnerable and unprotected against malignant forces. One misstep, she warned, could be catastrophic.

Amira promised Gloria that justice would be served to Ramona. Gloria loathed Ramona with every ounce of her being, as if her very presence were poisonous. Gloria clenched her fists in rage, feeling the heat of anger bubble within her. That wretched Ramona had been the cause of her suffering—the reason she had to flee her beloved home of Mexico. Gloria resented that, after years away, she still could not have a moment of peace away from Ramona's pure evilness.

The hairs on the back of Gloria's neck prickled as she felt the witch's eyes piercing through her family home. Every little sound and every creak in the floorboards gave Gloria a sense of unease that left her constantly on edge. She sensed the shadows lurking around the home, watching and waiting for their moment to be able to enter once again. Even almost a thousand miles away, Ramona was once again haunting her.

The shadows watched, haunting them once again with intensity. There seemed to be a steady chill in the air that only added to the growing sense of danger seeming to permeate everything around the home, even after the house was cleansed with sage. The wind carried whispers of curses and long-forgotten spells to tempt Gloria. Every creak of a floorboard or rustle of leaves outside sent her heart racing with fear, wondering if it was all just in her head or if something truly sinister was lurking in the shadows.

Gloria lit candles and placed them around the house, muttering prayers of protection as she did so. She took extra care to make sure every corner was cleansed with positive energy. If Gloria resorted to dark magic, Amira wouldn't be able to shield Miguel on her own. Despite her strength, Gloria was still vulnerable to temptation.

The malevolent call of dark magic echoed through Gloria's head, beckoning her to unleash her fury upon Ramona. Every muscle in her body tensed with anger, desperately fighting the unquenchable thirst for revenge that bubbled beneath her skin. She strained against the power of the dark magic, determined not to succumb to its temptation and take vigilante justice for what Ramona had done to her family.

THE RETURN

Topaz stepped onto the lawn, feeling the coolness of the freshly shorn grass beneath her flip flops. She took a deep breath and sighed at the sight. Izzy had asked Isaiah to mow the grass while she was away, and she was thankful for it. Her eyes swept over the familiar yard where she'd made countless memories. Stepping inside after so long away was strange; everything seemed smaller, and the house was deathly quiet. The house had an eerie stillness about it now.

She quickly stepped into a warm shower, letting the hot water cascade over her body. She squeezed shampoo onto her fingertips and began to scrub her scalp, feeling the foam soothe her tension as it ran through her long hair. Topaz finished washing her body and stepped out of the shower, wrapping a fluffy white towel around herself. She then carefully tucked her damp hair into a towel. As she brushed her teeth, the taste of minty toothpaste filled her mouth, causing her tongue to tingle pleasantly. She scooped a generous amount of lavender lotion onto her hands and glided them along her long legs. Her freshly shaven legs felt smooth as silk beneath her fingertips. Finally, she slipped into a short, satin nightgown that clung to her curves.

Topaz unwound the towel from her damp hair and held the blow dryer close. Her locks, now past her bottom, tickled the small of her back. Glancing up at the clock, she was surprised to see it was nearly 4:30 a.m. Despite her exhaustion, she ran a wide-tooth comb through her hair, determined to wash away the day's weariness before bed.

She slipped into the comfort of her crisp, white sheets and breathed in the familiar scent of the lavender fabric softener she loved. Her heart warmed at the thought that Izzy must have known she was coming back. It had been quite a while since she'd been here, yet her bed felt like it was freshly cleaned and waiting for her. Just as she dozed off, there was a knock on the door that startled her upright.

Topaz jolted awake, her heart racing as if pursued by a demon. Her feet pounded the ground with earth-shattering force, ready to confront whatever hellish creature dared encroach upon her domain. Striding through the living room, beams of light blazed into her sight, illuminating her path towards the door. She couldn't tell whether it was the moon or sun; all she knew was that she was bone-tired and utterly spent.

Fueled with adrenaline, she ripped the door open fearlessly, with zero fucks and ready to go up against whatever was disturbing her slumber. But... as soon as she saw Seth standing there, her courage melted away and was replaced with a profound longing. He pulled her into his embrace, his touch lighting up her skin like electricity. His lips moved hungrily against hers, and he muttered softly in her ear, "Let me make love to you," with his eyes full of fiery desire.

Topaz's heart raced as he grabbed her. "No... Fuck me," she pleaded as he lifted her off the floor with ease. She locked her legs around his waist, and their lips passionately crashed together. In a few strides, they were in her room, where he threw her onto the bed without mercy.

He roughly pulled her to him, one hand gripping her hip tightly while the other tore at the fabric of her nightgown that covered her body like silk. The garment rose up, exposing her warm, soft flesh beneath it as he laid kisses across her stomach and down further until coming into contact with the wetness between her thighs. Her panties had already been soaked from the anticipation of being with him. In one fluid movement, he ripped them away, unleashing waves of pleasure that had been gathering within her.

He began to devour her inner thighs with kisses, his lush hair creating a soft blanket around her as his hands slowly inched towards her core. His tongue now rolled around her clit, as she screamed out in bliss and arched her back from the pleasure, he was giving her. His body trembled with anticipation of what was to come as he felt her juices running down his chin. He opened her up with his fingers and entered her gently as if she were a temple, each thrust more enthusiastic than the last. She grabbed a hold of his hand and guided him into a storm of pleasure where thunder roared and lightning flashed within her. His expert fingers provided intense pleasure until she reached her peak, screaming out his name in pure ecstasy.

She knelt beside the bed and eagerly took him in her mouth, her throat convulsing as she gagged against his hardness. His size filled her mouth, and drool ran down her chin as she sucked and stroked his shaft with delight. He reached out to grip her hair firmly, pulling it back to expose her flushed face as he admired her enthusiasm. But he had no intention of ending it there. He stood, scooping her up easily from the floor as he ripped away the nightgown that blocked his view of her body. His lips caressed each breast hungrily until both nipples were so hard then finally met hers in a searing kiss that was passionate beyond belief.

Seth pounded into her on the bed, relishing in the sight of her ass cheeks shaking with his forceful thrusts. Taking her from behind, he felt her arch and tense as she screamed his name in release. Scooping her up in his arms, they staggered to the kitchen, where he sat her down onto a high back barstool. There, Seth took her even more savagely than before, pushing her neck back until she could barely move as he continued pounding mercilessly. Her wet pussy dripped onto the soft ivory-colored upholstery beneath them, each thrust driving her further and further over the edge into ecstasy until she quaked uncontrollably under him.

Topaz's eyes sparkled with desire as she looked up at him from the barstool, her body writhing beneath his touch. His hands provided a symphony of pleasure for her, and when he seemed close to cumming, she gracefully descended to her knees and placed his hard cock in between her lips. His taste filled her mouth as her tongue lapped up his salty cream, and her hand rhythmically stroked him until explosive waves of ecstasy spread through both simultaneously. She held onto him tightly as she savored every last drop of his pleasure, never breaking eye contact with him.

They found themselves in the shower, kissing and washing each other off before only fucking again. They collapsed in the shower, clinging onto each other as if this moment was their last. Seth loved this woman from the bottom of his soul, and her beauty consumed him like no one else ever had. Seth folded his immense wings against his back, careful not to crush them as he leaned into Topaz. He cradled her head in the crook of his arm and looked into her eyes— eyes that held a lifetime of love and longing—before their lips met. Despite the coldness of death, Seth felt like he was alive again with her.

As they lay together in bed, Topaz began to drift to sleep. Seth carefully draped his arm around her gently sleeping body, making sure to not wake her from her slumber. The tension of being apart for so long was finally lifted, and the warm embrace they shared radiated with love. As they held each other tightly, they both felt the presence of God in that moment, knowing the sacrifices they'd made were for a divine purpose.

When Topaz opened her eyes, the sun had moved across the sky, and Seth was still there, which surprised and elated her. Topaz was relieved that her time with him was not a dream. Seth held her in his arms, with her head pressed against his strong chest. His fingers gently stroked her hair as a warm feeling of love and gratitude washed over her.

He kissed her passionately on the crown of her head, inhaling the aroma of her hair. Locked in an embrace, neither said a word as they felt the electrifying connection between them, both wishing the blissful moment could stretch into eternity, and neither wanting it to ever end.

Topaz gingerly whispered, "I missed you," into Seth's ear. He looked into her eyes, admiring the stunning, brilliant shade of blue and green. Seth confessed he had missed her too. As he tenderly stroked her hair, the strawberry-scented shampoo blended with the freshness of a summer breeze and filled him with comfort. She adored having her hair played with; it was her favorite way to relax. Her eyes grew heavy as she softly drifted off to sleep in his arms.

Seth held Topaz tight in his embrace, basking in the warmth of her body. He was grateful for the strength she lent him when he was away from her, knowing that she was waiting for him back home. Topaz was his anchor, keeping him grounded despite how far away he felt.

Despite being dead, the horrors of war still weighed heavily on him, even as the heavenly being he now was. The sight of young men marching to their deaths was a sorrowful one, and he felt the weight of their families' anguish with each step they took. With every tear shed for lost loved ones, his heart ached in empathy and regret.

Seth felt the pain and anguish cascading from every family's grieving heart as if it were his own. His soul wept for each young life lost, mourning in silent agony. The shrill and guttural shriek of a mother receiving the news that her child is no more reverberates eerily in his ears as he crossed their souls over from this life into the next. The agony that wracks through the mother's entire being as she learns of her child's death is an agony like no other. The sound of her despairing scream echoes in the air and seems to reverberate from the depths of Hell itself—a long, tortured wail that pierces the heart like a thousand knives, never to be forgotten nor surpassed in its sorrow. It's a heavy burden, even for an angel of life to endure when they are upon our earth.

Topaz thought of Seth and the nightmare he was living in the warzone. She pushed back her own fear as she remembered the strength it took for him to keep going. This courage in turn ignited a spark inside her as she continued her task when she was away on her own journey.

Topaz was no ordinary woman. She had the power to see into the future, communicate with the spirits of the dead, and bend the fabric of space. She used this magic to help those in need, but it wasn't until Seth left on his journey that she felt something call her from beyond. On the night of the full moon, Topaz found herself in a dream state as she levitated into an alternate universe. Uriel, the Archangel, summoned Topaz. In her dream state, she felt herself levitate off the ground and be transported to a different realm. She saw Uriel, the Archangel of prophecy and wisdom, who shone like a star in front of her; he had chosen Topaz before she was even born to receive such special gifts.

Uriel was tasked with making an important choice. He knew that he must select someone from either Earth or the Kingdom to serve as the guardian of souls. After a long deliberation, he ultimately chose Topaz, an enlightened soul filled with grace and strength. A legacy of benevolence and powerful enchantment ran through her veins, yet Uriel was certain that her mother had instilled Topaz with the wisdom to use her gifts for divine purposes, not for self-glorification. Uriel easily recognized the greatness within Topaz.

Although Topaz was only human, she would make missteps and have urges for vigilante justice. Her intentions with her gifts were pure. Topaz would never intentionally use her gifts for her own gain but only to lend a helping hand or to protect others.

Despite her human limitations, Topaz felt a sense of purpose that drove her to fight for justice and protect others with every ounce of her being. Uriel saw Topaz struggling with the loss of what could have been between her and Seth and their daughter; thus, he knew this project would be the perfect distraction for her—even if it wasn't enough to make up for what was missing in her life without them.

Uriel offered her the project because he needed her in the trenches. She accepted the risk it would entail in keeping herself occupied while Seth was away. The task would provide her with a renewed sense of purpose and would push her to new heights in order to combat the worries she had for his safety.

Topaz was human, and the raging fire of her earthly desires burned like a furnace in her veins. Yahweh and Uriel felt compassion for her, understanding the grief that weighed down her heart and the hardships she had endured. Just as an understanding parent holds a child's hand through hardship, they extended their loving embrace to Topaz. The intensity of their love could only be described as eternal.

If Topaz and Seth's story had come to fruition, she would not only continue using white magic to protect those in need but would also be on a mission to rid the world of darkness. Even with her newfound family and relationships, the overarching purpose of her life would remain unchanged: stopping evil forces at any cost. All that would be different is that she would have had a family to love and cherish, something denied due to the free will of someone else.

Topaz mourned for the life she could have had—a life filled with grace and magic, centered around her gifted daughter. She felt a deep ache in her chest as she was faced with the harsh realization that she would never experience such joy and love. She envisioned a life full of grace and magic, where her daughter would serve as an oracle of hope and beauty. But instead, all she was left with was an endless void of sorrow that could never be filled.

Uriel's words vibrated through Topaz's core, his divine mission to deliver a message of free will igniting her spirit with a new fire. He spoke of the opportunities that lay ahead and the pages of her life awaiting to be written by her own hand. A messenger from Yahweh, Uriel offered clarity and balance, bestowing upon her an energy that would empower her to create her destiny—a destiny for others that needed saving.

His voice was like a flute, soft and calming. He floated as he spoke with grace. "Let the heavens be silent until God's hand moves to separate the righteous from the fallen. It is tribulation for us all, even for the angels..." He paused, looking upwards. "And for Yahweh himself."

His eyes shone like sapphires, and wings hovered gracefully behind him as he proclaimed the mighty words of Yahweh. "Until the trumpets ring in the sky, none are to enter the unknown depths of Hell. We must wait for our fate to be revealed... an arduous task even for angels and especially difficult for our heavenly Father," he said solemnly.

Topaz gasped in wonderment, transfixed by the archangel who appeared before her. It felt like she had died and was brought to Heaven itself; the angel was more divine than anything she could have imagined. His beauty transcended time and space, and the air around him seemed to shimmer with light. The very presence of the archangel stilled Topaz's racing heart, filling her with a newfound sense of profound peace as his words washed over her.

Uriel exposed Satan's wicked machinations, a diabolical plot to ensnare countless unsuspecting souls into the depths of Hell. Youthful soldiers were lured in with lies and deception, not knowing their fate until it was too late.

"I chose you because your soul exudes a power so strong that even the mightiest of demons tremble before it. Now I request you accept a remarkable challenge—something that only you can determine if you have the boldness to undertake. It is not something I am forcing upon you; rather, I offer it to you freely." Uriel explained to her as she looked upon the mighty angel.

As Uriel made his request, Topaz was immediately struck with reverence, almost as if the very air around her was charged with energy. She was honored to be asked and could feel the humility radiating off Uriel as if he were embarrassed that she might accept out of respect for him and not because it was her own true inclination.

Uriel gripped her with a powerful yet gentle embrace, instilling within her an unwavering sense of freedom and certainty. His fingertips burned hot against her skin as he traced the outline of her forehead, igniting her soul with an unshakeable purpose. She felt alive in that moment, empowered by what he had awakened within her. A soothing warmth spread across her forehead, and she felt the divine power of his touch, sending a chill down her spine as she understood the gravity of what was to come. Something she agreed to—of her own free will.

Topaz felt a wave of trepidation as she agreed to the dangerous mission. While her bravery was stronger than her fears, the risk of what could happen weighed heavily on her heart. She knew she must accept the task and leave immediately, but the nagging doubts held her back. Finally, with a deep breath, she pushed forward and set out just after stopping at the market to visit Molly.

Topaz was angered by the soulless manipulation of God's word by Satan, twisting it into an unrecognizable form to fuel hate and intolerance between those with different beliefs. It burned like fire in her heart when he saw people turning away from the truth of God's word, trashing it for their own agendas and stirring up animosity amid the followers of various faiths.

Topaz felt the claws of religion digging deep into the souls of mankind, oppressing its creations with guilt, shame and entitlement. Just as men hunted witches in a bygone era for their own motives, so, too, they hunt each other, weaving webs of sin and darkness that enshroud them like a cloak of paranoia and hatred. So... she understood the assignment from above very well.

The joy of Topaz's safe return was palpable among her coven, but no one could match the relief and pleasure of Seth. Unbeknownst to him, his beloved had ventured out into a world of danger, thrust onto the brink of life and death by Uriel's desperate plea for help. When Topaz left for her journey, Seth was unaware of her reckless venture. He would have been appalled if he had known that she had been asked to take on such a harrowing task.

Topaz was fully aware that if she were to fail in her mission, not only would her body leave this earth, but her soul, too, would be lost. Still, despite any misgivings or warnings, Topaz did not hesitate to accept the challenge before her—one that, had Seth known about, he would have stood in her way for fear of losing her for eternity.

Seth stepped into Heaven's grand gates, the gold and silver of which gleamed against the light of day. As he took his first breath of eternity, cheers erupted from the thousands of angels gathered in anticipation. Michael, Uriel, and Gabriel descended from the clouds and bowed before Seth in reverence. They raised Seth's hands in victory for his success in crossing over young souls into eternal bliss and love.

As Seth asked about Topaz with smiles on their faces, the archangels began to recount the tales and triumphs of his beloved Topaz. Seth was in shock, not expecting to hear the tales of her heroism. He was filled with a deep sense of pride and admiration for his wife's courage and selfless acts.

Uriel's request seemed impossible, as if it were a mission that no one would dare take on except Topaz. Her ability to transcend into Delta, and her previous venture to the depths of Hell, meant that she had to bravely undertake this task once more, despite the risks involved. The daunting but necessary challenge before her shadowed her thoughts, plaguing her with worry and fear. She could only hope that this visit would be easier than the last.

In her dream state, Topaz approached Uriel through a glimmering shower of sprinkles. The droplets felt cool on her skin, and the mist around her seemed to be washing away all the wrong she had ever done in her life. With each step she took, a wave of relief washed over her, knowing that if she could be absolved of all sin, Uriel believed she would go unnoticed in Hell while remaining an invisible void. Each sprinkle evaporated along with her worries, doubts, and guilt until only clarity remained. She moved forward without judgment or fear, undeterred by the pressure of perfection and confident that Uriel's holy water would make her invisible to the evil dwellers of Hell.

Topaz's robes felt strangely light as she waded through the milky pool, and she could feel the weight of her guilt slipping away with every step. Her bare feet glided along an amethyst floor, cool and smooth against her skin. An aroma of mint clung to the air, and a brilliant, golden light flickered in the distance. As she slowly moved closer, an overwhelming stillness filled Topaz's heart, making her wonder if she was already dead and at rest.

Topaz trudged through the dark forest, guided by Uriel's directions. She stumbled upon a moss-covered entrance to a cave underneath the earth. Inhaling sharply, she descended into its depths, not knowing what awaited her.

Topaz stepped into the darkness of the chamber. The floor beneath her feet was layered with thick sheepskin, and a chill filled the air. As she lay down, her eyes adjusted to the dim light that glowed from a few tapers scattered near the altar. Incense wafted through the room, and ancient chants echoed off the walls as the grandest high priestess of earthly magic uttered an invocation for safe passage into the underworld on her unprecedented task. With a final breath, she transcended into the underworld.

Chapter Fifteen

TALES OF TRIUMPHS

Seth heard tales of her thunderous triumphs yet was left unrewarded by the knowledge of the details of her ultimate victory. The archangels did not share that with him, as it was her story to share. Likewise, Topaz's admiration for Seth's feats was evident, but she hungered for a more intimate understanding in his successes of his grueling task.

Topaz tightly clutched Seth's hand as she asked, "What did you do when you were half a world away from me?" His eyes stared into the darkness of the night, tortured with memories of innocent lives he had witnessed falling victim to war. He squeezed her fingers gently and spoke in a low yet broken voice. "I brought young boys of no more than eighteen years of age to face their final moments. Their screams filled my ears, clamoring for help that I could not provide. I watched them suffer through unimaginable carnage—those who had lost limbs, those with gaping chest wounds, all dripping with blood until they took their last breath on this earth." The haunting image flashed across his mind as he finished his tale.

He told of innocent men brutally ripped apart by something beyond imagination. Men screaming in agony as their lifeblood pooled on the ground beneath them, their cries for help met with nothing but deafening silence. Seth looked deep into Topaz's eyes as he spoke the crushing truth: that he was no hero but had simply been a spectator there to pick up the pieces left behind—the destruction of young lives on this beautiful planet as he crossed their innocent souls into Heaven. A sad look was on his face as he finished recounting the madness he witnessed firsthand.

He fought against the rising tide of his memories that threatened to submerge his calm façade. Even Seth's heavenly body shook with fear as bullets whizzed through the air and deafening explosions rocked closer to the petrified boys. His ears were assaulted by high-pitched screams, like those of innocent children crying out for their mothers—the tails of their hymns begging for mercy—pierced his ears like a sword, reminding Seth that even in death, there are no atheists in foxholes. Seth felt the pain of their cries, shattering the illusion of safety as they screamed out for their mothers on this, their last night on Earth.

Topaz relived the terroristic moments the boys encountered as she lay with Seth, feeling his sadness. As the soldiers crossed the threshold of Heaven, they felt the Lord's presence, and their souls were filled with wonder. Every step they took was a holy pilgrimage, strengthened by divine might and power. The air around them crackled with glory as they ventured forward into a world of enchantment.

Although the young men no longer experience pain and fear, the lingering sadness of their family plagued Seth's mind. The heavy burden of their families' sorrows weighed on his soul like a boulder. Despite no longer feeling pain or fear, the sadness of the families continued to haunt him. His voice cracked as he spoke. "In Heaven, only peace exists. No stress, no heartache. But I can feel every ounce of their grief when I come back down to Earth." Topaz enveloped him in her embrace, and pressed her hand against where his heart would beat were he still alive, holding him tight to provide him some comfort.

The air between them throbbed with a thick, tangible tension. She looked up at him with an intense longing, and she could see he was wanting to break away from the heavy gloom that hung over them. Her gaze was met by his own—a powerful arctic hue that seemed to be filled with infinite kindness yet still demanded a response. He leaned in closer until their faces were nearly touching and spoke again. "Tell me of your task, my brave, beautiful wife." He sealed his words with a gentle kiss on her forehead.

"You don't already know?" she asked. She raised her eyebrows in surprise as he shook his head. He hadn't asked the archangels for any particulars, and they chose not to divulge them. Instead, they wanted her to share her story; it was hers to tell. The heavens were silent on Topaz's passage to Seth while he was on his own journey. When he would worry why he could not see Topaz, he was always assured she was safe by the archangels.

As she began recounting her journey, Topaz thought back to the moment she lay on the sheepskin in the cold void of the cavern. The chants of prayers for protection was ringing in her ears. She felt herself sinking into an abyss of fear and despair, struggling to keep afloat as she transcended into the realm of shadows.

Uriel and God selected Topaz to be the messenger of hope. Topaz descended into the deepest pits of Hell to retrieve the souls of those who had foolishly accepted their fate and resigned themselves to an eternity within its burning depths.

Seth, the angel of life, guided many young boys into Heaven while terrifying cries sounded from those who fell away in fear. Those that were left behind plummeted mercilessly into an abyss of writhing serpents, screaming out their regrets to an uncaring void, punishing themselves for deeds they considered evil and unforgivable. Finding themselves guilty of sin, they fell prey to Satan and his plans to damn the innocent.

Satan's lies spread like a plague, poisoning our minds and hearts with feelings of guilt and shame. God had seen enough, and he was determined to bring his beloved creations back into the fold. He wanted those who were beautifully flawed and burdened by pain, suffering, and worry to be saved from a life of darkness and fear.

Topaz opened her eyes, one a raging sapphire and the other a piercing emerald and looked ahead as she recounted her tale to Seth. She spoke about how she descended into the depths of shadows, sizzling from the searing embers that blistered her skin. She ventured past cores of blazing suns—one so hot it would scorch entire galaxies in its wake—until suddenly she had reached her destination and was ready to fulfill her destiny.

The air was thick with the putrid smell as Satan's demoniacs taunted the newly arrived souls with their twisted pleasure. The screams and cries of those who had already been condemned echoed through the void, a continual cacophony that only fueled the wicked joy of the damned. The bleakness of Hell intensified as an unnatural darkness descended, wrapping its sinister tendrils around all that dwelled there. Its toxic aura clung to every being in Hell like a suffocating blanket, bringing an unending sense of terror and dread.

Topaz stared, eyes wide with horror, as the ghosts of souls were ferried into the chamber of swarming serpents. The serpents breathed in the human essence as they rejoiced in the souls and their self-damnation. The demonic serpents began sapping away the souls' humanity until they could only be described as hollow husks of what they once were.

Satan's insidious lies filled the minds of the innocents like a thick, noxious smoke that smothered any hope of salvation. His demoniacs whispered damning secrets of unforgivable transgressions into their ears, and soon those lies were entrenched deeply in their thoughts. The selfless souls believed they were undeserving of any forgiveness, all thanks to Satan's venomous lies that saturated every aspect of their lives. And now... there they were—in Hell.

No being could ever be as maliciously cunning and conniving as Satan. No creature is as deceitful and manipulative as Satan, except perhaps mankind. That's what made Topaz the perfect aid in the plan to capture the souls that damned themselves for eternity. It was this shared wickedness she held—a human capable of free will and manipulation. This, along with her magic, is what made Topaz the ideal accomplice to craft a wretched scheme for ensnaring souls and keeping them from an eternity of damnation.

Topaz embraced her dark side, invoking her deepest flaws: selfishness, arrogance, doubt, mistrust, lies, manipulation, and the deep-seated loathing she unknowingly harbored in her soul. Her eyes blazed with a newfound intensity as she wielded the power of these passions like a weapon against the beast. She was determined to defeat him at his own game.

Topaz embraced the shadows of her soul, determined to traverse the depths of Hell among its wickedest inhabitants undetected. With a fierce resolve burning within her heart, Topaz squared up with the darkest adversary of Heaven that dared to defy Yahweh's will. She was there to scavenge from those whose souls should have been collected by Seth when they died. Ready to take on Satan's dark forces and collect the wandering souls, Topaz glided through the realm, stalking her prey with deadly intent like a lioness surveying its savannah.

BACK IN HELL

Seth closed his eyes and allowed himself to be taken away on Topaz's journey. He felt the searing heat of the abyssal pits when she first entered—a place that was brimming with fear and darkness. As she ventured deeper, she could still taste the holy water that washed away her sins, masking her presence from the demons. As she spoke, Seth could feel them both go back in time—back in Hell.

The blazing embers of Hell descended as Topaz pushed the boundaries of magic. She edged around the cursed pit, projecting her spirit into a murky gloom along the walls. Topaz maneuvered the treacherous abyss, concealing her soul in dark corners, hoping not to be discovered. Hell is massive in size, much grander in scale than you can fathom. Topaz had to make her way through many fiery abysses, looking for the cavern that harbored the ensnared souls tricked into entering Hell.

Topaz crept through the darkness, her thin frame shaking with fear. The smell of burning flesh was overwhelming, as were the screams of agony echoing off the walls of the first pit. Her brow furrowed in disgust as she approached a pit holding earthly monsters that enjoyed tormenting their innocent victims without mercy. The flames lit up the surrounding area with a blinding orange glow, and smoke obscured Topaz's view. She could make out their twisted faces and their malicious grins as they were when they lived. Topaz could see glimpses of their wickedness when they were on Earth. She could see how they tortured their victims. Her stomach churned at the horror of it all; she did not feel pity for these earthly monsters.

Their brittle, dry bones crumbled as they clawed desperately, attempting to inch out of the raging pit. They clawed, scratched, and pushed, but the walls were slick with boiling ooze, and they would fall further into the pit. Every inch was a titanic effort to conquer as white-hot flames licked and danced around them. Exhaustion weighed heavily on their skeletal frames as the stench of burning flesh and spilled blood filled their nostrils, reminding them that they were prisoners in this burning chasm for eternity.

Topaz cautiously stepped towards the edge of the infernal pit and peered down. A sickening wave of heat seared her face, and she could barely make out the gruesome scene below as fierce green flames crackled around it. She watched in horror as a never-ending cascade of souls had been thrown into the abyss, some writhing in agony, others screaming in terror, their faces contorted with anguish, their howls of agony reverberating off the charred walls. Topaz watched in silent horror as bodies were jumbled together in a grotesque pile of death, trying to claw out of the torment.

As she looked around, her stomach churned in fear as she recognized many faces. One face in particular was familiar to her: a man whose presence brought back memories of the church she attended as a young girl. Even then, she had followed her intuition and kept away from him. Now, knowing the person he really was—a cruel, murderous monster—made her feel nauseous and sickened. A wave of nausea bubbled up inside her like an erupting volcano as she slowly backed out of their eternal prison of depravity.

Her spirit flew through the cavern, its glow illuminating the murky darkness that filled the cave. As she descended lower, warmer air hit her face, and a low hum echoed from the depths. In the center of the chamber lay a boiling pit, writhing with scores of massive alligators and winding serpents. The creatures glowed red in the dim light, revealing their demonic origins.

The cambions—offspring of succubi or incubi—were as large as grown humans and lay among the other creatures in the dungeon. They had more human-like features than their demon parents, but an aura of malevolence clung to them. The cambions in Hell were consumed by Satan's seething hatred; their malevolent spirits intermingled with the worst parts of humanity—a legacy of pure wickedness that had been passed down through their cursed bloodline.

Every breath they inhaled spread their wrath like noxious fumes until it saturated the air around them, coalescing into something far more sinister than mere hatred. The cambions born in Hell were far more powerful and wicked than those born on Earth. They slinked through the fiery halls of Hell, writhing in the blackened shadows and radiating pure hatred. As they passed by their fellow demons, they seemed to emit a palpable cloud of wickedness.

Topaz trudged farther into the abyss, feeling assaulted by a stench that could only be described as death. The floor was thick with hot mud. Writhing in the mud were demons of all shapes and sizes—some engaged in lewd acts of fornication with one another, while others leered and poked at aggressive reptiles entwined within the pit. The serpents hissed and coiled around each other, as if conspiring against their demonic captors.

Topaz crept along the edge of the pit, her heart racing as she slinked through the caverns. She could feel the weight of the demoniacs' sinister presence swirling about. She feared the serpents sensed her; it was almost as if they were reaching out with their dark energy to taste her life force that hung in the humid air. The reptiles began slithering around and hissing, and she could hardly contain her terror. She knew one wrong move or sound could attract them all to her like a magnet. With every step, she prayed she would make it out undetected.

Topaz's shadow stretched eerily across the orange glow of molten rock, her nostrils filled with the acrid scent of rotting flesh, and the heat radiating from the lava began making her feel like her soul was burning. She was forced to hunch low as the overwhelming heat tried to ooze into her core, making it difficult to think straight. The ground shook continuously as lava spewed with each step she took, splattering against the dungeon walls that surrounded her.

As she stood at the entrance of one of the pits of murderers, her soul trembled as vibrations from the quakes in Hell rattled against the jagged rocks around her. The pit was endless and seemed to stretch into eternity, its depth unfathomable, like an abyss that ran even deeper than the Pacific Ocean. The gaping hole in the ground gurgled and steamed with an evil presence. Souls wailed in anguish from the depths, begging to be released.

One by one, the damned would claw their way to the top of the molten abyss, only to be dragged back down by repulsive demons with scaly bodies. The demoniacs' faces were contorted in rage and malice, their red eyes blazing like hot coals as each fresh victim was dragged from the top of the massive abyss into their merciless clutches, devouring them with their immense hunger. Each time the soul was snatched away, its cries reverberated through the air until it was swallowed into a prison more tortuous than the fiery pit itself. The cries of the doomed echoed deep within as they realized what was about to befall them: a fate worse than the soul-sucking pit.

Topaz's vision blurred as fear filled her body. A large, black silhouette appeared at the door of the cavern, and she felt its eyes fixed upon her. The demon approached closer, dragging heavy wings behind him as he looked around with his beady eyes glowing red. With each step of his cloven hooves, the walls of the dark cave rumbled. Topaz scrambled back into a corner; even if she wanted to scream, she couldn't as she was overcome with immense fear.

The fallen angel spread its wings and emitted a bellowing cry that reverberated in her chest. Like fiends summoned from the underworld, the demoniacs appeared in large, dark shapes—their coats a mix of black and orange. They moved quickly, sniffing through the smoke and flames with an eerie intensity, as if searching for any trace of a soul that may have escaped.

The beings tensed as they surveyed their surroundings. Topaz meticulously stepped through the death pits and into a hallway that seemed to stretch to infinity, descending further and further into the abyss. The walls on either side of her seemed to move like living creatures, expanding and contracting in time with some unseen breath. Fear ran through her veins as the depths of the abyss unfolded before her eyes, growing even larger in size.

Topaz fled desperately in search of safety, her mind racing with terror as she worried demons would soon discover her. Wheeling around a sharp corner, she stumbled blindly into a cavern that seemed to be tucked quietly away. She felt a sudden relief that this secret refuge had hidden her from her pursuers—she hoped.

As she recounted her journey, Seth began to feel dread, but of course he had comfort in knowing she was safe; she was there in his arms as she relived the experience with him. When she tucked into the cavern, her heart pounded. Topaz huddled in the corner of the dark, musty room, praying to go unnoticed. She began hearing moaning and smacking sounds coming from behind her, and she froze in fear. Her imagination ran wild with the possibilities. Was this Satan's lair, where he cavorts with his demoness harlots? She also knew Satan created monsters to reproduce with humans. Was he breeding his succubi and incubi in this muggy dungeon? She worried, slowly turning to look to see what was happening.

Topaz watched in horror as three monstrous figures rutted like animals over the writhing form of a petite succubus. One demon had her perched atop its loins while another forced his way between her legs from behind, making her moan and groan with excitement and pleasure. The third demon stood behind her with one hand clamped around her throat, thrusting his hard dick deep into her mouth.

The air was thick and heavy with lust as the succubus moved around the room, her curves a delicious invitation to any and all. A feral growl resonated through the room as each took turns enjoying the succubus' charms, a reminder that even beasts of Hell were not immune to carnal desires.

The demons and succubus writhed in pleasure, their passionate coupling creating a vibrant aura of chaotic energy. She couldn't help but feel shocked by their incestuous behavior, yet their insatiable lust didn't seem like it would ever be quenched as they continued to engage in vigorous intercourse.

The succubus, cursed with an unquenchable lust from the depths of Hell, was created to breed with humans, a task that she and her kin, the incubi, excelled at. Yet, here among the demons and Satan, she witnessed behavior completely unexpected: they were fucking other creatures in Hell too.

Topaz turned away, but she could still hear as demons ravished each other in a chaotic carnal orgy, utterly consumed in their desires. Topaz knew that although succubi and incubi were created only for reproduction, they were more than mindless drones—they possessed venomous tongues that could weave lies sweeter than honey and hearts blacker than coal. These entities will cloak themselves in perfect beauty when in their human forms as they perfume the air with an alluring scent that seems to enchant all who came near when they were on Earth. As Satan created them to possess humans, they were made without the same evil cunning instinct as other demons. These creations were subservient to the fallen angels and worshiped them.

The succubi were driven by an insatiable hunger—not for power but for the creation of their demonic spawn. They required nourishment from the pure seed of men to birth their cambions into the depths of Hell. The creatures would grow and mature in mere minutes, ready to follow their masters' commands, born to be loyal servants or unrelenting soldiers. Incubi craved the warmth of womanly passion and lust to birth creatures far darker and more insidious than any human. These Earth-born cambions exuded a charming aura, which would lure unsuspecting victims to birth impure human babies, never suspecting these babies would grow up with Hell coursing in their veins.

The incubi offspring on Earth grew and matured at the same rate as humans. They were smart and usually born into well-connected families of power. Like their Hell-bound cousins, they, too, were liars, thieves, and masterminds at luring humans to their demise. The demons arrived on Earth with a mission of corruption, tempting humans into the depths of sin and depravity with promises of pleasure. They sought to keep humanity from entering God's Kingdom, preying on their weaknesses for their own sinister gain.

On Earth, the creatures used their seductive powers to entice humans into a dark and twisted world of sin and deception, binding them in a prison and preventing mankind's access to Heaven. Topaz had been taught these monsters were just myths, but her intuition told her otherwise—and that intuition was proven right when she encountered them face-to-face, filling her with fear and dread.

More demons began to trickle into the room, and Topaz knew she had to escape the chaos quickly. She scurried out of the cavern and floated along the hallway, anxiety racing wildly. Topaz stared in awe as a radiant demoness stepped through the inferno and into the hallway. Her straight, silky-smooth hair seemed to absorb the fire and light up like platinum strands of starlight as she glided through the flames. The demoness had the same short, pointed horns that stood straight up from her skull as all of the other demonesses.

Her skin was flushed with a deep crimson from the heat of

hellfire. She moved gracefully through the flames, as though they were merely a light breeze that she could brush away with her delicate touch.

Shortly after she passed, another demoness appeared. Her wild, curly hair tumbled around her ample curves and framed her face like a halo of fire. Her stomach was taught and ripped with muscles that glimmered under the light. A sinister smirk stretched across her lips as she invited all who beheld her in, mesmerized by her blazing scarlet eyes that shone bright with a hint of danger hiding behind them. The air around her seemed to pause in admiration of her beauty.

The demons gasped as another demoness followed, strutting through the great hall, their eyes feasting on her every movement and breath. As if in a trance, they watched and ached for her to come even closer—but she kept walking, oblivious to their yearning as the demons hid in the shadows, observing the succubus.

After the demonesses brushed past them, a succubus emerged from the shadows. Her beauty was unmistakable in her humanoid appearance. She had her dark curls swept up and held in a high ponytail that bounced invitingly as she moved. Everywhere she walked, an invisible wave of lust trailed her wake.

As Topaz was about to exit, another succubus manifested before her eyes. She was a sight to behold, her beauty incomparable yet not as intimidating as the other succubi. Her hair glowed like a blazing fire, cascading around her in glowing rufescent locks, while her skin was as smooth as velvet. She stood slightly shorter than the others, but with swollen breasts and a protruding belly that screamed of an impending birth, she radiated power and awe. But what mesmerized Topaz most were her eyes—a soft amber hue so human-like, captivating yet ordinary in their brilliance. They held an inhuman depth, alluring and beckoning like a siren's song.

The pregnant succubus moved cautiously among the shadows that lined the walls, her large belly swaying with each step. Her breath came in gasps as the pain of labor tightened along her back. She slowly passed by the demons; her cold eyes filled with disdain for their presence. Their gazes followed her as she walked alone into the Devil's dungeon. With every surge of contractions, she snarled and snapped at them, her swollen face twisted in a grimace of agony, pausing every now and then as another contraction wracked her body.

The succubus trudged on, her swollen belly announcing an unholy birth. Topaz was overwhelmed by an urge to witness the abomination for herself. But she was filled with fear that the demoniacs would detect her, and even more so that Satan himself would recognize her presence. She knew if she were to be seen by him, her physical form on Earth would instantly perish, her heart would crush under the weight of such numbing terror, and her soul would be captured in an iron fist by the king of Hell.

Topaz felt her heart beating faster as she walked away from the demons that lurked in the shadows. Then a sound carried through the air—an unfamiliar sound in Hell. It was laughter—joyous and free. She looked ahead of her as her curiosity peaked and saw two demonesses embracing one another, entwined in passionate kisses. One had a mane of whisky-brown hair with silver skin that gleamed like light bouncing off crystal and yellow eyes radiating like stars. The other possessed deep, midnight-black hair with feral orange-red eyes that glowed hypnotically against her captivating rose-gold skin. Topaz watched with surprise at their delight with one another as she floated above the flames.

The sultry dungeon seemed to rise in temperature as their two bodies writhed together, fervor and desire coursing through their veins. She gasped as her lover licked and teased her ample breasts, each stroke sending a wave of pleasure over her body. Their moans echoed off the walls as they moved against one another, their hands exploring each other's curves with mounting intensity.

The demonic entities clung to each other, drowning in pleasure, until the steamy dungeon was bathed in ecstasy. They licked and sucked hungrily at each other's clits, pleasure radiating off them with every moan until they were overcome with desire. Flushed with exhilaration, the demonesses reveled in their passionate rapture, blissful exhalations filling the air.

Topaz spun around to leave, the shock of their unexpected intimacy catching her off guard. The demonesses' fluid and passionate motions swept Topaz away—despite the fleeting feelings of lust and drinking blood—and she wondered if demonesses were capable of more than hate and sexual desires.

Topaz felt a strong bond between the two and could feel something far greater than mere lust. *Could these beasts feel love?* Topaz wondered. The sight of the two together in harmony, without hatred or anger, was strangely beautiful—like a beacon of hope in the midst of darkness.

The demonesses' crave for one another was insatiable. Their naked bodies writhed and twined with each other as carnal desire peaked. They kissed hungrily, tongues intertwining, as they greedily tasted the blood that fed their hunger. Every taste of one another amplified their lust, amplifying their rapture as they lost themselves in a furious frenzy of passion. Topaz felt awkward and quickly looked around for a place to retreat and left the demonesses to momentary peace and privacy. Suddenly, the mood changed in the dungeon, catching Topaz off guard.

Their teeth began nipping and biting hungrily at the soft flesh of each other's necks and wrists. The taste of blood filled their mouths as they indulged in an unbridled display of blood lust. Their blood began pooling out—glowing red hot and before changing into a dark purple hue. Their teeth changed before her eyes from smooth to sharp and fierce. Their eyes blazed with radiance, as the color began to drain away from the irises and left them solid, pure black. The whites of their eyes went black as well, and then their irises began glowing red with power.

As Topaz looked on in horror, she watched the beauties transform into monsters right before her eyes. They began to tear at each other and ripped hunks of flesh away from one another's bodies, enthralled by the pleasure of feeling hot blood flow into their mouths. As they drank from one another, shrieking cries escaped them as they drank one another's boiling hot blood and tore into each other's flesh like starved animals. Blood pooled on the ground, soaked up by the smoldering ashes at their feet.

The intensity frightened Topaz. She began to sink away, but then her soul began to quiver in terror as her body on Earth convulsed without control. She could feel the looming presence of a powerful entity behind her. *Had I been detected?* Topaz worried. Resignation filled her as she realized that her mission was still incomplete and that all hope of success had dissipated. Death might come for her soon, but even more terrifying to Topaz was the thought of leaving this world with unfinished business. She was not going to go easy; she had souls to save.

The demonesses dropped to their knees, trembling with fear as a massive demon approached, looming menacingly before them. His dead-eyed gaze burned into their souls, knowing what they had been doing—a forbidden rendezvous. His low growl reverberated through the cavernlike thunder, and a chill swept over the two as if Satan himself had invaded the space.

Knowing judgment was coming, they scurried up onto the ceiling in a flurry of panic, clawing and scrambling desperately to get away from each other, as if some silent force had cursed them should they remain together. The demonesses parting was swift and silent—they both knew that obliteration would come before any more pleasure could be taken. Topaz, however, felt relieved that she still was undetected.

The demon's nostrils flared as he scented the air, searching for the source of his pleasure. Topaz could almost feel the scent of her fill his nostrils, but it was not her that triggered his senses. It was another he sought, and soon a cambion arrived as if summoned by the beast.

The alluring she-devil had long, shimmering strands of chestnut hair that framed her face and cascaded down her back. Her eyes were silver with a lavender haze that thinned to light violet around the soft circle of her irises. Smooth, creamy skin looked soft as satin to the touch, and vibrant pink lips were full and inviting—even to a demon. As the heinous creature embraced the cambion, Topaz knew he had been expecting her and chased away the demonesses.

The demon placed the cambion against the wall, his powerful arms pinning her in place as he looked into her eyes. She stretched her body up to meet his, wrapping her long, powerful legs around him and pulling him close to her. He ran his hands over her curves, squeezing and fondling, as her insidious laughter filled the air. While the cambion's moans of unbridled ecstasy distracted the large demon, Topaz seized the intense moment and slipped away, vanishing into the flames of hellfire.

Satan was a proud and discerning being, and it was said that he only ever engaged in intercourse with the most exquisitely beautiful of demonesses. The succubi were seen as unclean from having relations with mortals, while the cambions—born of half-demon, half-mortal unions—were looked down on even more by Satan. Topaz couldn't believe that the demons lusted after what Satan considered *lesser* beings in secret, but the demon's passions for these creatures were undeniable. Satan would not be pleased if he caught his servant angels laying with succubi and cambions as they were part human and made in God's image.

Satan thought little of these creatures... not trusting them. The mission of the incubi and succubi was to systematically pollute the lineage of mankind through repugnant copulation that birthed cambions. Satan, not God, created these entities to breed with humans to build his army. He created them to lure humans into carnal desires, not for playmates for his demons. The demons, however, lusted after these creatures that possessed humanesque qualities; they were drawn to them feverishly.

The most powerful demons soullessly mated with the succubi, reproducing offspring as needed. They considered cambions and humans to be inferior and abhorrent creations of God. Topaz knew immediately that the demon's intimate relationship with a cambion she just witnessed was his own dirty secret. The cambion, for him, was a risk worthy of annihilation if their illicit affair were ever uncovered.

Topaz slowly walked through the pits, her eyes darting in every direction as she tried to decipher which way to go. She hadn't realized how much she had come to rely on her developed abilities until they were suddenly gone. She felt powerless now that she was deep in the abyss of Hell.

Topaz heard a low, tortured wail from down the hallway, and her stomach lurched. The succubus was giving birth, and though Topaz was desperately curious, she was equally scared of what she might see. She froze, but curiosity battled with her fear. Then, as if it were tugging her forward, something deep within Topaz drove her down the hallway.

Topaz's steps were near silent as she descended the steep dungeon. Below, an eerie glow bathed the walls in shades of pink and purple. The succubus stood alone near the edge of a deep crevice that spewed forth flames hotter than any Topaz had ever seen. As if infected by her tears, the fire seemed to burn brighter, the indigo inferno licking the air with its howls and crackles. There was no sign of Beelzebub or the humanoid spawn.

Topaz watched in astonishment as the succubus heaved and moaned with each contraction. Finally, she pushed a grotesquely shaped pile of flesh onto the ground. The newborn cambion was still slick with blood, its skin mottled pink and red. Despite her labor, the succubus' body shimmered and shifted back to its original slender shape before turning away from the newborn. Without another glance, she stepped into the black pit of shadows on the other side of the room.

Topaz trembled in awe as she watched the spawn mutate before her eyes. The baby shot up inches at a time, muscles writhing beneath its skin as bones shifted and snapped to create a tall human form with an athletic physique. His features were hauntingly alluring as he scanned the room, his curiousness akin to that of a newborn discovering the world for the first time. He strode past Topaz, excusing himself as he brushed past her, leaving her trembling behind him in shock as he continued on his journey. The newly-born cambion detected her but did not know she was not supposed to be there.

Topaz's breath caught in her chest. The newborn entity had seen her! His gaze raked over her as if he were peeling away layers of her skin. She knew it was only a matter of time before she was discovered by other newly created cambions, succubi, or incubi—lesser creatures with a more benevolent relationship towards humanity than the demons of Hell. She feared their innocence could be used against her to reveal her presence and bring about her downfall.

Fear tingled through Topaz's spirit as she watched the cambion exit into the hallway. Something about the cambion's presence seemed so hauntingly familiar, and Topaz could feel a strange connection to him. As the other demoniacs welcomed him, Topaz observed as she slowly floated away into the darkness.

She moved like a ghost along the walls, careful not to draw attention to her soul. But then, a distant cry of agony echoed from deep within the lair, catching Topaz's attention and freezing her in place. She was torn between running away or exploring further, but something kept pulling her deeper into this abyss.

Seth was overcome with an incredible sight as he followed Topaz into the depths of Hell when she shared her story. He could feel the energy emanating from the entrance, and it seemed to reach out, like hands grasping at his skin. As Seth ventured further and further in with her, the darkness seemed to grow exponentially, and he found himself in awe; even a heavenly being could not comprehend such a vast expanse. Seth felt the sinister presence of evil, almost as if he had gone to Hell with Topaz. Seth became submerged in Topaz's experience as she relived her time in Hell. He could feel the very air choking the life out of him, making it nearly impossible to breathe as his vision blurred as the images of Hell warped and twisted around him.

Seth felt as if he were plummeting through the fiery depths of Hell, each agonizing step deepening his despair. The darkness and heat seemed to deaden every sense, leaving him with an endless void of nothingness. With each passing moment, Seth felt himself getting closer to Topaz's experience—the horrific screams, searing flames, and unbearable anguish that pervaded her memories. He could taste the ashes of death on his tongue and smell sulfur filling the air. Seth could see and experience everything Topaz experienced when she was reliving her time in Hell.

As Topaz stepped into the dark and desolate chambers of the dead, shadows seemed to move at their own will, and whispers of malevolent intentions echoed through the cavernous hallways. Topaz shuddered as she ventured deeper and deeper into the abyss of Hell, her heart pounding in her ears. Seth felt her fear like a jolt to his own heart, and he was in awe of Topaz's strength, feeling honor-bound to be in her presence.

Engulfed in fear, Topaz knew there was no turning back now; she had to press onward, trusting that her faith and courage would carry her—towards her mission and out from the depths of darkness.

Topaz shuddered as she narrated her time in Hell. Time seemed to stand still as she stumbled through the pits of despair, searching for lost souls. Seth was able to comprehend the level of dread she experienced as he relived that never-ending nightmarish journey with her. Weeks and months could pass on Earth, but while in Heaven, they could feel like only moments or hours.

There was no real concept of time there. She trudged through the murky depths of the Underworld, searching endlessly for lost souls that were taken away to this realm with no mercy. With every step that brought her closer to the center of Hell, she faced nothing but barren and scorching plains and fiery pits carved out for housing more condemned souls.

Topaz shuddered as she walked down the seemingly endless path that led her to towering flames, licking the top of the dungeons. Dread clawed at her heart as she felt herself sinking further and further into the abyss. As the intense heat and darkness grew stronger, Topaz's fear mounted, and her frustration boiled over—time was running out. Suddenly, chants echoed through the smoky air. Topaz perked up, for she knew these were prayers to God, emanating from deep within Hell. She could feel hope swell in her chest—she discovered where the souls were hidden and safeguarded away.

Topaz felt the flames of Hell surrounding her with a gravitating force as she buffeted through the wild, roaring flames. In their depths, she heard the desperate cries of souls dreadfully trapped. Seething embers rose even higher and hotter as she moved through the dungeon of prisoners, all pleading with Yahweh for salvation. In this pit of lost dreams, she realized that these too were young souls of soldiers that had died in war, intended for rescue by her companion Seth.

Her heart sickened at the sight of these sacrificed souls—so many taken from their families and beloveds too soon, stolen away to suffer here in the bowels of Hell. With heavy purpose, Topaz trudged forward to secure their freedom and bring them into God's grace.

Desperately begging for salvation, the desolate souls cried out, their calls reverberating through the air as they clung on to a fading hope of rescue from their suffering. Stolen breaths that were intended to be saved by Seth were tricked away into Hell. The *Master of Deceit* easily beguiled them into believing their transgressions could not earn redemption and dragged them straight to Hell. In their last moments, they realized too late that their fate was already sealed. These young souls, fooled into believing their sins were too grave and weighed heavily against them, condemning them unjustly to an unending cycle of suffering.

Her eyes were fixated on the pit of doomed souls who had been lured here in desperation. Sobbing, they begged Yahweh for forgiveness and rescue, praying for their lost souls to be found amid the ashes. With booming authority. All of these broken warriors, whose lives were taken too soon, fighting wars abroad only to be devoured by deceit and now chained to Hell. Satan intended for them to remain for eternity, but now they would finally have a chance at freedom with the help of an earthly priestess sent to retrieve them.

The souls were ensnared and hopeless, their cries of desperation echoing off the walls. Topaz could scarcely bear to witness it, yet he stood vigil in the flames. A demonic figure slowly descended into the dark abyss with wings like an eerie swarm of locusts and threw more fireballs into the inferno. The agonizing wails of the tormented souls grew louder with every additional ember as they suffered a fate worse than the most tormented death on Earth.

The demon's eyes glowed red with evil intent as he stoked their pain, throwing down a torrent of searing embers that caused the souls to cry out with even more anguish and despair made him giddy with delight. The sadistic demon laughed as the innocents howled in agony beneath his cruel lash. He delighted in their suffering, but soon he grew bored with the cruel game and departed. Topaz tucked herself into a corner of the burning chamber trying to stay hidden from the monster's gaze.

With a deep breath, Topaz lifted the veil of flames that shrouded the pit. A heavenly light like no other now bathed the doomed souls below, and their soft murmurs of hope replaced the screams of terror they once made. As she stretched out her arms with strength, Topaz commanded the stolen breaths chained by deception to break free from their captors and follow her out of their eternal prison God answered their anguished prayers, providing them salvation from the destruction and despair in which they were trapped. The souls of the damned were liberated from their hellish prison by Topaz, and they went on to seek their salvation.

Searing anger boiled through Satan's core as he woke in his bottomless pit, surrounded by his harlots. Flickering red eyes glittering with rage, he hurried through the depths of his dark kingdom, hearing the souls rejoicing as they ran towards the holy light and away from him. Fueled with vengeance, he unleashed a legion of demons to hunt for Topaz down on Earth. This is when her coven started being harassed, when Satan knew Topaz was wreaking havoc in Hell, bending magic, and helping innocent souls to be set free from his clutches.

He could *feel* her presence even though he could not identify her through her sins anymore, for they had been washed away by holy water. Knowing the angels and the absolved dead would never enter Hell, it could only be her causing such mischief. Beelzebub was determined to find her and take revenge, swearing to bring her body and soul back so she might suffer an eternity under his dominion.

Satan unleashed a primal scream of pure fury as he reached the pit of the lost souls, only to find it barren and empty. Satan's blood-curdling *ROAR* trembled the very depths of eternal damnation, reverberating through every crevice and every corner of Hades. His anger had become an inferno, fueled by jealousy over Topaz's growing power. He wanted vengeance—to cause her pain in every way imaginable. All those she loved could suffer his wrath.

Even the Beast's legion of demoniacs cowered in fear, their hands clapped to their ears as the tormented sound surged and overflowed. His rage was palpable; he would stop at nothing until Topaz felt his wrath, his burning hatred for her rivaled only by Yahweh himself. He craved to bring her pain, in all forms of agony imaginable. No matter who or what she loved—they could all be in jeopardy.

Satan felt the flames of fury rising in his core. He knew Uriel had something to do with this and that Topaz still had powerful allies in Heaven who would protect her from him. In desperation, he formed a plan to seek revenge on those she loved.

Her coven would be subjected to years of torment and taunting because of her involvement. The thought of Topaz crossing souls into Heaven enraged him beyond reason. A plan formulated in his mind. The followers of Topaz—her witches—were going to be taunted and tormented for years to come as payment for their priestess's transgression against him.

DESCENDING FROM THE DARKNESS

It was upon Seth's final delivery of souls into Heaven that the archangels greeted him, celebrating him, and sharing the news of Topaz's victory over a demon horde. It was then that the celestial angels instructed him to return to Earth to assist with Topaz's coven until she was able to return home.

With that, he was sent back down from Heaven. Gabriel had informed him of the demons' plan to pick off each member of the coven one by one and drag them back to Hell's bottomless cavern to punish Topaz for helping Yahweh.

As soon as Seth reached Earth, it was just as he had feared. Seth watched as a wicked figure flew through the night sky, Molly in his monstrous claws. Seth braced himself for battle, ready to destroy the beast that was harming Molly. In that moment, he saw a glint of moonlight embracing Topaz as she descended from the darkness, making her way to greet her coven, whom she knew was worried for her. Seth swooped towards Molly at lightning speed, shielding her from the demon's wrath.

Topaz leapt to the rescue as Molly tumbled from the demon's clutches, not realizing at that time that Seth had already stepped in. With Gabriel's guidance, Seth charged forward and forced the demons away from the coven, chasing them far from Earth, leaving nothing but darkness in their wake. The demon relinquished his grip on Molly, freeing her from his grasp as soon as he saw the presence of Seth descending upon him.

Seth couldn't contain his excitement when Yahweh granted the archangel's request to allow him and Topaz permission to reunite in the physical realm. The night passed by too fast, but not a moment was wasted. They hugged and kissed, caressed each other's skin, and made love with an intensity that could only come from knowing it could be their last time together on Earth and being able to experience physical passion with one another.

They wanted all of each other, tearing at the sheets and grasping at one another with desperate hunger. Seth and Topaz moved together in a passionate frenzy, their bodies entwined in an all-consuming embrace. They moved in unison, creating a delicious rhythm that built higher and higher as they clung to one another, until finally their love ended in a flood of passion that left them spent and trembling. The intensity of their lovemaking felt like it would last forever, as if they were devouring each other hungrily and merging into one being.

Topaz often lay in bed at night, imagining how their lives would have been together if it came to pass. She'd often pull the soft quilt tighter around herself and try to force away the loneliness that encompassed her. Topaz longed for the companionship of cuddling up close with Seth and feeling his body against hers.

Topaz knew even if they ended up together in Heaven, it wouldn't be the same; there would be no human pleasure or intimacy in Heaven, only a spiritual connection. There would be no dinner dates, hand-holding, or long nights of conversation. Even though they could never truly be together on Earth, this finite amount of time was all she had to share with him—she didn't want that time to end.

Topaz enjoyed Seth's kindness and couldn't get enough of him. His handsome face, his flawless skin that stretched over well-defined muscles, and his broad smile turned her on every time they made love. Seth lit a fire in Topaz that only he could fuel, and when she gazed into his eyes, she saw the universe shimmering with life.

Topaz hummed softly as she stroked his plush wings. "I love your wings," she whispered softly while smiling at him mischievously. He shivered as her hands moved from his wings to his body. She then began running her fingers softly along his side, admiring his perfect contour.

"You know what I love about you?" he asked as she giggled. "My ESP? My intuition, my badass ability to bend magic?" she jokingly suggested as he moved her onto her back and hovered over her. He glanced appreciatively at her curves before pushing her down onto the bed. As he leaned over her, his lips found her neck and lingered there as he softly kissed it, moving lower to her breast. His lips lightly grazed her breast as his tongue found its way around it, making her moan in pleasure. "You have the best tits," he growled, teasing her, making her blush with embarrassment.

She thrashed against him, trying to break free, but he held her tight in his iron grip, laughing with delight. Their playful embrace ended in an explosion of laughter. "This is the best day of my life," she pleaded as their eyes locked. "This is the best day of my eternity," he murmured as he moved closer, his lips and mouth covering hers as his tongue sought out her own in a tender embrace. His eyes smoldered with desire as he whispered in her ear, his voice deepening as he seductively coaxed her for another ride on his dick. Her heart raced with anticipation as their passion sent sparks of electricity through them both.

Time seemed to stop as they immersed themselves completely in each other's presence. Their conversations were never-ending, and numerous passionate kisses ignited fiery chemistry between them that expanded into a universe of heated lovemaking sessions. Every passing moment together was a montage of bliss, as if they were living out what could have been their married life. The house vibrated with the joyous sound of Topaz singing along to songs on the radio while she cooked, and he assisted her despite his lack of appetite. Even helping her with the dishes had become one of his favorite pastimes.

Topaz and Seth moved around her kitchen, exploring every inch of each other's bodies. They tangled their hands and lips together in a passionate embrace as they made love on the cold tile countertops, Seth fervently exploring her body with his own. When they finally moved outside, bare feet lightly trod across the shingles of her roof as they enjoyed the night air with its twinkling stars that lit up the dark sky.

Topaz and Seth stepped outside, the night sky a star-studded canvas above them. Topaz ran her fingers over his hands. She could feel the inevitability of his departure within them. They talked quietly, every word another reminder of how precious their time was together. They never spoke of the future, instead savoring each and every memory they made together.

During the daytime, Seth helped her in the garden, carefully tilling the soil and laying down mulch. As the scent of fresh-cut grass rose around them, he'd slide her sundress off her shoulders and pull her close, leaving only her sunhat on, shielding her face from the sun. She'd lean against him, feeling his warmth against her skin as he kissed away every worry on her mind. Together, they'd sink into the soft earth beneath them, indulging in each other's passions under the sky.

The days flew by in a blur of laughter and joy. Every moment they shared was precious to them, as if it would be their last. Together, they watched as the sun slowly set, painting the horizon in an orange hue. They talked about anything and everything until, finally, the stars began to twinkle in the night sky, bringing their magical day to an end.

Days drifted into weeks, each filled with smiles and laughter. Their mornings started before sunrise, watching the sun greet them from the roof of Topaz's house. Midafternoons brought picnics on a grassy knoll and long hikes deep into the woods. Evenings melted into star-filled nights where they talked until their breaths became heavy with sleep. Topaz finally got her dates with Seth, whom she thought she could only have in her dreams.

Seth's body tensed, and he slowly stood up from the bed. His eyes looked deep into hers, conveying a silent message she could feel in her soul. She wanted to keep him here forever. He broke their gaze and stepped closer, enfolding her in his strong arms. His embrace was warm and comforting as she breathed in his familiar scent, tears stinging her eyes. She kissed his neck tenderly before he brushed away her tears with his thumb. Seth lightly kissed her lips one last time and took one final look at her before vanishing, leaving for the heavens.

The pain of saying goodbye was intensified by the uncertainty of when they would meet again. Her mind raced, creating a timeline of possibilities: two days, two months, or twenty years? She felt as if her heart had been ripped from her chest, and he had taken it with him. She couldn't bear to speak to anyone or do anything that reminded her of him. For two days, she sat alone in darkness, missing his touch.

Topaz roamed the house with a hollow feeling in her stomach, stopping to examine any remaining traces of him she could find. She remembered his hearty laugh, the way his lips curled into an irresistible smile, and the cracks of blue lightning that sparked through his eyes. But he was gone, and she was painfully aware that their shared moments were finite, her longing for them growing ever stronger as days stretched on.

Seth was met with a rapturous chorus of rejoicing when he approached the gates of Heaven. The angels sang out his name in joyous celebration, and the souls of the saved clapped their hands in jubilation. Even the archangels seemed to understand the pain and longing that bound Seth to his earthly wife and showed him compassion, as if they mourned her loss right alongside him.

As Seth made his way through the entrance, he was overwhelmed by a sense of peace and joy. There is no sadness in Heaven, after all. Yet, as he stepped forward, the reality of Topaz's struggles on Earth without him lingered in his mind, only being comforted by the knowledge that Topaz was a badass and could get through anything, even Hell.

Seth was assigned to work in Heaven on souls who still needed growth or had yet to reach their spiritual journeys. No matter how hard he tried to focus on his job, Topaz's memory kept creeping back in. Not thinking of her was an effort as fruitless as trying not to breathe. For Seth, even in paradise, the thought of her was inescapable.

Topaz finally pulled herself together so she could check on the coven. Although she sensed all was fine, at least in that moment, she needed to see her witches. Topaz trudged slowly up the path to Molly's house, dreading what she would find. She pulled open the door, and Molly was leaning against the wall with her arms crossed. "It's about damn time; you've been missing sessions," she joked. Topaz entered, hung her head low, and began to explain, but Molly shrugged it off, she was only giving her a hard time.

Topaz nervously began to explain what had happened, but before she could finish, Molly interjected. "I know," she said as she took in a deep breath. When Seth rescued her from danger, he allowed her to read his thoughts, and she'd known of his impending visit. Which is exactly why the coven did not disturb her during that time. Molly shared with them that Topaz was with her soulmate.

Molly's voice rose as she exclaimed with a smile: "Everyone kept asking after you and wanted to know where in the Devil's domain you'd gone! We have been anxiously awaiting answers!" Topaz grinned mischievously and replied, "In Hell, lit-er-ally," she said, said slowly. Molly gasped in surprise as Izzy and Amira pulled up to the curb, alighting from Izzy's car like two flaming emissaries from the underworld. They *knew* Topaz finally had come out of hiding.

The two of them stood outside the door, their anticipation mounting. Topaz grabbed the handle and swung it open with a flourish. Her friends rushed her, arms wide in an open embrace, their faces alight with joy. As they settled in for tea, the other witches trickled through Molly's door to see Topaz.

Topaz described her time in Hell in vivid detail—from the giant pits of fire to the slimy dungeons full of souls all screaming for mercy, the heat, the smell—Topaz left no detail out as she shared her experience. The witches listened in rapt attention, their eyes wide and faces lit up with curiosity. Even the non-believers among them were enthralled by Topaz's story, recognizing that her own perspective was what shaped her experience.

Amira gasped in awe, her eyes growing wider with each new piece of information. Molly quickly grabbed Topaz and motioned to the transfixed expression on Amira's face. The witches cackled wildly as Amira hugged herself tightly, wrapping the blanket tighter around her body. Despite their teasing, she couldn't contain her shock and delight at the story they were telling. A hearty laugh escaped from her throat as she exclaimed, "I love story time!"

Topaz's grin quickly faded from her face as the memories of Hell flooded her mind. She winced at the sheer heat radiating from every crevice and shuddered as she recalled the echoing screams and sobs emanating from below. Her stomach turned at the thought of the despair that filled the humid air, and she shook her head in disbelief at the seemingly endless pits of flame and dark smoke that stretched out to infinity. Reliving the moment was stressful, but she played it off with jokes, comparing Hell to almost being as hot as Texas in July. In that moment, the witches could relate, having lived in Texas now for many years.

Topaz's voice raised higher; her expressive face held deep emotion as she described the vivid beauty of the demonesses. The witches were captivated and hung onto her words with morbid curiosity and held their breath in awe while Topaz spoke of the exquisite allure of these demonic beauties, created from Satan's own will for personal pleasure and service.

Eyes widened in disbelief at the thought of such beauty existing among a realm of gruesome demons crafted solely for war. Topaz shared her assumption that these beautiful monstrosities served no other purpose than to bring pleasure and servitude to the beasts and, of course, Satan himself. In stark contrast, the rest of Hell's inhabitants—fallen angels, other demonic entities, and the damned—served a purpose to Beelzebub solely for war and destruction. Entities Satan created to lure humans into a life of turmoil while defending Satan and the vast kingdom of Hell.

Topaz shuddered as she recalled the horrors of Hell, but what she saw next left her breathless. She could feel the peace of Heaven's light beaming down from above, and with a gasp of wonder, she saw the souls ascend to the gates in a flurry of joy and bliss. Even from where she stood, a lifetime away, the power of Heaven was overwhelming and filled her heart with hope.

She waxed poetically about the beauty and tranquility of the Kingdom of Heaven. When those she had rescued stepped into this realm of absolution, they were ecstatic and changed forever. Helping God's people who had been taken to Hell gave Topaz more joy and satisfaction than anything else in her life—a satisfaction that could only be rivaled if she and Seth had lived the life they were intended to.

The sun had long since set when the other witches left, but Izzy and Amira lingered with Topaz. Molly crossed her arms and leaned back in her chair. "So," she began with a sly grin, "tell us about your time with the stud." Amira erupted into laughter as Izzy chimed in, her voice rising high and loud, "YEAH *girrrlll.* Molly told us you were hooking up and we had to leave you alone. We know what you were doing!" Topaz's cheeks flushed crimson as they teased her.

Molly sneered at Topaz as she jeered the question, her voice booming through the air and echoing off the walls of the room. "Well, come on then, tell us," she spat. "Is your angel man hung like a stallion?" The other ladies cackled with glee as they waited for an answer from Topaz, taunting her and daring her to speak truthfully about her time with Seth.

Topaz smiled slyly, telling her friends to draw their own conclusions about her experience from the previous nights. Amira sat silently, her eyes sparkling mischievously like she had something to say but kept it to herself. Topaz kept it classy, to their disappointment; they were all about the smut talk.

They hounded Topaz, trying to get the scoop on her fantastical time with a heavenly creature. Topaz eventually recounted the nights spent with him, the wild passion of their sweaty bodies as they danced and their whispered conversations that filled her heart with an electric thrill. For Topaz, the serenity of being in his arms was like a drug, numbing her to reality and transporting her to a magical realm beyond our own. She held the details to herself but shared her blissful time with Seth with the ladies who were so happy for her.

Molly let out a booming laugh as she joked about big ole ding dongs in Heaven. Izzy followed suit, cackling with deep, throaty laughter. Amira stayed quiet, her lips spread into a thin line, her eyes darting around the room as if she was searching for something clever to add to the conversation. "ICK!" she finally squealed, sticking her tongue out of her mouth and scrunching up her nose. Izzy doubled over in hysterics at Amira's overly animated gesture. Amira met Topaz's gaze and tilted her head upwards slightly. "Men just aren't my thing," Amira stated matter-of-factly.

Molly and Izzy exchanged telltale glances before directing their attention to Amira. She sighed as realization washed over her face. She had been planning on coming out, but Molly and Izzy already knew. "Oh, so this was going to be my big coming out moment to y'all, and you all already knew?" she asked with amusement in her voice, her eyes twinkling with laughter.

"Did Topaz out me?" She turned to Topaz, who was rising from her seat. "Never! I would never betray your trust like that," Topaz said solemnly. "That's your news to share, not my own. I would never share your private thoughts or gossip about you. I am no grackle." Topaz assured Amira she could be trusted.

Molly and Izzy exchanged a knowing glance before confirming that no one told them, but they were thankful she chose to share her truth with them. The four witches had an unspoken, tangible connection between them, and secrets were hard to hide with a bond like theirs.

Molly's gaze softened as she made her way to the kitchen for another cup of coffee, shaking her head at herself before mumbling, "My life would be so much simpler if I liked women instead of men." Amira winced, her eyes flashing with indignation as she snarled, "You'd think so, but women can be as downright impossible and equally as frustrating as men!" Her voice rang through the room as they all agreed and giggled, knowing that they and all people were all difficult in their own ways.

Amira rolled her eyes as she told the other ladies about her short-lived fling. She had grown fond of the girl, but when she stayed over at Amira's place, she'd leave with her stuff—like the denim jacket she borrowed on a cool morning, Amira's favorite t-shirt, and even a pair of new sneakers. "I don't care how cute she is; that bitch isn't coming back into my house," Amira muttered under her breath as she got annoyed thinking about the girl.

Izzy suggested to Amira, "Just ask her to return the items?" But Amira snarled with a disdainful smirk. "Nah, she knows she took my stuff, so I put a hex on her instead. Take my stuff and suffer the consequences," she growled sinisterly. "Her mustache is coming in thick now. Once she returns my items, it will wane again." Amira was a master of passive-aggressive revenge, much like Izzy was. No confrontations, just swift and silent justice—all done with humor and cheekiness, of course.

"I just don't have the energy to invest in anything romantic right now," Amira shared as she expressed how little time she had to give to another person. She felt her life was so busy that taking even a few minutes for herself seemed like an impossible task. "You should make time for yourself. Life is too short not to enjoy it," Izzy replied. Amira agreed and realized she needed to make more effort to find time for family, love, and her true love—magic.

The group of friends were ecstatic to be reunited, but their joy was quickly overshadowed by the anger Topaz felt when they shared news of the demonic visitors. Topaz's face contorted in anger as they told her about the nightmarish ordeal they faced in her home, followed by the fear that filled Izzy's house as Kezziah wailed in terror from her crib. In a tense silence, they recounted their harrowing experiences while she was away, battling through Hell.

It was during that conversation that Amira confided some more upsetting news. Utter terror descended on the witches as Amira told them of Miguel's maddening nightmares—images of terrible creatures with horrifying faces and claws that seemed to torment him night after night, a lingering side effect of his demonic possession. Topaz could feel her muscles tense, and her heart raced in anger as she listened to the stories of the supernatural forces that had invaded their lives.

Miguel trembled as he told Amira of the witch tapping on his window at night. He could no longer contain his fear and pleaded with Amira to let him sleep in her room on the floor instead of his own. Although she welcomed him into her bed, she felt a heavy sensation that there was more to Miguel's terror than just a malicious spirit haunting him; something deeper and darker had taken control of him. His behavior became erratic and unpredictable; it seemed as though he desired the chaos that once possessed his mind and body.

Amira shared, in fear and awe, that she observed how Miguel began interacting with dark forces. She told the ladies how the winds seemed to rise at Miguel's command, each gust showering him with a flurry of leaves that swirled around his figure, lingering close like devoted admirers. Even with her trepidation, she could see how their attentiveness empowered him, his head held high in proud defiance of the elements. Slowly but surely, Miguel began to crave their presence, even as they continued to harry him. Amira could feel the evilness that still lingered around him now.

Topaz's heart raced as she sensed the sinister presence of Ramona lurking near Miguel, looking for any opportunity to invade his dreams and haunt him during the day. She could feel the demons lurking nearby, their malicious intent radiating off them like a cold chill. They seemed to sense his weakness and desperation, knowing full well that he was no match for demonic possession. Even with her strongest protection charms, Topaz couldn't stop the darkness from creeping closer to Miguel with every passing hour. Although he was young, he was old enough for free will, and he seemed to now welcome the power he felt when they engaged him.

Topaz had an ominous feeling. She knew in her gut that Ramona was lurking in the shadows, slowly making her way to Miguel in his dream state. No matter how hard they tried to keep them at bay, she and her cronies would relentlessly stalk the boy, waiting for any sign of vulnerability that they could use to possess him and take advantage of his gifts. He was too old now for Topaz to defend; he had free will, and the hard part was that he was welcoming his sinister visitors, making it that much harder for Topaz to keep them at bay. She could not force Miguel to want peace.

That night, Topaz cast a powerful safety spell on Miguel but cautioned sternly—it was up to Miguel to choose his own destiny. His will could not be bound or coerced, no matter the power of their magic spells; he would have to decide his own path, and that filled Amira with fear and dread.

Amira's unease around Miguel grew, dreading the power and magic he coveted. She could feel their presence lingering in her blind spots, hidden from her view but ever present in his life. At that time, she didn't realize that the more she became too busy to spend time practicing white magic, her blind spots grew. Amira became so distracted in her everyday routines, that she unknowingly made it easier for the witch and demoniacs to draw Miguel closer to their realm without her noticing.

Izzy was certain that Topaz had used not only a safety spell but another powerful magic to ensure Amira and her family's safety. Soon enough, an opportunity arose that took them far away from the state of Texas. Izzy felt strongly that Topaz had also cast a spell to send Amira away in order to protect her from harm.

The other witches in the coven agreed with this assumption: Topaz deeply cared for Amira and wanted her to have a peaceful life on Earth, watching over her brother and living peacefully with no fear. Though it was not stated openly, Topaz had willingly sacrificed her own desires by teaching Amira the ways of magic in exchange for Miguel's security. Topaz only hoped Miguel would resist the urge to surround himself with the power of dark magic.

Topaz and the coven ached with emptiness as Amira left, but they knew it was for the best. She had to go protect Miguel, no matter what the cost. As Amira settled into her new life, the witches felt themselves falling into a strange limbo. After years of being together constantly, distance began its cold embrace on them all. Even with Topaz, their conversations between her and Amira slowly dwindled away until there were only occasional brief phone calls in lieu of their daily contact—a reminder that time does not stand still even for the closest of friends, though the memories linger in emotion-filled silences.

No matter how far away or how much time passes, the bond between friends remains strong. Each thought of them, every missed moment, serves to strengthen the ties that bind them together in a way that cannot be broken by distance or time. Though far apart, the witches always thought of Amira.

Amira's chest ached with an intense longing for her beloved friends and her favorite state—Texas. The pain of losing her father a year after her family's move was still fresh in her mind. Gloria refused to leave the cemetery where she laid her husband to rest. The heaviness weighed on Amira like a blanket of dread, knowing that the right thing would be to keep them settled in their new life despite the tugging of her heartstrings to go back to Texas with the coven. Miguel was doing his best to come to terms with life without their father, but Gloria was deeply rooted in the cemetery, refusing to move away from her beloved husband's grave, and so... they stayed.

Time seemed to be slipping away faster and faster. The saying is true: days are long, but months and years are short. Amira had been gone for a long while. She was remembered fondly by her coven every day, though things had not been the same since she left. A few months after her departure, a young man from India named Devansh joined the coven, a highly gifted young man who brought with him an abundance of energy and enthusiasm. His grandfather and father worked with Topaz on a few occasions, so he was immediately taken into the coven with open arms.

Devansh's arrival was welcomed with open arms, as if he had always been a part of the family. He was 5'9", with bronzed skin that seemed to shimmer in the sunlight and dark, curly hair. His soft hair fell gently across his forehead, and his gorgeous, light maple eyes made the hearts of ladies his age race with excitement. His mouth— those lips—he had a dashing smile that turned serious when he spoke of magical matters.

Every now and then, Devansh would grow out his facial hair during the cooler months just to provoke the witches in the coven to swoon and compliment him—a reaction from the ladies that delighted him. He knew his beard made him look mature and devilishly handsome. They thought of him as a younger brother, and he considered each of them his sisters in magic.

Devansh had always returned to India in the summers after graduating from college, and he did so again after several years of being a part of the coven of white magic. But this year it was different. His father had fallen ill, slowly but surely succumbing to a disease that would take him from this world. He wanted to say goodbye to his family; he wanted to be with his mother, father, and sisters one last time. Devansh was so entwined with the heart of the coven that they grieved for him tremendously when he left.

Devansh's heart ached as he left the coven. The idea of not practicing magic with them made him feel like a part of his soul was slowly ripping away. He reveled in the way they openly shared spells, each member helping one another sharpen their skills; it was a true bond that had developed between them. But most of all, he would miss Topaz, who had taken him under her wing and adored him like a younger brother, much in the way she thought of Victor as being her brother too.

As Devansh left for India, Topaz felt the loss keenly. She missed his jokes and teasing—that special brand of affectionate torment that only he could get away with. Topaz cherished both his skill as a pupil and his teasing nature. He was the only one who could get away with riling up Topaz, but now he was gone—and things would not be the same.

As Topaz and the rest of the coven tried to carry on without Devansh, they found that something essential was missing from their meetings. Weeks before he left, Topaz began having recurring nightmares of ominous crows circling overhead, watching as one member after another drifted away from their tight-knit group. She knew instinctively that it was time for everyone to start going their separate ways—first Victor, then Amira, and finally Devansh. The sense of loss weighed on her heart like a stone anchor, but she knew there was no turning back.

Nothing lasts forever. Some relationships run their course, and people move along. Topaz knew their time together was drawing closer to an end. Sad as it may be, nothing lasts forever. Some of the witches would still practice magic in solitude as they focused on their families. The other witches would move on to other covens.

Topaz's heart ached with a deep pain that had become her

constant companion in the years since Seth had gone. With each breath she drew, a reminder of what she'd lost and what was yet to come resounded through her. She knew time was running out before she would have to bid farewell to this world, wondering if she would ever see Seth before that time came again.

The ravages of time seemed powerless against Topaz. Year after year, she retained her beauty with a strict regime of exercise, clean eating, and daily meditation. She kept her body lean and her mind sharp, so that even through the years, she glowed with an ageless radiance. Though the ladies accused her of keeping beautiful through the magic of witchcraft as a joke, it was mostly good genetics.

Topaz felt a heavy sense of dread creep in—the weight of an unseen task looming ahead. She tossed and turned as the nightmares took hold, crows flying away into a burning, flame-streaked sky. The dreams became more real with each passing night, her body wracked with fear and anticipation until exhaustion finally pulled her down into a dreamless sleep. She had a gut feeling that something was lurking in the near future.

An electric chill coursed through Topaz's veins as a distant voice called to her from the heavens. Her heart skipped a beat as she realized that the archangels would soon be summoning her once again, and with it came a sensation of anticipation that chilled her bones. As the silence lingered, the abyssal weight of their call closed in around her, but even more haunting was that she knew death was impending for one of her beloveds.

THE HARD GOODBYE

opaz had a looming dread hovering over her every time she thought of Molly. She kept having visions of her beloved friend soaring away with the crows that had been haunting her nights. Nudging and prodding, Topaz eventually convinced Molly to go to the doctor, despite her reluctance. Every time Molly tried to change the subject or roll her eyes, Topaz persisted in her hounding.

Molly's heart pounded with fear as the truth of her sickness loomed in front of her. She was the oldest witch in the coven and thought she knew better than to face her illness, but even she could not ignore Topaz's urgings to go to the doctor. Molly had no choice but to face the music, as each step that brought her closer to getting a diagnosis felt like a death sentence. Finally, the words of her ailment were spoken, confirming what Molly feared: she was very ill.

Molly had endured months of grueling treatments, but no matter how hard she fought, her health wasn't improving. Her veins were bruised from the countless needles and her skin sallow from lack of nutrition. She told Topaz it was time to stop—that pumping poison into her body only prolonged her agony. Together, with Molly's family, they made the agonizing decision to end treatment.

Molly decided to forgo the medications and treatments from her doctor, instead opting to live out her remaining days peacefully at home. Topaz tried all her best spells and healing rituals but was ultimately unsuccessful in reversing Molly's slow decline. Deep down, she knew that no amount of magic could counteract the inevitable: death was coming for her friend, and there was nothing she could do to stop it. As Molly's days began to dwindle, she gathered her closest friends at home for tea and small talk, trying to create as many memories as possible before the end arrived.

Molly's small frame was wracked with occasional spasms as she slept, and her voice would suddenly erupt in a ragged cry of "RAMONA!" that echoed through the room. Molly wasn't having nightmares about her, but Ramona was always right there at the top of her mind. Molly's worries grew more intense, fear of how her family and friends would cope without her pressing down on her heavily—especially about Amira and her family. As Molly's condition worsened, her worries about leaving her family behind intensified, though Topaz attempted to soothe them away by reminding her not to waste what precious moments she had left on pointless fretting.

Topaz sat patiently by Molly's bed, shushing away the fears when they threatened to overwhelm her beloved friend and taking care not to let desperation steal away Molly's last moments of life. Topaz would get comfortable in an armchair next to Molly's bed and open a book. Molly enjoyed Topaz reading to her. With each word, Molly would drift further away from the cares of adulthood, and Topaz could see her relax into a childlike peace.

When Molly was awake, Topaz would brew her favorite tea with milk and two sugars. Topaz would paint her friend's fingernails and toenails bright pinks and purples while she hummed soft lullabies. Through it all, Topaz never left Molly's side.

Molly slid further and further away from consciousness, her breathing growing shallower and slower. She would always murmur Amira's name, as if she could sense an invisible danger in the air. Through hazy vision, Molly could just make out the figure of the witch hovering over Amira's family like an ominous cloud. Even in her final moments, the witch's haunting presence lingered in Molly's mind.

Topaz often thought of the witch and her involvement with the occult. The witch had been a thorn in their side for years, but Topaz was forbidden to interfere with her free will. She longed to talk to the witch and persuade her to abandon Satanic rituals, but Ramona was too deep into the occult. On multiple occasions, the witch invited dark spirits to inhabit her body as she and other black-hooded cultists praised Satan.

Topaz began teaching Amira the shielding rituals, patiently guiding her through each step until she felt comfortable with their use. Topaz started with the basics, teaching Amira how to project a shield of protection from the witch's spells. She showed her the proper rituals, making sure she could recite each phrase correctly and didn't forget any details. "It must be you to protect your family now," Topaz claimed gravely, warning of the witch's presence lingering—waiting for an opportunity to break through Amira's defenses. Amira lived so far away now, and the distance did help. Out of sight, out of mind. The witches hoped the witch would find someone more convenient to latch onto.

Amira, no longer having help of her mother, Gloria, to guard against the witch, had to be up to the task alone now. Gloria had become withdrawn after her husband's death. A part of her seemed to have wilted away permanently, as if she wanted nothing more than to lay down beside him and wait for death. It was up to Amira to protect Miguel and Gloria now, and this gnawed at Molly on her deathbed.

Molly stirred in her bed as beads of sleet drummed against the windowpane. She opened her eyes to see her best friend, Topaz, curled up next to her, providing warmth and comfort. The room was dimly lit by a small lamp, which cast shadows on the walls. As if sensing her pain, Topaz leaned into Molly's touch, offering comfort and support. The room was quiet except for the rustling of sheets and the pattering of raindrops.

Molly let out a deep sigh, exhaustion etched across her face as she fought to get comfortable in the bed. Despite the warmth provided by Topaz's presence, she shivered from the cold that seeped into their humble abode.

As she lay there, listening to the sound of winter raging outside, she knew that Topaz would be there for her every step of the way, offering solace amid her suffering. The thought gave her some degree of peace as she drifted off into a fitful sleep.

Molly had been trudging through the same routines for weeks, her eyes bleary and dull. But one morning, the sun came up, and Molly awoke with a startling clarity—her brain alight with inspiration with an eagerness she hadn't felt in months.

Topaz was still asleep in her chair, hunched over Molly's bed as she had been every night. Molly gently moved Topaz's long hair that fell across her face as she slept peacefully so she could look at her sweet face. Molly watched her with admiration. Despite being admitted to the hospital and then placed in hospice care, Molly never felt alone with Topaz by her side every night. The quiet of the winter storm brought Molly comfort as she became lost in her own thoughts, listening to the sound of ice pellets tapping on the glass.

Molly found a strange solace in the sound of Topaz's breaths in between the beeps of the monitors. She listened to the melody of winter for hours on end, feeling grateful for every moment she had left, and watched as the sleet hit the window like tiny pebbles, clinging to the glass before being washed away by the cold rain.

Molly watched as the sunrays through the window illuminated Topaz's sleeping face. She softly touched her shoulder, and Topaz stirred, slowly raising her head and blinking her eyes to adjust to the light. When she saw Molly alert and looking at her, with her lips curved into a warm smile, Topaz returned the smile, letting out a content sigh.

Molly raised her arm and pointed to the wall behind Topaz. Swallowing hard, Topaz slowly turned her head in the direction Molly had indicated. When she saw what Molly was pointing to, a heavy feeling settled deep in the pit of her stomach.

Topaz stared at the wall clock, its hands spinning steadily and silently. She knew what Molly was trying to tell her without saying a word: it was time for her to go. Topaz could feel the salty tears stinging her throat as she tried to hold back the sob that threatened to escape.

Topaz tried to steady her breath, trying to calm the swirling emotions inside her. A lump formed in her throat, and she steeled herself against the tears that threatened to surface. She tried to remain stoic but could feel her heart racing. Her throat felt tight, making it difficult to express what she wanted to say. Saying goodbye to Molly was like saying goodbye to a part of herself—a best friend, a confidante, a sister in magic... her soul sister.

Molly's chest heaved gently with her labored breaths, each one weaker than the last. Topaz caressed her forehead and softly ran her fingertips over Molly's closed eyelids. Her voice cracked, and her chin quivered as she whispered, "It's time for you to find peace; it's time for you to let go, Molly." With one last rattling gasp, Molly exhaled her final breath.

Devansh sent his condolences to the family and the coven, his heart heavy from not being able to say goodbye in person. He wanted to travel to Molly's home and pay his respects but was unable to; his mother had been stricken with a stroke, and he was needed at her bedside. Despite being miles away, mourning washed over him like an ocean filled with sorrow.

Amira arrived in town, feeling the weight of the years between her and her dearest friends. She had come for a funeral, yet with each step forward, she wished to turn back time and savor the moments she'd missed with them. As she remembered the good times they shared, regret cut through her like an icy blade, reminding her how much time had passed away.

As Amira trudged through the cemetery, her steps were punctuated by short bursts of air and tears that left a salty trail on her cheeks. She could feel tears stinging her eyes as she hugged the necks of her closest friends, her tiny body shaking with suppressed sobs. But when she embraced Topaz, a guttural sound erupted from deep within her, and all the emotions and pain burst out uncontrollably.

As they embraced, the tears cascading down their faces clashed like a raging river as their shaking bodies clung to each other. Amira emitted a harrowing wail that practically shook the very foundation of the cemetery. Deathly silence was pierced by her plea for Molly not to be left alone in her grave. Amira could not stand the idea of her dear Molly being alone in the cold cemetery in the dark of night. Her sobs echoed across the graveyard, her anguish tearing her apart from within.

The knowledge that Molly's body was six feet underground, deteriorating alone in the cold darkness of the grave, caused Amira's heartbeat to quicken with sorrow. The pain of losing someone she loved consumed her like wildfire, burning through every bone and sinew until all that remained was an empty shell. Amira never could handle death well—every flicker of lifelessness reminded her of her father's passing, which still weighed heavy on her soul. With a heavy heart, Amira tried to reconcile with the fact that Molly was gone forever, never to return.

The coven gathered around the firepit in a quiet circle as the stars shone their silent vigil in Topaz's backyard. They gathered in a sorrowful silence, shrouded in darkness, on the night of the funeral. The atmosphere hummed with sadness and despair as they remembered the loss of Molly, whose life had been so deeply woven into theirs. The ladies clasped their hands together as the night wind rustled through the trees and carried with it memories of Molly's laughter and warmth. Tears welled up in everyone's eyes as their hearts ached as though they were their own soul being taken away. They spend time together, remembering the good times—grateful for one last opportunity to say goodbye.

Molly's deathly disease ravaged her frail body, sending the witches into a debilitating state of helplessness. No magical incantation, invocation or enchantment could combat the force of death; it brought them all to their knees with its power. Death was a humbling force that could not be subjugated by any of their powers. Death was not only the inevitable end but also a reminder of their own mortality.

As many of the witches bid their final goodbyes, Amira just stood there with a sour disposition as she watched them go. Izzy, of course, stayed with her at Topaz's house into the early morning hours. Topaz, usually stoic in the face of death, was visibly shaken by this one and quickly retreated to her room. Despite her best efforts to keep it together, the walls echoed with her cries for what felt like an eternity as she mourned into her pillow.

Izzy and Amira talked for hours like two old friends, lost in the depths of conversation. Izzy watched on with disbelief as she saw all the changes Amira had gone through over the years. Her silky hair now cascaded down her back, her face contour had sharpened and strengthened with age, and Izzy was now talking to someone who had grown from a young woman into a mature woman. Time seemed to stand still as they chatted and laughed, remembering their past together.

Amira's curiosity was palpable as she asked Izzy about Kezziah. Izzy pulled out photographs of the vibrant young girl that Amira barely recognized—she was already in school with pigtails tied up and a backpack on her shoulders. Amira felt a deep disappointment that so much time had passed between them; all the phone calls in the world couldn't replace a hug or face-to-face conversation. She wanted to see Kezziah in person, to hug her and hear her laughter echoing through the room. Amira felt saddened by the realization that Kezziah was very little when she left and would have no memory of her other than being the lady on the other end of the phone her mom spoke with occasionally.

Izzy leaned in and whispered, her voice low and conspiratorial. She recounted how Topaz had come to Kezziah's aid when her schoolteacher began harassing her, causing Kezziah to have nightmares of slithering pythons. With the deft manipulation of shadow magic, Topaz entered Kezziah's mind to observe the situation firsthand, discovering that the teacher possessed knowledge of forbidden magic taught to Topaz by their other beloved and belated friend, Victor.

The teacher's eyes glowed with suspicion as he studied Kezziah, sensing her family's connection to the realm of magic. He pestered her relentlessly at school with questions and accusations, driving Kezziah into a state of fear and unease. At night, his words echoed in her mind like howling winds, invading her dreams until she felt claustrophobic from his suffocating presence.

Izzy's voice rose in volume and intensity, her words like a shot of adrenaline into Amira. "Topaz insisted that Kezziah had to be brave and take control of her dreams—and she did! She seized that enormous python with both hands, despite the weight of his dragging her down and hundreds of pounds of writhing scales and hissing fury. Nothing could break Kezziah's iron grip on that beast!"

Izzy went on to explain that as Kezziah lay, sleeping, her mind was soaring into an ethereal realm. The looming presence of the schoolteacher cast a sinister shadow over her subconscious. The teacher threatened to overtake her soul or end her life if she did not stand against him.

Topaz lurked in the deepest crevices of Kezziah's subconscious, beckoning her to take action. She clenched her fists and felt the power of Topaz course through her veins as the serpent rose from the ground and looked into her eyes. Kezziah's eyes burned bright with an inner fire as Topaz whispered chants and Kezziah began repeating them, commanding the serpent to obey her or she would have no choice but to destroy him. During Kezziah's dream, the python hissed, thrashed, and writhed in agony until his death filled her hands with his lifeless body in her hands.

Izzy's words were like a thunderclap when she told Amira the chilling news that Kezzi's teacher had died in his sleep of a heart attack! Amira's eyes widened with shock, yet she couldn't believe that she had missed out on such an important event. With a bitter smirk, she joked about how the teacher should have known better than to trifle with Kezziah, a godchild of the most feared witch around—Topaz. After the schoolteacher passed away, Topaz finally revealed his true identity. The teacher was the young son of the witch whom Victor's mother had slain so many years ago in Peru.

Izzy and Amira discussed Isaiah's disdain for magic. Kezziah had grown to obey her father's wishes, erasing any traces of the magical arts from her life—even simple blessings were now off-limits. Topaz nodded in agreement with Isaiah's decision. Topaz explained to Izzy that it was Isaiah's right as a parent to shape his children's beliefs, and so Izzy respected that and kept magic away from Kezziah. Amira agreed that magic was something that needed to be approached with caution, only if both parents had given their consent and the student had a genuine interest in it.

Izzy's brow furrowed with worry as her thoughts raced about the potential damage Ramona—or even another sinister witch—could do to her beloved daughter if they sensed her magic. Izzy was in agreement with Isaiah and Topaz but still cast protective spells on Kezziah. Although Kezziah didn't feel inclined to learn magic, Izzy reasoned there were dangers out there that warranted protection, so she worked the spells in secret.

Amira concurred and said she still worked strong magic around Miguel, even though he seemed hell-bent on rebelling. She shared that she had been struggling with Miguel and recalled how she worked protective spells, despite Miguel thirsting for knowledge of dark, underground magic.

Amira and Izzy tiptoed into Topaz's room and found her fast asleep, tears drying on her pillow. Her face was pale and her breathing heavy, evidence of the months of stress she had endured by Molly's side. Amira bent down to press a kiss to her cheek, and Izzy carefully tucked the blanket around her figure before slowly turning off the lamp. They stole out of the room, leaving silence as Topaz's only companion.

Amira's deepening anxiety for Miguel seemed to take over the conversation, dominating her words as they delved further into her own family life. Amira's words seemed to become heavier, more desperate, until dawn threatened to break over the horizon. Amira and Izzy conversed until the first golden rays of dawn illuminated the sky. Amira realized how Izzy helped her relieve her worry about Molly slumbering alone on her first night buried in the cemetery.

The ladies stood in the sunlit kitchen, with Amira pouring coffee from a ceramic pot into two mugs. The fragrant aroma of freshly brewed coffee filled the kitchen as Amira spoke in hushed tones of her concern for Miguel, now an adult. He had taken up with a young woman named Lupe. But Amira didn't trust Lupe's intentions, suspecting that Miguel was clinging to her as he grieved another woman who had broken his heart. It bothered Amira that she couldn't read Lupe's thoughts. She was very strong, and she, too, seemed gifted with magic and was very mysterious.

Izzy's eyes lit up as she suggested having Topaz do a reading in her practice room. Amira nodded her head, but inside she seethed. She couldn't believe Lupe had talked Miguel into moving near her family in Mexico; the thought of Miguel being closer to Ramona made her stomach turn. Lupe was pregnant and wanted her family nearby, but Amira wished there could be another solution.   Lupe had spent years studying to become a teacher, working hard to earn her teaching credentials, and wanted to become a schoolteacher after her child was born. She always dreamed of becoming an elementary teacher in her hometown, so she insisted on going back home to Mexico. Lupe was eager to have Miguel take over the family business since her father's physical health had begun to rapidly decline. So, Miguel would oversee the lumber mill and three hardware stores. They had their plan in place, and Amira was in no way going to be able to stand in their way.

The only comfort to Amira was that Gloria agreed to go until the baby was born, so at least Miguel would have Gloria with him. Although Gloria didn't want to be so far away from her husband's grave, she knew she needed to be with Miguel and the baby. Like Amira, Gloria was fearful for Miguel to be so close to Ramona. Ramona was never far from any of their thoughts.

Izzy admitted that she sensed the presence of demons and shadows nearby; she was sure it was Ramona scouting out her and

Kezziah. Topaz would cleanse the house with sage and salt, driving away any negative energy, yet Izzy felt like the monsters were always lurking in some way. She had a sixth sense for when the witch was attempting to observe them.

The comforting sounds of Izzy humming as she prepared breakfast floated in from the kitchen woke Topaz from her much-needed deep sleep. The three ladies ate breakfast in comfortable silence, enjoying each other's company. When they finished, Izzy got up to leave, but Amira lingered on the sofa. She did not ask for a reading; instead, Amira put her head in Topaz's lap so she would play with her hair. Topaz hummed softly as her fingers ran through her sweet Amira's hair. As Amira began to nod off to sleep, Topaz kissed her forehead and smiled down at her.

Amira knew it was time to go home after a few hours' rest. Though she had found success in her nursing career after departing Texas, she began to feel the longing to return home and reunite with her dear friends if Gloria were to remain in Mexico with Miguel. Amira felt a tug of war between her professional life and the life that seemed so inviting back home. Although, being a nurse, she knew she could easily find a new job without any trouble.

Amira worked around the clock at her job, and despite the exhausting hours, she felt a change would be beneficial. She had friends that were accepting of her and unaware of her craft, so she never mentioned it to them. As free time was scarce, and not a single person was willing to help her hone her magical skills, magic plummeted down her list of priorities. I sympathized with Amira, knowing there was a possibility of something lurking around the corner but dismissing it because she was feeling safe, slipping into the distractions of everyday life.

Izzy's questions served only as a reminder that if she ever let her guard down, there would be consequences. Despite this danger, Amira lied to Topaz about her progress with magic, assuring her she was still working protection spells. She lied to Topaz and lied to herself even more. Topaz felt Amira was being dishonest—something she had free will to do of course, but Topaz was so grief-stricken about Molly, she didn't press Amira about her doubt.

Amira clinched her mouth, trying unsuccessfully to suppress a flood of tears as she drove. Dearest Amira was consumed—

overwhelmed—with grief at Molly's death. Dark thoughts of Miguel and Ramona crept into her mind and sent her heart racing. The pang of stress was undeniable. With every mile, she felt resentment rising like molten lava in her throat, each fleeting thought of Miguel doing what she explicitly asked him not to do, sparking an ever-increasing rage within her.

Amira knew she was running out of options and time. Topaz could be an answer, but Lupe stirred even deeper uneasiness within her. Lupe's unexpected pregnancy had altered the course of everyone's lives, and she was determined to move to Mexico with Miguel. Amira knew there was no way he wouldn't go.

Quitting her job to go with them was not a viable option—house payments, car payments, and bills needed to be taken care of—yet she felt like she should be with them. But she had not been invited, and Amira could feel Lupe's dislike for her. The feeling was mutual.

Amira felt that Miguel, although barely an adult now, needed protection. Gloria faced a similar internal battle, with which Amira could easily identify. The thought of staying behind while they ventured off filled her with overwhelming frustration, yet there seemed to be no clear solution.

As Amira trudged along her interminable commute, Topaz lay still at home. Her chest rose and fell heavily with grief in the dimness of her room, and her mind was heavy with exhaustion. Suddenly, she opened her eyes, alert to the world around her. The sounds of stirring next door caused a spark of anticipation within her, and she sat up in bed eagerly as Seth entered the room. His presence was like a balm to her soul. His handsome face and sexy body walking through her bedroom door was something she had longed for every day while they were apart.

Seth quietly entered Topaz's bedroom, his wings dragging against the floorboards. He was a glorious sight to behold; his plush feathers shimmered in the dim light and his powerful muscles shifted with every step. Upon seeing her distraught face, he quickly wrapped his strong arms around her and pulled her into a warm embrace. His protective embrace comforted her and reminded her of all the times in the past when he was there to lift her up when the world seemed so bleak. His very presence gave her a sense of security as she sobbed, and he held her trembling frame close to his body.

Right about the time Seth was consoling Topaz, Izzy awoke with a jolt. She was panting and drenched in sweat. She scanned the room for the source of the disturbance that ripped her from sleep then instantly thought of the dream she was having just before she stirred awake.

Her dream was vivid and terrifying. Swarms of black crows scattered around her yard and filled the air with their haunting cries. One by one, they plummeted from the sky as if pulled by an invisible force in her dream. As each crow struck the ground, it shook and shifted beneath Izzy's feet. She watched in horror as one of the birds fell into a chasm that opened the ground, never to be seen again. Izzy knew that this dream signaled trouble approaching.

Izzy nervously chewed on her fingernail as she dialed Topaz's number. Again and again, she called Topaz without an answer. She hadn't been able to reach her friend all day, and the worry that had begun to gnaw at her gut had grown into full-blown fear. She assumed that Topaz was trying to take her mind off Molly's death by burying herself in her work at the market, but Izzy couldn't help replay her own nightmare over and over in her head. It was a disturbingly vivid reminder that life can be cut short without warning. Izzy decided that if she didn't hear from Topaz within the hour, she would leave Kezziah with her husband and drive over to check on her.

Topaz collapsed into Seth's arms as the phone began to ring. She leaned into his broad chest, letting him hold her tightly as she felt her heart racing inside. He brushed her hair back and kissed her forehead softly, breathing in her sweet scent. With a heavy exhale, Topaz spoke up softly. "Did you help Molly find the light? Did you guide her home to Heaven?" Seth's grip only grew tighter as he searched her eyes for what felt like an eternity before finally releasing her. Topaz stared at him with a mixture of confusion and sadness as he remained silent.

After a few moments, she pulled away from him and searched his face for any sign of an answer. The silence between them was deafening as she waited for him to speak, but he only stared back at her with a pained expression. The ringing of the phone faded into the background as they stayed locked in one another's gaze.

The moment passed quietly between them, until finally, Topaz couldn't take it anymore. "Please," she begged, "I need to know." But Seth remained silent, just looking at Topaz. Finally, after what felt like an eternity, Seth spoke softly. "No," he mumbled, his voice barely audible. Topaz nodded slowly, still searching his face for any hint of an explanation. "I can't find her..." he confessed with a trembling voice.

Desperation shrouded Seth's face as he brushed Topaz's chin with his hand. His heavy words echoed in her ears. "I've looked everywhere for Molly's soul. I can't find her. Everywhere I have searched has led me nowhere, and now I am out of time. I must return to Heaven and pray the archangels can help guide me in my search. You must know something—some place I didn't think of looking. This is an unprecedented situation for me: a soul that I am assigned to guide has vanished." The gravity of the situation seemed to paralyze Topaz. Seth pleaded for ideas. He pleaded desperately as Topaz stood before him in stunned silence.

Topaz's eyes filled with tears as a flood of emotions threatened to overwhelm her. "Molly had a rocky past. Is she in Hell? Is she being punished for all the mistakes she made?" she almost pleaded. Seth took her by the shoulders and looked deep into her quivering eyes; his voice was resolute and sincere. He solemnly promised her that God had sent him to take Molly to Heaven, causing Topaz to exhale a sigh of relief. Even so, Topaz agonized over the thought that perhaps Molly was swiped away by Satan and drug into Hell. Desperately clinging to hope, Seth firmly told her he would find out what happened to Molly and escort her into Heaven.

Seth held Topaz's soft, smooth face in his strong hands and pressed his lips to hers. Her warm breath filled his lungs as he inhaled sharply through his nose. "I love you," he murmured against her lips. They broke apart reluctantly. Seth needed to find Molly, and time was not on their side. Topaz understood. She and Seth both knew the gravity of the situation: Molly had passed away, and her soul was missing. Time was running out to cross her into the light.

Topaz was certain that Molly's beloved parents, devoted husband, and precious infant son, who had sadly passed away shortly after birth, waited for their beloved Molly in Heaven. With a newfound determination, Seth left on a spiritual quest to consult with the archangels so they could provide guidance for him to find and retrieve Molly's soul. As Seth left, with a deep breath and determination, Topaz knew she would need to forge her own path to find Molly—

whatever it may cost her.

THE PRACTICE ROOM

Topaz's heels thudded against the creaky wooden porch as she approached Izzy's front door. She knocked and Izzy's daughter, Kezziah, answered with a grin. The scent of fresh cookies wafted out from the kitchen behind her. "Hey, there, sugar bee," Topaz giggled, her lips curling into a wide smile. "How was your day?"

Kezziah groaned, rolling her eyes dramatically. "Very good, but I just got a lot of homework." Topaz chuckled as she stepped inside and made her way towards the kitchen, looking forward to a few moments of comfort and relaxation with Izzy. Kezziah eagerly skipped into the kitchen after her godmother, Topaz. She was laughing and smiling, her eyes bright with excitement. Topaz chuckled at Kezziah's animated personality and winked at her. "No more issues at school?" she asked with a slight smirk on her face.

"Definitely NOT!" Kezziah exclaimed. "But I did have a dream that has bothered me. You went to a hot place with fires, dungeons, and crocodilians the size of dinosaurs!" A surprised expression crossed Topaz's face before she smiled and shook her head, dismissing Kezziah's nightmare. Kezziah hefted her book bag onto her shoulder as she crossed through the kitchen. She waved goodbye and darted out the door.

Just as Kezziah hurried off, Isaiah walked into the room and hugged Izzy and Topaz. His eyes shifted to the dining table as he shook his head in disapproval of the tarot card deck sitting on the table. "You ladies and your tarot cards," he scoffed as he scooped up a cookie to munch on as he exited the kitchen. As he left the room,

Izzy shook her head at him behind his back. "Mr. Judgey," Topaz picked up the cards and laughed aloud, a merry cackle.

Topaz handed the deck of cards to Izzy. "Shuffle," she demanded as she nibbled on a chocolate chip cookie. Topaz finished the cookie and then reached into her bag, pulling out a box of matches. She struck a match and lit the end of an incense stick, filling the room with a hint of sandalwood. Izzy stopped shuffling the cards, delicately placed them on the table, and leaned forward in anticipation as Topaz took the deck into her hands.

Topaz placed the tarot cards to the side without looking at them. Instead, she looked into Izzy's eyes and said, "I don't need to look at the cards to see that you're having nightmares. Tell me about your dream. I can sense that it has you worried about death." Izzy nervously bit her lip, her hands wringing together in her lap, as she described the nightmare in vivid detail. When she finished, Izzy shot a fearful glance at Topaz. "I know we just lost Molly. Losing her is all I can think about. Could this be why I had that dream, or could this be a warning of another death?"

Topaz cleared her throat. "I need you to come to my home with me later," she whispered, her words feeling stuck in her throat. Izzy shifted on her feet, hesitant but willing to go with Topaz. But something about the way Topaz asked made Izzy uneasy and suspicious; it wasn't like Topaz to be so secretive. Izzy nodded reluctantly, eager to get answers but full of trepidation.

As night encroached, Izzy hastened to meet with Topaz in her practice room, the place where secrets and magic were always safe. Topaz's voice shook as she spoke of her fears for Molly's safety, knowing that Molly would cling to her doll if ever there was danger. Topaz looked up at her with an anxious expression, fear for Molly evident in her worried eyes. "Where is she?" Izzy asked, worried for Molly's soul. Every second began to feel like an eternity as fear clawed at Izzy's insides and worry crept through the shadows.

Topaz reclined on the floor as Izzy lit the candles around her. Topaz sank into a meditative Delta state and began to review some of the most harrowing moments Molly had shared with her, in search of clues to her whereabouts. Her spirit wasn't tucked away in the nightmares either, which is how I escaped the witch and her fiendish monsters that hunted my soul.

Panic welling up in her chest like a venomous flame, Topaz declared, "Seth can't find her anywhere. It's unheard of, and time is escaping us." She was heartsick at the thought of what might have happened to her soul.

Izzy's heart was pounding as she frantically paced around the room, desperately trying to come up with a plan. "Is it possible...?" she began, before shaking her head sharply and looking at Topaz.

Though Seth had said otherwise, the two of them both feared that Molly had been sent to Hell for some unknown reason, unceremoniously written off without ever being granted salvation. Fury surged through Topaz at the thought, but it didn't make any sense. Even Heaven itself couldn't locate Molly. Determined to get to the bottom of things, Topaz knew she had to investigate further.

Izzy attempted to talk Topaz out of her plan, suggesting they wait or rely on Seth for help. But Topaz's brow furrowed, and she shook her head resolutely. She knew time was of the essence and that waiting was not an option.

Topaz and Izzy gathered in a solemn circle inside her practice room. Topaz held her hands over a bowl of holy water that the priest who frequented her market had given to her before she made her way to Izzy's earlier in the day. The ladies began to pray for protection. With each word, the air seemed to thicken and crackle with magic. When Izzy finished, she tipped the bowl over Topaz's head and let the cool liquid cascade down her body, washing away her sins in a sacred ceremony. Once the ritual was complete, Topaz took a deep breath and stilled herself. She softly thanked Izzy for her help before launching into incantations and spells to prepare herself for the journey ahead.

After the ceremony, before leaving for the cavern to meditate away from this world, Topaz sat with Izzy and wrapped her arms around her. Topaz poured a spell of love and protection on her. Reassuring a worried Izzy, "I will be fine," Topaz whispered. Topaz couldn't help but worry about Izzy's safety—even more than she worried about her own fate—as she would be in grave danger hunting for Molly's soul.

Izzy and Topaz steeled themselves against the demons that perpetually haunted their lives. Muscles trembling, they both trudged forward with determination—Izzy to her family home and Topaz into the cavern to prepare for another round of battle against the consuming darkness. Ramona's cruel presence hung heavy in the air as they departed, ominously watching them along with the demons. Satan wanted Topaz's soul more than he had ever wanted anything. Topaz feared that perhaps he was wanting to barter her soul for Molly's—a fear she did not speak aloud.

Topaz cautiously advanced towards the entrance of the cavern, her heart pounding with anticipation. Gloomy shadows danced along its walls while an eerie howl of wolves echoed in the distance. She steeled her nerves and readied herself for yet another agonizing journey to the land of despair—hunting this time for her beloved Molly.

As soon as she crossed the threshold of Hell, she was met with a chaotic battle between monstrous demons. The beasts crashed and collided against one another in frenzied wrath, their razor-sharp claws tearing through the air as they fought for supremacy over one another.

Topaz's entire being tensed as an energy approached in the dark. "It's about damn time, Topaz. I've been waiting here for you!" Molly cried out, her soul rushing towards Topaz's. With no time to spare, Topaz gripped onto Molly's soul and plunged them both into shadows and into the smoldering fires just outside Hell, narrowly avoiding detection. Monstrously colossal demoniacs lumbered into the underworld, their steps shaking the soot beneath them. The two souls stayed hidden in the flames, not daring to move until the demons were out of sight as the beasts entered the pickets of Hell.

Molly rolled her eyes. "You actually thought I went to Hell?"

Topaz took in the sight of Molly, seeing her as a young, vibrant version of herself. The two souls stood in a dark and eerie place just outside of eternity's grasp. The air was thick with the scent of sulfur and ash, and the marshy ground squished beneath their feet.

"And yet here you are?" Topaz asked, utterly confused.

Molly tugged on Topaz's arm and pulled her further away from the entrance of Hell. They huddled together, hiding in the shadows as evil spirits floated around them, searching for any signs of life to snatch into eternal damnation.

As they peered into the abyss, wormholes began to open all around them, revealing glimpses of Earth and other dimensions beyond.

Molly quietly explained, "As my consciousness began to slip away, I experienced a vision of divine clarity. The sensation was serene as I traversed the void and entered this plane. Never before had I encountered such an ethereal dream; it felt like my awareness left my body and joined with a higher power. I can't explain it fully, but as I began my transformation into Heaven, I felt myself transcending into something utterly perfect compared to anything I ever knew here on Earth. Before I reached forward, a nagging feeling in my core stopped me.

"I stopped going towards the light. Instead, I descended into the depths of darkness. Terror welled inside me until a flock of crows rose from their slumber and beckoned me forward. With no other choice in sight, I followed them towards here, the entrance of Satan's abode." Molly tried her best to describe the surreal experience to Topaz.

Molly declared, "I have a deep-seated conviction that I was brought here for you to join me on this path. Though it wasn't Satan's summons that called me here, I can't help but wonder if it was the voice of Heaven instead."

Topaz's mind raced with possibilities, making it hard to focus, as they had to lay low among the smoldering ashes just to remain hidden. Topaz nodded slowly. "I understand," she said. "As you were dying, Uriel sent you a message. He must have seen something. He knew I would look for you and guided you here to await me," Topaz whispered. "I can't help but wonder if the angels or…" Topaz hesitated and looked around furtively before saying in a barely audible whisper, "God himself knows that Uriel sent us here." Topaz paused only briefly, lost in thought, before they had to once again curl up among the smoldering embers, concealing their presence as best they could with a sense of dread tightening around their souls.

As the witching hour descended upon Topaz's part of the earth, the shadows of Hell's entrance grew eerily silent. Only a chill wind howled in the stillness, and with it came a sense of unease as the lurking onlookers slunk away from the gates of Hades.

Topaz's eyes widened in fear as she ventured into the immense marsh of Hell, a wasteland that stretched beyond what seemed like an eternity. The trees were dark and foreboding, their gnarled branches creaking and groaning with the weight of oversized bats that hung like eerie decorations from every branch. She felt a chill run down her spine as she stood there surrounded by a thick, ominous atmosphere.

The marshlands were alive with darkness, pulsing with sinister silhouettes. Crocodiles lurked in the crevices, their glowing eyes beckoning from the murky waters. Hellish snakes slithered through reeds, tongues like daggers, tasting the air for prey. A threatening tension hung in the air as these creatures of darkness roamed freely among the twilight between realms.

Orange fur-clad owls scanned the area with vigilant eyes, looking for souls—intruders. As Topaz noticed them, it hit her. These marshlands—this domain preceding Hell's gate—had been constructed to guard against any who attempt to trespass into the underworld. It was then that she knew it was built specifically because of her intrusions into Hell. Her heart raced at the thought as malevolent malice radiated from the wetlands, leaving a chill of dread in its wake. The sole purpose of all these beastly creatures was to devour her soul—or any soul that dared to enter unsolicited—into Hell.

Topaz shuddered as she watched the soulless monsters slither around the edges of Hell, their eyes trained on any lost soul who dared wander too close to the entrances to purgatory. A chill of terror ran through her veins as she saw them looming closer. She watched their baleful eyes searching for her, all too aware of her proximity.

Topaz held perfectly still, knowing her only hope was to remain unseen among the shadows that surrounded her, anticipating the fate they had in store. Trepidation held its iron claw on Topaz as the monsters began stalking closer to where she hid, waiting for their victims with sharp claws and menacing teeth ready to feast on any being unlucky enough to be lost between realms and wander too close into Hell.

The damp, sinister air of the swamplands hung heavy as gargantuan, bloodthirsty mosquitoes descended upon the marshy ground. Abominable crickets the size of small cats chirped deafeningly, while disease-ridden frogs, with grizzled gray skin and razor-sharp horns, hopped about and atop the stinking mud. Their morbid croaks seemed to be weeping for an end to the darkness that had plagued the land.

Topaz had a sense of panic that the creatures might detect their souls and consume them since Molly quickly saw her when she arrived. Topaz watched the beasts carry about, realizing with relief that their presence had not alerted the damned creatures of their souls. She knew if they had noticed them, they would have already tried to consume them, and they could have easily done so with a single bite.

The creatures were something out of a Jurassic nightmare—huge and menacing, with sharp claws and eyes that glowed with wickedness. They competed viciously for each soul, snarling and snapping at one another in a desperate bid to feast on the innocent lives of humans before delivering them to the gates of Hell to join the ranks of demons.

The soulless creatures of the Jurassic era loomed large, a plague of evil crashing through the realm. The smell of their hunger for souls permeated the air as they vied with one another viciously for the next soul to consume. Their long, piercing teeth snapped and snarled like wild beasts—an infernal chorus that echoes in the darkness. Each creature offered up its own sacrifice, hoping to earn a place in the company of the demoniacs while dragging another poor soul to Hell.

The air vibrated with the deafening whaling cries that began reverberating across the marshes. The ground shook beneath them as Molly and Topaz watched in horror, their eyes fixed on the sea of flickering lights in the far distant realm of Earth. Chants and laughter mingled with each other as more and more flames ignited, illuminating dark figures dressed in black robes.

"They are starting their sacrificial rituals," Topaz whispered grimly, her voice laced with both terror and disgust.

Molly's heart hammered in her chest as she surveyed the scene. The sheer number of people who had pledged allegiance to the dark lord and worshiped him like he was God was staggering. She felt a wave of sadness wash over her at the thought of all those lives lost to evil.

As the gravity of what they were witnessing hit home, Topaz knew they had to act fast. They were there for a reason, but bringing Molly into Hell with her was risky. What if Satan found out? He would stop at nothing to capture them both, and while she was prepared to go toe to toe with any demon, she knew Molly's soul would not be up to the grueling task.

Topaz spoke to her beloved Molly, "Thank you for bringing me here. I love you dearly and hope that you find the peace in Heaven for which you have yearned for so long. It is time for you to go now; blessed be." With a heavy heart, Topaz watched as Molly's soul was pulled away from the marshes, still undetected by the serpents below, and floated upward towards the dark moons above Hell.

In the stillness, Seth stretched out his wings, and a powerful current of energy surged through the air. Like an ethereal shield, they surrounded Molly until her soul glowed with intense warmth and security from the protection of his warm embrace. Topaz watched with tears streaming down her cheeks as Seth gracefully guided Molly to meet the Creator. A sense of calmness and reassurance overcame Topaz in that moment of magnificence.

Her gaze shifted skyward, knowing Uriel had sent her here for a reason. But she also realized Seth was aware of her mission, though, as a heavenly being, he could not enter the marshes or Hell without engaging in battle—something Yahweh specifically prohibited—at least for now. Any heavenly being was forbidden to enter the realms surrounding Hell without engaging in significant spiritual combat. Instead, God sent the Grand High Priestess, Topaz.

Topaz trembled as she faced the inferno that lay ahead, steeling herself against the wave of fear crashing through her. She took a deep breath and pushed all doubt from her mind, refusing to give it any chance of taking over. With determination etched into every movement, she stepped forward into the scorching abyss.

A turmoil of emotions warred within her as she gazed over the wicked landscape. Satan could sentence her to an eternity of suffering, a fate he had been aiming for since her birth. Her soul was at risk, and yet, despite all her fears, something kept drawing her towards the gates. The thought of venturing into the underworld filled her with apprehension, and yet she could not deny the curiosity that drove her forward.

Although she had uneasiness surrounding her assignment from Uriel, she put them all aside and plunged from the murky underworld into the dungeon of Hell. She didn't know what had prompted Uriel's enigmatic request of her, but Topaz knew that he must have a good reason for wanting her to take part in this mission, despite its inherent risks and unknown agenda.

OUI

Without Topaz, Izzy felt a deep emptiness and vulnerability plague her soul. The day Topaz set off to the mountains, Isaiah could feel the intense sorrow radiating from Izzy. Instinctively he knew the only cure was to get out of town—and fast. Izzy readily agreed, knowing it wouldn't be long before Topaz made waves in the underworld and brought unsolicited visitors right to their door. If they wanted to find them, they would.

Izzy hesitated before leaving, her eyes flickering over to the phone, knowing she needed to call Amira and check on her. Before leaving, Topaz begged Izzy not to tell Amira about her impending journey, knowing that would lead to Amira worrying immensely for her and Molly along with a plethora of questions. Topaz would never intentionally add so much burden to Amira, whom she loved and favored so much. On top of the worry for Miguel, the demand of working at the busy hospital had been unforgiving, and she was physically exhausted. Topaz didn't want to add to the weight of worry on Amira's shoulders. So, Izzy didn't say a word.

Seeing how stressed Amira already was, Izzy agreed with the decision. They withheld the information about Molly's soul and Topaz's dreadful journey. A pang of guilt tugged at Izzy as she packed her bags, thinking of Amira alone in that big house.

Later that night, after a long shift at the hospital, Amira trudged through her front door and collapsed onto the sofa. The silence was deafening, but she savored it before another grueling workday began. Amira's heart raced as the phone trilled in the next room, and she considered not answering. But after a few moments of hesitation, she forced herself off the couch and answered it.

A smile touched her lips when she heard Izzy's familiar voice on the other end. Amira was always delighted to hear from Izzy. Amira could feel herself relax as they began visiting. They made small talk about the weekend, with Izzy enthusiastically telling her about how Isaiah was taking her and Kezziah out for a small weekend trip away. Amira shared with Izzy how she wanted to use the weekend for rest but agreed to spend some time with work friends—one of whom was a new coworker that she had just met.

Izzy could hear the giddiness in Amira's voice when she talked about her new friend—a small spark flame that threatened to ignite into something much more than just a crush. Izzy felt a strange energy emanating from Amira and was perplexed by her lack of awareness of Topaz's secret. In that moment, she thought, *Perhaps Topaz shielded Amira from suspecting anything, or perhaps a consequence of Amira no longer using her magical abilities to trust her instincts and allowing her magic to become dormant.*

Izzy knew the dangers that were stirring in this situation, and she became overwhelmed with worry, but the best thing she could do was warn Amira to practice her magic and trust things would work out the way they always seem to. As she warned Amira, lecturing her about lurking dangers, Amira seemed to agree, and that provided Izzy with a great sense of relief.

The next morning, Izzy and her family headed to New Orleans, one of Izzy's favorite places. Isaiah and Kezziah stood on the deck of a riverboat, watching the skyline of New Orleans slip away in the distance. A steady breeze blew warm air up from the Mississippi River. The scent of flowers and trees was carried through the air by gusts of wind. The sunshine beamed late into the day, carrying with it promises of hot days ahead. Izzy stood next to Kezziah as she looked out onto the river. Izzy draped her arm over her shoulder and hugged her tightly. Kezziah gazed out into the city as well, a large grin spreading across her face.

Izzy enjoyed this moment, but the worry for Topaz and Molly was always at the forefront of her mind. She kept that worry to herself, trying not to let Isaiah sense her worry. With a painted smile on her face, she kept her concern off her face the best she could.

Izzy tried to distract herself from her fear as she and her family explored the vibrant restaurants in the French Quarter. The aromas of spicy jambalaya and rich gumbo filled the air with delight, and their laughter echoed down the street. But as night fell, nightmares drove Izzy from her sleep. She tiptoed over to the wardrobe, slipping on her shoes as soundlessly as possible, and scribbled a note for her husband in case he woke up and found her gone. The cobblestone streets of the Quarter were eerily quiet as she walked alone in the moonlight.

In her letter, Izzy stated that she desired some fresh air; however, she felt compelled to leave her hotel room. Her heart tugged at her to follow the mysterious pull she was feeling, so with a deep breath, she set out on an adventure of exploration. The bustling city streets were strangely silent as she meandered along, suddenly turning down a dark, winding road without any streetlights or the sound of life that seemed so present before. As she walked farther down the path, Izzy beheld a stately house tucked away from the rest of civilization, with acres of unmaintained land. In that strange moment, she didn't know if this was real or a strange dream.

Izzy stood on the street, a chill of anticipation running through her as she looked at the old house. Its windows were broken, and its paint had faded, but it seemed to call out to her. She could make out overgrown shrubs, wild ivy climbing up the walls, and an empty porch with half-collapsed steps. Then suddenly, from within the shadows of the doorway, a woman stepped out. Izzy's heart skipped a beat. This must be why she was here. The woman had a stern face, but when their eyes met, Izzy saw something glimmering beneath her gaze—a curiosity that mirrored Izzy's own.

The woman crept closer. Her slender frame was a stark contrast to her powerful presence. Every step she took was precise and deliberate. She wore her jet-black hair wound tightly around her head, almost like a crown of thorns. Light freckles sprinkled across her bronzed skin and sparkled in the dark like stars. With a deep and sultry French accent, she spoke. "What do you need?" The woman had a hint of European charm, but it was overshadowed by her overwhelming intensity that lingered in the air.

Izzy squared her shoulders, staring at the elegant French woman with suspicion. The abandoned house behind the woman seemed to loom ominously in the dark of the night. "And why are you here so late?" Izzy asked pointedly.

The French woman's eyes narrowed, but then her expression softened as she spoke. "My English... it is only OK" she said softly. "I am waiting for friends who will help me repair this house that was left to me by my family many years ago... Soon, I will sell it." Her lips twisted into a bitter smile as she gestured towards the dilapidated home. "It has been neglected for far too long."

Izzy felt a sting of discomfort as the stranger's penetrating gaze never left her. The beautiful French woman could sense that Izzy wanted something more from her, but the darkness of the night and Izzy's stare made it impossible for her to simply walk away. As she shifted uncomfortably on her feet, she anxiously glanced down the dark road, desperately hoping that her friends would arrive soon and this uncomfortable exchange with Izzy would come to an end. But still, Izzy kept looking at her, relentless and unmoving.

The tension hung heavy in the air as Izzy weighed the woman's words against her gut feeling. The French lady glared icily at Izzy, daring her to speak. Izzy knew the unspoken rule: the first one to talk loses. So, she stood motionless, refusing to be intimidated by the woman's gaze. After what felt like an eternity, the French woman sighed heavily, full of annoyance. She began to weave a painful story: Her brother and sister-in-law recently perished in a fierce inferno outside of town, leaving an orphaned little girl, Mae, for her to care for until their next of kin was located. She spoke each word with contempt, staking out her territory with a haughty indignation that oozed from every syllable. The woman was irked, and feeling she had to explain herself to Izzy caused her to become increasingly pissed off. As cars begin to arrive outside, the French woman casted a final scornful glare at Izzy before turning away and making her way back to the abandoned home.

Finally, Izzy nodded curtly and turned to go on her walk, but not without keeping one eye on the foreign stranger. Izzy found it strange that no one exited the cars as she stood at the edge of the road. Izzy also found it weird that such luxurious cars pulled up to the home—just before the witching hour no less—to help with repairs. It did not make sense to her. *If it doesn't make sense, it's probably not true,* she thought as she tried unsuccessfully to read the ladies' thoughts.

Izzy's heart raced as the fear gnawed away at her courage, sending a chill down her spine. Her eyes widened in horror at the thought of why cars were arriving at such an eerie hour. The woman's face seemed to take on a darker hue, as if she were trying to read Izzy's every thought, and without warning, Izzy knew she had to make a break for it from this spooky place back to the safety of the hotel. She sprinted through the night with a heightened sense of dread, knowing that something sinister lurked around every corner.

As she began to move away, she noticed the French woman watching her with a calculating gaze as she crept up the porch. With one hand gripping the doorknob of the house tightly, she watched Izzy walk in the darkness away from the home. It was clear that both ladies had a strange feeling about the other.

Izzy was instinctively aware that she had lingered too long and had an ominous dread fill her. She knew she needed to hustle back to her hotel. "Have a good night," she said with haste as she began her stride, head down and arms pumping, legs moving faster than Izzy ever could have imagined.

Izzy stopped in her tracks as she reached the end of the street. Her mind raced with thoughts of Topaz's courage to venture into Hell and her mother's, Victor's, Molly's, and Amira's bravery. A sudden chill ran down her spine, and her heart thudded painfully as a dreadful realization settled in: something was terribly wrong. She could feel it deep within the depths of her being... the oddness of the people lurking secretively in the cars, the bizarre timing of her summons to that house, the wicked stranger that fearlessly confronted her. All signs pointed to an impending disaster that she had no choice but to confront.

Izzy sprinted back into the city, her breaths coming in heavy gasps as she fumbled to reach the payphone to dial for help. Terror crept up her spine as she dialed the police, knowing that the darkness in the house had followed her and was threatening to consume her. The same dreadful force from her nightmares called out to her one last time.

She took a bold step forward, and the gravel alongside the dirt road crunched loudly beneath her feet. As she made her way back to the house, sweat began to bead on her forehead, and her breath came in short rasps that felt like fire. Her legs burned with fatigue, and her arms swung weakly at her sides. She tried to find a rhythm for her steps, but by the time she reached the old, abandoned house, her lungs felt ready to burst. *I really need to get back into shape,* she thought as she gasped for air.

She crept towards the door, trying to muffle her steps against the booming voices coming from the continuous chants in the living area. She peered into a broken window and saw an eerie sight: a circle of Satanists, lit up with candles, surrounding a young girl sitting alone and afraid in the middle. The occultists were all in black robes, with the exception of the French lady, who boasted a red robe, and it was clear she was the priestess of the sinister coven.

Izzy watched as the little girl cowered in the center of the room, her eyes darting from one person to the next. The candles she held illuminated her frightened face, casting wavering shadows on the walls that seemed to take on a life of their own as they writhed and shifted with each flicker of light.

Izzy's hands trembled with fear as she reached for the doorknob. Through clenched teeth and desperate determination, she braced her foot against the door and pushed with all her might, sending it crashing open in a flurry of splinters. Izzy was now faced with the unfathomable horror of what had been planned—a human sacrifice to Satan. Her heart raced as she contemplated the consequences of thwarting evil, but there was no other choice; she had to save the innocent girl from certain death.

As Izzy faced a daunting challenge, Topaz descended into the fiery depths of Hell. She passed by the screeching succubi and incubi, taunting her with their grotesque eyes, claws, and wings. The newly spawned cambions sneered as they lounged in the dungeons nearby. That made Topaz apprehensive, knowing one of the cambions had sensed her presence before.

She stealthily crept past the raging, colossal demons as they recklessly toyed with anacondas and alligators that were at least five times bigger than those on Earth. The volcano came alive as it spewed lascivious molten lava, rising up the walls with force and catching her off guard. Topaz moved swiftly through the ill-ridden dungeons, trying her best to evade the demons, along with the aggressive spouts of lava, as she steadily made her way through the dungeons.

Topaz hastened through the corridor, her heart pounding, knowing that she was risking more than just her life. She felt an instinctive urge to go deeper into the inky blackness despite her nagging fear. A primal force within her spurred her onward into the depths of Hell. She pushed herself further and further until she reached the entrance to a lower dungeon. Despite every warning bell ringing in her head, something inside her forced her to proceed forward. She took a deep breath, knowing that if she stepped over the threshold, she could be sealing her fate.

Topaz peeked through the door, her heart pounding. In the eerie light of the lower dungeon, she made out several demonesses flitting along the ceilings. As they glided closer to Topaz, she could make out the details of the monsters—razor-sharp claws, blood-red eyes, and menacing wings that seemed to ripple in the darkness. She held her breath and hid in the shadows as they passed, so close yet still unaware of her presence. The monsters moved gracefully above the massive snake pit, its contents slithering and bubbling beneath them. Without making a sound, Topaz followed behind the underworld goddesses as they descended further into the darkness.

The dank dungeon smelled of filth and stale urine. It was lit by a single torch that flickered, barely illuminating the moldy walls. Topaz could hear large rats scurrying through the darkness of the cavern. The demonesses then stepped into the abyssal pit—Satan's lair. It was a colossal dungeon where fear oozed from every corner.

The throne sat in the center of the chamber, an imposing monument to evil power, its massive structure perfectly molded to support his ominous presence.   Atop   the   throne   were menacing thorns larger than swords, along with three mocking and menacing crosses that were suspended upside down, each one dripping with a heavy static energy that filled the air with a sense of dread. This was the very throne on which the beast would rest. The throne itself was a despairing display, as Satan sat in it, daring the world to challenge him.

This was the very place where Beelzebub relaxed as his favorite harlots were nude at his feet. Satan loved to watch the most beautiful of the demonesses writhe together like snakes—their hands and mouths bringing each other to a mind-blowing orgasm as he watched in satisfaction. This was one of his regular routines. He enjoyed watching them carefully as they licked each other languidly while straddling one another on the molten floor.

This was the place he received his pleasure from the demonesses. After his time with his favorite harlots, other demonesses eagerly joined in, excited please Satan with depraved acts. As he pleasured himself the monsters gulped down his cum, thirsting for more and more. After reaching the point of ecstasy is when the bloodlust would begin. The demonesses descended upon each other; they bit into each other's flesh, tearing away flesh with powerful jaws and choking on the iron tang of blood. Satan thrived on their choking screams of pleasure while leaving nothing but pure carnage on the floor.

The room was soaked in blood after the feasting, yet they emerged from the dungeon unscathed, renewed, and stronger than ever. Their crimson eyes glowed with vigor; their fangs sharpened to perfection. Despite the carnage left behind, they boasted a newfound strength that made them even more beautiful, and they felt... invincible.

Topaz stumbled back in horror as she had visions of the debauchery that would take place in that dungeon—Satan's lair. The sounds of screams and ripping flesh filled her mind, while chaos lingered in the air. Her wits briefly abandoned her until she felt an invisible force urging her to flee, warning her that Satan himself would soon be present to revel in the carnage and lust for blood. Topaz scrambled to get away before he arrived, and the carnage began. With utter fear, she rushed out of his lair, desperate to escape this realm of hellish darkness.

As she turned to take her leave, the terrible shrieks of the demonesses filled the air, welcoming the beast as he made his way towards the dungeon. It was in that same instant of his arrival that Topaz felt a strong urgency to leave. Upon her exit, a strong feeling of relief washed over her body when she realized she narrowly missed Satan, who was so anxious to see the demonesses, he hadn't sensed her presence.

Fear and confusion pulsed through her veins like poison, making her feel disoriented and briefly robbing her of her intuition and instinct. As she crept further away, she could not help but feel relieved at having escaped before he arrived. Yet. She still felt utterly lost on why she was there and what she needed to accomplish.

Topaz's ears were filled with the sound of violent winds, as if a tornado were sweeping through the hall. With every gust, her soul seemed to flicker out until becoming one with the shadows that lurked behind as Satan snaked away from his lair, his evil cackle echoing in her mind as the demonesses scampered after him like rabid dogs. Despite knowing better, Topaz remained attached to the shadows as they followed Satan down that dark passageway. She was determined to seek out the consequences of her curiosity.

Her soul trembled as it lingered outside the depths of the menacing cavern's mouth. As she peered in, she witnessed an unholy transformation. She saw monstrous creatures shapeshifting from human forms into grotesque demonic entities. Some of these beings shapeshifting, Topaz recognized, as prominent, influential people on Earth. Topaz knew in that instance that she was seeing havacavters—Satan's strongest witches—achieving the ultimate accommodation in Satan's army.

These beings were, at their core, the darkest forces that freely live in Hell and on Earth. Topaz watched them bow to Satan. Their souls were glowing brightly with sinister power. Demons, witches and sacrificed—stolen souls—all joining Satan's evil army.

The havacavters were there, awaiting to welcome in a new witch that was expected to join their ranks—one that would soon be there after stealing away greatness from Heaven. Topaz could see that Satan was padding his army. Satan's army swelled with those who had been good, now corrupted and twisted by his wickedness until they had become unrecognizable monsters. Their allegiance to Satan was unshakeable, and it seemed as if he had expected this day from the very start, ensuring that no act of mercy or kindness would stand in his way when the *End* came.

"The ritual in New Orleans is almost complete," Satan declared to the monsters in the dungeon, a maddening cackle echoing in response. "You will go with the witch and escort the soul into an abyss of eternal torment that I have prepared for them." His laughter grew louder, vengeful, and proud, as if to proclaim his victory.

Topaz now knew why she was lured by Molly to the gates of Hell. Uriel had been pulling the strings from the start, luring them both to the depths of Hell—a test of their bravery that neither had foreseen. Not even Seth was aware of what was transpiring. After Molly finished her part, bravely waiting, luring Topaz into Hell, Uriel sent Seth to safely usher Molly to Heaven but left Topaz behind—alone and exposed in the depths of Hell, destined for an uncertain destiny.

Uriel needed her to join the fight against what lurked in the darkness, for the shadows were growing ever stronger. The stakes were high, and time was running out. Uriel needed Topaz to interfere so a strong witch would not reach her status as havacavter.

The witch was a force to be reckoned with; her power and strength radiated from her in waves, easily sensed by the archangels. Her wickedness and strength posed a great threat—one that could bring more enlightened souls into the hands of Satan, hastening the world's fate of destruction and despair. Her strength was unyielding and her presence undeniable. The archangels needed her plan disrupted, and they knew she could strengthen Satan's army immensely. Satan knew this too. They needed her to be stopped. If she wasn't stopped, they knew she would only hasten the impending doom that was about to consume the world.

Uriel wanted Topaz to observe his army of monsters, learn their secrets, and understand the power of the havacavter. He needed her to know the seriousness of the sacrifices of souls they feed on, creating an army of havacavters that would battle the archangels during Armageddon. With one glance, Topaz's soul thrust towards the entrance, racing through the blistering heat that emanated from deep within Hell's bowels.

Her soul buzzed through Hell as she desperately flew against time, barely skimming past chaotic pits that seemed to reach out for her as if begging her to stay. Topaz moved ever closer to the exit. But she feared there was no escaping Satan's will as the sacrifice grew closer to completion.

Topaz had explained this in her journal, which is when, with a sudden spark of inspiration, Izzy was summoned to action. Something powerful was at work—Izzy's presence on Earth became abundantly pivotal. A mysterious force, Topaz, had cued her arrival in New Orleans and set her on a path of higher purpose. This wasn't an ordinary fate. With the blessings of the archangels, it was, in fact, divine intervention.

Topaz stumbled through the dungeon, anxious to reach the end. As she made her way toward the final exit, a cambion pointed angrily and yelled, "Who are you?" Topaz didn't stop; instead, she ran faster, knowing she had been detected and burst out of the underworld with such force that she landed in the marshes. She sank deep into the swampy lands and felt stuck. Looking up, she saw glowing eyes of an alligator slowly closing in on her weary soul.

The tar-like substance gripped Topaz's soul like a cambion she crossed paths with before reaching down to free her from its claws. He pulled her beyond the wetlands carefully and tenderly, yet his eyes were narrowed in a skeptical glare. "I know you," he said, looking at her with skepticism. Not only could he sense her, but he could also see her.

Topaz froze as fear coursed through her. She was both mesmerized and scared of this creature—half human, half-demon—that exuded calm yet also unpredictable danger. Their eyes locked for what felt like eternity, neither one daring to break contact first. Then the darkness around them broke into a million shards of light as Topaz's soul illuminated brightly and intensely, revealing her powerful soul to the cambion that looked upon her.

The alligator's beady eyes glinted in the darkness as it watched the two—Topaz and the cambion—from a distance. Its tail flicked back and forth anxiously, stirring up the murky, simmering waters of the marshlands. The air was heavy with anticipation as it slowly crept closer to them, its nostrils twitching as it sniffed at them. "You're in danger in there," the cambion said while pointing to the inferno of Hell's entrance, and Topaz nodded in confirmation.

The cambion stood before her, his striking presence commanding the entire room. His skin was dark and glistened under the faint lights illuminating the fires of Hell. His skin appeared smooth with shimmering undertones that seemed to shift from faint yellow to dark orange. Thick, platinum blonde hair cascaded down his broad shoulders. But—it was his eyes that kept her attention. His eyes were solid black and all-consuming, like staring into the void of space itself. Every inch of him was domineering—tall and muscular with rippling muscles that bulged beneath his armor, a reminder he is a soldier for Satan—so Topaz kept her guard up.

The cambion grasped her hand and slowly led her away from the smoldering marshlands, the air thick with caustic fumes. The sludgy ground squished around them as they made their way above the marshlands that were blanketed in fog as thick and gray as smoke and laced with toxins. "Time to go," he said in a surprisingly gentle voice.

Topaz feared for his life and felt a moment of dread as they both contemplated their outlook. "Take me with you!" he begged. Without hesitation, she looked into his lifeless eyes and bound her own soul to his empty shadow. The cambions on Earth had souls, although different from humans since only part of them were human. Most of the cambions in Hell were born without souls in that alien environment, making do with just a shadow—a hollow shell where the soul should have been found.

As she took him into her consciousness, she experienced a wave of panic wash over her. Her breathing became labored, and her heart raced as she desperately tried to keep control of her emotions as he attached. The two escaped the depths of Hell and made their way up to where her body lay dormant on Earth in an extended slumber, well beyond Delta state of mind.

As Topaz awoke from meditation, she doubled over and coughed into the dirt, black chunks of tar and gravel splattering the ground. She stood only briefly before dropping to her knees and wretched until long strands of dark liquid splattered onto the ground in front of her. Her lungs burned from the noxious smoke of Hell, and her body ached from its presence. With each wretch, it felt like poison pumped through every vein in her body, making her feel weak and feverish. She struggled to her feet, wiping bile and sweat from her face as she used the last of her strength to steady herself, feeling lightheaded and unsteady.

Topaz cast the shadowing demonic spawn off her soul. As she was about to thank him for his help and ask if he would like to seek refuge from Hell, the cambion showed his true nature, that of a demon without remorse or conscience. His humanesque form grew taller, towering over Topaz. The face of the entity was handsome, with classic human features except for his dark energy, which seemed to suck the life out of the cavern. His dark aura radiated, and his solid black eyes began to glow red hot. The helpful cambion began to morph before her eyes.

The cambion's voice was low and raspy, and his eyes shifted from glowing red to a sinister yellow. He leaned in close to her face, a curl of smoke escaping his lips, and sneered. "You look like death warmed over!" His knuckles brushed her cheek, pushing her hair away from her eyes, and she could feel evil emanating from him. Skewed skepticism spread across her face as she withdrew from his touch.

Topaz's face drained of all color as she backed against the cold, damp wall of the dark cavern. She felt the chill seeping through her clothes and knew that she was facing death. "I cannot believe you fell for it," he sneered. "The first time I saw you, I knew you'd be back, and look at you—you nearly got away again. I didn't know the first time we crossed paths that you had such powerful enemies, but I do now." His voice boomed off the walls of the cavern. He took a step closer to her, and she was pushed back against the cold wall as his words hung in the air. "Even though I'm sure you're a fine lady, killing you will elevate my status in the ranks of Hell!"

Topaz's voice shook, and her eyes narrowed. She clenched her fists as she spoke, her words dripping with venom. "You're about to find out what happens when you cross me. I can be your closest ally or your worst nightmare." In that moment, Topaz was still recovering from her journey, not feeling quite herself, and did not know if she had it in her to fight this cambion.

The cambion's eyes seemed to glow as he used his power to draw her closer, despite her best attempts to create distance between them. His mouth opened wider than she expected, and a long, scaly tongue unfurled from his mouth and quickly wrapped around her body like a python. Its muscles undulated in an unearthly fashion, constricting her lungs and beginning to squeeze her life away. No matter how much she strained and thrashed against it, it only tightened its grip.

Topaz refused to surrender. She held her gaze on the cambion, hiding any doubts, standing her ground against the powerful and wicked creature that was hell-bent on snuffing out her life. Her gaze locked onto his sinister eyes. With a great shove, Topaz pushed against the cambion's tongue, which was wrapped around her neck. As it unwrapped itself, she felt its slimy texture sliver over her skin. She watched in surprise as the cambion stumbled back, his eyes wide with surprise at Earth's unaccustomed gravity. His tongue quickly slid back into his mouth, and he began to gasp, breathing oxygen that his lungs were not used to processing.

In his moment of weakness, she thundered, "I knew we were being watched, so I had to bring you with me and take a chance on your intentions!" She sneered at the cambion, who was gasping and struggling with taking in oxygen—something that comes naturally to us. He struggled on Earth the way Topaz's soul struggled to acclimate to Hell.

"I should have expected no less from one of your kind. My time in Hell has taught me how to prepare and wield my powers against those like you!" With a majestical wave of her arms, they began to light up into brilliant orange and purple flames. "You had better odds trying to kill me in Hell," Topaz said as struggled to breathe. She waited, refusing to win this way.

As the cambion caught his breath, he steadied himself against the priestess, Topaz. He contorted his face, looking more vicious and demonic than before. As he took a fighting stance, Topaz mirrored him. She was ready to battle this sinister monster and end him for good.

As he opened his mouth to send his tongue to smother Topaz again, she thrust her flaming hands forward, unleashing a storm of fire upon the demon, showering him in embers until he was engulfed in an infernal blaze. In a sudden flash of fire, he screamed as the heat engulfed him, melting off his skin as he began to char and blister.

Thick black smoke rolled up from his body, and the smell of burning flesh hung in the air. Still, he managed to laugh. "I was born in Hell of a succubus; I love a good fire." he snarled as he pushed through the pain he was experiencing for the first time. His taunting voice only made Topaz angrier, and she responded, transforming her hands from hellfire flames to red-hot blades of steel.

She was aware that his human side had been activated now that he was in our world. The thought of him feeling all that humanity could offer sent a wave of chills over her. His senses were alive, ready to experience all the joys, sorrows and beauty of Earth, but he would only know Topaz's wrath and pain would be his only earthly experience.

"Do you like the feeling of steel through your human flesh?" Topaz asked as her flaming arms hosted a surprise of hellfire steel as she pierced through his half-mortal body. The blades burned Hellfire hot as they pierced through his half-mortal body. He found out the hard way, on Earth, that cambions bodies can be vulnerable; their mortal form could be injured or even killed if they sparred with the wrong person.

Topaz growled in fury as she watched her enemy collapse before her. Her arms were returning to normal but still burning hot. Her words hung in the air as she declared with a powerful voice, "May you spend your eternity as you deserve!" With one swift motion, Topaz leaned forward, placing her mouth over his, and sucked the essence of the being from his body until his human form was drained dry. She then grabbed a blade resting nearby that she kept near her for safety. Topaz raised her sword and brought it down on the cambion's neck, cleaving his head from his body with one swift swing. The cambions lifeless corpse lay on the ground, a fountain of blood pooling around him. After she chopped off his head, she tossed it into the fiery pit. As smoke filled the area, Topaz watched with satisfaction as her enemy was burned until he was nothing but ashes inside of the cavern.

Topaz watched his lifeless body crumble to dust, and with a determined roar, she cast the tar-like venom of his essence she sucked in into a raging fire she lit to discard the poison from his body. She knew that if it escaped, the darkness of essence would follow, spreading like a plague across the lands. Seizing her last chance to bar its way from this world, she removed the clumps of toxins that remained in the ashes and then buried them deep into the ground.

The moment Topaz raised her sword and brought it down on the cambion's neck, cleaving his head from his body, the succubus who gave birth to him felt a sudden shift in her being. She knew something catastrophic had happened to him. Quickly, she flew through the night sky to inform Beelzebub of what had happened.

INTRUDING ON DARKNESS

As Topaz unleashed a torrent of power that annihilated the cambion, Izzy was engulfed in her own war against evil. Izzy kicked the door with such force that it flew open. Izzy clumsily stumbled into the room, kicking over a dozen lit candles in her haste. The worshipers jumped to their feet as the flames lapped at the tattered curtains, setting them alight and piercing the darkness with their orange and yellow glow. Standing before Izzy were imposing figures—shadow people, demoniacs, Satanists, and the French woman, who was the very witch Satan was waiting for in the depths of Hell to complete the human sacrifice.

"The name is Julia," she said in a slow, calm French accent as she stared into Izzy's nervous eyes. The witchy woman stepped forward; her face illuminated by the dancing flames from the burning candles. The witch's dark eyes fixed intently on Izzy, who stood nervously among a room full of enemies. "Your intrusion is rude. Can I help you?" she said in a slow, calm French accent as she stared unimpressed at Izzy.

With her chin raised in defiance, Izzy spoke with an iron will. "Oui, bitch...Julia." Izzy stepped into the satanic circle, her heart beating out of control in her chest. She saw the little girl huddled on the singed ground that was only a moment before surrounded by Satan worshipers. Izzy grabbed the fragile little girl from the center of the abhorrent circle and pulled her close to her side. The heat of the crackling fire was growing more palpable. The immense shadows looming ominously began creating a heavy and overpowering feeling over Izzy. She felt as if they wanted to devour her. The little girl was so frightened, though she did not understand the magnitude of the situation. The innocent girl could feel Izzy's strong grip on her hands, conveying a sense of safety despite the menacing presence of wickedness in every direction.

Julia's wild eyes were wide and unblinking as she brandished the long, silver knife and approached Izzy. "Oh, now that there's light, I can clearly see the resemblance," she said, her voice sharpening like ice. "You—you favor Lucrecia." Izzy watched with fear and fascination as Julia stepped closer to Izzy her, with her hand clutching tight around the knife handle. "Relative of yours?"

Izzy shivered as Topaz's words echoed through her head. Topaz had shared with her how Seth said her mother was a guardian in Heaven. Seth told Topaz how Lucrecia protected a French family. Izzy felt a chill run down her spine as she realized the family was being protected from a witch, and it was then she knew with confidence that Julia had to be the one Lucrecia protected the family from.

The witch ventured a great distance to be the guardian for her niece, who was barely more than a child. The witch thrust her hand towards her niece, a wide-eyed girl who grabbed onto Izzy's outstretched fingers with both hands and squeezed them painfully. Her grip was ironclad as if she was afraid that letting go would cost her... her life.

Izzy spoke up as the witch reached her hand out in a threatening manner, ready to cast an evil spell against her as she began. "Je t'ai jete un sort..." Izzy lifted her own hand, her fingers splaying wide, and the witch suddenly stopped speaking, lowering her taunting hand. It was then the witch understood Izzy was more than meets the eye. Julia was perfectly aware Izzy had knowledge of defensive magic. But... what she didn't know was that Izzy mastered defensive magic. The witch stepped back quickly as Izzy stepped towards her Izzy kept Julia away from the young girl, keeping her safe from harm.

The flames licked the walls of the darkly lit room, casting ominous shadows as Julia's followers tried to put the flames out in panic. The group of occultists were too preoccupied with saving their house of worship to pay attention to them, and Izzy felt relieved they were distracted by the fire. Izzy shuddered at the sight of pentagrams and 666 scrawled all over the walls that were a blaze. Izzy felt grim by the thought of what may have been if she hadn't followed the calling deep inside of her to save the little girl.

Thick black smoke filled the small room. Everyone began to cough and tried to wave the smoke away; their eyes were all stinging with tears. The occultist began circling Izzy and the witch's niece. Izzy feared for their lives but quickly found relief as red and blue lights flashed outside, illuminating the street.

The door burst inward, and police officers stormed into the room, guns drawn. Julia's heart raced as she tried to explain that Izzy had broken in, but the officers didn't seem to be listening. They looked around the room, taking in the bizarre symbols scrawled on the walls and the various occult artifacts scattered about, fleeing.

Their flashlights illuminated scattered tarot cards and sigils of unknown origin painted on the walls. They handcuffed Julia, as seeing her in her red occultist robe made them certain she was leading the ceremony that clearly led to the blaze. The officers led her out into the night, their footsteps echoing through the empty house.

Izzy gently scooped up the little girl, and as she handed her over to the authorities, she looked her in the eye and asked, "What's your name, sweetheart?" The girl trembled in fear, her tiny voice barely registering above a whisper.

"Mae."

Mae avoided eye contact with her aunt, the witch, as she waved goodbye to Izzy. The witch returned Mae's parting gesture with a menacing glare of her own as Mae was escorted away by the man from child services that was called to the scene to collect Mae. The young girl's aunt—the witch—retaliated with a wide, toothy grin. Julia glowered at Mae from behind her back, knowing the little girl wasn't aware of the power she had over Mae. Her caretaker could sacrifice the child's soul straight into Hell if it suited her occult ambitions. Before the man with child services could take Mae away, a handcuffed Julia broke away from the cops and ran to the girl, grabbing her hand, pulling her close, and whispering into her ear while looking at Izzy.

The gentleman from child services grabbed Mae and pulled her away from the witch, who became increasingly angry, screaming and shaking her fists. The police officers moved in quickly, surrounding her and dragging her away as she continued to yell. Meanwhile, other members of the coven were handcuffed and taken into custody for questioning in an effort to build a case against Julia. In the background, a group of shadowy figures watched silently.

Mae shared with child services and other officers how she felt the cold steel of the butcher knife pressed against her throat as her aunt's eyes burned with rage. Mae told them how Izzy, 'that nice lady,' barreled into the room to protect her.

As the officers began to place Julia into the car, the witch pulled off her greatest feat yet. With a wave of her hand, she cast a spell that sucked all light from the yard, killing the lights illuminating from their cars. They were all shrouded in utter darkness. In an instant, Julia vanished into the shadows and disappeared without a trace into the night.

Satan felt the energy shift the instant the ritual stopped. He was far from omnipotent and omniscient like God, so he sent three powerful demons to look in on Julia's sacrificial ceremony, unsure of why he could not sense what was transpiring. The air in the room changed abruptly as soon as the ritual ceased. Satan's anger seethed through his veins, and he felt an energy radiating from him, knowing something went awry.

Julia made a pact with the Devil to take Mae's life, her soul burning like fire in exchange. She knew that if Mae's pure and powerful soul were joined with her own, it would give her the strength she needed to become a creature of darkness. Nothing would stand in her way now as she prepared to commit this ultimate act of evil. With Mae's young, enlightened soul, and the witch's power—along with three demons that would join her body—Julia would be a step closer to being one of the most evil and strongest of Satan's creations, a havacavter.

As Satan was about to join in to investigate, a deep rumble shook the caves of Hell, reverberating through every rock and crevice. Satan's eyes burned with fury as he saw his meticulously planned ritual ruined before it even began. As he summoned the demons to investigate the situation, he stayed behind, ready to meet out punishment for those that were causing chaos in Hell. A cacophony of cries rose in the darkness as Satan stalked closer, radiating enough terror that even the damned cowered in fear.

The three powerful demons stood in a triangle as they united their power until it formed into one menacing entity. They chanted ancient words that vibrated throughout Delta, sending them hurtling towards the sacrificial site. The house stood eerily silent when they arrived. The demons could tell there was a struggle and things went horribly wrong as they separated and scurried around the smoldering house.

The police were still lurking around, trying to find Julia. They heard the faint sound of shuffling coming from the shadows. As they stepped further into the darkness, a chill ran down their spines when they heard harsh laughter from the demonic entities in the house. With each step the officers took, the entities seemed to grow more sinister and crueler; their shadows began to morph and pulsate with an evil energy as they shifted into their demonesque forms. Their faces contorted in wicked amusement as they advanced towards the officers, daring them to make a move and daring them to fight against something so powerful.

The officers felt a thick wave of dizziness wash over them as the demons' presence filled the room. They stumbled around, grasping at walls and chairs for balance while their stomachs roiled with unease. The nearer they got to the dark figures, the more disoriented and dizzy they became.

Izzy staggered back to the hotel, her clothes still reeking of smoke and ashes that clung to her, while the police fanned out across the large property, desperately searching for the witch with an almost animal intensity. The sky was just beginning to lighten as Izzy walked the eerily quiet streets.

As she walked, the wind was picking up speed, whipping her hair around her face. The trees along the path seemed to reach out to her, shaking their branches like accusing fingers as she began to jog. The gritty sand clung to her skin like a second layer of clothing as it flew in all directions, stinging her. Izzy clamped her eyelids shut as the force of the sandstorm pelted her face, but she couldn't block out the loud roar that seemed to be growing closer. She stumbled forward only to be met with an invisible wall that sent her tumbling to the ground. Before she could stand up again, she felt something push her back down and heard a grinding noise against her flesh as sharp rocks scraped against her hands and knees.

Julia charged towards Izzy with fierce determination, her body crackling with electric energy. She mobilized the shadow people and unleashed a torrent of pure rage against Izzy, who stole away her sacrifice. Julia was possessed with rage and determined to take back what was stolen from her, no matter the cost.

The demons abandoned the police officers in a chaotic flurry, cackling maniacally as they dove into the darkness after Julia. They roared through the night, gathering strength and speed, until they reached Julia, beckoning among the shadows. Their wicked silhouettes were tucked in close behind her like loyal familiars.

There, they fell silent, looming behind her like a wall of darkness.

The air around the witch was suddenly alive with thick, black soot that smelled like decay. From within it, Julia edged into view, her eyes glowing menacingly as she began to speak in rapid French to the gathering of shadows and demons.

Izzy's heart raced as she watched. These were no petty demons or harmless shadows; they had aggressive teeth, fearsome claws, and an unyielding aura of darkness. She could feel their eyes on her like daggers. But she was brave; she had no intention of hiding or running away. Somehow, she knew she had to face them. Izzy stood firm, ready to face any consequences that lay ahead for herself.

A fierce wind swept through the valley, carrying dust and debris with it. Izzy and the witch were forced to cling to each other just to stay upright. Izzy watched in shock as the demons swooped down and began circling the two women. The demonic shadows were dizzying as they wove in and out of the air around them. Julia forced Izzy off her with force, almost causing her to lose her footing.

The demons that had been stalking behind the witches dispersed into a wide circle around Izzy. Their dark silhouettes glided menacingly around her. The witch's eyes flashed with confidence, with her beasts standing firmly behind her. Julia pulled the large knife from her waistband. With a guttural yell, she lunged forward and thrust the blade towards Izzy's chest with enough force to drive it through the bone. Izzy could do nothing but watch in terror as the point of the knife raced towards her heart.

Izzy grabbed her arm forcefully, causing Julia to drop the knife. Julia grabbed Izzy and started to rain down a barrage of hard blows, her eyes wild with fury. Izzy's anger boiled over as she clutched her fist and delivered a punishing blow right to Julia's jaw. She delivered another fierce blow to Julia's nose, the force of it snapping her head back and sending a fountain of blood streaming from her face. Julia stood there with a shocked look on her face. Stunned and furious, she screamed in agony as the red liquid ran in rivulets from her shattered nose.

Suddenly, a bright orange ball spun around them, bouncing and rolling, until it came to an abrupt stop at her feet. Julia's face twisted in annoyance. Her voice rose above the wind. "Fuck off, Lucrecia!" Julia yelled desperately, her voice barely audible over the roar of the wind. The air suddenly stilled, and Julia began nervously shaking.

Mom? Izzy thought as her voice trembled with fear as she began to pray louder and louder as if her words had the power to keep the demons away. Lucrecia descended from the orb like a spark of lightning, touching down on the ground in front of Izzy. Her body glowed a heavenly white, crafted into that of a young woman—the very same image that had been burned into Izzy's memory since childhood. In the blink of an eye, Lucrecia transformed into an enormous, horned beast.

Lucrecia seemed to transform into a powerful being—taller than any creature Izzy had ever seen. Her face was no longer that of a mortal woman, but instead Izzy's mother had been replaced by a being with fearsome horns and glowing purple eyes. An entity rivaling the size and commanding presence of the fearsome demonic entities standing with Julia.

The demoniacs, eyes sunken and hazy, circled Lucrecia. Their inhuman tongues hissed and clicked as if speaking a language that only the depraved could comprehend. Despite not being an angel— just a guardian—they felt threatened by her power and hungered to devour her soul. Lucrecia kept them at bay with a grace that belied the danger of the situation.

The air around them crackled with energy, and the stench of brimstone hung heavy on their tongues. Izzy knew Lucrecia was capable of handling herself against the witch, although Izzy knew her limited experience was no match against someone who lived, breathed, and existed to pursue dark magic as Julia did. It was like watching a mortal struggle against an unyielding force of nature.

Lucrecia knew that her daughter was more than capable of handling herself against Julia's witchcraft, but even so, she worried for Izzy, knowing she could not overpower the demons. Izzy feared even Lucrecia descending from Heaven may not be enough to go up against a witch who lived and breathed the blackest magics and the beasts that were powerful agents of Hell.

As the circle of demons tightened around Lucrecia, she stood firm, her back straight and shoulders squared. Her eyes blazed with an inner fire as she faced the horrors that surrounded her. Izzy stood tall against Julia, and though sweat poured down her face and her heart raced in her chest, she refused to show fear or weakness. Izzy knew that if she faltered for even a moment, the sinister demons would strike—and there could be no telling what horrors they might inflict upon them.

Izzy was terrified of Julia and the demonic forces, knowing the power they could wield over her and Lucrecia with their sinister magic. Just as Julia began to cast a spell, Izzy threw all caution to the wind and threw a flaming right hook that landed square on Julia's mouth. Izzy wasn't one to normally fight, but her parents always taught her how to defend herself.

A spray of blood shot out from where Julia's lip had split open as the taste of her own blood filled her mouth. Julia was pissed off and she let out an angry yelp. Though Izzy was not as powerful of a magician as Julia, she knew how to make sure no one got away with messing with her or the spirit of her beloved mother.

Julia's face contorted with rage as she bent down and grabbed a fistful of earth. She hurled it at Izzy, but the clump of loam broke apart in mid-air, missing her by inches. Izzy seemed unmoved and Julia stood glaring, her eyes distant and cold, and her clenched jaw remained firmly set.

Izzy's voice was a murderous snarl as she threatened Julia. "Oui, bitch. I swear to God, if you keep looking at me like that, I will rip your fucking eyes out," Izzy spat coldly. Blind rage consumed Julia, and she quaked with rage as she barreled towards Izzy, wielded magic pulsating through her palms. Izzy stood her ground and faced her attacker with steely determination, expecting the worst. With a furious growl, Julia raised her arm to plunge the Devil's magic onto Izzy.

Julia's eyes widened in surprise and pain as Izzy, with an unexpected swift kick to her lower abdomen, sent her reeling backwards. As she fell to the ground, Julia picked up a large rock.

Julia's grip on the knife was tenuous as she stumbled and tried to regain her balance as she stood to her feet. Panting heavily, Julia let out a guttural scream and lunged at Izzy with the jagged rock raised in her hand as she charged towards Izzy.

Izzy darted away from the witch, Julia, as she swiped her hooked claws at her. Desperate to put an end to Julia's relentless pursuit, Izzy pushed her with all her might and knocked her to the ground. But in a split second, Julia was back on her feet and pointing her gnarled finger at Izzy, ready to cast a spell as she began to speak dark magic.

Izzy leapt onto Julia, tackling her to the ground again before she could cast a hex. Izzy pinned her arms above her head, pressing her skull into the gravel. Julia began trying to raise her head, her face pressed against Izzy's palms as she desperately tried to rise from the ground.

Imagine Izzy's surprise when the witch clamped down on her hand, biting her hard. Izzy winced and gasped as Julia bit down hard on her hand. The pain she felt was unlike anything she had ever experienced before. She could feel the unmistakable sharpness of Julia's teeth cutting deep into her flesh. With one last push of strength, Izzy flung the witch away from her. Izzy stood in shock as she observed the endless rows of jagged teeth protruding from Julia's mouth. Izzy described it as if Julia had more menacing teeth than Satan himself. As Izzy let off of Julia with her aching hand, Julia swiftly grabbed a jagged stone from the ground and thrust it into Izzy's thigh, forcing her up from Julia.

Izzy and Julia battled fiercely, and Lucrecia cautiously kept the demons at bay. As a gust of wind blew through the clearing, Izzy watched as her mother began to sweep away the demonic horde with movements that were both graceful and swift. She noticed Lucrecia dart around each tree, her arm outstretched in an effort to chase off a giant locust that seemed to be commanding the malicious swarm.

Izzy's grip on Julia tightened until her knuckles turned white, never relinquishing her hold. With a force of will stronger than iron, Izzy pushed aside her pain and grabbed Julia's hand that held the rock with such ferocity that it almost seemed as if time paused in its place. Izzy's voice rose among the air like thunder as she commanded an incantation against Julia, who quivered in fear and shock at the unexpected power of Izzy's words. Izzy stared deep into Julia's soul, as if to ignite everything within her with a single glance, while Izzy spoke words that bound her to do to herself as she would do unto others.

Izzy jumped to her feet as the police car's headlights illuminated the dimly lit dirt road. Julia was a twisted figure in the darkness, clutching clumps of her hair as she repeatedly bashed her own head against the ground while laughing sinisterly and calling out unintelligible words. The police stood stunned for a moment, watching Julia throw a fit, beating herself, before one of them radioed for an ambulance. The officers wrapped their arms around her as she screamed obscenities and thrashed around. A crimson river pouring from her forehead began to splash onto their faces and hands. Her movements grew slower and weaker until, finally, the paramedics arrived to find Julia's lifeless body on the ground.

The paramedics insisted on checking out Izzy as she limped to the back of the ambulance. They lifted her skirt and assessed the gruesome wound on her thigh. They rinsed off the dried blood and cut away at the dead flesh, then cleaned it out again before patching her up as best they could for transport. She insisted on waiting around a bit before letting them take her back to the hotel.   It wasn't the dread of questions from her husband on her mind, it was her hope of seeing her mother one last time. As the early morning transformed, she knew that Lucrecia chased the demons into Hell and was not coming back. Izzy knew her mother was aware she had successfully defeated Julia. Izzy also knew Lucrecia was likely already back in Heaven or off defending against another witch.

Izzy's heart raced as she trudged alongside her family, the journey growing more tiring by the mile. Her mind was filled with thoughts of Topaz and Victor's encounter with a witch who died at their hands and the possibility that Satan would appear to seek retribution. But before long, Izzy noticed the familiar sights of her hometown in the distance. Relief washed over her. Izzy felt both relieved and exhausted after a long journey that rattled her nerves.

Besides the bite marks on her hand and a wound on her thigh, Izzy had no other battle wounds left after a few days from her hellish battle with the witch. Sure, there was the possibility of invoking Satan and his army of demons, but Izzy worried most about Mae. She tried to call the child services department for updates on the little girl, but no matter how many times she dialed, they never gave her any information.

Izzy was overwhelmed with a wave of helplessness, unable to comprehend the child's future. Her mind raced with worry and dread while Isaiah tried desperately to comfort her, his words doing little to assuage her fear. Izzy had no choice but to lean into faith, clinging to her hope that things would turn out for the best despite her lack of control.

Izzy silently sent a prayer to the heavens, thanking God for guiding her to the little girl. She also sent gratitude to her mother for being there to safeguard her from evilness that would have outmatched her and left her for Julia to destroy. Izzy breathed in deeply, sensing something much bigger than herself at work.

Izzy couldn't help but think of New Orleans—the city of jazz—and Isaiah wanting to take her there on vacation. Everything was so serendipitous. It seemed that fate had taken her there for this very moment—to save an innocent life and to end the demon-like woman with supernatural powers who could bewitch even the darkest souls. Izzy never believed in such things as coincidences before.

Izzy was certain that destiny had been at work, bringing them to exactly where they needed to be. Izzy drifted to sleep, thinking of her mother, whose eyes seemed to sparkle like an angel that frightful night. She pictured her chasing away any demons that would try to hurt the little girl. In that moment, she smiled, knowing for certain she would once again see her mother... in Heaven.

Chapter Twenty-Two

CERTAINTY OF DEATH

After four days of being back home from her stressful vacation, Izzy was overwhelmed with anxiety, worrying about Topaz. Izzy grew tired of patiently waiting—something was stirring inside of her—and she decided to go to Topaz's to check on her house and at least feel close to her by being around her items.

Izzy felt a heavy sense of loneliness without her closest friends, and the fear for Topaz without the comfort from Molly, Amira, or anyone in the coven. Izzy wanted to reach out to Amira in search of help, but she was afraid her friend might be able to sense something was wrong with her and would try to pry it out of her. She didn't want to burden Amira with her worries, so she kept them all within herself.

Izzy started her car and began the long drive to Topaz's house. Her stomach twisted as she drove past fields of harvested corn and horses grazing in lush meadows. She said a silent prayer that Topaz was safe. The last time the girl had gone off on her own, it had taken months for her to return. As she pulled up to the driveway, she clenched her jaw, preparing for the sadness she knew she would feel going inside. In the back of her mind, she hoped sinister entities would not be awaiting there. Now that Molly was gone, and Amira was so far away, Izzy felt somewhat nervous facing entities on her own.

Izzy was startled when she heard a familiar voice coming from Topaz's bedroom: it was Topaz calling out for her. Izzy could almost feel the terror coming off her as she rushed to investigate the call coming from the bedroom. Her hand gripped the doorknob tight, and suddenly, Izzy hesitated. Her mind began racing with dark possibilities lurking on the other side like before. She steeled herself and flung open the door, half-expecting to face a demon instead of her beloved friend.

Izzy's heart raced as her emotions went between anguish and hope. Lying in the bed was Topaz, looking so fragile and distant—nothing like the vibrant soul Izzy had grown to love. She appeared very weak, with her skin pale blue and her lips dry and cracked as she spoke. Despite the weariness in Topaz's eyes, Izzy clung onto a sliver of hope that all would be alright.

Topaz tried to speak, her voice a raspy whisper. "Hi," she croaked out weakly, realizing how inadequate a phone call would have been when her body was so drained of life force. Izzy stopped her mid-sentence, recognizing the signs of exhaustion written all over Topaz's face. She rushed to help prop her up, coaxing small sips of water to pass through Topaz's cracked lips as Izzy looked on in desperation, fear glinting in her eyes.

Sometimes we all experience things that make us want to fall apart. Izzy trembled with fear for Topaz, whom she viewed as unstoppable. In that moment, Izzy realized the usually strong and resilient priestess was just a mortal too. A new wave of panic swept through her as she realized how vulnerable Topaz really was, leaving her powerless to protect her own flesh and blood. All Izzy wanted to do was make Topaz feel better.

Topaz smiled warmly at Izzy, but the moment was interrupted by a bout of wet coughing. Scarlet droplets spattered across the white sheets, and Izzy's eyes widened in shock. Tears spilled down her face as a lump rose in her throat. She wanted to say something comforting, but the words wouldn't come.

Izzy got up from the bed, her eyes bright with determination. But Topaz, her skin pale, hair matted with sweat, and lips cracked, grasped Izzy's hand, which trembled with fatigue. "It's OK," Izzy insisted. Topaz shook her head softly in response and offered a faint smile.

Topaz coughed harshly, and her mouth clamped shut as she struggled to contain the blood exploding from her lungs. She managed to push through her pain. "Or when you suck the life out of anacondas and cambions." The words dripped with defiance, a last act of rebellion before she succumbed to whatever fate awaited her.

"No magic can save me from what's next, but I don't regret going to Hell. It was my choice, and these are the consequences." She spat out the words with strong conviction. "We all die eventually, and if this is what it takes for me to do my part to help even one soul, then so be it. It was worth it." She leaned in closer, looking at Izzy, her eyes blazing with intensity. As she spoke, her eyes were borne of deep and profound knowledge. After all, she had explored the fiery pits of Hell, freed trapped souls, and spied on the beast himself, then returning to tell the tale.

Topaz warned Izzy of the havacavters, created by Satan, to wreak havoc on humankind and Heaven alike. Ready to pounce on Earth and Hell, they have only one mission: to steal souls and consume them to become powerful enough to destroy all life. But Satan's goal is for the havacavters to devour the archangels—his brothers he holds such resentment against—and take control of Heaven during the end times.

Topaz recounted in detail to Izzy her harrowing journey through the swamps outside of Hell, followed by the gruesome slaughter of the cambion on Earth. As she continued her story, Izzy listened with rapt attention as Topaz described how Mae's fate was so drastically changed due to her own quick thinking and courage. A slight smirk played across Topaz's face since she had a hand in Izzy being in the right place at the right time. Izzy beamed with pride, knowing beyond a doubt that her bravery had saved Mae from what would have been certain death, and she could see how proud Topaz was of her.

As Topaz reemerged from the depths of the cosmos, her journaling revealed a newfound clarity that she had failed to notice before. Every detail of her existence was illuminated, and she beheld herself with an unflinching gaze, embracing the good and the bad. Her epiphany was electric and life altering. At the end of her life, she even began to see the truth. She began to see herself... *differently.*

✳ Feeling the full weight of one's own truth, both the light and the darkness, is like having a crushing boulder sitting on your chest. No matter how hard you try to carry it or push it away, the immovable heaviness remains, forever reminding you of who you truly are. ✳

Topaz explained it best in her journal. The truth about oneself is a bitter pill that scrapes down your throat, scratching and clawing as it goes. It's an agonizing realization, watching as each flaw and insecurity is laid bare before you like a vivisected corpse. You want to look away, to hide from the reality of who you are, but you can't. Knowledge drags you under the waves, suffocating and drowning you in its embrace until there's nothing left but raw vulnerability.

Topaz was a great person—a dedicated priestess to her coven—and yet even she had an agonizing revelation, one that stripped away every façade and left her with nothing but the raw, unflinching reflection of her being.

We are all haunted by a truth that rips our insides apart, shredding them into millions of bone-drenched pieces. We know we must face what lurks beneath the surface—the grotesque parts of us that reek with embarrassment and shame. We dare not look in the mirror and see our true reflection—the monster staring back at us through shattered glass, its deliberate gaze burning through us to our core. Our sins, buried deep down, scream for attention, begging to be acknowledged. Do we have the courage to confront it and accept it, or will we forever cower away? Our secrets, so dark they eat away at us, demanding acknowledgment before we can find peace. Can we all be brave like Topaz and admit to ourselves who and what we really are?

Topaz remained tight-lipped about her worries and darkest secrets, preferring to keep them tucked away and isolated from Izzy so as not to trouble her. The night dragged on, with the two of them discussing all that had happened in their lives since they'd last seen each other, going over every minute detail that emerged since their previous conversation.

Topaz's voice drifted off, and her head drooped as Izzy spoke comforting words about the wonderful friendship they shared. Softly, Izzy placed the glass of water into her hands so she could take another sip before sleep overtook her.

Izzy ran her fingers through Topaz's thick mane of hair, feeling the softness beneath her fingertips. As she caressed it, she noticed large clumps coming away in her hand. Fear filled Izzy's face. She stopped and glanced at Topaz with wide eyes filled with fear. There was no way to tell her about the devastating news without breaking her heart.

Topaz opened her heavy eyelids and lifted her head to look at

Izzy. Her body felt weak, her skin pale and stretched tightly over her bones. There was heaviness in the air as Topaz took a deep breath and tried to summon the courage to explain the truth. "It's OK, baby," she said softly. "My body is preparing to journey to the next life. This is only temporary." Izzy's eyes filled with tears as she tilted her head up towards the ceiling so they would not seep out of her eyes and onto her cheeks.

Izzy's voice wavered, her throat clamping painfully. Her question was filled with anxiety and despair as tears blurred her vision. "What about Seth?" Izzy asked, wondering why he wasn't there while her body was withering away from her good deeds in Hell.

A soft smile graced Topaz's lips as she looked away. "I sent him away so I could see you one last time," she said, her gaze sweeping around the room and resting on the towering stacks of books and journals. "I pulled these out for you. These are yours now. I am also passing down many of Ana's crystals and Victor's herbs to you. Please pass along Molly's sacred scrying mirror and her crystal ball to Amira." Topaz said with her dry, crackling voice while pointing to the books and journals.

"The shadows of Satan and his wicked followers linger in the air, threatening and taunting. You must hold fast to your convictions, or else you risk being dragged into their dark world of sinister schemes," Topaz warned.

Izzy wrapped a light throw blanket around Topaz's shoulders as she dozed off, her hands trembling with fear. A lump had risen to Izzy's throat as Topaz started mumbling incoherently in her sleep. She rearranged the pillows behind Topaz again and again, desperate for comfort from a situation that seemed so far beyond her control. As tears welled in the corner of her eyes, Izzy dreaded the thought of losing her best friend.

Topaz asked Izzy not to say anything to Amira or the others about her condition—at least not right now. She needed silence and rest. She knew that they had busy schedules and much on their minds. She wanted them all to have a chance to process what had come into their lives without overloading them with additional worries or questions. After all, she knew death was inevitable—it had already come to her once with its beautiful face and luscious wings—so all she could do was wait now.

Izzy's mouth twitched up in a half-smile, half-grimace as the phone rang, and she felt the trepidation course through her body. She knew it was the others from the coven, feeling in the depths of their souls that something was wrong. Only Izzy lived close to Topaz now, so they couldn't simply pop in on her since they were all scattered around the country now.

As time and circumstances drove them in different directions and hundreds of miles apart, they had a bond that could never be broken. With a practiced hand, Topaz found the matchbook in her pocket, struck a match, and held it to the wick of the candle. The flame flickered to life and illuminated the room with a warm glow. She took a deep breath, then began to murmur an incantation softly. Her fingers trembled as she moved them in intricate patterns, casting a spell with each movement.

Topaz hoped it would be enough to shield them all from sensing or seeing into the room where she lay ill. Not only did she want to shield the witches from worry, but she also wanted to shield the beasts of the underworld from sensing her vulnerability. She cast a very heavy spell of protection over her home.

The air was heavy with the scent of sandalwood and rosemary mixed with the heady aroma of burning wax. Her voice grew stronger as she chanted the words of the spell. The candlelight danced across her face, throwing shadows that made her look both ancient and powerful.

Finally, she finished her incantation and blew out the match. The room was plunged into darkness once more, but Topaz could feel the magic humming through the air like electricity. She prayed it would be enough to keep them all from worrying about her well-being.

Although life had taken them down various paths, fate would always draw them back to Topaz. Izzy was the only one still living near her now, so that gave them some comfort. Izzy stayed by Topaz's side as her days began to wind down, doing her best to keep her beloved friend comfortable.

As Topaz lay sleeping, her body shaking with each heavy breath, she whispered words of comfort and resolution. "Don't be afraid of death—not for me," she murmured to Izzy as she gently caressed her hands. "I'm not afraid of death," she whispered, almost as if encouraging herself more than anyone else.

"I'm not ready yet; I must stay between worlds for now. Seth and God will have to wait." Izzy became distressed as Topaz's ramblings began to worry her. Topaz breathed in heavily, trying to find enough air—just enough to keep the death rattle from taking over her chest. But it seemed, even with her own words of comfort echoing in her mind, that she was still struggling to fight against her fate—a promise she was determined to keep even if it meant that she had to stay between worlds, hiding away from Seth and God until she was ready to face them. Each gasp became weaker, leaving only a death rattle in the still room. "I'm not. I am ready for what comes next and will be waiting on the other side to save her," Topaz said as she choked back blood that wanted to escape her lungs.

Isaiah watched with helpless dread as Izzy bore the burden of caring for Topaz alone. Desperate to keep Izzy from crumbling under pressure, he hired a nursing team to take shifts throughout the night to help Izzy, who wasn't sleeping in fear of Topaz needing her. Kezziah was a teenager by this time and stayed with her dad while Izzy remained at her best friend's house.

Kezziah loved Topaz and stayed stressed out, knowing her body was deteriorating. Izzy spent time at Topaz's house, doing what she could to make sure she went peacefully when the Angel of Life arrived. Izzy was with her all day and all night, just like Topaz had been with Molly. She read to her, read her tarot, and made small talk with her. Izzy's heart was heavy and dreaded the days to come as Topaz's condition declined with every passing day.

As the days dragged on, Topaz's grip on life slipped further and further away. Izzy questioned if it was her own selfishness that kept Topaz alive. She worried Topaz wouldn't let go because Izzy wasn't ready to lose her. Izzy could feel death making its approach, but she wouldn't let him near Topaz. She wasn't ready and begged God to work a miracle.

Izzy desperately clung to the thread of hope that, between Topaz's strength and God's ability to heal, somehow grace would be granted to Topaz. Izzy even felt somewhat angered, provided all Topaz did to help save innocents from eternal damnation. Izzy believed Topaz deserved better, she at least deserved an easier death. Izzy hoped for a miracle, but deep down she knew the insidious illness was winning the battle, and perhaps there were no miracles in the cards for Topaz.

Topaz lay in her bed, clinging to life, while Izzy held her hand. She remained strong and brave in the face of excruciating pain that wracked her body from the toxic assault of disease on her organs. Topaz held a quiet longing for death's sweet release. The air was heavy with the smell of death—a jar of burning incense on the nightstand attempting to quell the stench of decaying flesh. Topaz clutched Izzy's hand, her eyes wide, as she waited for the moment her soul would be released from the earthly suffering.

Thinly veiled sounds of distress trickled throughout the house. Izzy had been sitting beside Topaz, listening to the whimpers for hours. Izzy hated to see Topaz's torturous transition into the next life. Topaz would ramble about her time in Hell and things to come.

Izzy decided to make her way into the kitchen to brew some hot tea as the hospice nurse went to look in on Topaz. As soon as Izzy began pouring her tea, Topaz's voice pierced through the air with a shrill, angered shriek, followed by heavy banging against the wall— almost as if someone threw their fists in rage.

Izzy, caught off guard, jumped, sloshing hot tea over the rim of the cup and onto her arm. She winced as the liquid scalded her skin. The disturbance was so loud she feared the house would collapse. Izzy felt the blood rush through her veins as a piercing howl ripped through the air. Every step she took towards Topaz's room was met with an ever-increasing barrage of deafening cries and thundering booms that shook the walls around her. The clamor that filled the hallways grew to a crescendo as she reached Topaz's room.

Izzy swung the door open with panic. The room was dark, illuminated only by the silvery, glowing beams of the moon that shone through the windows. She surveyed the destruction: the bed sheet and mattress had been flipped upside down, the dresser drawers torn out, and a dusting of white pills covered the freshly polished hardwood floors. With her heart pounding, Izzy flipped on the light switch to see better, her eyes widening with horror when she took in the chaotic scene before her, and a deep dread filled her as reality slowly sank in.

Topaz held the nurse firmly against her body, one hand clamped over his face to muffle any cries. The nurse's legs flailed in vain as he tried to escape the iron grip Topaz held him in. Izzy froze when she saw the pair struggling. Izzy became mesmerized by Topaz's intense gaze that penetrated her soul, leaving her stunned and unable to move.

Until that moment, Izzy never knew Topaz to use her strength so freely. She knew Topaz could summon up enough magic to size herself up with any ordinary man, but this hospice nurse was far from average! The nurse stood much taller than her, the breadth of his chest and shoulders massive beneath the thin fabric of his shirt. His arms were corded with thick muscles. He towered over Topaz, who was a strong and formidable woman, yet his sheer size overshadowed her. His snarling rage, paired with his dominating size, seemed to fill the room with an intensity that felt almost suffocating.

Izzy didn't know what to do as her stomach lurched and she thought of Topaz harming her hospice nurse. Fear overtook Izzy, and she began feeling faint with fear. She watched in shock as Topaz, frail and ill, held the man captive. His face turned red with anger and humiliation, and Izzy was stunned, uncertain what to do.

Izzy opened her mouth to beg Topaz for the nurse's freedom, but her plea died in her mouth when Topaz spat out a string of words in an unknown tongue. Horrified, Izzy watched as the man's body twisted and turned like a puppet, his limbs jerking involuntarily as if they were being pulled along by invisible strings.

As the nurse's screams reached a fever pitch, a dark entity emerged from his body and filled the room with its unyielding, wicked presence. Izzy felt herself tremble as she looked upon the writhing mass, which spoke in tongues and crackled with an unearthly power. Izzy didn't know what kind of force she was dealing with, but she knew it was powerful—and certainly there to harm Topaz in her weakened state.

Topaz stared down the Devil's servant, undaunted by the imposing figure. She could feel her frail body gathering strength and radiating power as she prepared herself for one more battle against the demon posing as a nurse... Beelzebub's all-seeing eye, there to look in on her for the beast in Hell.

Topaz and the entity roared in a battle of wills. The demon's screeches and bellows were dripping with rage and malice as his eyes flashed with unbridled fury. But Topaz remained confident and spoke out loudly, her gentle voice overpowering the menacing creature until she had taken control. Izzy watched in awe at Topaz, seeing a woman who was completely in command of her own destiny—a woman in total control of herself.

Topaz's hands pulsated with otherworldly power as she unleashed a barrage of magic that tore the demon apart, its agonizing screams echoing throughout the house. Topaz's voice boomed as she took control of the demon. The ladies watched with grim satisfaction as the beast turned to ash as she banished him. Topaz stood with her arms outstretched in a powerful gesture of finality. The air crackled with energy as she lowered her hands, taking deep breaths to calm herself.

For a moment, there was silence. The ladies were unsure if the demon had been banished into nonexistence or sent screaming back to Hell, but he was gone nonetheless. The closer Topaz came to death, the more her magical powers seemed to grow.

As the room fell from quiet into an eerie stillness, the priestess declared her oath to never give in to the dark will of Satan. "He waits for me to die and become his ally, but I will stand ever vigilant and haunt him for eternity." Her words echoed around the room, lingering like a promise of retribution.

Topaz hacked and wheezed, her thin frame shaking with each labored cough. Izzy's stomach dropped as she watched Topaz's blood-stained lips part to expel a storm of lung tissue into the trash can beside her bed. "Satan sends his spies; I am sure he's a little wary to come face me himself," Topaz scoffed with a hint of determination in her voice. She paused to take a shallow breath before looking over at Izzy and winking. "If he comes alone and we battle, he might get more than he bargains for." Izzy nodded, then moved to help Topaz as she began picking up the mess from their struggle.

As Izzy desperately pleaded with Topaz to lie down for a moment and rest, an enraged Topaz spat her words like a venomous snake. "Satan's a coward! He thought he could take on God and gather his angels to fight against Him, only for them to be cast away like trash and forced to feed off each other's sorrow." She rolled her eyes in disgust.

Izzy wanted to lighten Topaz's mood, so she chimed in. "Fuck the Devil." She laughed. Topaz nodded and agreed, "Yes, he can fuck *allllllllllll* the way off!"

Topaz seethed with rage as she spat out her words, "Beelzebub wants to be the boss, but he isn't shit." Izzy snickered knowingly, her voice dripping with contempt. "Yeah, I know people like that too. They think they can control everything and everyone around them, yet their need for selfish ambition leads them down a path of destruction. All the while, it's hilarious to watch them spiral into... chaos. I try to tell 'em something, but their egos and greed are far too loud. It's truly pathetic," she scoffed. As she spoke, Izzy desperately hoped her words would settle Topaz's nerves down, changing the subject from Satan—the beast Topaz loathed.

Izzy tucked Topaz into bed, and as she did, the worry in her eyes betrayed her calm demeanor. She gently kissed her forehead just before Topaz let out a heavy sigh as she spoke reassuring words to Izzy. "Satan is somewhat afraid of confronting me and finding Seth, or the archangels here to protect me. He won't come here tonight, so please don't be afraid. I will be ready when it comes time for me to face him again—whether it be in this life or in the afterlife." Izzy sat beside her, grasping her hand and giving an affectionate squeeze before standing up to leave the room to get Topaz ice chips to crunch on.

When Izzy returned, Topaz was propped up against the pillows, her frail frame barely visible beneath a quilt. Izzy stood at her bedside, offering her a glass of ice chips, which Topaz ate slowly and laboriously. "We need to discuss my funeral," she said firmly. Izzy sighed and gently sat next to Topaz. "I don't want to talk about your funeral," she sniffled.

Topaz smiled weakly in response. "I know, but not planning won't stop me from dying," she declared softly. "I've put together instructions for you. A simple memorial is all I want." Izzy somberly shook her head with understanding and agreement.

Topaz asked to be dressed in her favorite black gown, the one she reserved for the grandest celestial balls. She made sure Topaz knew she wanted to be buried with the witch hat Molly had crafted for her years ago. It was a petite, bewitching black percher hat, adorned with exquisite vintage netting and an eye-catching rhinestone broach as the centerpiece. The broach was a gift from Ana—a gift that Topaz treasured deeply above all others. In this outfit, Topaz felt like a celestial goddess of power and grace. Topaz told Izzy that she was born a witch, lived as a witch, and will die a witch.

Topaz's eyes drooped while she murmured her words as she began to drift to sleep. "I have some more items for you in my practicing room under the altar floor. Just know that she's not going to listen—teenagers never do—but I won't allow her soul to be taken." Izzy thought Topaz was speaking of Kezziah being a difficult teenager and just rambling, but now, after everything, I do believe she was talking about me. Topaz must have known that I would fall prey to a witch who would torment my dreams as a young girl.

"It's time. We have only days now. Please summon the coven," Topaz humbly requested, her voice rasping with the effort of speaking. Her fellow witches gathered silently around her deathbed, their eyes glowing in the dim candlelight, their hearts broken. Devansh, who had journeyed across oceans to bid farewell to his dearest companion, stood grim at the edge of the circle. He was in shock and had a hard time watching Topaz struggle for breath.

As the night deepened and the air grew still, a shockwave of dark energy pulsed through the room. Everyone held hands as they gathered around their grand priestess. Topaz gasped her silent cries surrounded by love in her quiet room. As the air flowed from her fading lungs, her soul slowly released itself from her body, leaving nothing but a deathly hush behind. Topaz breathed in a strong, full breath into her lungs. With a final shudder, Topaz's breath of life slowly escaped her lips as it went softly into the light of the midnights... and faded away. A dreadful hush filled the room. The only sounds that could be heard were quiet whispers of goodbye as the coven realized their friend... their mentor's soul ascended into the next world.

When Amira saw the last of Topaz's breaths leave her body, she was in shock, though she knew it would soon happen. Suddenly, a loud screech escaped her mouth. Her entire frame shook with grief as she lumbered across the room and threw herself over her best friend's lifeless body. Tears streamed down her face uncontrollably, blurring her vision. The soft whimpers around the room were drowned out by Amira's whaling sobs, which increased in volume until they echoed around the cold room. She screamed at God. "It's not FAIR!!! She went to help you save souls. She went to help you, God. WHY!!!?" Amira and death did not have a good relationship.

Izzy pulled Amira into her arms and held her close. Her voice was soft and soothing as she spoke, her fingertips brushing away the tears from Amira's face. "Topaz wanted to do what was right, even if it meant danger. She did the right thing and saved so many innocent souls. Shhh... Everything is going to be alright. Topaz is no longer suffering."

Amira quietly slipped from the room and made her way towards the kitchen, trying to give herself space so she could be in solitude with her sorrow. As she walked down the hallway, the sobs emanating from Topaz's room made her heart even heavier, but she didn't turn around. In the corner of her eye, she saw Devansh reach forward and grab Izzy in a tight embrace. Izzy was heartbroken over his anguish as tears rolled down his cheeks, shaking with pain.

Izzy clasped her hands together and offered a comforting thought. "Topaz is with God now, and she's joined with Seth in eternal bliss. Let us be happy for them." Amira reentered the room, tears drying on her cheeks. She tried to offer a reassuring smile through quivering lips. "At least Topaz is with Seth and her family again—and our dearest Molly," her voice breaking at the mention of Topaz and Molly's deaths.

Izzy smiled so hard that her smile lines furrowed and deepened. "Molly is part of Topaz's family," she said in a strong voice, holding her hands out towards the other witches. They all began to gather around Topaz's bed, hands linked together. When their circle was complete, Izzy addressed the coven once again. Her voice was soft and soothing, like a warm blanket wrapping around them all. "We are all family in magic," she claimed adamantly. Every eye in the room was wet with tears as everyone banned together, one last time, in prayer for Topaz.

Devansh spoke up next, his voice steady and unwavering as he declared, "I hope she has the peaceful existence that she deserves." Izzy chuckled, though her voice quivered slightly. "Topaz is already in Heaven," she said with a smile, "barking orders at God, telling him how things should be run and plotting to take down Satan himself!" As everyone erupted with laughter, the air rang with a sense of reverence. It was both an absurd yet prophetic truth.

The sound of anguished cries ripped through the air like a horde of banshees, piercing the night with a macabre symphony. The dense fog smothered everything in its path, suffocating hope and shrouding the coven in a veil of despair that was almost palpable. They were trapped, held captive by their own sorrow, lost without their valiant protector— the savior of stolen breaths—their grand high priestess, Topaz.

Dressed in mourning, the shattered remnants of the once-powerful coven huddled together, seeking comfort from one another as they lamented their loss. With solemn gestures, each witch placed a treasured item into Topaz's casket. Some offered photos and letters, but Amira, with tears in her eyes, draped her beloved rosary necklace over Topaz's still chest. Devansh's heart ached as he placed a bracelet on her arm that had a petite golden bell that tinkled like a solemn death knell when it draped her arm.

Izzy approached the casket last, holding the very broom that Lucrecia used to escape to freedom—the same broom Lucrecia hung above Izzy's bedroom door for luck and protection when she was a child. Now, it would cradle the inside of Topaz's lifeless arm. As Izzy laid the broom next to Topaz, she hoped it would provide comfort on her journey to the beyond.

The air was thick with sorrow and respect as they each said their final goodbyes to their fallen priestess. As if on cue, the dense fog thickened into a poisonous mist, its tendrils wrapping around each member of the coven like snakes from the abyss. In this moment of total darkness, they feared that Topaz's protection had been ripped away from them forever.

Topaz left her home to the coven, her loves. After they split up the profits, each of them felt compelled to donate their portion to charities that safeguarded vulnerable children from forces of evil. They acted as one without discussion in honor of their dear friend who had dedicated her life to preserving innocence and preserving youthful souls.

DECEPTION OF EVIL

The coven of witches, once so tightly knit, slowly but surely drifted apart over the years. As the years passed, Kezziah married and started a life of her own. Time drifted slowly. The witches all grew older, many of them passing away due to natural causes, a stark reminder of all of their own mortality.

Devansh's passing shook Izzy. He was so much younger than her and it was completely unexpected. He lay in his bed, peaceful and still. His chest rose and fell slowly until, without warning, he took his last breath. The doctor confirmed it was an aneurysm that had taken him so quickly, yet mercifully without pain. Devansh had left behind a newborn daughter and Izzy felt her heart shred with sorrow and grief for the little one who would never know her father.

Shortly after Izzy received word of Devansh's death, Isaiah suffered a severe stroke. The long and emotional months that Isaiah's declining health consumed Izzy with sorrow. He passed only a month before my sister, Mia, was born. Another death, another reminder that no amount of magic could undo what felt like the end of the world—the silent, devastating way death and illness takes away someone you love without warning, leaving only haunting memories of their last days.

Izzy grieved deeply for Isaiah, and it seemed that the more grief-stricken she was, the less she and Amira spoke. Although they were still close, feelings of loneliness had been creeping in on both sides as they found themselves busy with their respective lives—Izzy mourning her husband, while Amira grieved the loss of Gloria, who passed away in her sleep while with Miguel, Lupe, and their young son.

Up until then, Amira had been wrapped up with studying long hours in medical school after deciding to become a physician while also working. Even though they kept in touch, Amira had yet to share details about her budding relationship with Sadie, a fellow nurse who now lived with Amira. Though...I'm sure Izzy knew somehow.

Amira juggled a job, school, her own life responsibilities, and love, but nothing as important as her endless worry for Miguel's safety. Whenever Izzy would call, Amira would always launch into a lengthy monologue about how worried she was about Miguel, who seemed so cold and callous when she called him.

Although he had become an adult, Amira could never think of her brother as anything other than the baby she had grown up protecting. But as the years went on, and he stayed in Mexico with his new wife Lupe, he slowly changed. He became a cruel stranger, unrecognizable from the person she'd known as a child. Izzy's heart ached for Amira and the relentless fear and worry that consumed her every day like a heavy weight on her tiny shoulders.

Miguel and Lupe's young son barely had time to get used to his three baby sisters before they passed away one by one. Amira had her suspicions about why, but Miguel didn't want to hear it, and the mere mention of Lupe or Ramona's name was enough to make him fly into a rage. He was not interested in Amira's unsolicited advice on his life.

Amira's fear pulsed through her veins like a dull river of dread. Her gut clenched as if warning her of something she could not face—something too sinister to accept. With magic slipping away from her, the blind spots in her intuition blotted out any certainty that once existed. She was no longer the witch she once was, and only her worry could lead her now—not her beloved magic or intuition.

The witch that she once was felt like a distant memory now so close to Miguel. This worried Amira. It now seemed like an unwinnable battle since he was determined to stay with Lupe in Mexico. She was his family now.

Amira desperately wished for Topaz to come to her aid but felt only the eerie emptiness of her absence. She knew Topaz was probably tasked with something far more daunting than looking in on Miguel, who was grown and capable of making his own decisions. Amira tried to sneak a peek into Miguel's life with magic, but everything was locked away and forbidden from her.

Amira's attempts to scry into Miguel's life with the mirror passed to her from Molly were always futile. All that lingered in Amira's mind were dark forces. She knew they were blocking her attempts to see around them. Amira, dabbling with magic after turning it into a stranger for so many years, was unhelpful to her now. Dark practitioners could easily deceive Amira, and she was very aware of her blind spots.

The malicious intent of those more experienced with the arcane arts left Amira helpless and vulnerable. Izzy sensed malevolence radiating around Amira, warning her to protect herself with *magical wards*. But Amira only promised that she would use wards of magic around her home for protection, she did not follow through. The beguiling power of magic remained neglected and forgotten. As a result, dark forces began gathering in the shadows, ready to strike at any moment.

Amira couldn't take it anymore. Something was wrong and she couldn't shake the nagging feelings deep inside of her; she knew in her core something evil was afoot. With a fierce resolve, she and Sadie began to craft their daring plan to go to Mexico and save Miguel. The uneasy feeling in her gut rumbled louder, urging her onward with a desperate need. She and Sadie packed their bags as they prepared to confront the danger that threatened Miguel and his young son's safety.

Sadie's heart skipped a beat as the thunderous knock shook the locked storm door, rattling the windows of the house like an earthquake. Fear raced through her veins, each surge of adrenaline making her pulse quicken with dread. As she cautiously approached the door, she had no idea what awaited her on the other side.

Sadie's hands trembled with fear as she hurriedly wove her short, glossy blond hair into a tight ponytail. With shaking fingers, she pushed her heavy dark-framed glasses onto her head, revealing wide, frightened brown eyes. As Sadie dashed to open the door, she encountered a stranger she'd never seen before.

Sadie's body quivered in fear as the monstrous man grabbed her, his vice-like grip crushing her against his firm chest as he entered the house. Sadie was no match for him. His grip was like iron as he violently seized her in his gloved hands, smothering her screams while terror burned through her being. She struggled to breathe, drawing shallow breaths as she felt the life slipping out of her. The room spun and faded to black as he effortlessly tossed her onto the cold, hard surface below. He lunged forward, towering over her with an inhuman strength that pinioned her beneath his vise-like grasp. She could feel his hot breath on her face as he slowly squeezed the air from her lungs.

The ruthless man's hands tightened around her petite throat until he felt the bones underneath her skin, buckling and cracking. The strength of his grip quickly extinguished any last breaths she had left, abruptly snatching away life from her fragile body. Her eyes flew open wide as desperation rose in her expression, and then suddenly turned to shock and emptiness as her soul was ripped from her limp form. As if a final act of humiliation, she involuntarily urinated on herself, and it was only at that moment the man knew for sure she was dead.

The murderous man stepped over the still body of Sadie as she laid in a lake of her own waste. The acrid smell of urine mixed with his cigarette smoke as he lit up and inhaled deeply, letting out an eerie chuckle that echoed through the darkness. His sick smile shone as he looked upon his lifeless victim, exuding a perverse pleasure from the carnage before him.

Izzy's hands trembled as she dialed Amira's number, her heart racing as dread seemed to seep into her bones. Upstairs, Amira swayed to her favorite song playing in her headphones as she lugged a suitcase onto her bed and stuffed it with clothes. In her blissful ignorance, she never heard the shrill ringing of the telephone, nor the commotion downstairs.

Amira was a shadow of her former self. She let her magic lay dormant for so long. Abandoning her powers. Amira had become... ordinary. This newfound freedom of not spending time with magic would now bring her life peril. There were countless unseen forces that had been tracking her every move over the years, waiting for the right time to strike.

After years of making big enemies and now not practicing magic, Amira had unwittingly placed herself in danger—grave danger. Instead of the all-seeing witch Amira had once been, she became vulnerable. Amira developed small blind spots in her visions, which grew over time into gaping blind spots. Not practicing magic, especially neglecting protective magic, left her vulnerable. The joy of a carefree life came at the cost of being hunted, unknowing and unprepared, while the darkness slowly gathered around her.

Amira's nose wrinkled as the acrid smell of cigarette smoke wafted through the air as she packed. She realized that it must be her neighbor, arriving to wish them farewell before their departure. He wasn't supposed to smoke inside, so Amira was ready to give him a hard time. She bounced down the stairs, carefree and even a little giddy knowing she would be seeing her brother and young nephew soon.

As Amira rounded the corner, a hammer careened into her skull with a sickening crunch. Shards of bone and brain matter flew out in every direction, covering the freshly painted walls beside the staircase. Amira let out an agonizing scream as her mind slowly processed what had happened to her, staring wide-eyed at the monster who had just changed the course of her life with one cruel blow.

Amira stumbled around her house in a trance, feeling the warm trickle of her own blood dripping relentlessly from her head. She crept into her bedroom and pulled out an old family photo album, flipping through its pages and grinning at the pictures of her parents' wedding day. Unfazed, she kept on flipping until she came upon a photo of her and her brother opening presents on Christmas morning. Her laughter soon gave way to tears as hot drops of red trickled onto the images, smudging each fond memory with a single brush stroke of death.

Amira stumbled into the kitchen, her throat dry and aching. Throwing back her head, she gulped down the glass of water, feeling an unquenchable thirst. The crunching of the ice between her teeth brought her temporary solace as she stared through the window at the birds gathered around the birdbath she had filled earlier that morning. Everything about this moment was overwhelming yet beautiful to her.

Amira gave the glass a thorough scrubbing, bubbles of soap floating on the surface before she rinsed it off. As she reached for a towel to dry the cup, she felt warm trickles fall faster down her face. Blood began to drip onto the just-cleaned glass as she placed it carefully back inside the cupboard.

Amira fumbled over to Sadie and kneeled beside her, shaking as she turned to lift the throw blanket from the recliner and draping it gently over Sadie's lifeless body. Amira stayed kneeling next to her girlfriend's body for a moment, while her blood seeped from the gaping wound in her temple.

Amira tried to stand up, but she staggered and fell, her body crashing next to her beloved with a sickening thud. Blood poured out of the gaping wound in her head, soaking her clothes and skin. She lay cold, shivering and alone in the pool of blood until she took in her last breath.

Her neighbor stumbled upon the gruesome scene about an hour after the women were slain. Izzy had been trying to reach Amira for hours when she discovered the horror of her brutal murder. It wasn't until the next day that Izzy learned the full extent of the bloodshed and terror that had befallen her precious Amira and her lovely Sadie.

Izzy was never the same after the day she learned of Amira's brutal death. She was shattered, like a mirror smashed into a thousand jagged pieces. The phone call replayed in her mind for years, like a sickening echo, every night as she tried to sleep. Amira, looking forward to seeing her family, instead met a gruesome death. She and Sadie deserved better. Casting magic aside ended up costing her everything—her life and the life of innocent Sadie.

The mutilated corpses bore witness to unspeakable violence. No one caught the killer, but to Izzy, there was something unworldly about the murder—something demonic—that lingered like an unspeakable curse. Ramona... Lupe. Izzy tried with desperation consuming her to vision and see who did this. She attempted to penetrate the veil that shrouded the truth from her without success. No matter how hard she tried, a powerful enchantment kept her sight obscured, leaving her blind to the source of this misdeed.

I trembled as I pored through the pages of Izzy's journal, the words describing Amira's demise blurring together until the scene was painfully clear in my mind. She had been so naive—so unsuspecting—not aware that her magic had been waning and its protection fading away. My heart filled with sorrow as I imagined what her last moments must have felt like, engulfed in a hopelessness she never saw coming.

Izzy was completely unaware of the impending disaster. Despite feeling a lurking sense of dread, her grief was too deep as she said her final goodbyes to her beloved husband. She struggled with his illness, followed by the busy days spending time helping with her granddaughter. Izzy stayed exhausted and distracted with daily life. The fate that awaited Amira was blurred by the haze of destiny and confused even the most powerful seer; not even magic could detect the monstrous malevolence on the horizon.

Those years were a living hell for Izzy. Her magical powers had become a burden, and her daughter, Kezziah, shied away from the dark knowledge of spells and rituals. Kezziah was afraid of the secrets she knew, as if every whisper of incantation held the potential to unleash something sinister into the world that she didn't want any part of.

The mysteries of magic that surrounded the family too much for Kezziah to bear. She felt helpless against its power and chose to abandon it, leaving her fate in the hands of destiny. Kezziah became so terrified of the dreams that haunted her each night, she refused to wield her witchy gifts like the other members of our family. The gap between Kezziah and magic widened until eventually there was an abyss between them.

Izzy refused to surrender to the darkness and diligently practiced her magic for the sole purpose of safeguarding her daughter, who had just started her own family. She vowed to thwart the dark forces of witchcraft and occultism with every breath she took until her last living moment. With absolute determination, Izzy embraced her magic and resolved to do whatever it would take to protect those she cherished. After Topaz passed away, she was certain the dark entities began to pluck the crows from the sky one by one.

Izzy was filled with an unwavering devotion to protect her family from the evil forces of darkness, so she delved into Topaz's powerful techniques of white magic from cultures around the world, determined to make sure that no malicious spirit would ever threaten the safety of those she loved. Each night, her fervent prayers would echo through the darkness as she devotedly studied and honored the teachings of Topaz—an angel on Earth, in her eyes, whose holy wisdom flooded her with light and power. She embraced her magical abilities with unyielding determination, ready to face whatever evil the witch and Satan threw at her. This is what kept the witch at bay while Izzy lived. This is the magic I was supposed to continue to practice.

I tremble in my bed as I feel the menacing presence of a dark force surrounding me, vying for control of my soul and shaking my very being. With every ounce of courage I muster, I remember who I am and what I can do. Steeling my mind against evil, I focus on Topaz's teachings and draw upon a power that had been passed to me through journals and books of magic. A wave of energy courses through me, filling me with strength and empowering me to protect myself from the darkness.

I brace myself for the bitter tap of the witch's bony finger on my windowpane. No longer will I cower and run in fear. This time, I stand my ground, a glint of steel in my eyes. With courage blazing within me, just like Topaz and Izzy before me, I ready myself for a battle against hordes of evil.

I am thankful for Topaz and Izzy. I know that without them, I would likely be damned to an eternity of torment. The books, the journals laced with wisdom, warnings, and magic—if it weren't for their foresight and bravery, the witch surely would have won and taken my soul, my breath of life, into Hell.

As I run my thumb along the rough edges of the worn journals, I begin thinking about how, without the information passed through them, I would have been able to survive the witch's magic. My sister and the brave ladies who rescued me had risked their own lives in order to save mine, but it had been the instructions that had been passed down by the brave coven of witches who faced the same malevolent forces before us that enabled them to rescue me.

The thought of being sent to Hell without a protector—a rescuer—like Topaz stirs deep terror within my bones. I can't help but wonder... are their other priestesses like her are out there, silently walking among us, protecting us from Hell?

My heart beats with anticipation as I await evil's arrival. I am not as strong or as gifted as Topaz or the coven of witches she trained and trained with. I only hope it is the witch I will face and not Satan. Everyone else believes the witch to be dead... gone—sent to Hell. But I know she lingers. I feel courage building in my chest as I study and learn the ways of magic. My courage—*daring me* to face the demons that have haunted me before. I will not run nor cower from evil this time. I am ready to fight.

Both fury and fear course through my veins as I take a ragged breath of accountability of what I have done, knowing full well that I invited the battle that I will surely be facing. I feel the consequences for what I've done closing in on me. The repercussions have been slowly gathering ever since I committed the atrocity earlier in the week.

Despite learning more about the effects of dark magic, I did it anyway. My selfish act suddenly left me exposed and more susceptible than ever to the punishment of Hell. My own anxiety began threatening to swallow me whole, even if, by some miracle, I was able to find a way out of my tangled web. As I tremble with terror, I await my retribution for my ultimate betrayal of using black magic.

Now that I have a new chance at life, you'd think my world is carefree. Instead, I await my retribution after seeking out vindictive justice— more than just unforgiving and wicked spells. I was supposed to being laying low, but I did something, and now I await my punishment for my reckless actions. My walls of protection have melted away, and now, here I lay—vulnerable, trembling in fear for the impending retribution for my sin.

I refuse to recede into the shadows like a coward. Maybe I was wrong for what I did earlier in the week, but I had released the world from an undeserving soul; after all, monsters do not deserve pity or reprieve. I had become judge, jury, and executioner all at once, playing God in my small corner of the world. I knew I was wrong, but even still, if I am being honest, I'd do it again. *He deserved it*, I thought as I tried to calm my nerves.   The swirling chaos of my inner thoughts gained more speed as my misdeeds echoed inside my head, despite trying my best to justify my actions. Evil looks in on me regularly, so I knew what I had done was not a secret, and it was only a matter of time before I was confronted as I made myself vulnerable. In the fear of the emissary of darkness, I study magic to prepare myself.

If the envoy of Hell ever dares to come knock on my door, I know I will have to stand firm and fight damnation itself if need be. *Should the Devil himself dare to come knocking at my door, I will be ready to face him. I am prepared to take on the fight*, I thought to myself as I began to drift to sleep.

My heart stopped as I heard the booming knocking at the front door. I ran into the living room as the room vibrated with each hit. The door shook violently, creaking painfully against its hinges as they strained to hold, begging for relief from what was trying to tear through. With every strike of a fist against the wood, I felt a piercing fear through my veins. The realization threatened to overwhelm me, as my heart sank to the pit of my stomach.

An avalanche of dread and regret cascaded down upon me with every beat of my heart, as I feared Satan was awaiting on the other side of the door for me. Thoughts raced through my mind faster and faster until I could hardly catch one before the door flew open—only leaving behind one raw thought:

*　＊　*　**Fuck—I'm not ready!**　*　＊　*